TETHERED hearts

STONE BAY SERIES

BOOK SIX

USA TODAY BESTSELLING AUTHOR

PERSEPHONE AUTUMN

BETWEEN WORDS PUBLISHING LLC

TETHERED *hearts*

STONE BAY SERIES
BOOK SIX

USA TODAY BESTSELLING AUTHOR

PERSEPHONE AUTUMN

BETWEEN WORDS PUBLISHING LLC

CONTENTS

BOOKS BY PERSEPHONE AUTUMN

Lake Lavender Series

Depths Awakened

One Night Forsaken

Every Thought Taken

Devotion Series

Distorted Devotion

Undying Devotion

Beloved Devotion

Darkest Devotion

Sweetest Devotion

Bay Area Duet Series

Click Duet

Through the Lens

Time Exposure

Inked Duet

Fine Line

Love Buzz

Insomniac Duet

Restless Night

A Love So Bright

Artist Duet

Blank Canvas

Abstract Passion

<u>Novellas</u>

Reese

Penny

Stone Bay Series

Broken Sky—Prequel

Shattered Sun

Fractured Night

Fallen Stars

Stolen Dreams

Raptured Souls

Tethered Hearts

Fiery Storm

Standalone Romance Novels

Sweet Tooth

Transcendental

In Knots For You

Poetry Collections

Ink Veins

Broken Metronome

Slipping From Existence

Poisonous Heart

Beneath Wildflowers

Chemicals Between Us

PUBLISHED UNDER P. AUTUMN

Standalone Non-Romance Novels

By Dawn

CONTENT AND AUTHOR'S NOTE

Tethered Hearts is a contemporary romance story with light suspense that spans seventeen years, not including the epilogue and bonus content.

Please be aware that Tethered Hearts contains sensitive subjects and graphic content in certain scenes that may trigger emotional distress in some readers. If you are sensitive to the listed triggers, this story may not be for you.

Please use your own personal judgement before proceeding, but know that everything is resolved and the book ends with an HEA. If you need more information, please refer to my website at https://www.persephoneautumn.com/tethered-hearts

- Grooming, manipulation of a minor (verbal)
- Homophobia (mentioned)
- People pleasing
- Mental health – depression, anxiety
- Parental neglect
- Emotional, psychological, and verbal abuse
- Degradation, non-consent, and sexual assault
- Underage drinking
- Substance abuse and addiction

Every 68 seconds, an American is sexually assaulted. And every 9 minutes, that victim is a child. Meanwhile, only 25 out of every 1,000 perpetrators will end up in prison. 1 out of 6 American women has been the victim of an attempted or completed rape in her lifetime. About 3% of American men—or 1 in 33—have experienced an attempted or completed rape in their lifetime. 1 out of every 10 rape victims are male. Native Americans are at the greatest risk—twice as likely—of sexual violence. More statistics can be found at rainn.org

If you or someone you know is a victim of sexual assault or abuse, I encourage you to connect with a professional who is trained to help. Call the National Sexual Assault Hotline at 800.656.HOPE, text HOPE to 64673, chat through WhatsApp, or chat online at rainn.org

If you or someone you know is a victim of emotional, psychological, verbal abuse, or neglect, or struggles with depression and/or anxiety, I encourage you to connect with a professional who is trained to help.

Resources are available online at psychologytoday.com/us/therapists **or** nimh.nih.gov/health/find-help. If you're in need of immediate help, call or text 988 or visit https://988lifeline.org/

Take care of yourself and those you hold close.

I love you,

Persephone

Through the years
you stayed at my side,
your heart unwavering,
the countless ways you made me laugh
instead of cry.

So many times,
I begged to be brave.
To step into your arms,
to fist your shirt with my hands,
to say the words that teeter on the tip of my tongue
every single night
and just as many days.

You have always been mine.
You will always be mine.

Even when I choose another,
even when I consciously ignore the tether
connecting your heart to mine,
even when I disappear
into the depths of my mind,
I never forget...

Until the breath evaporates from my lungs,
until my heart withers in its cage,
until I shatter into stardust
and leave this plane,
one truth remains etched on my soul.

You will always be mine
...and I will forever be yours.

RECYCLED WISH WITH AN EXTRA CANDLE

JET

Present

WHERE IS SHE?

Conversations carry on around me, but I don't hear a word as my eyes drift around Dalton's Pub. From one table to the next, I search for her in the crowd. *Again*. But Shanti's nowhere to be found.

My best friend.

My dance partner.

My reason for... everything.

Delilah wraps an arm around my shoulders and hugs me to her side, snapping my attention back to the table. "Having fun?" she shouts over the thunderous drumbeats, screeching guitar chords, and energetic vocals of Hailey's Fire, a local Stone Bay rock band. One of her best friends, Oliver, sits behind the drum kit.

Leaning into my older sister, I let go of my momentary frustration and soak up her warm affection. Relish the close connection I have with her and the rest of my family. Every chance I get, I thank the gods and goddesses for gifting me with this life.

A corner of my mouth curves up as I straighten in her hold

and nod. "I am. Thanks for putting this together." I lift my drink to my lips and take a hefty sip.

Pushing up on her toes, Delilah presses her lips to my cheek. "It's not every day my sibs turn twenty-four."

With a halfhearted chuckle, I shrug. "True." Twisting in my seat, my knees bump hers as I face her fully and quirk a brow. "But can we not use age as an excuse for next year's party? Let's just have fun."

I swear, since June—my twin—and I hit our teens, our elaborate birthday celebrations have been justified with a *you only turn (insert age) once.* Every time I hear it, it's on the tip of my tongue to say, *"Duh. We aren't stuck in some weird temporal loop where we repeat the same birthday each year."* But I keep it to myself. All the snarky comment would do is hurt feelings, and that is not who I am.

Parties don't bother me, nor does my age. June feels the same way. But neither of us wants to organize them. Just tell us you want to have a get-together, invite everyone, let us know where to be and when, and call it a day. We will be there, no questions asked.

Really, I get it. My family wants to make every milestone memorable. To fill each year with love, exuberance, and lasting experiences we will remember for years to come. To make this year's celebration better than the last.

As long as my favorite people are in the room, I'm happy. June too.

Delilah playfully rolls her eyes. "You know it's Mom making a bigger deal out of this than me, right?" Her gaze shifts to the next table, where Mom and June talk with a lady I have yet to meet. "Were it up to me, we'd be at the house watching movies and eating cake already."

Chair legs scrape hardwood as I push to stand. I offer a hand to Delilah, and she takes it without hesitation. With a swift tug, I haul her from her seat and pin her to my chest. My arms band around her middle a beat before I hoist her off the floor and hug the air from her lungs. "This is why we get along so well."

Laughing, Delilah playfully swats my shoulders. "Put me down."

I give her one last squeeze for good measure, then set her on her feet. "You love when I'm brutish," I tease.

"Says who?" She tugs at her shirt, straightening the unwrinkled cotton, then meets my eyes. "Besides, you're more of a cuddly puppy than a tough brute."

A snort comes from nearby, and I turn to see June at my side. I narrow my gaze at them before shifting back to stare down Delilah.

"Really?" I try and fail to sound irritated. Nothing my siblings do would upset me enough to treat them with disrespect. "A cuddly puppy?"

Delilah clamps down on her lips, the corners of her mouth twitching as she fights a smirk. Then she shrugs. "Calling it like I see it."

I quirk a brow. "Because you're the expert," I needle. "*Ow.*" Sharp pain ripples along my side as June jabs my ribs with an elbow. "What was that for?" I rub the fading sting.

Biting the inside of their cheek, June does their best to remain serious. But the hint of laughter at the corner of their eyes is unmistakable. On a deep inhale, June dons a pensive expression. "After a couple thousand romance novels, I'd say our sister is well versed in romantic partner archetypes."

Clasping my chin, I tilt my head and narrow my eyes, pretending to mull over their opinion. Not that I need to. Delilah lives and breathes romance stories. Every time I see her, she has a new book in her hands, on her tablet, or playing in her ears. She loves books so much, she works at the bookstore in town. From slow burn to erotica to shape-shifters to dragons, she has read every type of romance out there.

And good for her. I'm happy Delilah has something that brings her joy, boosts her courage, and allows her to safely explore love and sexuality without judgment. I'm glad she has discovered stories and characters she connects with. Words that give her the confidence to be unapologetically herself, especially with her girl-friend Phoebe.

Everyone needs and deserves love and the ability to be themselves without guilt or shame. We should all be so lucky as to figure out what makes our pulse soar, knees weak, and desire surge without worrying about what others think of us.

Delilah may not be a relationship expert—no one is—but she knows everything there is to know about love.

"Hmm. I suppose she does know a thing or two about romantic partners."

June snort-laughs while Delilah slaps my arm.

"You're ridiculous." Delilah twirls the paper umbrella in her drink. "Both of you."

"And yet, you still love us," June says as they hook their arm with mine.

"I do."

June rests their head on my shoulder as Phoebe garners Delilah's attention. For a beat, June and I enjoy our own little bubble. The pub is far from quiet, but everything seems to fade around us. Maybe it's our twin bond, I have no idea, but I treasure these fleeting, peaceful moments with June.

Dropping my head to lie on June's, I scan the crowd, soak up the atmosphere, and take mental pictures of my favorite people.

My parents and grandparents gather near a booth off to the side, talking and laughing with other townies. Mom's smile is infectious, and Dad looks at her like no one else is in the room. Delilah and Phoebe catch up with their friends—Skylar and Lawrence, Kirsten and Travis, and Levi, Oliver's boyfriend—over drinks and cheer on Hailey's Fire. A handful of dancers from the studio sip colorful mocktails and let loose on the small dance floor.

And then I spot Reema, Shanti's sister.

Is she here?

The thick, unyielding knot in my belly I've tried to ignore

eases a fraction as I scan the pub again. Breath trapped in my lungs, my gaze flits from one face to another. Searching. Hoping.

After what feels like hours, I spot Shanti at the bar. And she is not alone.

My shoulders slump as I breathe through the sudden, sharp pang in my chest. *Fuck*, it hurts. More than usual.

Through physical contact or our cosmic connection, June picks up on my unease immediately. Wouldn't be the first time, and it certainly won't be the last. Turning into my side, June wraps their arms around me, buries their head in the crook of my neck, and comforts me in a way only they can.

"Sorry," they mutter.

Hugging them with equal strength and comfort, I close my eyes and inhale a long, deep breath. "Thanks."

It isn't June's place to apologize. Not for this. Not when I could cut the cord and put an end to the longing, the heartache, the unnecessary pain.

I *choose* to be in this place—my heart tethered to Shanti Mahal, regardless of her lack of reciprocation. I *choose* to stay in her orbit, to remain close, even if the repeated sting of rejection hits me again and again.

I love her.

I have loved her for years.

And I know Shanti feels *something* more than a friendship love for me. She simply chooses to keep us in this place, distant and aching, because she has a strained past she isn't ready to process. No doubt, she fears what her life will be like if she unpacks all the hurt and rejects the drama at the core.

I can't fault Shanti for protecting herself. I would never.

If only she would let me in more. If only she would let me love her the way she deserves—something I have wished for countless times over the years.

From my spot across the pub, I trace the curve of her lips with my eyes as she smiles at the guy in her personal space. I have no idea who he is, nor do I care. It doesn't matter. *They* never matter. Not to her.

But I want to. Gods, do I want to.

I want her to look at me the way she always looks at them, and *matter*.

It's foolish. Juvenile. The most selfish and ludicrous notion to ever cross my mind.

Yet, it is what I crave. What I yearn for, year after year.

My blood boils and teeth gnash as the mystery guy leans closer, his lips brushing her ear as he says something. And as her smile stretches impossibly wide, I don't need to be at her side to know the obscene things he says to her.

They are all the same. Every single one of them. Attractive, charming, devious, and egotistical. And for whatever reason, she doesn't want someone better. She doesn't want someone who will regard her with respect and tenderness. Someone who will adore and cherish her. Who will *love* her with every breath, every heartbeat, every ounce of their soul.

Someone like me.

What about these nameless, unremarkable guys lures her in? What makes them so attractive she gives them her time without a second thought? What makes her give them a piece of herself without care? No matter how I spin it, it makes no sense.

Through all the ups and downs, through all the rejection and agony, one constant remains. One thing I can count on. One thing I continue to remind myself.

Her…entanglements always follow the same sequence of events. Smiles and flirtation, promises and sex, notches in the bedpost and no goodbye. Rinse and repeat.

Every single guy hurts her. Chips off a piece of her heart. Steals a shimmer of her light.

And it pisses me off.

Shanti can have anyone. A true partner who will give her genuine affection. Someone who will put her first, who will hold her in high regard and treat her like the goddess she is.

Someone like…

It doesn't matter. For years, it hasn't mattered. Shanti seems to repel love. To reject any form of real love.

The guy invades her space fully, and I curl my fingers into a fist. Disregarding the party and audience, the guy drops his mouth to her neck and nips and licks his way up to her ear, muttering something else.

Shanti shivers, and my palms scream as my nails bite my skin.

Beside me, June gives me more of their weight and strength. Consoles and keeps me rooted in place so I don't do something stupid like storm across the pub and yank the guy off Shanti. Wouldn't be the first time I barked at a guy for her.

I stay put, though. Taking several deep breaths, focusing on the comfort only June provides, I recenter myself.

I've waited years for Shanti. Sent infinite silent pleas to the universe when I thought *just maybe* we'd become more. During those rare moments when she held my gaze a little longer, lips parted and breaths shaky, I silently begged and incessantly fantasized what it'd be like to call her mine.

But the moment never comes. We never move forward. Forever stuck in some bizarre limbo, where we are everything except lovers.

More than once, I've questioned my sanity. Wondered if I am an emotional masochist. How can I not? Every time Shanti chooses someone else, it's a scorching blade to the heart. Yet, I stay in her life. I continue to wait for her. Wait for the day she will choose me.

Shanti Mahal has my heart. Since the day we met, I have been at her mercy. And until my final breath, I will voluntarily and contentedly hover in her orbit, a shadow-cloaked moon desperate for an ounce of her light.

Hailey's Fire stops playing, the pub falling silent. I blink a few times and glance around the room as the people here for my and June's party shuffle closer to us. My gaze finds Shanti's as she and the guy move with the crowd and join everyone to sing "Happy Birthday."

Bright orange glows from across the room as partygoers ease apart and create a path. On slow, steady feet, Mom makes her way to us with a simplistically decorated cake. I break eye contact with Shanti and smile at Mom as she slides the cake across the table to me and June.

When the song ends, I hug June to my side and give them a squeeze. Inching forward, we bend slightly and prepare to blow out the candles.

But before the breath leaves my lips, I lock on to Shanti's cognac-brown irises. One heartbeat, then another, time stands still. The unmistakable tether between us gives the faintest tug, my heart throbbing, quivering, aching profusely as the corners of her mouth lift in a soft, sweet smile. A smile she only gifts me.

The simple action snaps my attention back to the room, to our friends and family waiting for us to blow out the candles.

"Ready?" June whisper-asks.

They could have asked what was wrong. What had me momentarily frozen. But one of the best parts of having a twin is never having to ask. June and I share silent conversations, know each other's moods as if they're our own, and feel what the other is experiencing, even when we're apart.

I give them a gentle squeeze in answer, and we release our breaths, extinguishing twenty-four candles. Applause and cheers ring through the pub as we straighten. I plaster on the brightest smile and cocoon June in my arms, lifting them up.

Mom slices the cake and passes loaded plates to family and friends. The room buzzes with excitement as music from the jukebox stirs to life.

As I set June on their feet, Delilah sidles up to us.

"So, what'd you both wish for?"

June scoffs and swipes their pinched fingers along their lips. "You know it's bad luck to share your birthday wish."

Shaking her head, Delilah chuckles. "Only if you believe in

bad luck." Delilah nudges me in the ribs with an elbow. "What about you?"

My gaze flits back to Shanti, and I swallow. "Bad luck," I mumble, my mouth dry.

Delilah pinches my side, then June's arm. "You're no fun." She presses a kiss to each of our cheeks before grabbing two plates of cake and leaving us for Phoebe.

As my older sister walks off, I repeat my wish in my head. It isn't difficult to remember. Every shooting star, four-leaf clover, coin flicked into a fountain, wishbone, or birthday candle, I wish for the same thing.

I wish for Shanti to be mine.

And today, my wish was no different.

PART ONE

PAST

FROM THE START

ONE
FIRST STEPS
JET

Seventeen Years Ago

EVERYTHING IS SO BRIGHT. THE FLOOR, THE WALLS, THE LIGHT COMING in from the huge windows, and the reflection of it all in the biggest mirrors I've ever seen. It's like squinting in the summer bright. Or like that time Mom and Dad let us watch an eclipse with special glasses.

Way too bright.

What isn't bright right now? Me.

Black shirt, black leggings, black shoes, black hair… I am the complete opposite of bright. A lone storm cloud interrupting a sunny blue sky. A black swan drifting on the lake, alone.

But I don't mind. It doesn't bother me that I'm the only boy in the room. That I'm the only boy in town who wants to slip on ballet slippers. That I want to learn how to dance gracefully and beautifully.

A few years ago, my parents took me and my siblings to the performing arts center to see *Sleeping Beauty*. Stone Bay was the fourth Washington stop on the Pacific Northwest Ballet roster as it toured the state. Always eager to expand our view on the world,

humanity, and the arts, Mom and Dad bought mezzanine seat tickets and declared we were going to the ballet.

Before the announcement, I didn't know anything about ballet or formal dance. But the way Mom talked about it had me excited. She said ballet was fluid, elegant, and emotional. Moving art.

But it wasn't until the first male dancer came on stage that I truly paid attention and enjoyed the show. As a little boy, something about seeing a grown man slip out from the side curtains and move across the stage had me curious and spellbound. Onstage dance was new to me, and most of the ballet pictures Mom showed me online were ladies in pretty costumes. I hadn't seen any men until the actual show.

Watching them on the stage—strong, respected, unashamed—changed something in my young mind. It made my heart beat faster and stomach flip. When the audience clapped loudly for the lead man at the end of the show, his smile was so big as he bowed.

I'd never seen someone happy like that—like it was impossible to hold it in.

In that moment, I wanted to be him. I wanted people to look at me and think the things I thought when I watched him on stage. I wanted to be beautiful and elegant. A piece of moving art.

So when we got home, I asked my mom if I could learn how to dance like the men on stage. At four years old, she decided it best to start with at-home videos. After two years of repetitive videos and no solid instruction, I asked Mom if she would sign me up for ballet classes. My stomach had been in knots, but it was all for nothing because she said yes. I just had to wait for the summer class to start.

"Alright, class. Let's quiet down," Ms. Neesa says with a clap of her hands.

A girl with dark hair wrapped in a pink ribbon stands next to Ms. Neesa. Her whole body is stiff as she stares at the floor.

And I don't know why, but all I want to do is hug her and tell her it will be okay. That this class is fun. That I will be her friend if she needs one.

"Please welcome our newest dancer, Shanti."

"Hi, Shanti," we say in unison.

The corners of Shanti's lips twitch as she lifts her chin and a hand. "Hi," she says so softly I almost don't hear her.

"Everyone, find your places." Ms. Neesa rests a hand on Shanti's shoulder as she glances down at her. "We start class with warm-up exercises. Stand wherever there's space and you're comfortable. All we ask is for everyone to stand far enough apart that your hands don't touch when you lift your arms, okay?"

Shanti nods then shuffles across the wooden floor to an empty space near me. Tugging at the thick, tight straps of her leotard, her face turns sad.

I don't like it.

Turning toward her, I give her my biggest smile and wave. "Hi, I'm Jet."

A little of her sadness disappears, and it makes my chest feel better. "Hi," she mumbles.

I open my mouth to tell her this is only my third class, but Ms. Neesa speaks up and coaches us through warm-up exercises.

Gripping the barre, we push up on our toes then drop our heels to the floor over and over. We lift a leg backward and hold it, doing it fifteen times on one leg before switching to the other. Then Ms. Neesa has us stand wide and squat until my legs feel like they are on fire.

Once our muscles are warmed up, Ms. Neesa guides us through the ballet positions. Feet shuffle across the floor as she calls out, "Second position."

Shanti looks around the room, her eyebrows scrunched together, unsure what she should be doing. A moment later, her stance widens and she lifts her arms to mirror the rest of the class.

I remember my first class a couple weeks ago. I walked in, ready to be like the men I'd seen on stage, but was embarrassed when I missed step after step. My dream of becoming like the beautiful men on stage got smaller every time I messed up.

But Ms. Neesa said, "We all start somewhere. At one point, we're all beginners."

It was exactly what I needed to hear.

Scooting closer to Shanti as Ms. Neesa calls out for us to move into third position, I whisper, "Like this." I bring a hand to my belly as my feet move closer together, one heel pressed to the middle inside of the other foot.

Shanti wobbles in place as she tries to match my footwork. Without hesitation, I step out of formation and to Shanti's side, reaching for her arms to stop her from falling down.

"It's okay, go slower than everyone else. We're all beginners." I smile. "I'm new too. This is my third class."

After a deep breath, she looks less nervous.

My chest feels warm like it does when I do something nice for my family.

I stay by Shanti through the rest of class, helping her with the things I know and stumbling next to her with the things I'm not good at yet. When class ends, the smile on Shanti's face is almost as bright as the dance studio.

I like her smile. I like her happy. And I like the pink ribbon in her hair so much, I tell her it's pretty.

Her cheery mood makes me feel good. It makes me feel special.

"Time to go, Shanti," a lady near the door says. She has the same pretty hair and smile as Shanti, and I assume it's her mom.

But when I look back at Shanti, ready to say I'll see her at the next class, the smile she had seconds ago is gone. Like when she stood in front of the class, she stares down at the floor.

My belly hurts at seeing her sadness.

I don't like that her mom makes her upset.

"See you next week," I say. "We can fall over together again."

This makes her laugh a little, and the ache in my belly eases some.

"Bye, Jet." She gives me a stiff wave.

"Bye, Shanti."

TWO
WHAT A PAIR
SHANTI

Fourteen Years Ago

THE TRANQUIL NOTES OF CLASSICAL MUSIC FLOAT THROUGH THE room, a symphony piece I've listened to so many times I've lost count.

When Ms. Neesa announced the title of our fall recital, Under A Spell, I thought we'd be doing something fun and witchy. Instead, each dance in the production is gentle and spiritual—but not in a God-like way. And since the announcement, my parents have played the song Jet and I are dancing to every minute of the day.

I'm ready to shred my leotard and scream.

Somehow, I don't.

Not sure how I feel about the routine yet. The dance doesn't seem like something kids our age would perform. It's eloquent, sophisticated. The complete opposite of children in grade school. But what do I know? Maybe some kids are like that—refined, stiff, quiet.

Sometimes, it feels like that is how my parents expect me to be.

Regardless, I keep dancing. Keep hoping I will eventually

connect with the music and flow. Keep wishing I'll love this as much as my friend and partner, Jet.

Arms out wide, I ripple them up and down in delicate, slow waves as my foot glides across the floor, pauses, and points before my other foot sweeps behind the first in a point. The ball of my back foot flat on the floor, I push up on my toes then drop down in a plié. My arms lift high over my head as the music shifts, and I cross the room, tall on my toes, in several tiny, quick steps that make me look like I'm floating.

Jet moves from his position in the corner to a couple feet behind me, just off to the side. And then we move in sync, his arm and leg movements ten times more fluid and precise than mine.

When Jet dances, everyone in the room stops to watch him. Without effort, they see and feel how much he loves to dance. How much he lives and breathes his art. How he was born to be on the dance floor.

Watching him makes my face hot and heart pound. It makes me angry at myself for not liking ballet and being forced to do it anyway.

But my frustration fades away when Jet is here, at my side, helping me become a better dancer. It disappears completely when we meet at his house to practice—like right now—and goof off every once in a while.

It's hard not to smile when Jet is near. He makes all of this more bearable. He makes me forget about all the upsetting comments and demands my parents make after dance class.

Perfection. That is what is expected of me.

Unfocused, I move in the wrong direction and my back smacks into Jet's front. We lose our balance and tumble to the floor.

"Ow," I cry out as my butt hits the floor. On the next breath, my entire body goes hot with embarrassment. Covering my face with my hands, I scream into my palms as my feet slap the floor again and again.

The fall hurts nowhere near as much as my pride.

Jet scurries to my side and touches my arm. "Are you okay?" he asks, a hint of worry in his voice.

I like that Jet worries about me. He and my sister Reema are the only people who treat me like a person instead of some moldable doll.

"Yeah," I grumble as my hands drop from my face and slap the floor. "I'm fine."

Bending so his face is in front of mine, his gray eyes turn too serious for a ten-year-old before they study my eyes, my mouth, my cheeks. Were it anyone else, I'd get up and walk away. But not with Jet. His stare is gentle, peaceful, friendly.

With Jet, I always feel safe. Free to be myself.

"It's okay if you're not," he says softly.

Is it, though? My parents have expectations for me and Reema. Being anything other than perfect and capable are not on the list of those expectations. I know this because they've sat us both down several times and told us as much.

"I never get it right," I say with a huff. "No matter what dance we do, I always do something wrong."

"Dancing isn't about right or wrong."

My brows tug together as I squint at him. "No one wants to watch us do it wrong. Especially not my parents."

His lips curve into a small smile as he nods. "That's probably true about some people. And I'm sorry your mom and dad feel that way."

I don't say anything. What can I say?

I'm glad he doesn't admit his parents wouldn't care. But after coming to his house to practice several times and spending time with his family, I know none of them would care if he missed a step or landed on his butt. Well, they would care if he hurt himself. But they wouldn't worry about what other people think. They wouldn't worry about how a misstep or tumble would reflect on his future or their image.

I wish my parents cared more about *me* than their self-importance.

Jet drops to the floor and sits in front of me cross-legged. He lifts a hand and presses it to his upper belly, just beneath where his ribs connect. "This is where I feel it." He closes his eyes and takes a deep breath. For a moment, he is quiet, calm. Peaceful. His fingers tap his chest twice. "Deep inside, I feel this... energy when I dance." His eyes open and he smiles big. "Mom calls it my chi."

Huh?

Jet smiles bigger at my confusion and shrugs. "Dance is my spirit animal."

Hmm. Okay. I definitely don't feel that when I dance. I don't really feel anything other than frustration. But I'm not saying that out loud.

Instead, I nod.

His hand drops into his lap. "Where do you feel your love for dance when you're on stage?"

I freeze and stop breathing. My heart bangs so hard in my chest it hurts. Sweat dampens my skin as I try to figure out what to say. Each second without air makes me a little dizzy, so I close my eyes.

This is Jet, not my parents. Whatever I say won't make him like me less.

Swallowing, I remind myself to breathe as I open my eyes. I'm about to open my mouth and admit I don't feel it anywhere, but stop myself. Rather than confess I don't love ballet, that I only do it because my parents make me, that I only enjoy it because he is in the class, I lift my hand and place it on my belly like he did.

"In the same place," I lie, and my tummy twists immediately.

His eyes hold mine for a few heartbeats before he nods.

Does he know I'm lying? God, I hope not. But Jet always understands me better than anyone else, so maybe he does know.

If he does, he ignores it.

Instead, he holds out his hand. "Come on. Let's try again."

I groan, and he chuckles as we stand.

"We got this."

"Sure we do," I mumble.

Jet helps me up, and we prepare to start from the beginning. As the music echoes through the room once more, I glance over my shoulder at Jet and smile.

Whatever brought us together, I am grateful.

I may not like dance, but without it, I wouldn't have Jet in my life. I wouldn't have him as a friend. My best friend.

THREE
THE TWINKLE OF A STAR BEING BORN
JET

Thirteen Years Ago

"Attention, class," Ms. Neesa calls from the front of the room with a clap of her hands. "We have a special announcement."

Finishing my current warm-up exercise, I straighten and shift my focus to Ms. Neesa, Mr. Aurelio, and the woman standing with them. Tall and poised, the woman's gaze scans the dancers in the room. When her eyes pause on me a moment, a strange twinge tugs in my belly. Kind of like when I eat something bad. The moment she looks away from me, the cramp eases.

What the heck was that?

I've never felt anything like that before. Tight and tense and something else I don't know how to describe. I bet if I told Mom about it, she would say it's my intuition telling me to be alert.

But why?

I don't know this lady or anything about her. Still, after one look, she makes me uncomfortable.

"Please welcome Ms. Vivienne." Ms. Neesa turns toward the woman and holds a hand in her direction.

The class applauds then quiets.

"Ms. Vivienne is from the Northwest Evergreen Ballet Company."

Gasps echo through the room as a few dancers cover their mouths with a hand.

I glance at Shanti to see if she has heard of the instructor or school. Shanti gives a subtle shake of her head and shrugs.

Not just me in the dark. Good.

The excitement tapers, and Ms. Neesa continues. "I'm sure many of you are curious why Ms. Vivienne is here." A big smile plumps her cheeks as she clasps her hands beneath her chin. "We've been invited to participate in this year's Pacific Northwest amateur ballet competition."

Squeals fill the room. Veronica, Blair, and Sabrina go from calm to unrestrained in a heartbeat. They jump and hug and shriek with excitement.

Shanti and I simply stare at them, confused. Thrilled as I am for us to be invited, I can't quite grasp their level of excitement. I love dance, but I don't do it for fame or prizes. I dance because I was born to.

At least I'm not alone in my muted enthusiasm.

Ms. Neesa allows them a few seconds, then claps to bring their attention back to her. "Alright, ladies."

Veronica, Blair, and Sabrina quiet down and resume their spots, still fidgeting as they wait for more information.

"Let's give our full attention to Ms. Vivienne as she shares the details of the competition." Ms. Neesa clasps her hands in front of her waist and turns her gaze to the guest instructor.

Over the next few minutes, Ms. Vivienne explains the competition and how we came to be chosen to attend. Earlier this year, Ms. Neesa submitted our school for consideration with a video of our most recent recital. Along with more than a dozen other studios in the state, we have what the competition is looking for. At least, according to Ms. Vivienne.

She goes on to explain her role. As a chair member for the competition, it is her job—along with the other chair members—to assist the schools invited. Each répétiteur—expert choreographers who share their vision and lead the rehearsals and performances—is assigned a studio to instruct leading up to the competition.

Blair raises her hand and asks if Ms. Vivienne will judge the competition. I know the answer before it is said—no. It'd be unfair for the instructors to determine which school is the best. Each would choose the school they represented.

"The theme this year is A Breath of Summer," Ms. Vivienne announces. "After reviewing the video Ms. Neesa and Mr. Aurelio sent in, I've choreographed variations and pas de deux with select dancers in mind. Everyone will be part of the performance, but some will have more stage time. If you weren't selected for a solo or duet, it's not because you did anything wrong." A soft smile curves Ms. Vivienne's lips as she surveys the room. "You're all wonderful, talented dancers, and choosing who would perform specific roles was a difficult decision."

As one of two male dancers in our class, a buzz of excitement finally sparks in my chest at the mention of pas de deux. I don't want to assume we are guaranteed the dances, but it's hard not to.

The energy in the room is contagious as we wait to hear who will dance variations and pas de deux. Time seems to slow as the room falls impossibly quiet. Then Ms. Vivienne announces the roles.

Veronica and Blair cheer and leap when their names are called as two of the variation dancers. Luka and Sabrina get one of the two pas de deux, and Shanti and I earn the other. Ms. Vivienne states each dancer in the pas de deux will also have brief variations.

A hint of sadness colors the expressions of the dancers not selected for solos or duets. Then Ms. Vivienne reminds them they are the backbone of the performance. Without the corps de ballet, the entire story couldn't be told. This lifts their spirits and makes them a bit more enthusiastic.

Shanti inches closer to me and whispers, "I'd give someone else my role if I could."

My chest warms at her confession. "That's really nice of you."

Her pretty brown eyes on the group of girls not selected for variations or pas de deux, she swallows, shrugs, then turns to look at me. "I don't like dancing on stage," she admits in a whisper.

Confused, I narrow my eyes as I study her expression. "Since when?" We've been in six performances since we joined Rhythm and Flow. Not once has she said she didn't want to do it. And I never remember her looking uncomfortable.

She exhales a heavy sigh as her shoulders sag. "Since forever." Her gaze darts around the room a moment before returning to mine. "I don't like being the center of attention."

My face tightens as I think back on all the times she has been in the spotlight in class. I recall her smiles and appreciation as she demonstrated in class or danced at the front of the ensemble in a performance. She always looked ecstatic. Grateful. On top of the world. When the audience applauded, she smiled brighter.

Or did I imagine that?

Unsure what to say, I fumble over my words. "I don't... What do you..." I pause and inhale slowly. On the exhale, I say, "Why didn't you tell me?"

Before Shanti replies, Ms. Vivienne steals our attention and breaks the class into groups—variations, pas de deux, and ensemble. Laptops are set up for each group, then we watch the choreography for our routines. Luka and Sabrina will perform a different dance than me and Shanti, but we are asked to learn both.

After the third watch, we practice each dance while the video continues to play. Although Shanti and I have danced together in the past, we haven't done a true pas de deux. Maybe it's our age, maybe Ms. Neesa didn't think we were ready, or maybe it's something you get the opportunity to do once you've danced a certain number of years. I have no idea.

But dancing as a duo with Shanti feels natural.

Ms. Vivienne stands off to the side, gaze critical and head

tilted as we fumble through the routine. The way she watches us makes me queasy, but I try to shove the feeling down and focus on dancing.

When we reach the end, Ms. Vivienne approaches us, her blank expression not giving anything away. And then, a smile lifts the corners of her mouth. "Bravi." She applauds quietly as she closes the distance. "First run of the routine and you've confirmed I made the right decision."

Elation hums through my body as I stand taller. When I glance at Shanti, expecting her expression to mirror mine, my exhilaration fades at the look on her face. Posture stiff and eyebrows bent inward, she forces herself to smile.

But Ms. Vivienne doesn't pick up on it. Or she chooses to ignore it.

"Your connection on the dance floor is seamless. Beautiful. Rare." Ms. Vivienne circles us, her gaze curious. "I've not seen anything like it in dancers your age." Stopping at our side, she rests a hand on each of our shoulders. "There's nothing more powerful than the bond between dancers."

I shift my gaze from Ms. Vivienne to Shanti and really look at the girl a foot away. My skin and chest warm at the sight of her. Our bond isn't the same as the inseparable one I share with June, but it's a close runner-up.

"She's my best friend," I say without hesitation.

Shanti meets my gaze and slowly smiles, and it's the biggest one I've seen in weeks, maybe months. It's in that smile I see some of her worry disappear. "And he's mine."

"It shows," Ms. Vivienne says. "Connections like yours are lifelong. They're also the heart of every celebrated dance duo." A dreamy sound leaves her lips. "Keep at it and you will have incredible dance careers."

At this, Shanti lights up. The sparkle she rarely shows is in her eyes and tugging up the corners of her mouth.

And it is in this moment I realize she *needs* praise from someone other than me or our usual teachers. From the times I've practiced at her house, I know compliments are rare from her parents. Why? I wish I knew. But the lack of encouragement and commendation has obviously stolen some of her confidence.

But hearing the praise from a renowned dancer is exactly what Shanti needs.

"Thank you," Shanti says softly, her cheeks pink and eyes glassy.

After I thank Ms. Vivienne, she tells us to run the routine until the end of class, then she leaves us for Luka and Sabrina.

"Ready?" I move toward the laptop to start the video over, but pause when Shanti doesn't answer. Peering over my shoulder, I meet her eyes. "Do you need a minute?"

She nods.

I return to her side. "Everything okay?" I whisper-ask.

Dropping her gaze to the floor, she tugs at her skirt. The longer she stays quiet, the more it bothers me. Seconds ago, she was so excited. Thrilled to be here and chosen for this role. Then Ms. Vivienne walked away, and it was as if she took all of Shanti's joy with her.

How do I get it back for her? What can I do to give Shanti back her happiness?

"You don't know what it's like," she finally says.

When she doesn't say more, I speak up. "What?"

She toys with her skirt more, her fingers twisting the fabric. "To constantly be told you can do better. That being good isn't enough because you need to be the best."

Reaching for her, I clasp her elbows and wait until she looks at me to speak. "No one is perfect. No one is good at everything. And whoever is the best at something today might not be the best at it tomorrow."

Shanti shifts her weight from one foot to the other. "Tell that to my parents."

Someone should, but it won't be me. They wouldn't listen. I doubt they'd listen to my parents either.

"I wish I could make it better. You know I would."

Shanti nods. "I know."

Instead of spending useless energy on her parents, I decide to look at the positive. I want to encourage her to do the same.

"While we're dancing, focus on the routine and ignore everything else. Don't let the things you can't control take away your happiness. You're a rising star, Shanti. The only person who can change that is you."

She playfully shoves me away. "You're wise like an old man."

I release her and smile. "Thank you." I bow. "That's the best compliment I've gotten in a while." I want to tell her she is wise beyond her years too, but I keep it to myself.

Most kids our age care about video games, playing outside, junk food, apps on phones, and television. But those aren't our top priorities. Or secondary priorities. Dance, sports, and other extracurriculars tend to change your focus. Some make you mature at a younger age. Work harder because you want to prove you can do it all.

But it's okay to not do it all. It's okay to say you need a break. And no one should judge you or be cruel because you need to take care of yourself. Especially someone who says they care about you.

Shanti rolls her eyes. "You're a dork." She points at the laptop. "Let's practice."

"Fine," I say jokingly.

We go through the routine again, and I notice a difference in Shanti's footwork. I pick up on her boosted confidence. With each pass, she gets better, stronger, more in tune. With each pass, she is more alive.

When Ms. Neesa wraps up class, we go to our bags by the wall to change our shoes. As we sit, Shanti nudges my side with her elbow.

"Thank you." She gives me a gentle smile.

I lean toward her and bump her arm with mine. "For what?"

"I couldn't do this without you," she admits quietly.

"Do what? Dance?"

Shanti nods.

"Pshh." I shake my head. "Not true. You're a great dancer."

She shrugs. "Maybe, but I would've given up a long time ago if you weren't here."

I don't think that's true, but I keep that to myself. "Well, then I'm glad I'm here." I pause for a moment as I slip on my second shoe. "Wouldn't want anyone missing out on how amazing you are."

We stand and hook our bags over a shoulder. When I glance over at Shanti, a playful smile lifts the corners of her mouth.

I want her to smile more. I plan to make her smile twice as much in our next class.

Shanti opens her mouth to say something, but before she gets a word out, her mother's voice echoes through the room.

"Shanti, come."

I fist my bag strap at the way she speaks to Shanti. As if she isn't a person. As if she doesn't have feelings. As if she is something her parents checked off a list and are now doing the standard follow-through.

"We have important things to do before going home and"—she glances at her watch—"your class has made us late."

Shanti deflates faster than an untied, released balloon. Lifting a hand, she waves goodbye. "See you next class." And then she rushes past her mother, her head down as she darts out the door.

"Bye," I mumble, wishing there was more I could do.

FOUR
BOYS SUCK
SHANTI

Twelve Years Ago

"Ugh," I groan as I stare at the stack of books off to the side. "You didn't warn me I'd be doing homework until my hand cramped." Bringing my eyes back to the algebraic equations in my math text, I sag against the couch. It's not that I don't know *how* to do it. It's that I don't *want* to do it.

Beside me on the floor, hunched over his science book on the coffee table, pencil pressed to notebook paper, Jet chuckles as he scribbles.

I twist in place and narrow my eyes at him. "Are you laughing at me?"

He sets his pencil down, picks up his water bottle, unscrews the cap, and shrugs before taking a sip. "Not *at* you, just the situation."

I jab him with my elbow, and he all but chokes on his water.

"What was that for?" he sputters between coughs.

"You're a jerk."

Leaning away from me, he takes another sip of water. "How am I a jerk?"

"You're making fun of me." I cross my arms over my chest and dare him with a fierce gaze to challenge me right now.

He takes a slow, deep breath then shakes his head. "Promise, I wasn't teasing you." I open my mouth to disagree, but he holds up a hand to cut me off. At the same time, his expression softens. "I would never."

Warmth blankets me as my eyes dart between his. The way those three words came out… I believe him.

A hint of a smile tips up the corners of his mouth. "Two years ago, I was where you are—overwhelmed with a new school schedule, endless homework, extra dance practice, and spending time with everyone."

I turn back to look at my current assignment and mull over his confession. I think back to two years ago and try to recall a time when Jet seemed stressed. Sifting through countless memories, I search for any when he came off as frustrated or swamped. But I don't find a single one. Every memory of him is the same—full of smiles and his usual light, breezy mood.

"How?" My single-word question comes out in a cloud of disbelief.

Jet bumps my arm with his. "What do you mean?"

Uncertainty has my brows tugging together a beat before I meet his curious stare. "How did you do it all and not let it eat you alive?" I drop my chin to my chest and exhale a heavy sigh as I close my eyes. "I've had this workload a month and I'm ready to pull my hair out." Lifting my head, I gesture toward him with a hand, waving up and down his body. "But not you. After two years, you're cool and calm."

He snorts. "On the outside, and maybe a little on the inside." Running a hand through his longer-than-usual black strands, he sags against the couch. "But I swear, I felt everything you're feeling right now. Some nights, I did homework past bedtime. And on the days when it all felt like too much, I thought I'd have to give up dance."

"Really?"

Lips pursed, he nods. "Yeah. June picked up on it and went to our parents. The next day, Mom and Dad sat me down, and we had a long talk. They helped me work through my frustrations and told me they'd back whatever decision I made. They gave me guidance on how to juggle so many things, and if I still wanted to quit dance after a few months of trying, they'd support my choice."

God, how I wish my parents were as encouraging and understanding as Aurora and August Fox. I'd give anything to have parents who cared about *me* and not what I could potentially offer the world.

I am more than my intelligence.

I am a simple girl who wants to be loved. A soft girl forced to behave like a rigid, detached machine.

Unfortunately, my life was mapped out long before I took my first breath, and there is nothing I can do about it. Not until I'm of age, anyway.

"Will you help me?" My question is barely a whisper.

"Always." He smiles, soft at first, then so bright it makes my heart race. Then he tears a blank page from his notebook and starts ripping the paper to bits.

"What are you doing?"

"Shh." A mischievous smile plumps his cheeks. "I'm concentrating."

I roll my eyes and wait for him to wrap up his unexpected art project.

A few more tears, and he holds out his hand, palm open. "For you."

In the center of his palm is a lopsided paper heart. Jagged edges and minor indentations from the page he wrote on above it. It's plain and wrinkled and the best gift anyone has ever given me.

The backs of my eyes sting as I reach for and take the precious heart. "What's this for?" The words come out garbled, and I clear my throat.

"A token of my… friendship. Something to make you smile when times are hard." He shrugs then switches gears. "Come on. Let's finish what we're working on then give our brains a break with dance."

His logic makes no sense, but I slowly nod anyway. "Okay." I blink away the threatening tears then tuck my most prized possession in the front pocket of my backpack.

"What was that?" I catch myself before I twist my ankle, which wouldn't happen if Jet were focused. Once I have my footing, I spin around, prop my hands on my hips, and glare at him. "Your hands slipped on my waist."

"Sorry, sorry, sorry." He runs his hands through his hair as he walks circles in the living room.

Half an hour ago, we started our brain break. But it seems as though Jet's brain abandoned ship.

In the five years we've danced together, he has never put me in danger. He has never given me a reason to question him. Jet has always had my back—literally and figuratively. But right now, his focus is nowhere to be found.

Our conversation from earlier pops into my head, and I question if he is more overwhelmed than he wants to admit. Is he balancing too much? Giving just enough to each, but not his all?

Is that how he is doing everything without losing it?

No. Not Jet.

On a slow five-count, I summon every ounce of calm and make my voice neutral as I say, "You never slip."

He stops pacing, curls his hands into fists in his hair, and grunts before dropping his hands to his sides. "I know." He tips his head back, closes his eyes for two breaths, then meets my gaze. "I'm so damn sorry."

Hour-long seconds pass as we stare at each other. I study his gray eyes, the corners more crinkled than usual, the faint darkness I'd miss beneath them were I not looking so intently.

How did I miss his exhaustion?

Jet is my partner. How did I not know something was bothering him?

"What's wrong?" I ask before I can stop myself.

His brows twitch. "Nothing."

"Liar." I shake my head. "Did we not just have a conversation about our hectic schedules? You said you found a way to make it all work." I point to where we were dancing a moment ago. "But that…" I cross to him and *really* look at him. "That slip tells another story."

A storm swirls in his eyes as we stare off. As he decides what to say next. And then he exhales, his frame deflating.

Now, it's my turn to listen. *Really* listen.

I reach for and take his hand. "Talk to me."

For a moment, he stares at our clasped hands as he pieces his thoughts together. "It's a lot," he finally says. "And sometimes I get distracted. I start thinking about a project or an assignment while doing something else." Worry flickers in his gray eyes when they connect with mine again. "But not usually when we're dancing."

I flip my hands to hold his tighter. To comfort him. "Why didn't you tell me that an hour ago?"

He shrugs. "It hasn't been that bad. And we were talking about you. I wanted you to know you're not alone, but not steal the spotlight."

I've always known Jet to be selfless, but this… He'd let himself suffer to lift me up. It's not a bad trait to have, but it's not great either.

His feelings matter as much as mine. And I want to be a safe space for him to share them. Him being able to express what he is going through won't steal anything. I believe it gives space for both of us to shine brighter.

"Thank you." I squeeze his hands then let them go. "But we

should be able to share anything with each other. I don't want our relationship to be one-sided. You're my partner, Jet. What affects you affects me."

Bending at the knees, Jet lowers himself to sit on the floor. I mirror his position and cross my legs. He runs his hands up and down his thighs, his eyes following the repetitive action. The silence stretches between us, but I remain quiet.

This is his moment.

"I still love dance, but…"

My heart stops, my breath caught in my throat as my chest catches fire.

Is he giving up dance?

"My head is all over the place."

Since the start of the school year, my mind has felt like a never-ending tornado, spinning violently and turning everything upside down. The only thing that has kept me sane is Jet and our time on the dance floor.

In the past five years, Jet has become my biggest source of peace.

"Mine too. But you always level me out."

His brows pinch together. "I do?"

"Mm-hmm." I drop my gaze and pick at the hem of my skirt, unable to look at him as my next words come out. "When we're together, everything feels better. Safe. You give me so much strength. You make me feel like my true self." My mind drifts to the paper heart in my backpack, and I swallow hard. "When we dance, I feel capable. Free." The last word comes out so quiet I barely hear myself.

His hands stop on his knees, and my pulse soars.

Did I say too much?

"You are all those things, even without me." Emotion laces his words.

Jet Fox… will he ever take credit for all the good he puts into the world? No, probably not.

I lay my hands over his on his knees. "Is it school?" I pause, dreading the answer to my next question. "Are you thinking about quitting dance?"

His eyes fly to mine. "Not quitting dance," he says, tone firm as he shakes his head. "It's my escape. My happy place."

"Okay." I rise to stand and offer him my hand. He takes it and gets up. "Enough of that for now, as long as you promise to talk to me before it gets bad again."

"Pinkie promise." He holds his hand between us, pinkie extended. "But only if you promise the same."

We hook pinkies and squeeze, swearing to not let each other get to this place again.

The next half hour of dancing feels lighter, happier, back to normal. When the final song ends, I turn and give him my biggest smile. My chest turns warm and bubbly when he returns it.

Sweaty and flushed, everything feels right. Perfect. Back to how it was before all the crazy school schedules.

His phone chimes with a notification, and he crosses the room to the table. Wiping his forehead with a towel, he swipes up his phone and unlocks it. A bright smile lights his face as his cheeks turn a darker shade of pink.

I love that smile. But my stomach twists at the thought of him giving it to someone else.

"Who is it?" I ask as I reach his side.

His fingers fly as he types out a reply. "A girl in my grade. We've been talking."

My body stiffens as the world wobbles beneath my feet.

He is talking to a girl in his grade? Since when? Who is she? Why hasn't he brought her up? What does she look like?

I bet she is pretty. Only someone real pretty would be Jet's girlfriend.

Is she his girlfriend?

I think I'm going to puke. But only after I hit something. Hard.

We just talked about sharing stuff with each other. That we wouldn't hold back. We promised we'd say if things were hard and ask for help when we needed it.

But he completely left out the fact he has a girlfriend. I bet that is where all his time is going.

Fired up, I ball my fingers into fists as he keeps texting. "No wonder you can't focus," I grit out.

His fingers freeze as his eyes dart from the phone screen to me. "What? No." He shakes his head.

My nails dig into my palms. "You have a girlfriend." The last word comes out like sandpaper.

Tossing his phone onto the couch, he grips my biceps with a gentle yet firm hold. "She's not my girlfriend." He bends his knees so we are eye level. "I swear."

I clench my teeth. "But you want her to be."

He doesn't say anything, and the fire in my chest burns hotter.

"Whatever." I tear myself from his hold and start to gather my stuff. This is the last place I want to be right now.

"Why are you so mad?" It's a genuine question. "She's just a friend. The same as you."

I stop shoving my books into my backpack and look at him over my shoulder. "So now I'm just a friend."

"You know what I mean." He lets out a frustrated sigh.

"Aren't you too young for a girlfriend?" I toss over my shoulder. I'll be lucky if my parents let me near any boy other than Jet until I'm eighteen.

"Shanti, will you stop. Please." He plops down on the couch. "It's nothing serious. Callie is a friend."

Part of me believes him. But the upset part of me won't listen right now—her thoughts are all over the place, and she wants to leave. Now.

So, I do.

With the last of my things in my backpack, I sling it over my shoulder, stand up, and head for the door. The moment I step outside, I dig through the front pocket of my backpack and retrieve the paper heart. I stare at it for one, two, three breaths before I shred it and toss the litter on his porch.

Boys suck.

FIVE

GIRLS SUCK

JET

Eleven Years Ago

LIMBS ACHING AND EYES WEARY, A YAWN LEAVES MY LIPS AS I SHUFFLE through the entrance of the connected middle and high school campus. In no rush to start another lackluster academic day, I mosey into the open courtyard with my peers. Those of us who arrive early meander to our usual bench, patch of grass, picnic table, or spot on the stone wall surrounding the garden at the heart.

June bumps my arm in a silent *see you later* then wanders off to sit with their friends.

It isn't often I get to sit around and do nothing. Most of my day, week, and foreseeable future are mapped out. Between dance, academics, family time, and the occasional stint spent with friends, free time isn't something I have much of. So the fifteen-ish minutes of solitude I get from when I arrive at school to when I head to class aren't taken for granted.

Slipping in my earbuds, I tap on my extensive morning playlist, amble over to an unoccupied evergreen, and lower myself to the ground with the thick trunk at my back. The rock song I'd hit pause on yesterday transitions into a hip-hop number.

And for an uninterrupted, blissful moment, I close my eyes and get lost in the track.

The balance I've struggled with the past couple of years whispers in the back of my mind, begging for attention, but I ignore it. I shove it down and focus on the music flooding my ears. The sweet relief I don't get enough of.

Something has to give, or ease or become second nature, not only for me but also my family.

It's in the small details that I sense their concern over my stress and hectic schedule. June checks on me more frequently, asking if there is anything they can help with. Dad hugs me harder, longer, and always ends each embrace with a *you know I'm proud of you, no matter what, right?* And Mom... gods, she is an open book. Obvious. Beyond transparent. She wears her empathy on her sleeve. Speaks her mind more honestly and tenderly than anyone I know. And she has the uncanny ability to let you know how she feels with a single look.

I don't take their love for me for granted. I wouldn't be who I am without them.

But this—my jam-packed, endless itinerary—I need to figure out on my own. I need to learn how to balance everything I want in my life. Better to figure it out now before more gets piled on.

The song transitions to a calm piano piece. I take a deep breath and slowly open my eyes. Scan the bustling courtyard, searching for the same person I do every morning.

Shanti.

Things have been... off between us. Not in a bad way. Just different. Our focus and priorities have changed.

While I continue to seek balance, to find a way to keep doing dance—something I love—while more is added to my academic workload, Shanti spends more time with friends. As far as I know, her grades are fine. She still shows up at dance class, does what is expected of her, but doesn't seem to want to be *better*. From the outside, it looks like she is doing the bare minimum. Enough to get by without receiving the wrath of her parents.

As her dance partner and closest friend, someone I spend a great deal of time with, her apathy feels like a festering wound niggling beneath the surface, itching to be set free and spread like a virus. But I can't say that with certainty. And I definitely can't say that to her.

Maybe it's hormones. Maybe it's peer pressure. Or maybe it is a deep-rooted need to defy anyone who tells her what her life should look like. A relentless impulse to push against every boundary, claw at every decision made by someone else for her. I honestly don't know.

Maybe I'm looking at this from the wrong angle.

From what I've seen, her parents are good people. Strict and a little cold, but otherwise good. Yes, they do things differently than my family, but that isn't necessarily a bad thing. Then again, maybe I'm unable to see the whole picture. Maybe in the comfort of her home, her life isn't the same as what she lets me see.

Whatever the reason, I miss my friend. I miss how we used to be. Miss the younger version of us. Miss the way I was her favorite person, and she was mine.

Shanti is still my favorite person. She always will be. It would take something extreme to change that.

Rather than disturb the peace, rather than act selfishly and whine about my temporary misery, I keep my thoughts to myself and trudge forward. I continue to do things as I always have.

Rising from my spot beneath the tree, I wipe the dirt from my jeans, pull my earbuds out, and head for the hallway entrance.

Everything will work out. It always has.

Textbook tucked to my chest, I shut my locker and cross the hall for my last class, English lit. Although it's not my favorite subject, I do love how the teacher challenges our mindsets. How they ask us to read books that make us think deeper and see the world through someone else's perspective. How they encourage us to write essays and stories that provoke others to question societal "norms."

I wish more teachers would push our boundaries and comfort levels in this way. To make us want to question why some things are considered acceptable while others are not.

"Afternoon, Jet," the teacher greets as I enter the room. "Good day?" They sort through a stack of papers on their desk.

"Better now that it's almost over," I answer with a hint of laughter as I take my seat.

"How is Monday always the longest day?"

I shrug in answer, then sift through my backpack for my English folder.

Students file into the room, most of them after the warning bell rings. Seconds before the final bell, an unfamiliar boy approaches the teacher's desk. A green shirt clings to him like a second skin while light denim rests loose on his waist and legs. Black slip-on Vans on his feet and a hoodie draped over his arm, he stands tall and confident while the teacher studies the paper he gave them. A moment later, the paper is handed back and the teacher gestures to the empty desk next to mine.

"Class, we have a new student. This is Mason. Please make him feel welcome."

The class is a mix of greetings, grunts, hand waves, and some giving zero attention to the teacher or Mason.

"Hey," I greet with a smile as Mason sets his backpack on the floor. "I'm Jet."

Mason gives me a casual, well-practiced smile as he sits down. "Hey."

I open my mouth to offer notes or help if Mason needs them to catch up, but don't get the chance.

"Alright, class. Let's get to work. Pull out your copy of *To Kill a Mockingbird*." The teacher grabs a worn copy from the bookshelf and brings it to Mason. "Use this copy until you have your own. All I ask is that you not mark it up."

Class carries on per usual, but something feels *different*. A faint energy hums in the room that didn't exist until Mason came in. It feels familiar, but I'm unsure how.

Peeking at him out of the corner of my eye, I study his features a little more intently. Long, dexterous fingers that slowly lead to slender yet strong forearms and sun-kissed skin you rarely see in Washington. For someone our age, his biceps are sculpted, his muscles flexing the slightest bit when he digs through his back-pack for a pencil and paper. And when I reach his face, I turn my head a little more in his direction for a better view. There is some-thing… regal about his features. Refined. Honed. But I can't quite place it.

Something about Mason is familiar, but I can't quite put my finger on what it is.

And then, his gaze lifts and meets mine across the aisle. Neither of us smiles, nor do we offer a response. We just stare at each other. It isn't uncomfortable or awkward. It just… is.

The teacher asks the class a question and it snaps my attention away from Mason. For the rest of class, I focus on our assignment. But the entire time, Mason lingers in my periphery—physically and mentally.

When the bell rings, I hang back rather than bolt out the door. While I gather my belongings, I turn to face Mason. "If you need a study buddy or just a friendly face to hang out with, let me know."

Zipping up his backpack, a lighter smile plumps Mason's cheeks. "Thanks. Worst part about moving is making new friends."

"Not your first move?"

Mason shakes his head. "I've lost track. With my mom's job, we move a lot. Dad works remote, so it doesn't faze him." His expression falls, as if all the joy has been sucked from the room. "It's cool to see new places, and I'm grateful for everything I have, but it sucks to not have a place to call home."

Rising from my desk, I sling my backpack over my shoulders. "Maybe this time you'll get to stay. Stone Bay is a great town." I meet his gaze and hold it. "And you're welcome at my house any time."

"Hopefully." Mason grips his backpack straps. "Thanks, Jet."

Leg on the barre and arms outstretched, I bend forward, grip my foot, and press my chest to my thigh. A faint stretch warms the hamstring and calf muscles in my leg as I breathe slowly and count to ten. Straightening, I back off the stretch for a count of five, then repeat. When I've done the same on the other leg, I switch to lunges. One move after another, I move through the rigorous warm-up routine I've done for years.

Halfway through quad stretches, Shanti steps into the studio, sets her bag near mine, and starts the same routine in the spot next to me at the barre. Silence stretches between us, but it isn't uncomfortable. There is something magical about the energy Shanti and I have shared as partners for years. It's akin to a cozy favorite blanket you can't help but wrap yourself in and sigh. It's safe and intimate—like home. It sets the tone of our headspace during dance.

Slowly, fellow dancers filter into the studio and start their own warm-up routines. I acknowledge them with a smile or nod but otherwise focus on myself.

Then the door swings open and a new but familiar energy tugs at my attention.

Lifting my head from my knee, I sit up in a full split and glance toward the door. When I spot a head of short, sandy-blond hair, my pulse races in my chest.

Palms planted on the floor, I steady myself as I rake my eyes down his slender frame. Sculpted muscles on display, I ogle Mason's biceps longer than usual before moving to the cotton shirt hugging his torso. Lean but prominent pecs stretch the material. Inch by slow inch, I trail my gaze down, down, down until I reach his waistband. Breath held, my chest burns as I take in the black leggings snug on his chiseled glutes and thighs.

My groin aches as my eyes drift to his for a beat. Swallowing, I shift my attention to the floor, swing my legs out of the split, and take a few meditative breaths to ease my impending hard-on.

Mason isn't the first guy I've been attracted to, but he is the first to make me lose focus so easily. When he enters the room, something primal inside insists I pay attention. And without hesitation, I obey.

I feel something similar with Shanti. Always have. But her energy, her gravity is different. Softer. Sweeter. Quieter.

But Mason… his aura is loud. Bold. Colorful. It reaches out its proverbial hands, grabs a hold of you, and says *Look at me*.

And I do exactly that.

His gaze meets mine as he crosses the room, two deep dimples appearing as he gives me his smile.

I rise to my feet, praying any sign of my possible erection is absent. "Hey, man," I say as he reaches me. "Didn't know you dance."

Unhooking the duffel from his shoulder, he tips his head toward the wall in a silent *walk with me* gesture, and I follow. "Yeah, it's not something I bring up." He sets his bag down, unzips it, then strips off his shirt and stuffs it inside.

The air evaporates in my lungs.

He's so comfortable in his skin. His beautiful, soft, sun-kissed skin.

I shake off the thought and swallow past the dryness in my throat. "Why not?"

Green eyes meet my grays and hold them for a beat. A grimace tugs at his lips as he shrugs. "Most guys our age don't get it."

My brows pinch together in confusion.

He rolls his lips between his teeth, and the action is a direct link to my dick. With every ounce of mental strength, I demand that my body not physically react. At least not now.

Mason shrugs. "They don't understand why we dance." He toes off his sneakers, stows them in his duffel, and takes out a pair of black leather split-sole ballet shoes, slipping them on as he continues. "The name-calling and jabs get old fast. Especially when you're the new kid. So I don't bring it up."

I haven't been the new kid in a long time, yet I understand where Mason is coming from. The taunts are rare in Stone Bay, but not nonexistent. Same with the homophobic slurs. Because, for whatever reason, a select few of the jocks in town see formal dancing as effeminate. And to show off their "masculinity," they ridicule and bully guys like me and Mason.

Although I've only experienced verbal abuse, it somehow feels worse than any physical blow.

With a nod, I roll my shoulders and start my upper-body exercises. "Yeah, I get it. But now, if you want to talk about it, you have someone on your side."

"Thanks, Jet." He zips up his bag and turns to face the room. "Where do you warm up?"

I lead him to my usual spot near Shanti and offer him the barre since I don't need it. As Mason props his leg on the barre, Shanti lifts her chest from the floor and takes a deep breath, slowly bringing her feet back to center from a side split.

With a soft groan, Shanti glances up and meets my eyes. "Will you help stretch my—" Her question dies on her tongue as her attention shifts to Mason. An unmistakable blush colors Shanti's cheeks as she openly stares at him.

My stomach sours at the sight.

Am I guilty of doing the same a moment ago? Yes. No sense in denying my interest in Mason.

But something about Shanti's fixation feels different. The way she... *admires* him wrings my insides. And I don't like it. At all.

"Who's this?" she asks instead of finishing her previous question.

I inhale deeply and shove down the twisty, anxious sensation simmering in my chest. "This is Mason. We're in English lit together. He recently moved to Stone Bay." I turn to face Mason and the unsettled feeling in my belly amplifies tenfold as I take in his beaming smile... aimed at Shanti. Clenching my teeth, I continue the introduction. "Mason, this is Shanti. *My* best friend. *My* partner."

Mason appears oblivious to the emphasis of my words. But not Shanti. The second I stop speaking, she breaks eye contact with him and looks at me. For a split second, the irritation and apprehension fade away. Until she rolls her eyes.

Shanti rises from her spot on the floor and closes the distance between her and Mason. "Nice to meet you." She jerks her head in my direction. "Ignore Jet's less-than-warm introduction." Her blush deepens as her lips curve into an unforgettable smile. "Obviously, he's in a mood."

I open my mouth to respond, but get cut off by Ms. Neesa calling class to order.

Shuffling to my usual spot on the dance floor, I take a deep breath and try to let go of the past few minutes. Now is not the time to focus on my newfound jealousy. Now is the time to focus on why I'm in this studio—dance.

After we go through the start-up routine, Ms. Neesa and Mr. Aurelio demonstrate new choreography for us to practice. Then, they do it again. In addition to the steps everyone performs, Mason and I are asked to do two other arrangements. Once we have the footwork down, we will work with partners.

The room around me disappears as I pour my energy and soul into the choreography. I replay the moves in my head a half second before my body mirrors them. My muscles burn as sweat dampens my skin, but I keep going, relishing the sensation. With a slight bend of my knees, I straighten and push up on my toes, lift a foot to my knee, then extend it back and up, holding it for a count of two before planting it on the floor.

Time feels infinite as I glide through the room, as I soar through the air, as I tell a story with my body rather than my voice. Every kick of my legs, lift of my heels, spin on my toes, burn in my muscles, reminds me why I was born to dance. Why I wouldn't be whole without it.

When I reach the end of the choreography, my eyes search the mirror for Shanti as they have every other class. The moment I land on her, my body stiffens.

A hand over her mouth, she tries to hide her smile. But there is no use. Nothing can hide the most radiant smile I've seen her bear. A smile aimed at Mason as he fakes not being able to do part of the movement.

Tightness forms in the center of my chest as I stare in disbelief, the two of them behaving more like longtime friends instead of new acquaintances.

It's not until Mason meets my gaze in the mirror that my frozen form begins to thaw. The corner of Mason's mouth lifts into a sly smirk. His brows waggle. And then his attention is back on Shanti as he purposely fumbles a move.

The tightness in my chest turns painful and hot as I clench my fists. But my agitation is short-lived.

Mr. Aurelio sidles up to me and coaches me on my performance. His critique and direction are enough to distract me from whatever is happening between Shanti and Mason.

After I go through the routine again, Mr. Aurelio praises my technique and gives me a few more pointers. I give him my full attention and absorb every word, mentally correcting the moves in my head for next time.

"Ready for the male solo routine?" he asks.

Thrill blooms in my chest as my pulse quickens. "Absolutely."

The class shuffles to the back wall, light chatter filling the room as Mr. Aurelio takes the floor. A new song echoes off the walls a beat before Mr. Aurelio starts the dance choreographed specifically with me in mind.

The studio disappears as I study every placement of his feet, every lift and bend of his legs, every jump and more. I etch every move into my mind. Memorize the way his body flows with the dance, as if he is the music and the story.

When he finishes, I step forward, ready to pour my soul into the routine that's already replaying in my head.

In position, the song starts over. And for the next few minutes, I bleed art and beauty. There is no *me and the dance*. I am the dance. The dance is me. We are one and the same, and I've never felt more alive.

Applause fills the room when the song ends. My heart hammers in my chest as immense joy and pride fill my veins. It's one thing to do what you love. But it's much more fulfilling when others celebrate your accomplishments with you.

"Magnificent, Jet," Mr. Aurelio reveres, a sparkle in his eyes. "Everyone, back to practice. Jet, I'd like you to alternate between both routines."

Cheek-stinging smile on my face, I nod, then head for a larger space off to the side. Wanting to maintain this happy buzz, I don't seek out Shanti or Mason. I focus on the routines and my form in the mirror. For thirty blissful minutes, I ignore everything except what matters—my artistry.

But it isn't long before reality hits again. And when it does, it's as if I've landed in some parallel universe. I cross the room with slow steps, soaking up the sight of my best friend, my partner, giggling with and hanging on the new guy in town.

Jealousy roars to life in my chest once more, and I mentally work to stomp it down. I'm not that kind of guy, nor do I want to be. Shanti can befriend whoever she wants, and I should be happy she has more people in her circle. Whatever this newfound jealousy is, it's petty and foolish.

I should be supporting her, not trying to win her like a prize.

Sidling up to them, I take off my shoes and swap them for my sneakers. "How'd you do with the new routine?"

Shanti tugs an oversized shirt down her body, one of her shoulders exposed. "Good. Need to work on a couple of the transitions, but I have it down."

Wide smile aimed her way, I bump her arm with mine. "You're incredible." I meet Mason's eyes. "What about you?"

Mason gives a noncommittal shrug. "Fumbled a few times, but

Shanti swooped in to save the day." His gaze flicks to Shanti as a flirty smile dances on his lips.

Ignore, ignore, ignore.

"Shanti and I study after class." I sling my bag over my shoulder. "We should get going so we don't lose time."

"Come with us, Mason." It's more a command than suggestion as Shanti waves him our way. "We don't mind, right, Jet?"

Actually...

"Of course not," I say, my need to keep the peace strong. The last thing I want is Shanti upset.

The glee on Shanti's face gnaws at the building tightness in my chest. And on the next breath, I decide I can't do this—spend the next couple of hours watching them flirt with each other.

So, I do something I've never done before.

I pretend to be surprised a beat before I reach in my duffel and pull out my phone. I tap on the message icon and open the text chain between me and June. I read an old message from yesterday, but act as though it was sent seconds ago. And then, for the first time in my life, I lie to my best friend.

"Crap."

Shanti's brows scrunch. "What's wrong?"

"Totally forgot Mom organized some special dinner for tonight." I feign being upset. "Sorry, but I have to skip studying today." I swallow past the thickness in my throat. "You two go ahead."

"Oh." Shanti tilts her head for a breath as she studies my face.

Before she says anything else, I turn and head for the door on fast feet. When I step outside, I suck in a sharp breath and hold it for five, four, three, two, and exhale.

The ache in my chest from earlier comes back stronger, and I gasp at the foreign pain. Rather than call my older sister or one of my parents for a ride, I trek through neighborhoods until I reach Granite Parkway. I trudge down the main road in town and get lost in the noise as residents shop and dine.

My feet eat up the distance as I work through the hurt, a heartache I've never experienced until now. And by the time I make it home a couple hours later, my mood is calmer, and my next steps are clear.

Shanti is my best friend, my dance partner, and that is all. I will do anything to keep her in my life, to see her happy and thriving.

So instead of making a decision that can ruin everything, I make one that will keep the peace... even if it is not what I want.

I shove down every emotion other than friendship for Shanti. I let go of my jealousy so she can soar.

PART TWO

PAST

SOME THINGS ARE INEVITABLE

SIX
SO, THIS IS LOSS
JET

Nine and a Half Years Ago

IT STARTS AS A SLOW DRIP. AN UNHURRIED YET STEADY PITTER-PATTER. You see it, hear it, know it is happening, but you can't move. Can't seem to turn off the drawn-out, eventual death of it. Even when it breaks your heart. Even when it hurts unlike anything you've ever experienced.

In the past year and a half, I've learned there are different types of loss. And this one, as of now, is the worst.

Losing someone little by little but watching them come to life with someone else, it's a blunt object to the heart.

Mason, the boy who claimed he could never make friends or put down roots because his family moved too often, is still here. Because for whatever reason, fate is on his side. The gods have decided to cut him a break and let him have stability.

Although him staying in Stone Bay has had an unpleasant impact on me, I still find a way to be happy for him. Because Mason makes Shanti smile more than I did for years. He makes her laugh and feel lighter. With him, she shines brighter.

And I refuse to be the person to take that from her. Not when all I've ever wanted for Shanti is for her to bloom and excel.

Seeing her carefree and thriving is the only gift I need. Or so I keep telling myself.

"Has Mom let you practice driving more?" Delilah asks, snapping me out of my thoughts.

Twisting to face her in the driver's seat, I trace the lid of my water bottle in the cup holder with a finger. "No. Said she doesn't want us to be *too* good before we get a permit." I chuckle then fall quiet. "I think she's just worried June and I will leave home sooner if we're more self-sufficient."

Delilah briefly glances my way, sympathy coloring her expression. She has firsthand experience of Mom's subtle melancholy over her children *leaving the nest*. We all witnessed it, but none more than my big sister.

When Delilah left for college in late summer last year, Mom became someone else. She wasn't her usual joyful, lighthearted self. Sure, she smiled, laughed, and loved just as hard. But anyone who really knows her was able to see the difference in her spirit. You felt it in the way her hugs were a touch firmer and lasted a little longer.

Mom wants us to live and love and do what makes us happy. She wants to see us thrive and do incredible things. But she also selfishly wants to keep us tucked under her wing for as long as we will allow her to.

Not sure I have the heart to step out from under her protective shield anytime soon. Lucky for Mom, she has June and me for no less than three and a half years before the subject comes up.

A soft smile curves Delilah's lips. "I easily picture you exploring the world. Hiking miles of national parks. Traveling to other countries to visit monuments and castles." Her smile widens. "Although your roots are deep and resilient, you're a free spirit, Jet Storm Fox." She flips on the blinker, pauses at a stop sign, looks both ways, then turns. "June loves those things too, but is happier here. They'd enjoy seeing the world, but not the same as you. June prefers repetition and routine. They would be happy staying in Stone Bay and working at Sage Whisperer with

Mom until the shop is passed on to them. You, my brother, are an adventure waiting to happen."

If Delilah hadn't already chosen her college major, I'd suggest she take psychology. Her ability to read people is uncanny. And the way she always searches for the positive is admirable.

"I love how well you know me. June, too." I lean across the center console and press a kiss to her cheek. "Best big sister anyone could ask for."

Delilah steers the car into the dance studio parking lot and pulls up to the drop-off spot near the doors. "Love you too." She reaches over and ruffles my hair. "Want me to pick you up after class?"

"Please. I should be ready to go in a couple hours," I say as I grab my duffel from the floorboard and exit the car. "Thanks for the ride."

"Have a great session," she says with a wave before I shut the door.

Gods, how I've missed her. Not that I spent a great deal of time with Delilah before she went off to college. When there is a five-year age difference between you and your older sibling, after a certain age, your interests aren't the same.

Delilah has always been a sounding board between me and June and our parents. A happy middle person who explained our perspectives in ways each of us could understand. But she also has this beautiful energy that makes everything better when she is in the room.

Thank goodness her winter break coincides with mine this year. I miss movie nights with too many salty and sugary snacks. I miss how she listens without judgment and offers wisdom on what to do next.

As far as big sisters go, June and I lucked out with Delilah.

Setting my duffel down, I peel off my layers, ditch my fur-lined boots, and slip on my split soles. Ms. Neesa waves from the office, currently open to the classroom. I return the gesture before crossing to the barre to start warm-ups.

Per usual, I'm the first to arrive. It'll be at least ten minutes before the next person shows. A couple years ago, the next person would have been Shanti. Not anymore.

Since Mason came to Stone Bay, Shanti only sees him. Instead of dancing with me at the studio, now she dances with him. Rather than come to my house after dance ends to do homework, she leaves and goes somewhere with him.

As I stretch and twist my body, as sensation ripples and nerves fire beneath my skin, as I get lost in my head—my new normal when Shanti is around—I remind myself it isn't all about me and my happiness. Remind myself I don't exist alone in the world. Remind myself I am fortunate to have an amazing circle of people who love me as I am.

Since Mason's arrival, I've become a distant star in Shanti's sky. A shimmering light in the background, struggling to stay in her line of sight.

And I'm exhausted.

The rest of the class trickles in over the next thirty minutes. We go about our typical before-class routines until Ms. Neesa and Mr. Aurelio stand at the front of the room.

My gaze flits to the wall of mirrors, searching for Shanti or Mason. But I don't find either of them. Maybe one or both are sick. It is flu season.

Ms. Neesa asks everyone to quiet down, then goes into what we will be working on today. Just as she and Mr. Aurelio start the demonstration, the door flies open.

Shanti giggles and Mason snort-laughs as they enter, the sounds echoing loudly off the bare walls. All eyes shift in their direction, a few looks of irritation in the group.

"Nice of you to finally join us, Ms. Mahal, Mr. Powell. Places. Quickly and quietly." The hint of sharpness in Ms. Neesa's tone states she does not take kindly to her class being disrupted. "All eyes on the instruction."

Everyone snaps their attention to the demonstration. A

moment later, in my periphery, Shanti and Mason shuffle to their usual spot on the floor... without warming up.

After a second run-through of the dance, we work on the routine solo before pairing up. Since Mason joined, Shanti and I rarely partner up. Lately, I've danced with Blair. Although our flow is a little less than smooth, I enjoy working with her.

When Ms. Neesa is satisfied with our solo technique, we shift to working pas de deux. Not a minute in, giggling erupts in the back of the room.

I don't have to look to know who it is. Until Mason showed up, there was no goofing off in class.

Rather than get frustrated and upset over something I can't change, I zone out and put all my energy into my dance with Blair. Focus on my footwork, jumps, as well as hers. Keep my body strong and tall, but my limbs loose and delicate. Replay the dance in my head a second ahead of my own movements, preparing for the upcoming lift.

My fingers curl around Blair's ribs a breath before I lift her off the floor. Her legs gently kick once, her arms extend wide at her sides, and then I gracefully lower her to the floor. As we transition into the next step, a scream echoes through the room.

Yanked from my focus, I glance around the studio. When my eyes land on Shanti on the floor, my insides twist.

I dart across the room and drop to my knees at her side. Tears flood her eyes as she clutches her hip.

"What hurts?" I ask as I scan every inch of her.

Shanti sniffles and taps her hip.

"I'm sorry, Shan," Mason whispers from behind me.

"Aurelio, call the nonemergency line," Ms. Neesa hollers.

Fire roars in my veins. His apology is my tipping point, and I whip around to face him.

"Get the fuck away from her," I yell. "You may have seriously hurt her. Your apology is bullshit."

Mason shrinks back at my words. He opens his mouth to say something else, but snaps it shut, probably for the best.

Turning back to Shanti, I soften my gaze and voice. "Can I check you?" I hold a hand over her hip.

A tear rolls down her cheek as she nods. "Yes." The single word cracks.

With the barest of touches, I palpate her hip, thigh, and calf. I unlace and ease off her pointe shoe, then continue checking her foot. I'm no doctor, but it feels as though everything is where it should be. No broken bones.

Thank goodness.

I sweep an arm under her knees and ribs and gently lift her into my lap. Leaning into her, I embrace her with the utmost care and drop my forehead to her crown.

"I've got you," I say, a breath above a whisper. "You're safe now."

Shanti shakes in my arms as she fists my shirt. "How could I be so stupid?" Her sobs come a little louder.

Swaying side to side, I do all I can to comfort her while we wait on the medics. "Shh, shh, shh."

"I'm sorry, Jet. So, so sorry."

The backs of my eyes sting as emotion clogs my throat. "It's over now. I've got you."

"Thank you." She wipes at the tears on her cheeks. "For always being there when I need you most."

Warmth floods my chest, and I tighten my hold on her. "Always." I inhale a shuddering breath. "I'll never let you fall."

OVERPROTECTIVE MUCH?

SHANTI

Nine Years Ago

SWEAT ROLLS DOWN MY SPINE AS I BEND AT THE WAIST AND BAND MY arms around my legs, hugging myself close. A familiar ache flares in my hamstrings, a noticeable tug in my calves, but I ignore the hint of pain that comes. The regular, ordinary throb in my muscles I've grown accustomed to over the years.

Closing my eyes, I inhale deeply and slowly twist my torso to the side. A sharp, fiery stab of pain ignites in my hip and lower back. The same pain I've dealt with for months. Since the day Mason dropped me.

The backs of my eyes sting as I exhale a shaky breath. *Pain is part of the process. Push through it.*

Taking another deep breath, I move back to center a moment before twisting to the opposite side. The fire dissipates as I settle into the new stretch, and I sigh in relief.

The fall happened a little more than six months ago, yet I still haven't completely recovered. After X-rays and MRI scans, the doctor assured me, my parents, and my dance instructors I had no breaks or fractures. Once my scans were clear, they did a series of

muscle tests. Unfortunately, those did not have as happy an outcome.

Manufactured sympathy curved their lips as the doctor shared the diagnosis. Muscle contusions on my lateral and posterior hip and strain to my hip flexors and IT band. The relaxed tone of their voice unnerved me as they rattled off my treatment plan—lots of rest, ice on the affected areas no less than five times a day, compression wrap on my thigh until the strains heal, frequent limb elevation, over-the-counter pain meds, and physical therapy once able.

They made it sound so simple. As if I'd just *bounce* back after halting my daily stretches and regular dance routines for weeks. All I'd wanted to do in that moment was tell the doctor off.

Now, half a year later, I still struggle to hit my mark on the dance floor. Still grapple with my body not performing the same as it did before the fall. But most of all, I still haven't come to terms with the mental and emotional side effects.

Since that nightmare of a day, I've fought against the undertow of my thoughts. The whispered words in the recesses of my mind telling me I'll never be one of the greats. I'll never live up to my parents' expectations.

That my dance career is over at thirteen.

Straightening to my full height, I flex my leg, grab my foot, pull it up and into my body, and stretch my quads. A more tolerable fire lights as I engage my main hip flexor. I take a deep breath, then another as I hold it. The irrational part of my mind tells me to lift my leg higher, to tuck the bottom of my foot to my back and breathe through any pain. And for a moment, I give the idea serious thought. I consider pushing my boundaries.

Until I spot Jet crossing the curtained-off area behind the amphitheater stage. At the sight of him, all temptation to indulge in my reckless thoughts evaporates, and I relax my grip. As I release my leg to stretch the other, he sidles up to me and starts another round of warm-ups.

"Remind me to *never* sign up for outdoor performances in the summer again," he says, humor lacing his tone.

Twisting to meet his gaze, I arch a brow. "And miss the opportunity to listen to you complain all day? Where's the fun in that?"

Jet scrunches his lips and nose as he narrows his eyes. "Ha ha." Arms up, he rotates his shoulder joints in large circles. "Heat waves and impermeable materials are not a good combination." He snaps the waistband of his leggings.

My ensemble will need a thorough cleaning after today. I've never sweat in so many new and uncomfortable places.

"Can't argue with that." I switch from lower to upper-body stretches. "How much longer until we go on?"

"Fifteen." Jet hums. "I overheard Mr. Aurelio assuring Ms. Neesa everything would be perfect. Seems she's worried the town won't enjoy today's performance."

In early February, two major events happened. The first is why we are here. The second…

When the mayor stopped by the studio a week into February, he had an exciting proposal for the dancers of Rhythm and Flow. A half hour on stage at the annual Independence Day festival. A perfect opportunity to show the town ballet isn't just graceful and delicate.

Ms. Neesa and Mr. Aurelio said yes without hesitation. Since mid-February, we have worked hard on today's show. With modifications and extra hours once I was cleared by the physical therapist, I learned the routine and kept pace with the rest of the class.

The day after Valentine's is when the other event happened.

After my fall during winter break, Mason and I drifted apart. While I was immersed in anger and tears, Mason drowned in guilt and worry. For weeks, he called and texted and expressed his sincere apology for what happened. Like my moods, my response —or lack thereof—varied.

It wasn't until his text on Valentine's Day that I felt something other than hurt.

MASON

One day, I hope you find it in your heart to
forgive me. If you do, I'm just a text away. Happy
V Day. Until our paths cross again xo

The last line of Mason's text had several horrific thoughts running through my head, and I called him immediately. We talked for over an hour, and for ten minutes, he swore that last line of his message didn't mean what I'd interpreted it as. He had no intention of harming himself. Mason assured me he'd be okay —eventually.

Like me, he spent a lot of time in his head over what happened. Wondering if things would be different now if he'd acted differently then. I told him there was no use in asking endless what-if questions. What's done is done. Verbally, he agreed, but I picked up on the doubt in his voice.

As the call went on, as we got past more apologies, I figured out the context behind the last line of his text.

Mason was moving again. The next day.

"This was the first time I let myself hope." His sigh echoes through the phone. *"I really like it here. It was nice to have friends, even if I messed things up."*

And for weeks following that call and his departure from Stone Bay, guilt clouded my mood. I'd spent so much time being angry at Mason over the fall, I never once considered how he felt about it. That my injury and distress took their toll on his happiness as much as they did mine.

Mason has texted once or twice a week since his move to check in. He shares what he loves and dislikes about living in the outskirts of Denver, sends jokes that make me snort-laugh, and occasionally tells me he misses me and hanging out together. I pass along the newest drama in Stone Bay, send him pictures of my latest disastrous attempts at cooking, and tell him I miss him too.

The one thing neither of us brings up... dance. I don't ask if he is at a new studio, and he doesn't ask about my recovery or if I'm back full time. It's better that way.

I miss Mason and his ability to make me feel weightless. But a part of me is also happy he moved away. With the exception of my fall, I have countless wonderful memories with him. Smiles and laughter and zero pressure to be anything other than myself. But I think I always knew my time with Mason would be fleeting.

Unlike my relationship with Jet.

Although we have never been more than friends, it is impossible to ignore the permanence and protection I feel when I'm with Jet. Maybe it's because we have known each other more than half our lives. Maybe it's because we have to trust each other implicitly as dance partners. Or maybe it's some mysterious, ethereal tether connecting me to him.

Whatever the reason, I'm lucky to have Jet. My best friend. My partner. My person.

"If someone doesn't like our performance, they obviously need more art in their life." I shrug then bend to stretch my obliques. "I'm not worried."

Jet chuckles. "Me either."

Silence stretches between us, a tinge of discomfort lingering in the air. The same unease that has existed with us since Mason and I got close, and I spent less time with Jet. Over the last six months, the awkwardness of returning to how we were has lessened. But it still exists. And I still feel guilt over it.

One day at a time.

Peeking at Jet from the corner of my eye, I note his furrowed gaze on me. Specifically, the leg I landed on when I fell. My skin heats—in anger, frustration, and... appreciation. As if he senses my sudden emotional shift, his eyes lift until they lock with mine.

Cheeks ruddy with embarrassment, his expression turns sheepish as he swallows. "Sorry."

I groan and transition to my final stretch. "I'm fine," I lie, my voice a sharp blade.

In truth, I shouldn't push myself as hard as I am. I shouldn't do stretches or techniques that set my muscles on fire and exceed my body's boundaries. Instead, I should give myself grace. Unfortunately, I can't. Weeks with almost no activity, and I'm still making up for the loss of time, training, and physical strength. And for some inexplicable reason, my parents can't comprehend the healing process or setbacks my injury has caused.

So, I continue to push my limits and ignore the pain. What other option is there?

Jet's shoulders cave forward as he drops his gaze to the floor. "I know." He clenches then flexes his fingers. "But is it such a bad thing for me to worry about you?" His voice is barely a whisper, but I hear every word.

I open my mouth to say yes, but snap it closed. Were our roles reversed, I'd be just as on edge as he is.

Light-gray eyes full of warmth and adoration lift and lock with mine, and I stop breathing. He takes a step closer, his fingers tapping the side of his leg as his eyes dart between mine.

My heart hammers in my chest, my skin glistening with a new layer of sweat that has nothing to do with the hot July air.

What is he doing?

"I care about you, Shanti." He swallows. "So much." His tongue peeks out and wets his bottom lip. "Not sure I have it in me to feel otherwise."

"Jet..." His name is raspy on my tongue.

Another step closer, and he reaches up to toy with the pink ribbon in my hair, his gaze shifting to watch his fingers. "It's okay. You don't have to say anything." Releasing the ribbon, his eyes come back to mine. "Just wanted you to know."

I open my mouth to tell him I care about him too. That I always have. But I don't get a word out.

"Three minutes," Ms. Neesa hollers. "Find your places, everyone."

Panic widens Jet's eyes slightly. "Please don't be mad, but I'm asking again." He inhales deeply. "Are you sure you're ready?"

I purse my lips. "Yes." *No.*

He nods. "We need a code word."

My brows pinch together. "A code word?"

His gaze becomes distant for a beat. "In case you need a moment or something's wrong."

"Jet, I'm fine," I grind out. "I don't need some Shanti-needs-to-quit-for-the-day word or hand signal."

"It's just a precaut—"

"No," I say, cutting him off.

He holds his hands up in surrender. "Okay. I'm sorry." On the next breath, a crooked smile curves his lips as Jet holds out his hand. "Come on. Let's show this town how incredible we are."

And just like that, the subject is dropped, and we are back to us.

With a mirroring smile on my face and his admission repeating in my mind, I take his hand and let him lead me to our place onstage. And for the next thirty minutes, I mull over the possibility of something *more* with my best friend. Something deeper.

My parents have been adamant about Reema and me not dating until they say we are ready, and they approve of the would-be partner. But my sister and I have our ways of working around the rule. I wouldn't say I've technically *dated* someone. But Mason and I kissed… a lot. I most definitely considered him my boyfriend. To my peers, friends, and family, though, Mason was a schoolmate and guy I danced with at the studio.

Something about the idea of hiding how I feel about Jet from others, about keeping him a secret if he becomes my boyfriend, makes me nauseous.

"Thirty seconds," someone shouts.

I shift my attention to Jet and find his eyes on mine. Time stands still for a heartbeat, but it's all the time I need to decide what happens next.

A love stronger than what I feel for anyone else pulses in my chest. But I won't indulge in it. Not when it means I could lose the person who lifts me up when I'm down. The person who adds sunshine to my days and stars to my nights. The person who makes me feel courageous, beautiful, and whole.

"You've got this," he mutters a beat before the music starts.

And then we dance as if no one else is watching.

EIGHT

WHAT THE FUCK WAS THAT?

JET

Nine Years Ago

A NOTABLE BUZZ VIBRATES THROUGH THE STUDIO AS THE REST OF THE students file in and warm up. The same effervescent hum that has existed since our Independence Day performance.

Hearing the town residents gasp, whistle, and applaud our hard work was the best reward—and motivator.

When Ms. Neesa and Mr. Aurelio announced we'd start working on the fall performance today, everyone's attention snapped into focus. More so than any other seasonal ensemble we'd done. After our dance at the Independence Day festival, the fall show just felt more important. Life changing. Magical.

Clapping echoes off the walls as Ms. Neesa and Mr. Aurelio enter and walk to the front of the room.

"Quiet down." Hands propped on her hips, Ms. Neesa sweeps her gaze from one dancer to the next. "Places, everyone."

We shuffle across the room and take up the place most of us have held for years during practice. Before long, the room falls silent and still.

Releasing the grip on her hips, Ms. Neesa presses her palms together in prayer and holds them in front of her lips, her soft

smile growing more and more with each passing breath. Without a single word, her excitement for today is palpable. As the other students start to fidget, I know they feel it too.

"I have the most wonderful news." Ms. Neesa drops her hands to her sides, straightens her spine, and squares her shoulders. Ever the lithe and beautiful ballerina. "After seeing our performance last month, an instructor from the Northwest Evergreen Ballet Company wants to assist us with our fall show."

Soft gasps float through the air as several sets of eyes go wide. When I peek over at Shanti, shock and awe highlight her features.

She meets my gaze and mouths, "Oh my god."

I match her expression and mouth back, "I know, right?"

An instructor from one of the top ballet companies in the Pacific Northwest wants to teach us. They want to help us reach our full potential after seeing what we can already do.

This is huge.

My fingers twitch at my sides as thrill ignites in my bloodstream. Unable to contain my exhilaration, I lightly bounce on the balls of my feet.

"Class, please welcome back Ms. Vivienne Bellecourt."

Audible gasps fill the room a beat before soft applause bounces off the walls. When I glance at the opposite side of the room, admiration glows in Veronica and Blair's eyes. Obviously, they respect and idolize our guest instructor. A few others— Mahida, Mary, and Shannon—regard her with familiarity but not reverence.

When my eyes connect with Shanti, she shrugs. I nod and mirror the action. My gut doesn't twist quite the same as it did the last time Ms. Vivienne was here. Still, something about her puts me on edge.

For now, I'll suppress the niggling sensation in my gut. Regardless of what I feel, having a guest instructor from a premier school guide us is exceptional and the chance of a lifetime. I'd be a fool not to take advantage.

"Thank you for such a warm welcome," Ms. Vivienne says as

she takes center stage at the front of the room. "It's a true honor to be here again. The talent in this room is a true inspiration, and I'm grateful to work with each of you." An easy, friendly smile curves her lips as she paces the length of the room, gaze studying each of us in turn. "Over the next few weeks, I'll be instructing you alongside Neesa and Aurelio. We'll be pushing you harder than ever."

Pivoting, she paces in the opposite direction. "Many of you are at a turning point in your ballet career. An age where decisions need to be made regarding your future. If you want to attend one of the top dance schools, now is when you put on the performances of your life. Now is when you show everyone you are a force. A powerhouse worth remembering."

Those last two lines repeat in my mind and settle firmly in my bones.

I am a force. A memorable powerhouse.

From a young age, dance has been my one constant. The dream I knew without a doubt I would achieve and succeed at. The day I slipped on my first pair of ballet slippers, a foreign yet familiar comfort settled over me. An inexplicable certainty. An overzealous joy.

At four years old, I discovered my love for dance. At seven, I knew with one-hundred percent certainty dance was my passion, my heart, what I was born to do. And now, I have the opportunity to prove it.

"This isn't like your previous performances." Ms. Vivienne pauses in front of me and Shanti, regarding us with more scrutiny. Her keen eye makes my stomach cramp. "Instructors, principal dancers, artistic directors, and more will be in the audience."

Gasps of shock filter through the room.

"They will be here to enjoy the performance. They will also be critiquing you. Pointing out areas in need of improvement. Discussing who they feel has the most potential to turn their passion into a career."

The buzz in the studio grows tenfold, more than half the class unable to stand still.

Crossing to center stage once more, Ms. Vivienne's expression turns serious. "Many of you are excited, and I love your enthusiasm. But I'd be remiss if I didn't warn you."

The class falls eerily silent.

"Some, if not all, of you will receive harsh evaluations." She purses her lips as her eyes flit from dancer to dancer. "Many of you will say you want brutal honesty... until you get it. But at this stage of your dance career, you can't afford anything other than candor. So, prepare for the worst and hope for the best."

Internally, I wince—more for others than myself.

Honesty is essential in my family. My parents and grandparents have always shared the truth and taught us to do the same. Lies, even if said with the intent to soften the blow, only bite you in the end.

"Those who have a future in dance will receive additional instruction from me or another instructor from the company."

A sense of euphoria floods my veins with each piece of news Ms. Vivienne delivers.

This is it. This is my chance to prove I was born to dance.

Straightening to my full height, I draw back my shoulders, secure my feet in first position, and lift my chin. Arms and hands poised at my sides, I exude every ounce of professional ballerino in my soul.

Ms. Neesa and Mr. Aurelio join Ms. Vivienne at the front of the room. They talk quietly among themselves, Ms. Neesa occasionally covering her mouth with a hand. After a moment, they break apart and turn to face us.

"If everyone will please step back to the wall, Ms. Vivienne and Mr. Aurelio will demonstrate the updated choreography for the fall dance." Ms. Neesa waves a hand toward the wall without the mirrors.

Once we are out of the dance space, they assume their positions in the center of the room. Off to the side, Ms. Neesa gets in position for the part of the routine others will fulfill. A breath later, somber music floats through the room and the instructors begin to move.

Eyes locked on our mentors, no one breathes or speaks as they drift through the room. Some, including myself, clone the movements with small waves of the arm or shuffles of the leg or feet. We absorb every chassé, pirouette, dégagé, relevé, and arabesque. Every longing stare and wistful glance. We become the dance, the emotion, the soul of the performance.

When the song and dance end, we all stand in silence, breaths held until they come out of character. And then, deafening applause roars to life. My hands sting as I clap and clap and clap. Our instructors curtsey and bow before moving to the center of the room, signaling us to quiet down.

"Glad you all enjoyed the performance, To Love Persephone," Ms. Vivienne says, her cheeks rosy as she smiles. "First, we'll work on the corps de ballet, followed by the variations. Then we'll move on to pas de deux before we blend everything."

Once we're back in our spots on the dance floor, we shift our feet into position as all three instructors stand at the front of the room, guiding us. After we go through a section a few times, we perform on our own as the instructors observe.

In the mirror, I study my footwork and occasionally watch how others move. As Ms. Vivienne gets closer, I hear her offer ways to improve technique to my peers. When she reaches Shanti, I pay more attention. Note the way Ms. Vivienne walks more slowly around Shanti. Notice the difference in how she stares at Shanti—a little longer with a harder level of focus. Her eyes cascade over Shanti's body, but not in the same way I've seen countless times from Ms. Neesa or Mr. Aurelio.

Something about the way she regards Shanti sours my stomach and makes my skin crawl. It sets me on edge. Her observation doesn't look professional or for instructional purposes. It almost appears… lewd. Creepy. Gross.

I don't like it. At all.

When Ms. Vivienne moves in to correct Shanti's posture, placing her hand far too low on Shanti's back, I freeze.

What the actual fuck?

But as quickly as the touch happens, Ms. Vivienne pulls her hand away. And for an hour-long second, I question my sanity. Question if that just happened or if the angle of my view messed with reality.

I have no clue.

Movement in my periphery snaps my attention back into focus, and I pick up where I left off in the routine. Ms. Vivienne steps into my space, circling me in the same manner she did Shanti.

Nausea rolls in my stomach as bile claws at the base of my throat. My skin prickles with unfamiliar awareness. I do my best to ignore the horrid sensations churning through my body and put all my energy into the routine. But dismissing my instincts is damn near impossible. Because the way her dark eyes *revere* me is inappropriate. Scandalous. Revolting.

Then, she closes the distance between us.

I think I'm going to be sick.

Pausing a couple feet away, she meets my gaze. "Jet, correct?"

I nod and swallow. "Yes." It's all I can manage to say.

"Your love for dance shows." She gives me a well-practiced smile. "But as with everyone, there is room for improvement. If you would… Relevé."

Inhaling deeply to settle my wayward pulse, I bend slightly at the knees and then rise up onto the toes of both feet. A tinge of fire burns in my ankles and calves as she circles me.

But the blaze in my legs fizzles out the second her hand touches the lower curve of my spine and stays.

"Bring your shoulders back more," she says, voice steady as she keeps her hand on my back.

I do as she says, hoping she will remove her hand.

She doesn't.

"Better," she praises, her gaze sweeping the length of my body.

Bile hits the back of my mouth, and I swallow.

"Continue to work on your posture. You have a magnificent form." As she steps more in front of me, her hand glides lower, pausing just beneath the waistband of my leggings for two stunted breaths.

The world stops spinning. I stop breathing. My heart bangs, bangs, bangs loudly in my ears. Every cognitive thought ceases, and I turn to stone.

And then, she walks off as if nothing other than performance critique happened.

I drop my heels to the floor, press a hand to my mouth, and breathe through my nausea.

What the fuck just happened?

NINE
FINDING BALANCE IN THE IMBALANCE
SHANTI

Nine Years Ago

Ms. Vivienne has been the best thing to happen to our dance studio. Since she walked through the door of Rhythm and Flow, I've felt more seen, understood, and coveted as a dancer. More important, appreciated, and worthy.

And I will do whatever it takes to stay in her good graces. Whatever it takes to keep this feeling alive.

Over the past month, Ms. Vivienne has devoted an hour a day, five times a week, to working alone with me. When she first brought up the idea, I worried how I'd make time and still get my classwork done. I feared my form needed more work than that of my peers, seeing as no one else was asked to put in extra hours. But the more she explained why she wanted the solo time with me, the more I relaxed.

Ms. Vivienne sees my potential, my abilities, my strength. The future I can have if I hone my craft better. In such a competitive industry, she also knows how easy it is to get overlooked when up against equally talented young dancers. If I want to be a principal dancer, I need more than what my small-town teachers have to

offer. I need expertise from someone outside the Stone Bay borders.

So when Ms. Vivienne offered individualized time, I jumped at the opportunity. I'd be a fool to turn down such an incredible gift. Under her tutelage, my chances of making it to the big stage are greater.

During our sessions, Ms. Vivienne shares her tips and wisdom. Shows me how to correct my center of gravity when I'm less than stable. Divulges what has worked for her and her previous students. Guides me on how to make some of the trickier transitions easier and less stressful. Pushes me harder than anyone and doesn't soften her criticism to placate my feelings—something I didn't know I needed.

But more than that, Ms. Vivienne boosts my confidence. I stand taller on my toes with my chin higher because of her encouragement and enthusiasm. My feet move with surety and grace because of her trust and unrelenting support. Every move I make on the dance floor is second nature, flawless, definite. All because of her.

Ms. Vivienne has helped me fall in love with dance again.

And with all the other pressure on my shoulders, I need something, anything, to love.

Initially, I worried the extra hours devoted to dance would throw my life off-balance. But somehow, it had the opposite effect. Somehow, the additional time and focus enhanced other areas of my life and gave them balance.

"Beautiful lift, Mr. Fox," Ms. Vivienne praises Jet as he sets me back on my feet. And then her gaze lands on me. "Elegant and ethereal, Ms. Mahal. Brava."

My skin warms under her compliment, and I smile so wide my cheeks sting. "Thank you, Ms. Vivienne."

Beside me, Jet shifts from foot to foot before he mutters, "Thank you."

Brow furrowed, I peer at him from the corner of my eye. And what I'm met with makes my chest ache.

Eyes downcast, he studies the floor with too much intensity. His shoulders slightly caved, Jet rolls his lips between his teeth over and over. And the more I study him, the more I don't like what I see.

Jet always exudes this effortless competence, nobility, and ambition. Happiness, inspiration, and peace. Whenever I struggle or want to give up, he is the one person I can count on—to share my thoughts with, to remind me why I still put on my ballet slippers, to encourage me when my parents make life difficult. Whenever he is in the room, life is simply better.

But this version of him is unfamiliar. Unsettling. An ache in my belly that refuses to ease.

I don't like him like this. At all.

Inching closer to him, I crane my neck and whisper-ask, "What's wrong?"

Subtly, slowly, he shakes his head. "Nothing." He runs a hand through his hair and sighs. "Let's just practice. We only have a little time before the show starts."

Every cell in my body screams to ask more questions, to probe until he yields and shares what has him on edge. But as I open my mouth to say something, laughter bounces off the backstage walls and cuts me off.

Now isn't the right time.

But when *is* the right time?

Our lives are so busy, so scheduled, so overwhelmed with schoolwork, dance, pressure from our peers and family. The weight on my shoulders to get good grades and be at the top of my class, to push myself to my physical limits so the *right person* notices me while I dance, to give back to the community so colleges will see I'm well rounded with academics and social skills... it all feels endless. And that is only what my parents put on me.

Jet, being a couple years older, has a different level of pressure and less time to manage it.

But I can help him as he has me so many times.

There is never a *right time* for anything. Waiting for it is just an excuse to put off what could be a painful situation. But no matter how long you wait, the feeling will still exist. The reaction will still be the same because the people involved are the same.

For the rest of our preshow practice, I focus on the choreography and don't say a word. I pay just enough attention to my body and his to not miss a step, but I let my mind sift through all the possibilities of what weighs Jet down.

Is he worried about his grades or college acceptances? Jet is so smart and pretty low stress when it comes to school, so neither of those seems plausible.

It can't be anything at home. His family is one of the nicest in Stone Bay. Laid back and cheerful, his parents only want him and his siblings happy, whatever that looks like.

My mind spins and spins, but nothing stands out. And then, I have a eureka moment.

The only time he seems not himself as of recent is when we are at the studio. When it is the two of us before anyone else arrives, Jet is his usual warm, friendly, extroverted self. But as the class commences, he all but shuts down. Goes inward. Becomes this vacant version of my best friend.

But why?

"Excellent, Shanti. You're landing every move beautifully," Ms. Vivienne says, snapping my attention into focus. She aims a wide smile in my direction. "I'm so proud of you. All the extra hours and hard work are paying off. The crowd will applaud you tonight."

Squaring my shoulders and holding my head higher, I beam under her praise. "All thanks to you."

"It's been an honor to enhance your skills." Ms. Vivienne pivots and turns her attention to Jet. Frame somehow bigger, more imposing, she narrows her eyes and purses her lips for a split second. "I wish your *partner* was as dedicated." The sharpness of her tone as she speaks about Jet, the way she looms over him, as if to intimidate him, makes me uneasy.

She circles us, her eyes assessing in a way that makes me shift in place. As my gaze lands on hers, I note her eyes are locked on and sweeping over Jet—and only him—as she continues her inspection. I shift my focus to him and am immediately aware of his closed-off demeanor and rigid posture.

The niggling sensation in my belly expands, tightens, grows almost unbearable. Somehow, I resist the urge to rub the building ache at my solar plexus.

What is going on?

Resting one hand on his hip and the other on his lower back, Ms. Vivienne tweaks Jet's posture to make him stand taller, more centered. It's nothing new. Something she has done with me on several occasions.

But Jet... his face twists with a level of discomfort I've never seen.

"Remember, Jet, your center of gravity is different from your partner's." She shifts more to his side, her hands still on him, his body statue still. "It's important to maintain your balance, so neither you nor your partner is injured." Slowly, she removes her hands. A little too slowly.

What the hell is happening?

Jet nods and steps back from her.

"Ten more minutes," Ms. Vivienne calls out to the class. "Finish warm-ups and head for your places." Her eyes survey Jet for a beat before they shift to meet mine. A manufactured smile plumps her cheeks, and then she turns and walks toward the exit.

"What the hell was that?" I blurt out the second she leaves the room.

"Shh." Jet's gaze darts around the room as he presses a finger to his lips.

I inhale a deep breath, attempting to settle the nervous energy swirling beneath my breastbone. Then, I eliminate every inch of space between us. "What's going on?" I ask only loud enough for Jet to hear.

In my periphery, Jet taps his thigh with his thumb again and again. His typical carefree aura pulses with tension and alarm. His gaze flits from one person to the next faster than my erratic pulse.

"Talk to me," I plead. "Please."

Turbulent gray eyes latch onto my golden browns a beat before his brows pinch together. Minute-long seconds tick by in silence. The more time that passes without him answering, the more the pang in my chest hurts. And just when I think he won't say anything, when I open my mouth to beg him to say something, he finally speaks up.

"Not much to say," he says so softly I almost don't hear him.

My head jerks back as if I've been slapped. It feels like I've been slapped. But I do my best to swallow down the hurt. This isn't about me.

"How long have we known each other?" I know the answer, as does he, but I ask anyway. I don't want the actual answer. He knows I don't. Because the only reason either of us would ask this is to tell the other *you know me as well as I know you*. It's a nonchalant way to call each other out when we say nothing is wrong.

He hangs his head, inhales a slow, methodical breath, then closes his eyes as he exhales. "It's probably nothing."

I take his chin between my thumb and finger, lifting until his closed eyes are level with mine. Then, I wait.

The last of the dancers leaves the room, and I know we don't have much more time. But I refuse to leave this room until he says something to relieve his pain and my anxiety. Neither of us needs to carry this on stage and lose focus.

"*What* is probably nothing?" I ask when he opens his eyes.

I've never seen him so uncertain and reticent. It makes the ache in my chest morph into something new and unnamable. Foul and repellent.

Jet is my best friend. The one person I hold in high esteem, look up to, regard with so much... love. No, not love. Something between really like and love. He is my support system as much as I am his. Without him, without this connection we share, I'd be lost.

He reaches for and takes my hand, guiding us to the exit. "Like I said, it's probably nothing," he mutters. "But I get a bad feeling…"

We move down the short, narrow hall toward the main stage. When he doesn't continue, I prompt, "A bad feeling?"

Pausing next to the door that leads to the side stage, he turns to face me, both his hands holding mine now. He nods. "A gut instinct. About Ms. Vivienne."

Nausea instantly churns in my stomach as I recall the way she looked at him only minutes ago. "Did she do something?"

Please say no. Please, please, please.

He shakes his head.

Oh, thank goodness. But as soon as the relief hits, it vanishes.

"Does she make you uncomfortable?"

He gives a halfhearted shrug. Might as well be a yes since it wasn't a definitive no.

"Promise you'll tell me if something isn't right?"

Jet squeezes my hands for a heartbeat, then slowly nods. "Yeah. I promise."

I study his gentle gray eyes and try to discern if there is truth behind his words. Right now, it's difficult to tell. But this is Jet. All he has ever given me is honesty. So, I'll assume that is what he's giving me now.

My thumbs stroke his hands a beat before I release him. "I'm here for you, Jet. Always. No matter what."

The corner of his mouth tips up slowly, his dazzling half smile making my pulse quicken. "Same." He lifts a hand to my hair and toys with my ribbon. "Always."

TEN

I LOVE YOU, I'M SORRY

JET

Just Over Eight Years Ago

THE FIRST WEEK OF SUMMER BREAK HAS NEVER BEEN LIKE THIS. FOR the first time in I don't know how long, I'm able to take a full breath, to relax, to be myself. It sounds absurd, but for the first time in years, I have freedom. An entire week of zero obligations—no schoolwork, no helping out at Mom's store, and no dance classes.

For one week, seven glorious days, I get to be a typical teenager. Well, my version of typical.

Shanti laughed at me the other day when I pulled out a piece of paper and asked her all the things we should do. I let her make a mockery of me as I scribbled *Jet & Shanti's Fun List* at the top of the page. Because as soon as the week kicked off, I knew she'd ask what we should do, and I'd be prepared.

At least one lazy, movie-marathon day, just me and her. The other items on the list can be just the two of us or with friends. Putt-putt golf, galactic bowling, a full day at the beach, hiking through the nearby forest, camping. If one of my older friends was up for the drive, a day in the city.

If we tackle everything on the list, it'll be a week to remember

for years to come. If we only tick off a few items, I'll be happy with that too.

So long as I get to spend time with Shanti, it doesn't matter what we do.

"Please tell me you have more Reese's Pieces," Shanti says as she digs through the box of candy my family keeps in the pantry. The desperation in her voice is cute.

I close the microwave door, press the popcorn button, then shuffle closer to her. Dipping my chin until my lips are a breath from her ear, I hum. "There should be another pack. I bury them at the bottom so no one else eats them."

Her hands freeze in the middle of their forage as she inhales a slow, shaky breath.

Warmth blankets my skin at her reaction to my proximity. In all the years we have known each other, we have been in close contact more often than not. But this—me in her orbit, an ever-present moon in her sky—is different. Because this isn't some scripted move a choreographer told me to make. This is me *wanting* to be closer. *Needing* to be closer.

Minute-long seconds pass, neither of us moving, breathing, speaking. Every hormone-laced cell in my body begs me to erase the last bit of space between us, but I don't move a millimeter. Not only will my parents have my head if I make a move on someone without their permission, but I'll also be mad at myself for years to come.

Yes, I am a hormonal teenager. But that is no excuse to overstep someone's boundaries. I don't get a free pass to make anyone feel uncomfortable or unsafe for any reason. Ever.

After what feels like an hour, Shanti audibly exhales, her hands resuming their task. "Thanks." The single word comes out quiet, hoarse. She swallows once, twice. "Always looking out for me," she says, voice clearer but just as soft as she grabs a Butterfinger—one of my favorites—then continues her search.

Popping sounds behind me and startles me back to reality, and I take a small, reluctant step away from Shanti. Not that we won't be inches apart on the couch soon to continue our *Friday the 13th* marathon.

"Always." One word, two syllables, six letters, and yet it holds so much significance. More importance than any other word I've said to her. So far.

Arms loaded with candy, popcorn, napkins, and drinks, we amble into the living room and plop back down on the couch. I hit play on the remote as we situate in our seats. As the intro to the movie fills the screen, Shanti lifts her legs and crisscrosses them, her knee resting on my thigh like it has countless times.

The only difference now… my heart pounds so hard in my chest, I swear she should hear it. The spot where her body touches mine feels alive, electric, on fire.

For three slow, measured breaths, I close my eyes. As the room disappears, I focus on where her bare leg touches mine. I bask in the heat, the hum, the way it feels different from every touch before it. And during that last breath, I memorize the contact and how it makes me feel.

When I open my eyes, I lean a little more of my weight into her side. Gain more points of contact. Revel in how easy it is to be with Shanti, in every way.

And for the next two hours, I forget about the movie.

Two days ago, Shanti whooped my ass in Putt-Putt. Truly and thoroughly wiped me off the putting green early on. The entire game, she teased me and my lack of skills without mercy. Did a cute little shimmy shake every time she sank her ball several strokes before I did mine. Told other players, strangers, how she was far more superior at Putt-Putt than I will ever be.

All I did was laugh.

Most guys my age would have been embarrassed. They'd wave off her words and maybe tell their friends they let her win to fluff their egos. But I didn't give a damn if I won or not.

Shanti's victorious smile was prize enough.

Yesterday, we met up with friends at the bowling alley. Again, Shanti beat me, but only by a few pins. At least I wasn't at the bottom of the roster. Shanti and I were comfortably sandwiched in the middle, not that anyone seemed to care about keeping score.

Our time at the bowling alley was about laughter, conversation, and having another great day without a schedule or responsibilities. About being young and carefree.

It was about fun.

Today, unfortunately, we have to be a little more serious. But only because a group of us is headed into the woods to hike for hours. Fun is still on the agenda, but none of us are fools. The forest isn't our home, and the wildlife owes us nothing if we stumble upon them.

"What the hell did you put in here?" I tease Shanti as I hoist her backpack from the trunk and hand it to her. Her pack isn't heavy. By the weight and size, I'd guess she has a few bottles of water, a handful of snacks, basic first aid supplies, and a change of clothes.

Shanti snatches the pack from my hand then playfully shoves my shoulder. "The stuff you probably forgot." She loops her arms through the straps and lifts the pack onto her shoulders, buckling them together across her chest.

"Probably right." I shrug on my own pack then step closer to her. "Let's just hope I don't need more than chocolate chip trail mix."

Of course, I'm joking. I've hiked enough times to know what necessities to bring.

Mom and Dad learned early on, I have an affinity for the forest and exploring. So they taught me about hiking safety at a young age. What I should always have in my pack, what I should watch for in the woods, proper foot placement when on unstable surfaces, how to make shelter if I needed to, how to not panic if I got lost.

They kept their lessons exciting and interesting. It made me love exploring nature more.

Shanti snickers and rolls her eyes. "Is that really all you brought?"

I school my features and force myself to appear serious. "Yes." But my solemnity falters a breath later when Shanti's eyes go wide. And I know the second she sees my mask slip.

Her shock morphs into exaggerated irritation. "Not funny, Jet."

Pinching my thumb and forefinger close together, I say, "It was a little funny."

She wraps a hand around my pinched fingers, curls her fingers into a tight fist, and squeezes the blood from the two digits. "Is it still funny? Hmm?"

Firm as her grip is, it doesn't hurt. Not even a little. But she doesn't need to know that.

I wince and halfheartedly pretend to yank my fingers free. "Okay, okay. It's not funny. I'm sorry."

"Are you sure?" She narrows her eyes, uncertainty crinkling the corners.

A very loud voice in my head says to keep playing along. To say I'm *not* sure. Just to stay in this moment, this bubble neither of us will admit exists. The place where Shanti feels like more than my friend, more than my dance partner.

But I ignore the loud voice, only because I suddenly feel the stares of our friends on us.

"Yes." I nod for emphasis. "I'm sure."

She releases my fingers, steps into me—so close I feel the heat of her on my chest—and lifts her chin. "Good. Now turn around."

I bite my lip to cut off the more-than-friends retort on my tongue. The last thing I need to say in this moment is something about her spanking me because I've been bad.

When I don't move immediately, she makes a spin gesture with her finger. As soon as our eye contact breaks, it emboldens me, and I open my mouth.

"Am I in trouble?" I glance toward my shoulder, catching her profile in my periphery as she clasps the zipper of my backpack. "Are you going to punish me?"

Her hands freeze. The world around us goes silent.

Too far, you dumbass.

Sweat slicks my skin, which has nothing to do with the warmer temperature outside. My heart pounds a vicious rhythm in my chest the longer the silence stretches. Every possible apology I can spew rattles through my brain. And when I finally choose one to say, not a single word leaves my lips.

Laughter rips through the air, loud and obnoxious with the occasional snort. And I've never heard anything so wonderful in my life.

Shanti smacks my shoulder, then proceeds to open my backpack. "You're ridiculous, you know that?" She pulls something out, walks around me so we're face to face again, and holds out the bug spray in silent request.

"I do know." I take the spray from her, drop down into a low squat, and look up until her gaze locks onto mine. "But that's one of the reasons you love me."

Her cheeks immediately flush red, and it lights some deep-rooted spark in my soul.

"Will you two hurry up? We'd like to reach the peak before the sun melts us," one of our friends hollers from the trailhead, where everyone is gathered and waits on us.

I make quick work of covering Shanti with the repellent, and she returns the favor. Then we rush up the path to join our friends.

The first quarter of the hike, Shanti chats with a couple girls in her grade. I hang closer to the back with a guy I've had in a couple classes over the years. We get on fine, but I wouldn't say we are friends. He comes off as the quiet one in the group—loves hanging out but doesn't say much unless it's important or relevant.

We reach the peak an hour later and decide it's the perfect spot for lunch. I check in with Shanti and offer to share my wrap with her, but she opts to sit with her girlfriends. The entire time, they whisper and giggle, and I wonder what the heck they are talking about.

After we clean up, we start the second half of the trail. And this time, I change my pace and position to walk with Shanti. Not that it's difficult, because she seems to do the same.

"So what has you and the others all giggly?" I ask, voice only loud enough for her to hear.

Fingers curled around her backpack straps, she peers up at me briefly then shakes her head. "I'm not telling you."

"And why not?"

She pauses, grips the branch off to the side, and slowly steps sideways down the bumpy decline in the path. When we are level again, she continues. "Because I'd break one of the biggest rules in girl code."

Girl code? Do I even want to know the girl code rules? No, I don't.

So, I switch topics.

"Thanks for hanging with me so much this week."

The barest of smiles curves the corners of her lips. "It's not a hardship, Jet."

I chuckle. "I'm not sure, but I'm taking that as a compliment."

She rolls her eyes but doesn't say anything.

"Anyway..." I bump her arm with mine, keeping my eyes trained ahead as I continue. "I've loved spending this week together. It's been nice to do something other than work and dance. To escape reality with you."

Several steps pass in silence, and I worry I've crossed some invisible line I shouldn't have. But when I chance a look at Shanti, my concerns fizzle out. Her cheeks are red again. Her lips are fighting a smile.

"We definitely need this more often," I add.

She pauses and glances up to meet my gaze. A world of mystery swirls in her pretty golden-brown eyes. "We do."

Our friends and their conversations disappear, along with the sounds of the nearby river and forest animals. For a small moment in time, it is only me and her and whatever this magnetic force is between us.

Until someone's shriek pops our bubble.

Blinking a few times, Shanti faces forward on the trail and starts walking again. And I fall in line beside her.

"So..." She fumbles with her backpack straps.

"So..." I repeat, clenching my straps to resist reaching for her hand.

"How've things been with Ms. Vivienne?"

One question, and the mood automatically veers in the opposite direction. But I refuse to let anything sour today or this week, especially Vivienne Bellecourt.

I shrug and go for nonchalance. "Fine. Nothing worth mentioning." At least nothing I want Shanti concerned over.

When it comes to Vivienne Bellecourt, I've remained tight lipped. I'm saving those conversations for Ms. Neesa and Mr. Aurelio. And maybe my parents. I haven't decided yet. Plus, I still need to figure out what to say and how to approach it.

Her actions are far from acceptable, especially since they make me uneasy. But how do I bring it up? How do I tell her peers or my parents that this highly respected dancer touches me in a way I find inappropriate?

Would anyone believe me? A young man who dances ballet. Of the stories I've seen online about boys or men who come forward, they are less believed than girls or women.

Would anyone consider her hand on my lower back indecent? How about the way her touch lingers longer than necessary? Or the way she visually studies me?

Nothing has ever been physically sexual. But does it need to be? If it puts me on edge, if it makes me queasy, if it makes me want to stop doing something I love, something isn't right. Her actions may not be overtly sexual, but I often question if they toe some invisible line.

More than anything, I don't want to cause an uproar. Don't want to spark unnecessary conflict.

When Vivienne isn't around, everything is fine. And right now, she isn't in Stone Bay.

"Remember what I said," Shanti mumbles, snapping me out of my introspection. "Remember what you promised."

"I remember." Needing a physical balm, something to ground me and bring my mood back into the light, I reach up and tug Shanti's hair ribbon free.

"Hey," she protests.

My smile is automatic and wide. "You won't miss it." I bunch the ribbon in my hand and clutch it like it's my salvation. In a way, it is. As is Shanti. For more than half my life, she has been my one constant that isn't family.

"Because I have an endless supply of hair ribbons," she teases with a roll of her eyes.

Over the years, Shanti has become one of the most important people in my life. Someone I care for deeply and think about often. Someone I want to share all my secrets with because I trust her implicitly, just as she does me. Shanti Mahal is someone I want as more than a friend and dance partner. She is someone I don't want to live without.

Halting on the trail, I tuck the precious pink ribbon in my pocket. And when Shanti stops, her brow furrowed as she takes me in, I inhale a deep, shaky breath.

"I love you," I say in a strange blurt-whisper.

Shanti stares up at me, eyes wide and jaw slack. Shock. She is in shock.

Guess I would be too.

I mean, what almost sixteen-year-old tells his fourteen-year-old best friend he loves her in the middle of the forest? What almost sixteen-year-old really knows what romantic love feels like?

Hell if I know.

But if the way she heats my skin, makes my heart wild, and has me thinking about things other than friendship is any indication… I am head over heels in love with her.

The only problem? Maybe she doesn't feel the same.

And I probably just ruined the best and most important relationship in my life.

"I shouldn't have said that," I say, eager to fill the stifling silence. My knuckles burn as my nails bite my palms. "I'm sorry."

Fuck. Fuck, fuck, fuck.

Shanti subtly shakes her head, blinking a few times. Then she swallows. "Jet, I—"

"Hey, slowpokes." Brock sidles up to Shanti and wraps an arm a little too comfortably around her shoulders. "Thought maybe you got lost." He turns his attention to me, a teasing smile on his lips. "Forget your compass, hike master?"

It's a joke. I know it's meant to be funny. But all it does is irritate me, something that doesn't happen often.

I tap the compass dangling from the hook on my backpack strap. "Not lost, man. Just talking."

Brock glances from me to Shanti then back to me, an eyebrow arched. "Odd place to talk, but who am I to judge?"

Why is he still here? And why the hell is his arm still draped around Shanti like she is his?

Before I get the chance to tell him we will catch up with everyone in a minute, he speaks up first.

"Come on, sweet Shanti. Everyone's waiting for you." Without another word, he steers Shanti away from me and down the trail toward our friends.

Stuck in place, I stare after them. Silently beg for Shanti to duck out from under his arm, turn around, and come back. But the longer I watch them, the more I realize that isn't going to happen.

Just before they reach the bend in the trail, Shanti looks over her shoulder and meets my gaze. For a split second, hope soars in my chest. But as quickly as it bloomed, it fades away.

Because Shanti breaks eye contact with me and smiles up at him. And then, she vanishes from sight.

I once heard love makes you a fool. Not sure who said it, but I suppose they are right. It made me confess my feelings, put my heart out in the open, put everything on the line. And for what?

Obviously, for nothing.

I should have known better. That was my mistake. Lesson learned.

Now, I have to accept reality. I don't know what real love is. Because if it was real, Shanti would feel it too. It wouldn't be so easy for her to walk away and not say a word.

But she did.

So, I should too.

If she is happy, then so am I, even if her happiness comes from someone else.

ELEVEN
SUMMER LOVE GONE WRONG
SHANTI

Eight Years Ago

"WANT TO GET OUT OF HERE?" BROCK CUPS MY JAW, HIS THUMB stroking my cheek slowly, tenderly.

I love when he touches me like this. As if I'm precious, rare, beautiful. My entire body heats up when his hand is on my cheek, my neck, my waist. And when he adds a little pressure, just enough to silently let me know he loves his hands on me too, I melt into a puddle.

It's been a month since Brock put his arm around me on the hiking trail and called me his sweet Shanti. One month since he all but claimed me as his in front of several mutual friends. And one month since I walked away from Jet, moments after he told me he loved me.

A pang twists in my belly, but I shove it down. Ignore the hint of guilt that makes an appearance whenever I think of that day. Instead of seeing the hurt in Jet's eyes over and over, I choose to focus on the happier memory.

Brock.

Since that day in the woods, Brock and I have spent most of our waking hours together. My hand in his while we sit in the

theater with a mountain of snacks. His lips so close to my ear, his breath warming my skin as he whispers blush-inducing words, our friends only feet away in the arcade. My back to his front, his arms around my waist, and his chin resting on my head as we hang out at the beach with schoolmates.

This has been the most adventurous, carefree, and fun summer of my life. And I owe it all to him. Brock.

"And go where?" I lean into his touch, into him, silently begging him to kiss me already.

A corner of his mouth kicks up into a half smile I've become addicted to. He inches impossibly closer, the heat of him blanketing me from my thighs to my cheeks. "Does it matter?" The question comes out low and throaty.

My pulse throbs in my neck and whooshes in my ears. And for a split second, I dizzy. Mentally wobble.

Please kiss me.

Swallowing, I give a slow shake of my head. "No."

His light-green eyes twinkle with excitement a beat before his gaze drops to my lips.

This is it. Oh my god, he's finally going to kiss me.

When he doesn't make a move to close the last little bit of space between us, I give him a little incentive. A final push and my consent. I wet my lips with my tongue, then roll them between my teeth.

His grip on my jaw tightens, but isn't painful. And then, he demolishes those last pesky centimeters of space between us. Presses his warm, soft lips to mine. Once. Twice. Tenderly. Purposefully.

My eyes roll back and close. Fever blankets my skin as exhilaration ripples through my body. I fist his shirt at his hips and pull his body flush to mine.

A muffled groan vibrates his chest a beat before his fingers are in my hair, his hands angling my head as his tongue sweeps across the seam of my lips. He is everywhere and everything, and all I can think is *more.*

But this isn't the time or place.

We've only been dating a month—secretly, because my parents would lock me away if they found out. And all this is new to me. The physical stuff, anyway. The last thing I need to do is rush into anything I'm not ready for. Especially at fourteen.

So, as much as I'd love to kiss him until my lips fall off, I do the opposite. I break the kiss and add a little space between us.

"Sorry," he whispers, running the tip of his nose along the length of mine. His thumbs caress my cheeks once, twice, and then he lowers his forehead. "Hope that was okay."

I clutch his shirt tighter and subtly nod. "It was perfect," I whisper, breathy.

He presses his lips to mine once more, and I feel him smile just before he breaks the kiss and takes a step back. His fingers weave through mine and give a gentle squeeze. "Let's go explore by the lighthouse loop."

The lighthouse loop.

My mouth goes dry as my heart pounds for a new reason. Because the lighthouse loop isn't a place to explore or watch the sunset and sunrise. No, every teenager in Stone Bay knows exactly what happens at the lighthouse loop.

Sex, or so I've heard. It's also known as *the* make-out spot. Not that I would know from personal experience.

But I'm ready for that to change. I'm ready to be reckless and fun. To be a teenage girl and enjoy my summer vacation. To check *make out at the lighthouse loop* off my mental things-to-do-before-I-die list.

Inhaling a deep breath, I straighten my spine and swallow past the dryness. "Yeah, let's go explore."

"Skip dance and come play with me," Brock pleads, his hands in prayer position at his chin as he gives me his best puppy eyes.

Why is he ten times cuter when he begs? Because he knows exactly what will make me say yes.

And god, do I want to say yes. With every lovesick cell in my body, I desperately want to tell him yes.

But I need to say no. I've missed too many classes since Brock and I started dating, and I'm feeling the physical side effects.

Shouldering my duffel bag, I slip on my shoes. "I want to." I head for the door and wait for him to follow. "But I can't miss any more classes."

Brock rises from the couch and crosses the room, the muscles in his jaw flexing. But as quickly as I pick up on his annoyance, it's gone, replaced with his dazzling, irresistible smile.

He stops a breath away from me and lifts his hand to cup my cheek. "I understand." His grip on me tightens as he lowers his mouth and takes mine in a hungry kiss. "What if we hang out after? I'll get my girl her favorite pizza, and we can watch a movie at my place."

Pizza and a movie at his place... also known as eat one slice, get comfortable on the couch in his basement, and ignore the movie while he tries to make it to third base. Again.

It's not that I don't want his hands on me... down there. But am I ready for that? Am I ready for what comes after?

Without a doubt, Brock will shoot for the final base once he passes third. But I need to be honest with myself. I need to listen to my intuition. I need to ask myself why I haven't let him go further yet. There's a reason, whether it's my age or that we've only been together six weeks, or I just don't want to.

The reason doesn't matter. I'm not ready. Period.

But I don't want to upset him. I don't want him to feel like he's done something wrong. "Pizza and a movie sound great."

Our fingers intertwined, Brock drives me to dance class. Before I exit the car, he kisses my knuckles and says he'll see me soon.

When he picks me up an hour and a half later, the rest of the day goes as predicted. Brock tries to cross the invisible line and slip his hand down my shorts.

Panic explodes in my chest as I shoot him down for anything more than third with clothes on. The basement goes eerily quiet as I wait for him to say something. Anything. And then, he surprises me. Says it is okay, that we are okay. He calls me his sweet Shanti, wraps an arm around my shoulders, and curls me into his side.

Every ounce of concern I had disappears as I snuggle deeper into the most amazing boyfriend.

Waves crash along the shore as birds soar and squawk overhead. The sun warms my skin, and I tip my head back to stare at the rare, cloudless blue sky. Distant laughter rings through the air from farther down the beach, Stone Bay residents and tourists taking advantage of the beautiful day.

"Got us turkey and cheddar to share," Brock says as he pulls a box out of a paper bag. "And some of Rosenberg's famous potato salad."

Humming, I drop back onto my elbows and expose more of my bikini-clad body to the sun. "Sounds great."

I barely have the words out before his hand is on my thigh near my knee. "Why did I wait this long for us to have a picnic on the beach?" A low, throaty sound vibrates his chest now pressed to my arm. And then, his lips are on my bare shoulder. "You in this bikini..." His lips kiss their way to my neck as I wait for him to say more, but he doesn't.

When Brock suggested a day at the beach, I assumed it'd be more than the two of us. That is the way it's been all summer when we've gone outdoors.

I figured it'd be safe to wear a swimsuit that shows more skin than usual. I expected others would be around to distract Brock, to keep him from groping me in public.

How many times have I heard the adage about assuming? Enough to know I am an ass for counting on others to keep my boyfriend entertained most of the day.

But I shouldn't *need* to worry about what I wear or who I'm with, in public or private. I should be able to wear whatever I want, be with whoever I want, and feel confident about myself, my surroundings, and my safety. I should be able to be my authentic self without being visually, verbally, or physically mistreated.

Since the movie night in Brock's basement last week, he has been a gentleman. With every move, every touch, every kiss, he has respected my boundaries. He has asked before doing anything more than I've given him permission to do previously.

But I'm not oblivious to what he wants. What he has tiptoed around for days since suggesting *this great, quiet beach at the end of a hidden trail I found.*

Brock wants to take the next step. The big step.

And I'm not ready. Which only makes me more nervous.

The people down the beach—they're too far away to see anything. Probably too far to hear anything other than screams. And I don't like it.

But I try to push it all down. Try to tell myself Brock would never do anything to hurt me. Brock likes me and would never do anything malicious.

Right?

When his lips reach my mouth, I kiss him back with equal enthusiasm. Show him how much he means to me without words.

His hand comes to my cheek, his thumb stroking softly once before his hand slides to the back of my neck. Fingers thread through my hair and clutch me tighter as he switches the angle of his head and deepens the kiss. And then ever so slowly, he shifts his weight over me and blocks the sun with his body. He lowers me to the blanket and puts one of his legs between mine.

I turn my head, trying to break the kiss, but he shifts with the move. Then, I do it again, and he mirrors the action once more.

Shit.

I fumble beneath him until I grip one of his biceps and press against his chest to push up. "Stop," I mumble, his lips still on mine.

His hand on my neck drifts down and grips my forearm, lifting it above my head. Breaking the kiss, he lifts enough to look me in the eye. What stares back at me makes my stomach churn.

"Such a fucking cocktease, Shanti." He grinds himself against my hip. "I've been pretty damn patient. Played the perfect secret boyfriend for weeks." His grip on my forearm tightens to a bruising strength. "Now it's time for you to pay up."

His last words hit the hardest. I use them for strength to get me through this moment. To get me *out* of this situation.

"Pay up?" Incredulity laces my words. "That's not how relationships work. Being kind doesn't equal sexual favors."

Shaking his head, he scoffs. "You seriously think all I want is to make out and follow you like a puppy? How did you not think this"—he trails his nose up my jaw—"would lead to sex? Are you really that stupid?" He puts more of his weight on me, drags my other arm up and pins them both with one hand. "I'll get what I want. What you *owe* me. You can scream or cry, I don't care. No one will fucking hear you. Not here." He drops his mouth to my collarbone and sucks at the flesh just below it.

My mind races for ways to get away from him. Brock easily has six inches and fifty pounds on me. But I'm strong. I've spent years conditioning my body for dance. If I really want to, I can shove him off me. I can hit him hard and where it will hurt.

I just need to get my hands in the right place. I need to get out from under him. And the only way I can think to do that is to make him think he has won. To make him think I am ready to take the next step, but that I want to be on top.

Inhaling a shaky breath, I close my eyes and do my best to release the turmoil flooding my body. I tell my limbs to relax. Tell my mind to quiet. Convince my breaths to even out. And when my body calms, I purposefully roll my hips and moan.

His smile against the swell of my breast is immediate. "There she is." He kisses and licks his way up my body until his face hovers over mine, our gazes locked. "Knew you were ready." The smirk on his face has bile climbing up my throat.

"I am." My tongue darts out to wet my lips. "It's just…"

He drops a kiss to my lips, and I make myself kiss him back. "What, my sweet Shanti?"

I break eye contact and clamp my lips between my teeth, attempting to appear shy. "I'm nervous," I whisper. "I've never…" I meet his waiting gaze. "I'm scared it will hurt."

For a moment, his expression softens. For a split second, he looks like the guy I met on the trail at the start of summer. Then, he opens his mouth and shatters it all.

"I'll make it good for you." He caresses my cheek with his free hand. "I promise."

Forcing what I hope is a smile of gratitude, I pray my next words come out genuine. That he believes my lie.

Please let him believe me.

"I've heard from other girls, it helps to be on top the first time. That it hurts less."

I have no clue if that is true. Hopefully, he has no idea either.

Seconds feel like hours as he stares down at me, his green eyes boring into my soul. The longer he studies me, the longer he remains silent, the more doubt creeps in.

But then he turns his head and looks down the beach. Seemingly satisfied, he eases some of his weight off me and starts to roll us. "You want to ride me, sweet Shanti? I'd be a fool to say no and deny my girl."

As his back hits the blanket, he brings my hands to his chest and pins them in place.

I continue to play dumb and fumble over his lap, giggling. "Will you help me?"

He releases my hands, moving for my hips. But he never gets ahold of them.

With my hands and weight crushing his chest, I rear back my leg between his and drive it forward until my knee connects with his groin. Hard. Immediately, he howls and curls in on himself.

I wiggle free from him, but he reaches for and grabs my leg. "Fucking bitch!"

Tightening my fingers into a ball, I hurl my fist at his exposed solar plexus. It's enough to make him release my leg. I shuffle backward, grab my bag, and run for the trail.

Twigs and rocks stab the bottoms of my feet, but I've experienced worse in my pointes. Ignoring the pain, I push harder. Run faster. Bolt down the path toward the lot where Brock's car is parked.

I need somewhere to hide.

When I reach the lot, I scan the tree line in search of temporary shelter. Several feet from the trailhead is a bathroom. I make a run for it, dash inside, go into one of the stalls, lock the door, climb on top of the seat, and squat so I'm not visible from above or below.

Quietly, I riffle through my bag and find my phone. Unlocking it, I pull up the text history with my sister. I close my eyes for a moment and contemplate what to say. When it comes to the important stuff, Reema is one of the few people I can talk to without worrying about judgment. But not sharing anything about Brock with her… she will be so upset, hurt.

But she can yell at me later—once I'm far away from him.

> Hey, can you come get me? I'm not safe.

Within seconds, dots dance in a bubble on the screen.

REEMA

> Where are you? Should I call anyone else?

I send her my location.

> I'm in the bathroom. And no.

> On my way. Don't come out until I say the code phrase.

> Okay

When I first started school, our parents gave me the code phrase they gave Reema five years earlier. A safety measure. A phrase anyone who said they were sent to pick us up had to know. As Reema and I got older, she said we'd keep using it in case we ever got into a bad situation.

Until today, I've never had to say or listen for it.

I could really go for some mint chocolate chip right now.

It's something anyone might say. Common. And anyone within earshot wouldn't think anything of it.

But that line is a source of refuge. Protection. A simple phrase with a complex meaning.

Never thought I'd ever be in a situation where it'd get used. But here I am, trapped in a bathroom stall. Hiding from a guy who claimed to be kind and tender but turned out to be a monster.

At least I'm safe. I got away. And help is coming.

Not everyone can say the same. Not everyone is as fortunate.

TWELVE
HOW DO YOU STOP LOVING
SOMEONE?

JET

Eight Years Ago

Something is wrong. Really wrong.

The entire summer and first month of the new school year have been a blur. A haze of distraction and desolation. Swirls of confusion with a touch of pandemonium. Some days, I don't know which way is up. What day of the week it is without checking my phone. What I absolutely need to get done without looking at my planner.

Wish I could blame my murky thoughts on my full schedule and heavier workload. But then I'd be lying to myself. And what good comes of that?

This funk, this state of uncertainty… it exists for one reason.

Something is wrong with Shanti.

The worst part? She won't talk to me—about whatever happened, about anything. When I approach her, she shuts down any form of conversation and makes an excuse to leave.

If she shows at the studio for practice, Shanti dances solo and away from the rest of the group. Every time I glance in the mirror, hoping to make eye contact and silently ask her what is wrong,

her gaze is on the floor as she robotically performs the current routine.

Shanti is a literal shell of herself, and I don't know what to do. I don't know who to talk to about it without coming across as a gossip or sparking concern. I don't know if I should ignore her or insert myself into the situation.

All I want is to know she is okay. Or on the path to being okay.

As teenagers, it isn't odd to change your whole persona over the summer. But most of my friends don't turn inward, or stop talking to everyone, or wear twice as many clothes, covering every inch of skin from neck to ankle. Usually, it's the opposite.

Why won't she confide in me? We may be in this odd place after my confession, but I'm still her friend. I'm still here for her.

But it isn't just me she is shutting out. I haven't seen her talk to anyone—at school, at dance.

And where is Brock in all of this?

Most of the summer, Shanti has been glued to Brock's side. When I helped out at Mom's shop, I saw them stroll hand in hand past the store several times. The way she smiled at him, stared up at him, it was as if he was the air she breathed.

And now, nothing.

Did he break her heart? Was she a summer fling? A conquest before his senior year?

Fire roars in my veins at the idea of Shanti being some douchebag's box to check off. I swear to every deity, if he pressured her to do something she didn't want, I will end him.

Sitting under a tree in the school courtyard, I study Shanti from a distance. Her monochroic attire, listless expression, and crumpled frame. The book she has open in her lap, but isn't reading. The cardigan she tugs tighter around her torso anytime someone walks within five feet of her. The way her knee bounces almost imperceptibly over and over.

It shreds me to see her like this. Reluctant. Jittery. Despondent.

I miss her strange sense of humor, her smile, the way she rolls her eyes at me when I am goofy, how she checks in on me and I her. Our friendship is far from perfect. We've had just as many downs as we've had ups. But this, her shutting down and keeping me at a distance, is unlike anything from our past. Usually, after a day or two, we open up to each other. Mostly.

A pang flares in my solar plexus as guilt rears its ugly head.

How can I expect Shanti to be vulnerable with me when I still haven't done the same? I still have skeletons. Still harbor suspicions about Vivienne Bellecourt I have yet to share with anyone.

Expecting Shanti to spill everything when I haven't is unreasonable and inconsiderate.

Our relationship isn't a quid pro quo scenario. But if I want Shanti to share what is bothering her, I have to reciprocate. I need to share the things that keep me awake at night. Even if it feels I might be making something out of nothing.

Picking up my backpack, I sling it over my shoulder, take a deep breath, and wind my way through the crowd. As I cross the courtyard, my eyes never leave Shanti. And for the entire twenty-two seconds it takes me to reach her, I mull over what to say.

I want to come out and ask her what is wrong, but decide against it. All it will do is make her shut down and bolt. Instead, I opt for more neutral territory. Something we'd normally talk about that has nothing to do with us.

"Hey," I say, halting when I reach the invisible boundary she has erected around herself. "Good book?"

Shanti blinks a few times, her brow furrowing a beat before she glances up to meet my waiting gaze. "What?"

I gesture to the well-loved paperback in her hands. "The book. Is it good?" I drop my gaze to the cover and read the title— *Wuthering Heights*. Required reading for freshman English.

Two years ago, that was on my list of books to read. Although it took some time to adjust to the older style of writing, I enjoyed the story. It isn't as steamy or emotional as the romance books my older sister Delilah reads, but it left a mark.

Shanti dog-ears the page, closes the book, and shoves it in her bag. Without a word, she rises from her spot on the ground, shoulders her bag, and shrugs. "It's fine." Evading eye contact, she steps toward *B* wing. "I gotta go."

"Wait." I reach for and take her elbow.

Her entire body locks up long enough for me to notice. Then she rips her arm from my grasp and shuffles back, her eyes glued to my face, the muscles of her jaw taut. "Don't."

Startled, I lift my hands in surrender. "Sorry. I just..." A soul-deep ache thrums in my chest as I hold her weary, anxious gaze. Slowly, deliberately, I lower my hands and shove them in my pockets. "I just want to talk." I swallow past the lump building in my throat and lower my voice. "I miss you."

For the briefest of seconds, the tension in her jaw softens. The shield she has up lowers. For a blip in time, Shanti is herself again. My dance partner. My best friend. The girl I fell for.

Then, I blink. And in an instant, she raises and fortifies her shields. She shuts me out again.

Arm tightly banded across her chest, she glances behind me, off into the distance. The muscles of her jaw flex once, twice, before she purses her lips and nods. "Yeah." Her eyes snap back to mine. "Well, don't."

The ache in my chest morphs into a kaleidoscope of hurt, frustration, rejection, and uncertainty.

Over the years, I've experienced almost every emotion with Shanti. It's what makes us good dance partners. But no matter what happened, I always knew where we stood. I always knew we would get past whatever landed in our path. That we would always be there for each other.

Now, I am at a loss. A dead end.

And I have no idea what to do. Or how to make it better.

So I let the throbbing pain beneath my sternum take hold. I quit fighting my feelings. Stop shoving them aside and allow myself to be selfish for a moment.

I did nothing wrong. I am not at fault for whatever happened to her.

I may love Shanti, but I will not be her punching bag.

With a subtle nod, I clamp my lips between my teeth and take a step back. "Done." Retreating another step, I break eye contact. "Sorry I bothered you." I pivot, give her my back, and head for the building that houses my locker.

She doesn't call out to me, doesn't come after me, doesn't make any attempt to forge the expanding fissure in our relationship. And her silence, her easy dismissal of me, is all the answer I need.

It is time to accept that how I feel about her is not enough. I am not who or what she wants. Maybe I never will be. Or maybe the way I feel about her is too much. Overwhelming. Scary.

I get it. We're teenagers, young. Our schedules are hectic. We are under constant scrutiny and pressure.

Who has time for love?

More recently, I've also questioned if what I feel for Shanti is actual *love*. Hell if I know. It could be some weird mix of hormones playing tricks on my mind. It could be that we have known each other so long, have spent so much time together, she is a safe space. A form of comfort. Familiar. My constant.

Or at least she was. Now it seems as if we are none of the above. Nothing at all.

Maybe this is for the best.

Shanti wants someone spontaneous, exciting. Someone who tells asinine jokes and makes her laugh. Someone new and different who knows nothing about her life. She wants fun, frivolous, and easy.

And I will never be any of those things. Not in her eyes.

So it's time to let go. To abandon my feelings for Shanti. To set her free and move on.

"You have a date for homecoming?" June lifts a hand to cover their mouth.

My neck and cheeks heat with a blush, and I make no move to

hide it. A wide smile stretches my face as I nod. "Yeah. It's a little last minute." I shrug. "But I don't care."

June grabs my hand and hauls me to the couch. The second our butts hit the cushion, they turn to face me, crisscross their legs, and bounce excitedly.

"Tell me everything."

It isn't often my twin and I discuss the romantic side of our lives. Not because we shy away from sharing our feelings. More like there isn't much to tell. Our dating lives are mediocre at best, and June is pretty private.

Mirroring their position, I start, "You know Maverick from chemistry class?"

June nods. "The guy on the swim team?"

"Mm-hmm."

Their eyes widen. "He asked you to homecoming?"

My smile grows impossibly bigger as I slowly nod. "He did." The image of Maverick rocking back on his heels in front of me filters in. "At lunch, he asked to sit with me."

"At the table under the trees?"

"Yep." I rarely see Maverick during lunch. Most of the jocks sit with their teammates in the cafeteria. I prefer to be outside, away from the noise and crowd. "Walked right up and asked."

"Of course, you said yes."

"I did." Something new and thrilling lit inside me when I saw how nervous Maverick was—his tray lightly shaking in his hand. I had no idea why he wanted to sit with me, or why he was nervous, so I let him spark the conversation. "At first, he talked about how hard the last chemistry test was."

"Common ground."

I nod. "He said it's getting harder to maintain the GPA his parents set for him to stay on the swim team. I told him I understood the pressure because of ballet."

At the mention of dance, my thoughts momentarily shift to Shanti. It's been a week since she let me walk away. A long week of distractions and accepting my new reality. And I am mentally exhausted.

But Maverick approaching me, the flash of his cute, boyish smile, the way he fidgeted with the hem of his shirt... He is a breath of fresh air. The sun peeking through my cloudy sky. A welcome light bringing me out of my momentary darkness.

"He asked how long I've been dancing, and I asked about swimming."

June shoves at my knee. "I wasn't even there, and I'm giddy."

I chuckle. "Twin sense," I tease.

They roll their eyes. "Duh. Keep going."

Thrill swirls in my belly as the day replays in my head. "Lunch was almost over, and out of nowhere, he blurts, *'Will you go to homecoming with me?'*"

"Just like that?"

I nod. "Well, he kind of fumbled over the words. But yeah."

June grabs my knees and squeezes. "Did you hesitate to answer?"

"A little." I wince. "But only because I wanted to make sure I heard him correctly."

"That's a good reason." They squeeze my knees again. "So are you just going to homecoming? Or is it more?"

After I said yes to Maverick, I had the same question. Was asking me to homecoming his way of asking me to be his boyfriend? Or did he only want me to go to the dance with him? I didn't want to assume anything, but the way his bright-hazel eyes held my grays, the way he gave me his smile so effortlessly, I wanted him to be more.

Biting the inside of my cheek, I fight and fail to hide my smile. "I told him I was good either way, but asked the same question."

When I don't say anything for a moment, June glares. "And? You're killing me, J."

I drop my gaze to my lap and shrug, doing my best to appear nonchalant. "Maverick wants to be my boyfriend, so..."

"You have a boyfriend." June lunges forward and wraps their arms around my neck. "Oh my goddess, J!"

Laughing, I hug them back. "I have a boyfriend."

As the words leave my lips, I'm weightless. Buoyant. Dizzy with excitement. Thrilled and eager to see him again.

And I welcome every single emotion with arms wide open. Because I deserve happiness.

"You are not leaving this house until I get a picture of you," Mom declares, holding up her phone. "It's not every day my little boy puts on a suit and goes to homecoming." Mom rests a hand over her heart. "You're so handsome."

Maverick pins my boutonniere to my lapel, his eyes focused on the task, a shy smile on his lips. "You do look really good in a tux," he says, only loud enough for me to hear.

"Yeah?"

Red rose in place, he lifts his gaze to mine. With a lick of his lips, he nods infinitesimally. "You have no idea how hard it is to not kiss you right now."

Heat blooms on my chest, my neck, my cheeks as I swallow past the anticipation whirling in my belly and rising in my throat. It'd be so easy to lean into him, to erase the inches between us, to chastely kiss him in front of my family. But I refrain.

Maverick may have taken the first step and asked me out, but we have yet to discuss how comfortable either of us is about public displays of affection. Yes, he has held my hand at school and the couple of times we've met up for dinner or to hang out. But we haven't done more than that.

Once it's just the two of us, I'll ask. Because I really, *really* want to kiss him out in the open. To let everyone know he is mine and I am his.

Mom takes a couple dozen pictures with her phone while Dad takes exactly three with his thirty-five-millimeter camera. It's funny how opposite and ironic my parents are. You'd think Mom would want all the nondigital things since she owns a metaphysical shop. Nope.

Once we say our goodbyes, we get in Maverick's car and head for the school. Hip-hop plays quietly in the background as he drives with one hand on the wheel. I reach across the console, take his free hand, and thread our fingers. The gentle squeeze he gives my hand makes me all warm and gooey inside.

"Question," I say.

He hums, his thumb stroking my hand.

"How do you feel about kissing in front of others?"

His thumb pauses for a beat then resumes its leisure strokes. "I'm not against it." We stop at the red light, and he glances my way. "But you're the first guy I've openly dated." He shrugs. "My family and friends know I'm bi, but I've never been in a relationship where I've been publicly affectionate."

"Because you were uncomfortable?"

He shakes his head. "No." The light turns green, and he faces forward. "It just never happened," he says matter-of-factly. "Maybe it was the other person or nerves." He gives another shrug. "Don't really know."

Inhaling deeply, I dig for the courage to say what I feel. On the exhale, I tighten my grip on his hand and say, "I want to kiss you out in the open."

The corner of his mouth curves up, his dimple making an appearance. "I'd like that very much."

Homecoming is as expected—hundreds of bodies packed into the gymnasium with loud music, shiny decorations, sugary punch, and salty snacks. A handful of people have flasks and have spiked as many ladled drinks as possible. Every direction you look, someone's ass is grinding against another person's crotch.

It's the first time since the start of summer break that I've felt like a normal teenager.

After Maverick introduces me to a couple people on the swim team, he hauls me to the dance floor. "Show me what you got, big boy."

Something about the way he says *big boy* gets me all hot and bothered. And when we find a place to dance, I spin him around so we're face to face, yank him forward, fist his hips, and drop us into a low crouch, grinding myself against him.

He clutches my biceps. "Fuck," he groans, dragging the word out. Then his hands slide up and behind my neck, his body moving in time with mine. "Ruining me for anyone else already."

I chuckle. "You're welcome."

As the song ends, it fades into a slower one. Straightening to our full height, he threads his fingers through my hair at the nape of my neck. I band my arms around his waist and breathe in his earthy, sweet cologne. Maverick rests his head against the side of mine.

"Never thought I'd enjoy slow dancing," he whispers, then ducks his chin and nestles in the crook of my neck.

Out of nowhere, Shanti surfaces in my thoughts.

I slam my eyes closed, tighten my hold on Maverick, bask in his warmth, his smell, his affection, and shove every idea of Shanti away.

She rejected you. You told her you love her, and she dated another guy. Let. Her. Go.

Maverick hums, and the vibration of it is enough to bring me back to him. To someone who wants me.

As he lifts his head, I open my eyes. His hands untangle from my hair and slide to frame my face. Those sparkling hazel irises lock onto mine, and I'm flooded with adoration. Warmth. Then his gaze drops to my lips.

Heat ripples over my skin as desire pulses in my veins. The room and everyone in it disappear. In a single breath, it is only him and me and the kiss lingering between us.

Slowly, ever so slowly, he dips his chin and lowers his mouth to mine. And the moment our lips connect, all I feel, all I know, all I want is Maverick.

In the middle of the gymnasium surrounded by our peers, I slide my hands up his body, his neck until I clutch his cheeks. Somehow, I pull him impossibly closer. Tilt my head and take his mouth from a different angle. Lick the seam of his lips, slip my tongue along his, and moan when I taste him for the first time.

The kiss is heady, potent, volatile. He takes as passionately as he gives. The fire, the energy, the power of our kiss is explosive. Greedy.

Maverick breaks the kiss and rests his head on mine. "Wow," he whispers. "So much better than I imagined."

My thumbs stroke his cheeks as I run my nose along his. "Stole the words from my mouth." I drop a peck on his lips and lean back enough to meet his gaze. "You imagined us kissing, huh?"

A shy smile tugs at the corners of his mouth. "Several times."

My brows rise as I bite my bottom lip. "Really?"

He nods then brings his lips within a breath of mine. "Jet, I've wanted to ask you out for years." A ruddy blush colors his cheeks. "I finally found the courage to do it."

When his lips press mine again, the only person on my mind, in my world, is him. Maverick. The guy who has pined over me for years.

THIRTEEN

I HATE IT HERE

SHANTI

Just Over Seven Years Ago

Have you ever felt like your entire existence is against you? Like, no matter what decision you make, it always seems as if it's the wrong one?

Yeah, that has been my life for almost a year now. And I honestly have no idea what to do next. At this point, I wonder if it matters what I do anymore.

Should I even bother trying? With anything?

What the hell is the point? Right now, I'm not seeing one.

Before Brock, everything was good. Not perfect—that's impossible—but good. Until the last few weeks Brock and I were together, life was phenomenal. I was so happy. More than I have ever been. Then I met Brock's dark side and everything went to shit.

For months, I crawled inside my mind and isolated myself from everyone. I shut down and ignored the most important people in my circle. And when they tried to help, I shoved them away. I let them think I wanted nothing to do with them. In truth, I needed them more than ever. But I had no idea how to ask, how

to tell them what happened, how to explain I needed *them* but not their sympathy or pity.

Now it's too late.

Because the kindest, most thoughtful person in my life, the guy who told me eleven months ago he loves me, is with someone else.

And I don't know how to fully articulate it, but the loss of him, his friendship, his affection I took for granted, is unlike anything I've experienced. The hurt is a rusty, dull blade to the chest. A scorching-hot branding iron to the heart. An anchor tugging me down, down, down when all I want to do is soar and escape.

I wish I knew what happens next. Wish I could see the future, only far enough to know when this period of torment ends. Because it will end. It has to.

Rising to my toes in my pointes, I cross the dance floor in small, rapid steps, my spine and arms bowing forward then backward over and over. When I reach my mark, I drop into fifth position, glance over my shoulder briefly, take a breath, then jump sideways in pas de chat.

As I perform the final jump in the move, the door to the studio opens and sniggering echoes through the room. My feet wobble as my eyes flick to the door in the mirror, but I catch myself before tumbling over.

Arm draped around the guy next to him, Jet shuffles into the studio with the biggest smile I've ever seen on his face. Jet leans into Maverick, lips so close to his ear it looks as if he's kissing him. But when Maverick grins a second later, Jet's shirt clutched in his hand, I realize it was so much worse. Jet is whispering sweet nothings in his boyfriend's ear. Or perhaps his words are the opposite of sweet.

My knuckles ache and burn as I curl my fingers into fists. The skin of my palms stings, but I ignore the bite of pain. Instead, I fuse every ounce of hurt, frustration, and rage in my body and hurl it mentally toward the one person who was always there for me and no longer is.

Don't get me wrong, I'm happy for Jet. He found someone who cares about him. Someone who makes him smile, laugh, and enjoy life. Someone who gives him time and exactly what he needs. What he deserves.

But I won't lie. I hate I'm not the source of his happiness.

I squandered the possibility, and it is a hundred percent my fault.

Still, it fucking hurts. A lot.

"Sit," Jet says with a titter, his finger pointed at the ground beside his duffel bag. "Be a good boy."

My gaze fixed on them, I grit my teeth as Maverick steps into Jet, his lean body pressed into him, his hands on Jet's hips and lips at his ear. Fury flames my skin as my heart thrashes in my rib cage.

But I can't look away.

Not long ago, I was the center of his world. Not long ago, Jet loved me.

"And what if I'm not a good boy?" Maverick taunts, and I wonder if he is intentionally speaking loud enough for me to hear.

If so, he's an asshole.

Jet grabs his chin and jerks it so their lips are a breath apart. "Then you'll miss out on the reward."

Maverick arches a brow. "Reward?"

With a subtle nod, Jet smirks. "But only if you behave."

Hands on Jet's hips, Maverick presses their bodies flush and kisses him. Hungrily. Possessively. Libidinously. As if they've done way more than kiss and touch each other.

The dull, rusty blade in my chest twists and twists at the idea, and I close my eyes.

Taking a deep breath, I attempt to center myself. Remind myself that for the next hour and a half, Jet is *mine*. To look at, to touch, to share an incomparable intimacy with.

No matter how absolute or fierce their relationship is, Maverick will never have what I do with Jet. Ever.

When they finally detach themselves from each other, Jet saunters across the floor, finds his spot, and starts his warm-up routine. "Morning, early bird."

I glare at him in the mirror, a fake, forced smile on my lips.

"Or not." He playfully rolls his eyes then breaks eye contact.

While he warms up, I finish the routine I was practicing. Not long after, the rest of the dancers funnel in and Ms. Neesa starts the class.

Music filters through the room, and we rehearse the choreography for our next performance in the summer, Swan Lake. The familiar tap of pointe shoes on wood blends with the symphonic melody as we flutter and glide, rise on our toes and lower on our heels.

Gaze fixed on the mirror, I study my every move and occasionally glance at my peers. And when I notice we're in sync, I smile.

And then my attention shifts to where Maverick sits at the back of the room. My eyes catch on his face, his expression as he stares at Jet. Pride shines in his eyes. And something else. An emotion I don't want to name. A feeling that makes my stomach churn.

Distracted by Maverick and his... adoration of Jet, I slip and bump the dancer next to me. My face grows hot as everyone stops dancing to look in my direction.

"Sorry," I mutter, hanging my head for a breath. "I misstepped."

The young woman waves me off. "Happens to all of us. I'm okay."

I give her a tense smile. "Thanks. Again, sorry."

As she steps away, Jet takes her place, concern wrinkling his brow. "Are you okay?" He drops his gaze to my feet. "Didn't twist or sprain anything?"

His worry softens my embarrassment temporarily until the reason I stumbled in the first place flashes in my mind. The moment it does, anger filters in.

"I'm fine," I bite out. "Just got distracted." I shift my attention to the back of the room for a second, but long enough for him to know *who* I'm looking at.

Before he has the chance to respond, Ms. Neesa gets us back in position. "Shanti, are you good to continue?"

Inhaling, I nod and give a soft smile. "Yes, Ms. Neesa."

"Wonderful. Let's practice the pas de deux."

Great. Just what I need. To dance with Jet while his boyfriend stares at us.

All but our understudies clear the floor. I close my eyes, take a deep breath, center myself, remind myself what matters right now, then open my eyes.

The music for act two starts and Jet begins. When I hear my cue, I move from the side stage and begin my part of the dance. We dance next to and with each other until I lower to the floor. When Jet reaches me and I take his hands, I grip them firmer than usual. We ebb and flow, dancing in sync, his hands gently on my waist. The next time he takes my hand, I repeat the same strong hold. His brows twitch a split second before he releases me. I gracefully fall backward, and he catches me.

I don't meet his expectant gaze. Instead, I zero in on the music, hit my marks on time, and zone out from anything other than this moment.

Halfway through the dance, the intimacy of the performance changes. When he reaches for my chin to make me look at him, I press into his palm more than necessary, look into his gray eyes more than required. There is no time to see his reaction, but I *feel* his confusion.

I bask in it.

And when the dance brings us closer together, I lean more into him. Then he lifts me high, moves across the floor, and slowly lowers me against his body. As he does, I subtly arch into him. Let him feel me more.

Each look, each touch, each embrace, I give more. Every chance I get, I remind him I'm still here.

When we reach the end of the dance, Jet creates distance

between us, tilts his head the slightest bit, and narrows his eyes. Then he plants his hands on his hips and inches closer. "What was that?" he says only loud enough for me to hear.

The music starts over, and the next group of understudies takes the floor.

Jet pulls me off to the side. His brows lift as he waits for me to answer.

But I'm not feeling very chatty right now.

A muscle in his jaw flexes a beat before he huffs. "That wasn't you." Lips in a flat line, he shakes his head. "That was something else. What's going on?"

Crossing my arms over my chest, I shrug. "Nothing." I match his expression as I peer toward Maverick. The glint lasts all of a heartbeat, but it's long enough. My irritation flares anew. "Can you not bring him?"

Jet follows my line of sight, and I watch as his lips soften into a smile he once gave only to me. It pisses me off.

"You have a problem with my boyfriend?" His gray eyes are a winter storm waiting to let loose.

Go ahead, bring on the monsoon.

I shift my hands to my hips and purse my lips. "Yeah, I do." I step within a couple inches of him and lift my chin. "When he's here, you're distracted."

His eyes dart between mine, searching. For what feels like an hour, we have a stare off. Then, infinitesimally, he shakes his head. Laughs under his breath.

"What?" I bite out when he doesn't say anything.

One, two, three breaths pass before he speaks up. "Jealousy isn't a good look for you, Shanti."

My face flames, and I open my mouth to tell him I am not jealous. But I don't get a word out.

Jet closes the last of the distance between us and lowers his chin, bringing his lips within an inch of my ear. "I told you how I felt. I told you I love you." He pulls back until our eyes connect. "And what did you do?" His nostrils flare. "You walked off with

Brock. You started dating him on the day I spilled my heart to you."

The backs of my eyes sting, but I blink away any possible tears. I don't say anything, don't open my mouth to argue, because there is no point. Jet is right.

"Obviously, you only care about me when it's convenient," he says, plunging that dull, rusty blade from earlier deeper. Then he chuckles again. "Regardless, and for some stupid reason, I still love you."

I gasp at the same time he sucks in a breath and holds it.

On the exhale, his hands shake. "I still love you," he repeats quieter. "Even when I know you'll never love me back. I guess that makes me a fool." His eyes flick to Maverick for a beat. "But it's time for me to care about someone who will return my feelings." He rolls his lips between his teeth. "It's time I move on."

With that, he storms off toward Maverick. They exchange hushed conversation while Jet changes his shoes and slips a graphic tee over his head. Maverick rises from his spot on the floor, takes Jet's hand, and guides him out of the studio. Neither of them spares me a glance.

The moment they're gone, the ache in my chest amplifies. The moment I no longer feel Jet in my orbit, my heart weeps.

What the hell have I done?

FOURTEEN
MINE, ONLY IN MY MIND
JET

Seven Years Ago

"Does it freak you out that I'll miss you?" I reach for and clutch the cotton of Maverick's shirt over his abs. "Can't believe you'll be gone an entire month."

The smile I've come to adore curves his lips. "Nah. It doesn't bother me." He ducks his chin and drops his gaze to the ground, his foot nudging the rocks.

The subtle shift in his demeanor makes me wonder if my admission does bother him. Like I've overstepped some invisible boundary. The line between telling each other you really care about each other to saying the *L* word.

Aside from my family, Shanti is the only person I've said I love you to.

Although the past nine months have been incredible with Maverick, I'm not the type of person to tell someone I love them so easily. Do I have deep, intense feelings for Maverick? Absolutely. He has been the best boyfriend and companion anyone could ask for. He's kind, affectionate, and damn can he kiss. And he does this thing with his tongue…

But do I love him? As badly as I want to say yes, I can't

without hesitation. And with that smidge of uncertainty, I have my answer. No, I don't love him. At least, not fully.

I tug his shirt, hoping he will look up. "What's going on in that head of yours?"

Taking a deep breath, his bright hazels slowly lift to meet my grays. For two shaky breaths, his eyes dart between mine. Then, he swallows.

Each move is small, subtle, but it sets my nerves on edge.

"I was thinking…" He bites the corner of his bottom lip.

When he doesn't say anything for a moment, I tug his shirt again then release it. "What?" The single word comes out soft, shy, reluctant.

Maverick's brows pinch together, a faint ridge forming in the middle. "I've never met anyone like you."

My stomach twists as nausea climbs up my throat.

"And god, I waited so long to ask you out."

I force a smile and do my best to not appear concerned. But his tone, his words, his expression, it's difficult to *not* be worried.

"Wish I wouldn't have waited so long," he mutters.

Why? I want to ask, but don't. If the sudden cramp in my belly is any indication, I won't like his answer. Something is different— with him and between us. Whatever sparked this abrupt shift, whatever caused him to go from doting boyfriend an hour ago to this awkward and uncomfortable version of himself, I won't like it or where I think it may lead.

I almost open my mouth to tell him we have plenty of years ahead of us. But I bite my tongue. Swallow down the urge to speak.

In my periphery, he reaches for my hand. Before he makes contact, he pulls back. "You've been the best boyfriend," he says, licking his lips. "You know that, right?"

My eyes narrow as I tilt my head. For a beat, I simply study him, every line in his expression, the way he fidgets. "Thank you?" My response comes out more like a question because I have no idea if he's giving me a compliment or insinuating something else.

Feels more like the latter.

He chuckles, but it sounds all wrong, uncomfortable, forced. Then, he goes silent. Still.

And I can no longer stand the stifling, anxious energy between us. "Why does it sound like you're breaking up with me?"

His eyes widen a beat before red blooms on his neck and across his cheeks. It isn't suspicion or rejection I see staring back. It's shock, surprise... because I figured out why he is so nervous.

The backs of my eyes sting as I stumble back a step, yet I can't seem to look away from him. Not even when the first tear rolls down my cheek.

You're great, but I don't want to be with you. Like, who thinks that? Who breaks up with someone they care about?

What the actual fuck?

"Jet..." Maverick reaches for my hand again, but this time it's me who denies the touch.

I blink away any other tears, curl my fingers into tight fists, and give him a pointed look. "Are you?" I ask, my voice stronger, harsher.

He takes a step toward me, his eyes pleading with me to understand. "It's not what you think."

Crossing my arms over my chest, I infuse my expression with every ounce of hurt coursing through my veins. "And what exactly am I thinking, Mav? Hmm?"

Exhaling a shaky breath, his face twists with hurt. A second later, he smooths his expression and takes another step in my direction. "When I started high school, my parents stressed how important it was to do well academically and with my extracurriculars. They also told me it's important to be young, have fun, and enjoy these final years of my youth."

I relax a little but keep my guard up. "Okay."

His gaze drops to my lips for a split second. Had I blinked, I would have missed it.

He doesn't want to do this. So why is he?

"A few weeks ago, my parents sat me down and flashed me a super-serious look. I thought they were going to tell me one of them had a terminal illness." His lips stretch into a flat line as he shakes his head. "Nope. Thank goodness." Then his expression morphs into a grimace. "They spent over an hour telling me it'd be best if I enjoyed senior year without an attachment. The entire time, I argued they were wrong."

The smallest glint of hope sparks in my chest. "Then why are you doing this?" I hold my hands out to my sides. "Why are you still breaking up with me?"

"I don't want to," he says louder.

"But you are." I scoff. "You have yet to tell me otherwise."

Maverick sighs. "Both my parents regret not enjoying their last year of high school single. They feel like they didn't get the full experience. And I get where they're coming from. I get that they want my senior year to be fun and exciting and something I'll cherish when I'm older."

It all sounds so ludicrous. Absolutely absurd. And the only thing I can do is laugh. It beats the alternative—crying.

"Why are you laughing?" Maverick has the audacity to sound offended.

And it pisses me off. "Would you like me to cry? To spill my heart out and beg you to not do this?"

He opens his mouth to answer, but I hold up my hand and shake my head.

"No. You don't get to ask me on a hike and hold my hand for the first half of the trail. Tell me I'm a great boyfriend, but you want to break up, then get upset when I react differently than you expect." I slap my hand to my chest twice. "It fucking hurts, Mav. You are hurting me."

"I'm—"

"No," I repeat, almost yell. "Do not apologize. If you didn't *want* to do this, you wouldn't. Any time over the past three weeks, you could've come to me and talked. We could've figured it out together." I take a step back, then another, and another. "If you wanted to keep me, we would've brainstormed a better solution. Obviously"—I start walking backward, my eyes locked on his—"you don't feel for me what I feel for you."

Before he gets a word out, I pivot on my heel, give him my back, and run away. When I'm far enough that I know he can't hear me, I unleash the other tears I held back.

This fucking sucks.

The dull, throbbing ache in my chest. The burn behind my eyes and frequent urge to cry. The lack of energy to do anything other than stay in bed, stare at the past nine months of pictures in my phone, and question for the millionth time why Maverick broke up with me.

Because it still doesn't make sense. He used the conversation with his parents as an easy out. But why? We were happy. Nothing he did prior to the breakup makes me believe otherwise.

Maverick cares for me, still. The way his expression shifted as he delivered the blow... I know he didn't want to rip us apart. Yet, he still did. All for the sake of zero attachments in his final year of high school.

"Ugh," I huff out as I toss my phone across the bed.

Heartbreak and I are far from strangers. Seems like I've been in a repetitive cycle of it for so long. Too long. And damn is it exhausting. Bone-deep, soul-level weariness.

Nine months. Maverick and I were together for nine months. He says he still cares about me deeply. That this wasn't what he wanted. And yet, he released me like a balloon. Watched me disappear without any true attempt to catch me, to pull me back in, to apologize and say fuck what his parents told him.

To Maverick, I am not worth the risk. He'd rather disappoint and hurt me than go against his parents' ideals.

Coward.

My phone vibrates as a text notification pops up on the screen. It's embarrassing how fast I move to swipe up my phone and tap the notification, hope surging in my veins. But when it doesn't open my chat history with Maverick, I deflate and slump back against the headboard.

JUNE

Did the bed eat you? Do I need to come in there and rescue you?

For a split second, I smile.

Thank the gods for my twin. June is the one person who gets me like no one else ever will. We could be miles apart and still know the other is upset or injured, or just not right. It's the coolest, weirdest, most unique connection, and I wouldn't trade it for anything.

No bed monsters. No life rafts necessary. Your text is exactly what I needed.

And I mean it. One simple, silly text from them and I feel a little lighter.

If I don't hear or see you out of your room in the next ten minutes, I'll assume the bed monster texted me this and not my sib.

I laugh.

Thanks, J

Any time, J

I force myself out of bed, take the shower I needed to a couple days ago, get dressed, and head for the kitchen. As I enter, June slides a mug across the counter with a smile on their face.

"Damn." They chuckle into their own mug. "I really hoped I'd have to come up there and save you." June taps the back side of their hip. "Even picked my weapon of choice."

Taking a sip of coffee, I lean a little to the side and peer down at said weapon. Again, June makes me laugh. Because poking out the back pocket of their shorts is the small rolling pin Mom let us use when we were little. It's half the size of a normal rolling pin and lightweight.

"You were going to save me"—I point to the implement—"with that?"

June shrugs. "Nah. But I knew if I walked in with it wielded, you'd have gotten up."

I smile at my favorite sibling. "You're right."

"I know." They down the last of their coffee and set the mug in the dishwasher. "How are you?"

It's my turn to shrug. "Not great. Heartbroken. Upset. Confused."

June sidles up to me, wraps an arm around my waist, and rests their head on my shoulder. "I'm always here." They leave it at that—simple, straightforward, open. There is no pressure to say anything now, to spill my guts.

"Thanks, J. I wouldn't be me without you." I press a kiss to their hair.

"Want to do something today?" They straighten and turn to face me more. "You need some vitamin D."

I narrow my eyes at them. "Is this your polite way of telling me I look pasty?"

June pinches my side then steps away. "Maybe."

Drinking the last dregs of my coffee, I set my mug in the dishwasher. "How about we do something outdoors tomorrow? Today, I just want to chill on the couch and watch mindless TV with you."

What I don't tell June is that I also want to reach out to Shanti. Our last conversation was not great. Shanti was jealous, upset, angry. And I threw it in her face—not something I would normally do.

At the time, it felt good, cathartic, to tell her *Now you know what it's like to be on the receiving end*. But in my super-emo, post-Maverick state, guilt has wiggled its way in. I've spent so many hours in my head, it's impossible not to question everything I've said or done since he and I got together.

I wouldn't say I'm sorry for *what* I said. But I am sorry for how I said it.

By nature, I'm a warm, affectionate, caring person. And the day I hurled her feelings in her face, I was not that version of myself. I was someone I never want to be again. Insensitive. Bitter. Careless.

I need to make amends.

"I'm down for a lazy day on the couch." June moves to the pantry and starts sifting through the contents. "Who am I to say no to good company and snacks galore?"

Sidling up to them, I reach into the pantry and grab the bag of kettle corn. I'll come back for candy after I polish this off. "Anything you want to watch?" I ask as I tear off a few paper towels.

"*Jurassic Park* marathon?" June suggests.

"Dinosaurs… the perfect antidote." I chuckle.

"Exactly." June pokes their head out of the pantry. "Dinosaurs and sharks are always the answer."

I tilt my head toward the living room. "I'll go get us set up."

"Drink?" June hollers as I leave the kitchen.

"More caffeine, please."

While June gathers more snacks, I drag the oversized ottoman closer to the couch, gather pillows and blankets for our seats, and search for the first movie in the series. When I'm done and June still hasn't entered the room yet, I take out my phone and open my text history with Shanti.

The time that's passed since we last chatted feels like years ago. Sure, I've seen her at dance. But we haven't interacted outside of what is absolutely necessary in class.

Before I was with Maverick, before she was with Brock, we really knew each other. Every little thing that made us tick. Every single thing that threw us off our game. When Shanti was upset, I almost always knew what to do to console her. And she would probably say the same in regard to me.

But now… Shanti is practically a stranger.

And I hate the way the truth of it twists my insides.

> Hey. Sorry I haven't reached out in a while. How are you?

I stare at the sent message on my screen, read it a few times, and question if I sound desperate or like a jerk. Feels like I'm a little of both.

Shanti hasn't answered by the time June meets me in the living room. So I lock my phone, set it beside me on the couch, and focus my attention on spending time with June.

Halfway through my kettle corn, the movie starts to shift from *oh that's cool* to *who's about to get eaten*. It's also when my phone vibrates against my leg. When the phone lights up and a text notification with Shanti's name appears on the screen.

My heart races as I wipe my hands with the paper towel. My stomach knots as I reach for the phone and unlock it. And my knee starts to bounce when I open her message and read it.

SHANTI

Like you care

I swallow down the urge to mutter that I've always cared. That would be an automatic movie-pausing moment and June would hound me with questions.

Trying to be discreet, I type out my reply.

> Of course I care. I always have.

Got a funny way of showing it

It would be so easy to argue with her right now. To throw in her face all the times our roles were reversed—where I felt like a convenient backup plan when something great in her life vanished.

But I'm not an asshole. At least, not *that* kind of asshole.

> What can I say? I got wrapped up in Mav. But that's over now.

My fingers almost typed out that he made me happy, cared about me, and wanted my time. Somehow, I restrained myself.

> So now that he's gone, you have time for me?

Her words are more than a slap, a gut punch, and laced with venom. They're cruel and toxic. Manipulative. Ironic and downright selfish.

How many times has she abandoned me and our friendship for someone or something else? I don't have an actual number because I'm not the kind of person to keep track of someone's choices. But it has been more than once.

Will I call her on it? No, because that isn't who my parents raised me to be.

Rather than answer her question, I ask what I want to know.

> Can we hang out? Catch up?

I almost added that I miss her. Thankfully, I hit send before I did.

She doesn't respond before the screen dims then locks. Instead of sending another message, I set my phone down and return my focus to the movie. I stare ahead and get lost in the world of dinosaurs on a remote island far from here.

Close to a half hour later, my phone vibrates again. I inhale a slow, methodical breath and prepare for the possibility of Shanti shutting me down.

Why should I say yes?

Because I said yes when our roles were reversed. Any time you've needed someone, I've said yes. I have been your best friend for most of our lives and, until last fall, always did everything with you in mind.

Going out with Maverick was the first time I was one-hundred-percent selfish. Now I need to learn to be both selfless and selfish again.

I miss you. I miss my friend, my partner, who we used to be. Is that wrong?

Of course not

But we can't just go back to how things were

Things are different now

I know. I still want to see you.

Those pesky little dots dance in the bubble on the screen then disappear. This happens a few times, but nothing comes through.

So I type out another message.

I'm sorry things happened the way they did with us. I still love you. And I know I already said it, but I miss you. Our friendship means everything to me. What we share is irreplaceable. You are irreplaceable.

My free hand starts to shake as I read the sent message. I shove it under my thigh and read the message again. And again.

I sound like the literal definition of a desperate idiot. Maybe I should give my phone to June and tell them to hide it.

Maybe. I'll think about it.

A step in the right direction, even if it's a baby step.

Cool. I'm here whenever you're up for it.

Too much? Don't know, don't care.

I'll let you know

Locking my phone so I'm not tempted to type more foolish texts, I set my phone down and go back to watching the movie. But the more I sit, the more I let my mind wander.

Shanti opened the door to let me back in, but not fully. But I'll take every little opening she gives.

I wasn't kidding when I said I missed her. And it isn't only because Maverick is out of the picture. Maverick was just really great at distracting me from thoughts of Shanti. He gave me the attention I always craved from her. He made me feel wanted and loved.

I miss him, but not in the same way I missed Shanti when she was with Brock. Maverick had my heart for almost a year. Shanti has had my heart—in some capacity—for a decade. The loss of Maverick versus Shanti… they are nowhere near identical.

Maverick could have been so much more. Permanent. Lasting. But I accept that the universe has other plans for my future. That I was only meant to have Maverick's love for a short time. Perhaps it was to show me what it feels like to be so lost in another person, to be so adored and cherished by them your logical brain goes out the window.

I love Shanti, but I've never experienced what it is like to be loved by her. We fell into each other's lives. Grew together. Became a unit, a pair. Neither of us went through an infatuation phase with each other like Maverick did with me. Shanti hasn't experienced—at least, not to my knowledge—the level of pining I have felt for her.

Maybe my time with Maverick opened her eyes. Maybe it dawned on her that I won't always sit around and wait for her.

I may love Shanti Mahal, but it isn't healthy to wait my entire life to be loved by someone who may never love me in return. Not in the way I want. Deserve. Maverick taught me it is possible to have my affections reciprocated. That I am worthy of more than a one-sided romance.

But what if one day Shanti does return my feelings? What if she becomes mine?

My heart pounds viciously against my rib cage as nervous energy builds beneath my diaphragm. I close my eyes, drag in a slow, quiet breath, let my imagination run wild until my lungs burn, then I exhale and open my eyes.

No matter how much time passes, no matter who steals our attention for a stint, one thing will always remain true.

Shanti is mine, and she always will be, even if only in my mind.

FIFTEEN

SPARKS IGNITE

SHANTI

Six and a Half Years Ago

ALTHOUGH THINGS AREN'T QUITE THE SAME, JET AND I ARE SLOWLY getting back to us. Well, a newer version of us. A variation molded by happiness and heartbreak.

It's been almost six months since Jet texted to apologize and ask how I was. Six months since he told me he missed me, that I am irreplaceable. Six months since I let go of the foreign jealousy I felt while Jet dated Maverick.

Part of me didn't want to give in so easily. I didn't want to let him waltz back in as if the distance between us wasn't real.

The chasm forged between us while I was with Brock and then when he was with Maverick was very real. A fissure so deep and wide, either of us would be foolish to not question how it came to be. Maybe it formed because our connection wasn't as strong as either of us believed it to be. Or… maybe that canyon tore wide open because our bond is *more* than either of us recognizes.

The urge to dissect every nuance of our friendship, to study every pivotal moment in our history, is strong. But what if I'm wrong? What if I dig too deep, overanalyze every aspect of him and us, and come to the wrong conclusion?

I will never be able to unsee it. Never be able to look at Jet the same way. Nor will what we have be the same.

After all we've endured, I won't risk losing him—in any capacity. Not again.

The door to the studio opens, and a faint smile curves my mouth as I lift a leg onto the barre and lower my torso to my thigh. Soft footsteps echo through the room as I wrap my fingers around my foot and drop my forehead to the top of my shin.

The delicious stretch behind my knee is no match for the way my pulse races in my chest. The way it has the past three months —when Jet and I drifted back into our routine of spending almost every day together. I don't quite understand why my heart gets so excited, why him being in the same room makes my skin warm and tingly. But I also don't question it.

He quietly pads across the room to the barre, but I hear every step he takes. A moment later, his black ballet slippers appear in my periphery. I bite the inside of my cheek to keep from smiling bigger.

"Hey," he greets as he lifts a foot to stretch his quads.

Inhaling deeply, I release my foot and slowly straighten to my full height. "Hi." Despite my best effort, I flash him a smile. "Late morning?" I ask as I switch to my other leg and drop into the stretch.

Jet grumbles. "Overslept. Then the cat tried to make a scratching post out of my leg."

Turning my head, I study the disgruntled look on Jet's face. I clamp my lips between my teeth to stop myself from laughing. But when he glances my way and rolls his eyes, I can't contain it.

For a beat, he laughs too. Head shaking and tears in his eyes, he pauses long enough to say, "It's not funny."

Silence stretches between us for one breath, followed by another as we stare at each other. Then, the most embarrassing snort-laugh leaves my lips. His eyes widen as mirth shines in his captivating gray irises.

Coming out of my stretch, I turn to face him. "It's a little funny."

With a scoff, he rolls his eyes and switches to his next move. "To you. But that's only because you haven't experienced Rebel's version of love yet."

A few years back, when Jet's sister Delilah was in college, their Mom said the house was quieter with one of her children gone. She knew it wouldn't be long before Jet and June also discovered their independence. So, Aurora adopted a cat. Rebel loves Mrs. Fox. Unfortunately for everyone else in the house, Rebel doesn't share the same affection with them. It's comical to witness.

I snicker. "After the stories you've shared, I'm smart enough to stay away from her."

Jet harrumphs. "Lucky."

Silence stretches between us as we finish our warm-up routine, but it isn't uncomfortable. If anything, I enjoy it. Relish it. Breathe it in and absorb every second. With our hectic schedules—mine more jam-packed every month as my parents add new places for me to volunteer—the quiet is welcome. Desirable. Appreciated. Whether five seconds or an hour, I bask in the muted, tranquil moments I share with Jet.

"Ready for today?" he asks as he rotates his shoulder joints.

The soft creak of door hinges, followed by hushed conversation, rings through the room as a few of our classmates enter the studio. Displeasure heats my skin, and I hate that we no longer have the place to ourselves.

Ignoring the chatter behind us, I nod. "Feels like we haven't rehearsed for a performance in years." In reality, it has only been months. "It'll be nice to have a project to focus on."

"Agreed."

Over the past few years, our class has graced the stage four to six times a year. But that has changed. Earlier this year, Ms. Neesa said she wanted to lessen our onstage time so we could strengthen our techniques and focus on any moves we hadn't quite mastered. Because many in our class are preparing for what comes next.

College and possibly working with a dance company.

My parents have nagged me a few times since school resumed, but I dismiss their needling. I'm a sophomore, for crying out loud. It's too early for me to apply to college or dance schools. Not only do I need more hours under my belt, I also need more extracurriculars and volunteer time—which my parents are so graciously piling on. The only thing applying now would do is start a rejection pile. Not that it would be steep since I only plan to apply to one school. But no one wants to open the *we're sorry to inform you* letter from their top school choice.

School drama aside, I have wondered about Jet's college applications. How many schools has he applied to and where? I want to ask, but every time I think about it, anxiety sets in. I lock up mentally. So I haven't brought it up.

He hasn't mentioned applying anywhere, which seems odd. It's halfway through his senior year; he must have applied to several schools by now. Right? Maybe he has and isn't ready to tell me yet. Maybe he has a stack of rejection letters—a ludicrous thought. Or maybe he has all acceptance letters.

Thrill and nausea roll through me simultaneously.

You know what? I don't want to know. Not yet. Not when things are finally good between us again.

Clapping echoes through the studio and pulls me out of my momentary spiral. "Good morning, class," Ms. Neesa greets as she glides to her place at the front of the room. "I trust you're all enjoying the start of winter break."

Several say yes while the rest stay silent.

"I know it's a bit late for us to start rehearsing a winter performance, but you're the best this school has to offer, and I know we'll be ready to put on a stellar show in a month."

Muffled conversation erupts in the room, but Ms. Neesa cuts it off with another clap.

"With focus, determination, and some additional hours each

week, I'm confident every one of you will be ready. But if you're still not convinced, here's another reason." Ms. Neesa gestures toward the door with her hand.

Every head in the room swivels to see what she is referring to. A second later, the door opens and in walks someone we haven't seen in years—Vivienne Bellecourt.

A chill rolls down my spine. Goose bumps ripple over my skin. Unease flares in my stomach. I can't tear my eyes off her. I refuse to. Following her every move, I curl my fingers into loose fists as she saunters across the room to stand beside Ms. Neesa.

Jet never explained the specifics as to why he doesn't like this woman, but she puts him on edge. Stresses him out and steals his focus. Unsettles him so much he doesn't want to be in the same room as her.

But I don't need specifics. If she makes him uneasy, it's reason enough.

"Class, please welcome back Ms. Vivienne."

Excited greetings float through the air from everyone except me and Jet.

"We're very fortunate Ms. Vivienne will help us prepare for our next performance. And it's with her assistance I know we'll be ready in time."

While Ms. Neesa and Ms. Vivienne discuss the performance, I peer at Jet from the corner of my eye.

Jaw tight and gaze on the floor, Jet clenches then flexes his fingers over and over. Irritation and agitation color his aura a grim black, something very out of character for him. If given the chance, he would've bolted the second she entered the room. But Jet doesn't like to be the center of attention. He never has.

"Hey," I whisper. When he doesn't say anything or meet my gaze, I speak a little louder. "Jet. Look at me."

The muscle in his jaw tics once, twice before it relaxes. On his next inhale, he lifts his chin and twists to meet my waiting stare. His nostrils flare, but I don't take his reaction personally.

"Do you want to leave?" I ask, my words as serious as my expression. "Because I'll walk out the door with you."

His features soften a beat before his shoulders relax. "You'd do that?" The simple question is laced with awe and a hint of incredulity.

Eyes locked on his, I nod. "In a heartbeat."

The corner of his mouth twitches, but he doesn't smile as his eyes search mine. Warmth and comfort and some unnamable sensation bloom in my chest. The studio disappears around us. Time ceases to exist. For hour-long seconds, his gentle gray eyes hold me captive. Keep me shackled to him. But it's no hardship. I'd gladly stay tethered to him.

Dizzy from my thoughts, I break eye contact.

I trail my gaze down his face until I reach his soft, full lips. Light pink, the bottom plumper than the top. God, how I've fantasized about kissing those lips. So many times. Probably too many.

With a blink, I drift lower to the faint shadow of his freshly shaved jaw. Sharp and prominent yet delicate and understated. Often, I wonder what he'd look like with facial hair. A light dusting of scruff. Would it be thin and soft or thick and coarse? And how good would the scrape of it against my skin feel?

Shaking off the thought, I continue my descent. Finally, my gaze lands on his Adam's apple. I visually trace the distinguishable bulge. Imagine pulling him close and running my tongue over it.

Fire scorches my cheeks. My heart hammers in my chest.

Then Jet swallows, and my gaze flies to his.

Every ounce of outrage and discomfort he had moments ago is gone. In its place is something heady, alluring, inviting. His gray eyes are liquid silver. A fiery storm of desire and hope.

My lips part as I gasp. And just as I'm about to take a step toward him, clapping echoes through the room and breaks the spell.

"Shanti and Jet, Sabrina and Luka, you'll perform pas de

deux," Ms. Neesa announces. When she moves on to the other roles, I tune her out.

Nervous energy thrums through my veins, and I lick my lips. My palms sweat as I take a tentative step toward Jet, then another. His eyes never leave mine as we slowly close the distance between us. When we finally meet in the middle, the heat of him warms every inch of my skin.

I've known Jet most of my life. We've laughed, cried, hugged, and gone off on each other. But in the almost eleven years we've been in each other's lives, I've never felt *this* with him.

And if the look in his eyes is any indication, he knows exactly what I'm feeling. Because he feels it too.

"Dance with me," he says, his voice low, raspy, needy as he offers his hand.

I slip my hand in his and shiver when his warm fingers curl around mine. Swallowing past my sudden nerves, I nod. "Always."

And like we have hundreds of times, we glide across the floor together. Synchronize our bodies, our every move, until we are one. We practice the beginning of our first routine until it becomes second nature. Until we *are* the roles we're portraying.

Then we start the next segment of our routine and everything changes.

Fluttering across the floor, my chin over my shoulder and gaze aimed at Jet just behind me, I sway my body left then right as his hands take my waist. It's a simple move, one we've done countless times, but it feels different now. And as I spin on my toes to face him, I swallow when our eyes connect and hold.

His gray irises shimmer in the light as he lifts my arm, steps closer, and trails his fingers lightly down my palm, my wrist, my forearm. My eyes drift closed for a breath, opening when his hand stops at my waist. And then his grip on either side tightens, just above my hips, and he lifts me into the air.

The hypnotic trance I've been in wanes when our eye contact breaks. While Jet dances across the floor, my arms ripple like waves as I draw one foot to the opposite knee in a pirouette, then switch to the other foot and knee. On Jet's next step, I mentally prepare for him to lower me to the floor.

What I don't anticipate is the slow, deliberate way he moves. How he pins me impossibly close to the front of his body as every inch of the front of mine drags down, down, down every muscled inch of him. When the platform of my pointe shoe hits the floor, when my golden browns lock back onto his grays, the air around us charges. Becomes electric. Hums with the undeniable chemistry between us.

And then, with a single word, it evaporates.

"Bravo," Ms. Vivienne cries out as she applauds less than a foot away.

Jet goes stiff as a statue, his grip firmly on my waist. And his reaction to her lights a fire in my veins.

I have no idea what the deal is with this woman, but I don't care. She makes Jet uneasy, and that is enough to piss me off.

As if it's part of the routine, I spin us and put myself between her and Jet. Then I turn, face her, and shift just enough to block Jet from her view.

With a curt nod, I say, "Thank you, Ms. Vivienne."

As if she senses my need to protect Jet, she gives me a clipped smile. "This is what I want to see," she says loud enough for everyone to hear, her eyes never leaving mine. "Passion, beauty" —she pauses and tilts her head—"longing."

My eyes narrow as my lip curls. Fury boils beneath my skin, but I don't hide my animosity. Or my disgust.

I don't know what this woman's deal is, but she needs to back the fuck up. Now.

As if he hears my thoughts, Jet tightens his grip on my waist. I let that subtle squeeze fuel my next move.

Tilting my head, I lift my hands and lay them over Jet's as a smirk tips up a corner of my mouth. Jet and I may only be friends, but he is mine. And I won't let her fuck with him. I won't let *anyone* hurt him.

"We really should get back to dancing," I say, my voice as saccharine sweet as the fake smile I flash her. "You understand, right?"

She arches a brow then takes a step back. "Let's take it from the top, everyone." And then she returns to the front of the room, far away from us.

The rest of class feels cold and stiff. We go through the routine, nail every move, but all of Jet's warmth from earlier is absent. He is here, but only in the physical sense.

It grates on my nerves that this woman has the ability to steal his light.

When class ends, we swap our shoes, don our coats, and shoulder our bags quickly. As we head for the door, I loop my arm in his. "You okay?"

He leans into me and nods. "Yeah." His arm clamps onto mine as he stops us under the awning outside. "Want a ride?"

I scan the parking lot and note that neither my parents nor sister is here, honestly not surprised. "I'd love one."

While the car warms up, I contemplate my next words. The last thing I want to do is upset Jet, but I need to know if there is more going on with Ms. Vivienne than he's shared. He did say he'd tell me if anything happened, but that was before Brock, Maverick, and the rift between us.

There is no perfect way to ask, so I just go for it. "Did anything ever happen with her?" Facing forward, I peer at Jet out of the corner of my eye. I figure not staring directly at him will help him feel more comfortable.

Silence stretches between us, and I let it. I resist the urge to say anything else. He may need a moment to gather his thoughts.

In my periphery, he shakes his head. "Nothing anyone would deem inappropriate."

What does that mean? I shout in my head.

"But something did happen?" Hesitation laces my tone.

He drops his head back to rest on the seat and audibly exhales. "It all feels like this huge gray area. Like she's dancing on the edge of unacceptable behavior but stays just inside the lines of what's allowed."

As much as I want him to expand on what he means, I also don't want to upset him further. So I take a different approach.

"Did you ever speak with Ms. Neesa or Mr. Aurelio about it?"

He turns to look at me. "No. I don't want things to be weird."

Without hesitation, I reach for and take his hand. Lace my fingers with his and anchor him to me in every possible way. "I get that." A sympathetic smile tugs at my lips. "Really, I do." I give his hand a gentle squeeze. "But what if you're not alone in this? What if there are others? Maybe they're too scared to speak up. What if your bravery helps them and you?"

His brows twitch then relax. He gives a halfhearted nod and says, "Maybe you're right." Closing his eyes, he takes a deep breath, swallows, then meets my gaze. Confliction darkens his gray irises. "But not today, okay?"

I brush my thumb over his and give him a gentle smile. As much as I don't like his answer, I won't push him to do something he isn't ready for. "Not today," I agree. I face forward in my seat, but don't let go of his hand. "Let's get out of here."

The corner of his mouth curves into a half smile. "As you wish."

Instead of driving me home, Jet takes me to his house. And I have to admit, it feels different, better, more. Unlike any other day we've spent together. Something about it feels perfect.

Every day should end like this. Just me and Jet and the undeniable tether between our hearts.

PART THREE

PAST

LOVE IS FICKLE

SIXTEEN
AND JUST LIKE THAT, I LOST HER...
AGAIN

JET

Six Years Ago

"Look at my grandbabies," Grandma Amelia says, emotion clogging her voice. "All grown up now." She loops arms with Grandpa Zach and leans into his side. "I refuse to believe it."

Grandpa chuckles and hugs her closer. "No matter how old they are, they'll always be our grandbabies, my love." He kisses the top of her head. "Only now, they get to travel the world on their own and share their generous hearts."

"Zachariah Fox," Grandma scolds as she playfully slaps Grandpa's chest, tears rimming her eyes. "Don't you dare make me cry."

June plucks a napkin from a nearby table and hands it to Grandma. "Just in case."

"Thank you, my darling June bug." Grandma dabs at the corners of her eyes with the napkin. "Can't have mascara running down my cheeks. It's a happy day, after all."

A month ago, June and I earned our high school diplomas. Neither of us wanted a party or fanfare. Holding the certificate and not having to wake up at some horrid hour was reward enough.

Obviously, our family wasn't satisfied with that response. So, when it came time to organize our eighteenth birthday, the details were kept quiet from me and June. All either of us knew was that we needed to be home on the big day. We agreed.

Fast forward to today, June and I are being doted on as though we missed the past five birthday celebrations. The morning started with a full breakfast of funny-face pancakes, cheesy scrambled eggs, crispy hash browns, and fresh fruit—a tradition our parents started on our fourth birthday. As we ate, the decorations went up. The cakes were made. Finger foods were prepared.

Yes, this birthday is a major milestone and worth celebrating. But neither of us expected this—decorations galore and what feels like half the town in our house. It's a tad overwhelming—more for June than me—but we are taking it one cheery congratulations at a time.

"Have you decided what happens next?" Grandpa asks then takes a sip of his drink.

This isn't the first time the question has come up. For the past year, I've heard it at least a couple times a month. There is zero pressure for me to apply to colleges or dance schools. More like my family wants to know what my plan is for the future, whatever it may be.

June is skipping the college experience. They signed up for online courses for a business degree and will work full-time with Mom at the Sage Whisperer. The shop is perfect for June. Like Mom, they enjoy being in the metaphysical store, surrounded by crystals, soothing energy, and like-minded individuals. June just wants to expand their knowledge of running a business because one day the Sage Whisperer will be theirs.

As for me, I'm in limbo. It's probably foolish, but I've postponed applying to colleges and dance programs until Shanti mentions her plans. I haven't asked where she wants to submit applications, but I have my suspicions. The last thing I want to do is be another nag in her life. From what little she shares about her parents, they do a standup job of stressing her out. I won't add to her anxiety. Plus, she still has time.

The idea of leaving Shanti for a long-distance dance school makes me twitchy. The thought of not seeing her, of not dancing with her, of not being in her orbit several times a week turns my stomach.

I've never considered myself insecure or possessive, but sometimes I wonder if I'm forgettable.

My right pocket grows hot suddenly. The small box tucked in there abruptly heavier.

Shrugging, I inhale slowly and meet Grandpa's waiting gaze. "I'm taking a year off while I narrow down the dance schools I want to apply to."

Grandpa unhooks his arm from Grandma and pats my shoulder. "Nothing wrong with weighing your options. Better to make a solid, informed decision when your happiness is on the line. We'll support whatever decision you make, whenever it happens."

Love and warmth bloom in my chest as his gray eyes—a shade darker than mine—hold my gaze. "Thanks, Grandpa Zach." The backs of my eyes sting for a beat. "That means a lot."

Setting down his drink, he hauls me into a tight embrace. "I'll always fight for what's best for this family." After a breath-stealing squeeze, he releases me, picks up his drink, and takes Grandma's hand. "We've hogged enough of your time. Go. Be with your friends."

I chuckle, then lean in to press a kiss to Grandma's cheek. "Love you."

They return the sentiment and then wander off to chat with Mom's parents.

"If you need me, I'll be in the library with enough snacks to hold me over until cake," June declares.

The library is June, Delilah, and Grandma Amelia's favorite room on the Fox estate. Floor-to-ceiling windows on one wall, bookshelves lining the other three, a grand fireplace, and cozy places to read. What's not to love? The most incredible part is all the books inside.

At least five generations have added books to the shelves. From classic literature to romance to scientific studies to paganism, those shelves hold every type of book imaginable. Most of the older texts are now stored in a climate-controlled case to prevent the pages from deteriorating, but it's so neat to own books from the late 1800s.

What started as a lavish, four-hundred-square-foot office and study with a single bookcase for James Fox, one of the town founders, slowly morphed into a personal library with more than three thousand books. It's our own little bookstore.

"Keep you posted on the cake," I promise as June heads for the food table, and I weave through the crowd for the back doors.

Laughter and conversation fill the house and patio as I step outside. Several people congratulate me or wish me happy birthday as I pass. People I don't know. Thanking them, I cross the yard for a quiet spot near the garden.

Sitting on a bench, I bend and pick up a leaf. Tear at the edges until a familiar shape appears—a heart. Closing my palm and safeguarding the leaf, I scan the crowd. Look for the one person I want to spend time with today.

Shanti.

Just as I'm about to give up my search, I spot a head of dark-brown hair with her signature pink ribbon tied around her ponytail's elastic. My pulse soars, whooshing loudly in my ears as I rise from my seat and make my way toward her. A few feet from her, she spins around, annoyance coloring her expression as she crosses her arms over her chest.

My brows tug inward as I follow her line of sight. A guy I've never seen before says something to her, and she shakes her head. As he says something else, he reaches for her arm and grips her elbow, but she yanks free and steps back.

Everyone else in the crowd disappears as I storm across the patio for her. The heart-shaped leaf in my hand is crushed to bits. I don't know who this asshole is, but he better not fucking touch her again.

I never condone violence, but I will protect the people I love. By whatever means necessary.

"Is there a problem here?" I ask, voice loud enough for others to hear as I sidle up to Shanti. Brows raised, I glare at the guy. All but goad him to piss me off.

The douchebag smooths his hands down his *sport coat* then tucks them in his pants pockets. Is he from the 1980s? Why the hell is he wearing a sport coat in the middle of June?

"No problem at all." His gaze flits to Shanti, and my blood boils. "We were having a conversation."

I shuffle closer to her and wrap an arm around her waist. "Looked like you were harassing her."

"Jet…" Shanti mutters. "It's fine."

Narrowing my eyes at him, I speak to her. "Anyone who makes you upset or uncomfortable is not *fine*."

"Ah," he says, a smirk on his pretentious face. "You're the *friend* with the birthday."

The way he says *friend* grates my nerves. *Pompous dick.* "And you are?" I ask, tightening my hold on Shanti.

He opens his mouth to answer, but Shanti speaks before he has the chance.

"Jet, this is Rohan." Shanti shifts her weight, and I take my eyes off him to look at her. "A family friend."

Doesn't matter who he is; the way he treats and talks to Shanti is unacceptable.

A curt smile tugs at my lips as I offer my free hand. "Jet, Shanti's best friend and dance partner."

He takes my hand to shake, and I tighten my grip. His wince is a shot of pure gratification. He tugs his hand from mine, flexes his fingers, then wipes his hand on his pants.

Prick.

"Rohan, premed, with a focus on pediatrics." He makes a show of surveying the patio. "What are your plans? Attending college in the fall? Dance, I assume."

Shanti fidgets in my hold but doesn't try to wiggle free. I stroke my thumb over the curve of her waist and bask in the sensation that small action elicits.

I shake my head. "Nah, deferring for a year. Still reviewing my options. Too many top schools to choose from."

"Really?" Shanti mumbles, a hint of mortification in her voice.

"It's okay, Shanti," Rohan says, a smug look on his face. "We guys are known to brag about our merits." He softens his expression a beat before meeting her gaze. "Especially in the presence of a beautiful woman."

"Ugh." Shanti slips out of my hold and takes two purposeful steps away from us. "Please, just stop."

I open my mouth to tell Rohan to quit acting like an arrogant ass, but he cuts me off.

"Would appear you haven't told *your best friend* about me, Shanti." Satisfaction glints in his eyes, and my stomach sours at the way he emphasized my role in her life.

Shanti pales at his words. "Rohan, don't," she commands, but the directive falls short.

"What's he talking about?" I ask, even though I'm not sure I want to know.

Absolute delight colors his smug face. "Yes, Shanti, what am I talking about?"

Shanti groans. "You're such an asshole." She shakes her head then turns my way. "I literally just found out." She closes her eyes for two breaths then opens them, pleading. "It's nothing, I promise."

Rohan scoffs. "Nothing?" He laughs a little too loud. "We're betrothed."

My head jerks back as if I've been slapped. *Betrothed?* First off, no one our age uses the term betrothed. And second, I've not once heard of this guy. If Shanti was actually promised or engaged to someone—which sounds all kinds of wrong considering she's sixteen—I would be the first to know. Right?

She said she just found out.

Based on the smarmy look on his face, he knows he got under my skin. That he has someone I want and there isn't a damn thing I can do about it. The egotistical smile on his face stretches wider, and it makes me want to hit something.

"You aren't anything." The declaration comes out harsh and conclusive. "Shanti isn't some bargaining chip. She's a person with her own mind." I shuffle closer to the prick, tilt forward and hover inches above him. "Only she decides who she belongs with."

Rohan shakes his head on a laugh. "And what? You think that's you?" His eyes gleam as he tries to make himself appear taller. "Sorry to break it to you, *friend,* but this was set up years ago by our parents. Shanti may not have known the details, but we aren't strangers."

His words eat away at my insides and I can't help but wonder if Shanti had her suspicions. At some point, her parents had to have mentioned this to her. Mr. and Mrs. Mahal are not the type to skirt around the truth. They are the definition of straightforward, regardless of your feelings.

As if she senses my apprehension, Shanti closes the distance between us. "Jet, please look at me."

The small box in my pocket scalds my thigh as my pulse throbs in my ears. I inhale a lungful of air and slowly release it before shifting my gaze from him to her.

Shanti takes my hands in hers, and the subtle contact cools the inferno in my veins.

"I swear to you, I didn't know about this. Yes, I know Rohan. But only because our parents are friends." She tightens her hold on my hands. "I haven't seen him in years. Then, two hours ago, he showed up at the house and my parents told me everything." She steps impossibly closer. "I haven't even had time to process my own anger. So please don't be mad at me."

Those final words stomp out the last of my rage. I lift a hand to her hair, my eyes following the action, and toy with the ribbon tied there, the one that looks identical to the one I took from her years ago. The pink, silky piece of fabric I still have. "I'm not mad at you." I tug lightly on the ribbon, release it, and trail my fingers down her jaw. "I could never be mad at you."

Time stands still for what feels like hours as we hold each other's gaze. And in this small blip of time, I swear I see everything I've felt for her staring back at me. Thumb and forefinger on her chin, I tilt her head back and bring her lips a fraction closer. Inch by slow, painful inch, I lower my mouth to hers. And just as my eyes roll closed, a throat clears and makes me freeze.

"Seriously?" Rohan chastises. "I'm right here."

I bite my tongue to stop myself from telling him I don't give a fuck. And apparently, neither does Shanti, who has yet to pull away.

"Shanti, let's go."

That, however, steals the moment and stirs my irritation back to life.

My gaze flits to the prick behind her, far too close for my liking. "Back. Off," I grind out. I don't miss the way Shanti wilts in my grasp.

Rohan grips her forearm. "You wished your friend a happy birthday. It's time to go. We have a lot to talk about."

Against every instinct, I release Shanti's chin, straighten my spine, and glare at the asshole with a colossal ego. "What's your problem?"

I become acutely aware of how quiet the patio is and look away long enough to see everyone watching us. *Great*. The last thing this situation needs is an audience.

Rohan tugs Shanti aside and comes toe to toe with me, over-confidence radiating off him in waves. "Right now, you are my problem. You may want her"—he points behind him and almost smacks Shanti in the face—"but she's not yours to have." He jerks his chin up and taps his chest. "Like it or not, Shanti is mine."

Pain radiates in my jaw as my molars gnash. I let the sensation fuel my rage. "That's where you're wrong," I say, voice low. "She will *never* be yours." We come chest to chest as I tower over him. "Not in any way that matters."

We stare daggers at each other, the air around us thick and stifling. And then he cocks a brow, takes a step back, and keeps his eyes locked on mine as he says, "We're leaving, Shanti. Now."

Before he yanks her away, I invade her space and wrap my arms around her. "You don't have to go."

Her arms circle my waist a beat before one of her hands trails up my spine. "I should. He's caused enough of a scene already."

Hugging her tighter, I lower my mouth to her ear. "You know where to find me if you need anything. Day or night." I drop my nose to the crook of her neck and inhale her subtle orange-blossom-and-honey perfume. "Any time you need me, I'm here."

Her fingers clutch my shirt then relax. With a nod, she releases me and steps back. "Happy birthday, Jet." Glassy eyes hold my stare. "See you soon."

Rooted in place, the backs of my eyes sting as I watch her walk away with *him*. When she disappears from view, when the noise of the party resumes, I move through the crowd for the yard and go to another bench beyond the garden.

As I sit, a corner of the small box in my pocket jabs my thigh. I don't fight the sting. Don't shove away the feeling of my heart breaking once again. Lowering my elbows to my knees, I drop my head in my hands and laugh without humor. Because what else is there to do?

The next morning, I do something impulsive. Something I thought I would never do.

I drive to the northern outskirts of town, park at the plaza with only two occupied storefronts, and enter the smallest one. A little over two hours later, I leave with a new pain. A permanent reminder etched in my skin.

In black ink, a lone feather now follows the curve of my hip bone. Next to it are the words *never let her fall*.

And I never will. Not physically or emotionally or in any way that matters. Regardless of what happens between me and Shanti, I will always lift her up and keep her safe.

Always.

SEVENTEEN
ALL I DO IS GIVE AND GIVE AND GIVE
SHANTI

Five and a Half Years Ago

THE CLOSER I GET TO ADULTHOOD AND TRUE INDEPENDENCE, THE LESS free I feel.

Most parents are supposed to mold and guide you into a decent human being. When you make a decision that will steer you the wrong way or cause you harm, their job is to nudge you back onto the correct path and explain why. When you slip in school—I'm talking grades that will keep you from moving forward, not getting something other than an *A*—their job is to encourage, to help in any way possible, to boost your esteem when you feel like you're failing. And when you are passionate about something, their job is to build you up, motivate, inspire, and be your biggest champion while you pursue your dreams.

Most parents want the best for their children, even if their future isn't as predicted.

Unfortunately for me, my parents aren't like most.

Don't get me wrong, I'm grateful for everything I have and all the things their bountiful careers have gifted. My years in ballet and friendship with Jet wouldn't exist without it.

But sometimes, all I want is a hug. A few motivational words

to show their support of me and the future *I* choose. A single *I love you* without an ulterior obligation or meaning tied to it.

But that isn't the life I live.

Slowly, my parents are tightening their reins. Squeezing my proverbial character mold more. Thrusting me into new activities that will *look better* on my college applications, which means less time for the projects I'm already committed to.

My entire future is this intricate, grand plan splayed out in diagrams and spreadsheets on their computer. A comprehensive blueprint I've not seen, nor had a say in. An elaborate outline of who they have cast their youngest daughter to be, without regard for her own thoughts or ideas.

For almost seventeen years, all I've done is try to please my parents. And for just as long, I've never earned their approval. No matter how much I sacrifice, no matter how much I deplete my soul, what I offer is never enough. And I'm just so damn exhausted.

My phone buzzes on my dresser, but I ignore it and finish getting dressed. Without looking, I already know who the text is from. The same person texts me at this exact time every single day.

Rohan. The additional nuisance in my life.

Six months have passed since my parents let me in on the biggest, most archaic decision they've made on my behalf. Promising me to their friends' son before I took my first step.

I mean, who does that?

Who sits down with their friends and says, *"Hey, I've got a great idea. How about your son marries my daughter when she turns eighteen? That way, they can focus on intelligence instead of love and we'll have brilliant grandkids. What do you think?"*

I shiver at the thought.

A couple days after my parents told me, after Rohan texted me over and over, I turned off the *read receipts* function on my phone. I stopped answering my phone unless it's someone I want to talk to. Almost everyone gets sent to voicemail. If Rohan leaves a message—voicemail or text—I delete it.

A yawn escapes my lips as I tug a hoodie over my head. I lift the collar to my nose, close my eyes, and slowly inhale. The faint smell of clean cotton and something distinctly Jet lingers in the fabric. The comforting scent isn't as strong as it was a couple weeks ago when he lent me the hoodie after dance class, but I pick up the faint notes.

I'd recognize his distinct, calming smell anywhere.

"I miss you," I whisper to myself as I cross my room and grab my backpack from the bed.

Since Jet graduated, I see him even less. Not because he went off to college or has a job that consumes all his time. But because Jet doesn't fit into the grand design my parents envision.

For years, I took for granted the additional time I got with my best friend—before school, lunch, hours after school for dance and homework, days off. I was foolish to think I'd have those small moments forever. That I'd have *him* forever.

Now, I'm lucky if my parents let me go to dance class—the only time I get with Jet.

As of recent, I get voluntold to attend or help at charity events in my imaginary spare time. Not because my parents believe in worthy causes—thank goodness, all of them do—but because the specific foundation names will shine brightly on my college applications. As if the gift of my time at a lesser-known organization is a waste—insert dramatic eye roll.

A huff of bone-deep exhaustion leaves my lips as I exit my room, plod down the stairs louder than necessary, swipe a banana from the fruit basket in the kitchen, and head for the front door.

"Don't forget about—"

My mother's words are cut off as I step out onto the porch and close the door. It's better than me going off on her over Rohan and his parents coming for dinner tonight. A meal I'd rather skip but am not allowed to. Because, of course, they will be discussing my life as if I am not in the room. As if I were some doll to dress up and parade around. As if anything I want for my future is pointless.

Right now, everything feels chaotic and pointless.

Sliding into the driver's seat, I crank the gently used car to life and let it warm up. I type out a quick text to Jet, letting him know I'll be at the studio soon, but only have a half hour to practice. Then I connect my phone to the car and hit play on my current favorite playlist and let the music ease my frustrations.

At the start of fall, my parents gifted me the reliable SUV so I had a way to get from one appointment to another without relying on them. All I heard was that I needed to do more and their lives were too busy to participate.

When I get to the studio, Jet is already inside. A light dusting of snow crunches under my boots as I cross the lot. After a quick swipe of my feet on the mat, I speed walk to the room we usually practice in, set my bag down, and start peeling off my layers.

"Everything okay?" Jet sidles up to me as I begin an abbreviated warm-up routine.

Thankfully, I did ten minutes of stretches before I dressed. "Not really, but I don't want to talk about it." My lips stretch into a sad smile. "Maybe later. I don't have much time, and I'd rather focus on dance right now."

Jet trails the back of his fingers down the length of my arm. "Whatever you want."

Thirty minutes breeze by far too quickly. When the timer on my phone goes off, I groan. It feels like we started practice seconds ago.

"Ugh." My shoulders sag as I walk toward the wall where my bag is. "Not sure how much longer I can do this."

Jet drops down onto the floor beside me as I don my sweatpants and his hoodie. "Wish there was a way I could help." He traces the tip of his finger over my name stitched onto my bag.

"You're doing it," I whisper, and he glances up. "This. Being here when I need you. Sticking by my side while my parents rip my life to shreds... it all helps." I tug on a boot. "You keep me grounded, as close to whole as humanly possible. If I didn't have you..." I don't voice the rest of my thoughts.

The last thing Jet needs to hear about is the dark rabbit hole I'd be in without him.

"I'm always here," he says, the promise so soft it's barely audible.

Holding his gaze, I give a subtle nod. "I know." I reach for my bag and sling the strap over my shoulder as Jet rises from the floor. "Thank you." It feels weird to thank my best friend for being there for me, but I need to say *something*. I owe him so much for keeping me levelheaded over the years.

We're quiet as he walks beside me to the door, his pace matching my slow one. I want to drag out my time with him. Stretch it impossibly long so I don't have to go back to my sad reality. Not yet.

The light dusting of snow crunches beneath our shoes as he walks me to my car. When we reach the driver's door, warmth blankets my back and arm a beat before Jet trails the tips of his fingers from my elbow to my wrist.

I suck in a sharp breath and hold it. Every cell in my body begs me to lean back, to fall against him, to press my back to his front and soak up the heady mix of longing and comfort I only feel with him.

But I don't. I can't. As much as I want to, I can't give in to the ache in my chest. All it will do is hurt us both more than we already do. Because no matter how much I fight it, I'm currently *promised* to someone else... even if only by a verbal contract my parents constructed.

"Jet..." His name is a plea on my lips. A whispered prayer. A murmured invocation. It's heavy and loaded, delicate and fragile, the most precious word and vow.

He ducks his chin, his breath warm on the curve of my shoulder. "Day or night, no matter what's going on, I'll come if you call."

And god, I know he will.

Tears sting the backs of my eyes as I lean into him for one shaky inhale then force myself to step out of his orbit. I swallow past the emotion building in my throat and unlock my car. Then I do my best to school my expression as I face him. "Don't know where I'd be without you." I close my eyes for one, two, three seconds then meet his steady gaze. "I have to go."

He reaches for and takes my hand, giving it a gentle squeeze. "Love you, Shanti." Then he releases my hand, pivots, and dashes back to the studio.

While the car warms up, I let my tears flow freely.

———

"Did you fill out the applications your father and I suggested, Shanti?" My mother takes a sip of wine and stares expectantly, hoping I won't embarrass her in front of company.

But it's just Rohan, and I don't care what he thinks of me or my family.

"No." The single syllable comes out sharp and irritable. I almost open my mouth to tell her I did apply to one school, but she'd be angry with the answer. Juilliard is my dream, not hers.

My parents may have started me in dance class, but they never expected me to stay. Maybe they wanted me to get just enough time under my belt to make me appear "well-rounded" when I speak of my experiences. Now, I bet they wish they'd put me in science camp.

"Shanti, I will not be spoken to with that tone." She sets down her glass and picks up her fork. "And you will fill them out. Now is not the time for games or childish behavior."

I fist the napkin in my lap and fight the urge to tell her I am technically a child. But all that will do is create more animosity. And I'm so tired of fighting.

"Perhaps Rohan can be of help," my father says, his eyes shining at his prearranged son-in-law-to-be. "It wasn't long ago he was applying to colleges. He may have some tips to make the process easier."

No way am I asking Rohan to help me fill out college applications I have no intention of submitting. The less time I spend with him, the better.

"Sure," I say, my voice as saccharine and artificial as the smile I give my father. "Whatever *you* think is best."

Because my opinion doesn't matter. Not to them. Never has.

"Well, I'd say dinner is officially over," my mother announces.

Thank god.

"Rohan, why don't you and Shanti go wander through town and look at the lights. I hear the displays are lovely this year." My mother blots the corners of her mouth with her napkin. Forever prim and proper.

The chair across from me slides out, and Rohan stands. "Sounds like the perfect way to end the evening." Rohan meets my gaze. "I'll get our coats."

Wiping my mouth, I toss the napkin on the table. "Fine."

The moment Rohan is out of earshot, my mother turns her fiery expression on me. "That's enough, Shanti. You will respect me, your father, and any guest we host. Do you understand?"

A cringe-worthy screech echoes through the room as I shove back in my chair harder than necessary. "I do understand." I rise to my feet and clench my fists at my sides. "Doesn't mean I care." Then I storm off for the door.

The ride into town feels hours long. Dark clouds loom on the horizon, the dismal energy mirroring my mood. Banding my arms tight around my chest, I lean against the passenger door and as far away from Rohan as possible. But no matter how small I make myself, no matter how tight I make my body, he still tries to invade my space. Tries to rest a hand on my thigh. Tries to spark conversation as if I want to be anywhere near him.

He asks if my family has traditions this time of year. When I stare out the window and ignore him, he blathers on about how his family celebrates the holidays.

My skin itches. My stomach churns. Pain pierces my palms as my nails dig, dig, dig into my flesh. But I welcome the burning sting. The vicious bite gives me something to focus on.

Because all I want to do is tip my head back and scream to the heavens. Release a banshee cry to relinquish my frustration and anger.

I didn't ask for this—to be put on an invisible, impossibly-high pedestal, to be in an undesirable relationship, to be treated as if my thoughts and feelings are irrelevant. And I'm just so damn exhausted.

Rohan parks across the street from RJ's Diner on Granite Parkway. "We'll see more lights if we start near the end of the storefronts." I feel his eyes on me as he opens his door, but I don't look at or acknowledge him. He sighs dramatically, exits the car, and slams the door.

I jump slightly then straighten in my seat as he rounds the front of the car.

Am I being a bitch? Absolutely, and I don't care. If our roles were reversed, if he was being thrust upon someone at his parents' behest, if every single aspect of his life was being dictated, if he had seemingly no say in his future, he would be miserable too.

But because he has a penis between his legs, he gets a say in the direction of his life. I'm sure the only reason he is okay with the situation is because it guarantees him sex and a wife—not that I plan to give him either. I will fight both to the death.

He opens my door and offers his hand. "Come on, Shanti. Let's look at the lights."

I ignore the gesture and slip out of the car, shoving my hands deep in my coat pockets. "Whatever," I mumble.

Rohan leads us south on the sidewalk, and I try to keep a foot or more between us. As we pass the bowling alley, Rohan inches closer to avoid townies gazing at the lights display. When he makes no move to add the previous distance, I do it.

A white puff clouds the air as he huffs out his annoyance. "Quit making this so fucking difficult," he grouses.

As we near the small gym, raucous chatter and music from Dalton's Pub hit my ears. Unless patrons are within five feet of us, they won't hear him berate or belittle me. No one will pay attention to two teenagers bickering in public.

And the knowledge gives me a boost of confidence. It pushes me closer to the edge. It tempts me to let go.

So, I do.

Jerking to a stop, I twist to face him and jab a finger toward his chest. "Quit acting like this is fucking normal." Fire surges in my veins and heats my skin. I take a step closer and shove at his chest. "I'm not a damn doll to pass around." Another step. Another shove. "I'm not a prize bitch to train, dress up, and parade around." I shove him until he stumbles and falls into a shrub. Patting my chest, I practically yell the next words. "I am a fucking person. I say who and when. I decide. Not you. Not my parents. Definitely not your parents." Stepping back, I poke my chest with a finger. "Me."

I need to get the hell out of here. Now.

Checking for cars, I cross the side street and jog toward Dalton's. As I reach the next stretch of sidewalk, Rohan's voice cracks through the air.

"Don't you walk away from me." Venom laces his words, his footsteps loud and harsh. "We're not done talking."

A couple outside the pub glances my way, and my cheeks heat with embarrassment. Or maybe concern. But I ignore the emotion swirling in my chest. I'll deal with it after I get away from Rohan.

Whirling around, I straighten my spine, square my shoulders, and lock my posture. "We were done before we started."

Rohan looks over my shoulder, no doubt seeing the couple watching us. He reaches for and takes my wrist. "Shanti—"

"Don't touch me," I say loud enough for the others to hear as I yank my arm away.

His nostrils flare as he snarls. "Such a petulant little bitch." He closes the distance between us, but I hold my ground. "Game time is over," he bites out. "Accept it."

The couple behind me moves into my periphery, but they don't step in. I hope they don't need to.

"Never." I shake my head for emphasis. "You may want this, Rohan, but I never will. And I'll fight it every damn day." I lift my chin and hold his angry stare. "Don't contact me. Don't touch me. Quit forcing this on me. And get it through your thick skull, no matter what anyone says, I am not yours. I never will be."

Taking a step back, I spin on my heel and head for the pub entrance. Breath trapped in my lungs, I hold my head high and maintain my composure.

I refuse to break in front of him. I refuse to let him see me fall.

As I reach the open door, Rohan bellows, "The sooner you realize this is inevitable, that you *will* be my wife, the happier we'll all be."

Not sparing him a glance, I keep walking. It's not until I reach the farthest table from the door that I stop and take a seat. My hands tremble and my lungs burn. I release the breath I'd been holding, count to five, and inhale deeply.

A woman sidles up to me, concern etched in the lines on her forehead. She was one of the people outside. "Are you okay?"

I give her a sad smile and nod. "For now."

EIGHTEEN
SHE IS MINE
JET

Five and a Half Years Ago

RED. ALL I FUCKING SEE IS RED AS I EXIT CHEESE US PIZZA WITH June.

Roughly a hundred feet away, Shanti and Rohan are toe to toe in front of Dalton's, yelling. And despite her fierce demeanor, Shanti looks ready to crack.

I hand June my leftovers. "Be right back." When I know they have the box, I let go and stride toward the pub.

As I take my fifth step, Shanti disappears inside Dalton's. Rohan doesn't follow her.

Good.

In three anger-filled breaths, I reach Rohan on the sidewalk. Before he faces me, I shove at his side, making him stumble.

"What the fu—"

"She said no, asshole," I bark out, not caring who sees or hears. "Leave her the fuck alone."

Rohan straightens to his full height and steps toward me without an ounce of concern. He brushes over the front of his dress shirt as if I've soiled it. And then he glances up to meet my furious gaze, a snide grin on his lips.

Pompous prick.

In two strides, he erases the distance between us and has the gall to thrust his chest to mine. "Mind your own fucking business, *friend*. Shanti is no longer your concern."

This piece of pretentious trash. Who the hell does he think he is?

Tightening my core, I bump his chest with mine. Unable to hold his ground, he stumbles backward. It's laughable—all bark with zero strength or balls to back it up.

"Shanti will always be mine to worry about. And nothing you say or do will erase that. I don't care what kind of fucked-up bullshit your parents and hers have concocted, it doesn't change reality."

Rohan messes with the collar of his shirt as he puffs his chest out again. At least this time, he is smart enough to keep his distance. Then he chuckles, the sound all wrong, hollow, malicious.

"You still don't get it, *friend*." He shakes his head, his dark laughter mingling with the pub music. "Whether she likes it or not, Shanti is mine. Hate me all you want"—he shrugs—"she's still mine." His brow cocks as a devilish smile tugs at his lips. "And there's not a damn thing you can do about it."

Shanti doesn't need a savior. She doesn't need someone to defend her honor or fight her battles. She doesn't want someone who will steal her voice or decisions. Doesn't want someone who will rob her of her happiness and passion.

What she does need is someone at her side when she fights her battles.

And I will always be that person for her. Will always step up and join her crusade. Will always be her pillar when she needs extra strength or encouragement.

Because that is what you do when you love someone. You let them shine on their own. You lift them up when they need a boost. And you hold them close when life presents obstacles.

I sweep my gaze down and up Rohan. "What a sad, pathetic

little man you are." Scoffing, I shake my head. "Shanti bows to no one. Especially not pricks like you." The corner of my mouth twitches and I bite the inside of my cheek to curb my smirk. "And the more you push her, the more she'll resist."

"You would know," Rohan spits back. "Seeing as you've been friend-zoned since the beginning."

Dangle the bait, asshole. Unfortunately for you, I'm mature enough not to take it.

"True," I admit. "But at least I'm not so insecure and incompetent that I depend on my parents for a life partner."

"I don't depend—"

"I'd love to keep debating this with you." I chuckle. "Who am I kidding? No, I wouldn't." I jab a thumb over my shoulder toward the pub door. "I should get going. Shanti *needs* me. You understand, right?"

Rohan's face turns a bold shade of red. "Stay the hell—"

I step into him and peer down my nose. "It's in your best interest to not finish that sentence." I shove him back, turn, and head inside Dalton's. As I reach the door, he calls out, and I pause.

"I'll back off... for now. But it won't change anything."

Peering over my shoulder, I take in the smug look on his face.

"We're still betrothed."

What does he think this is, the eighteenth century?

"That's where you're wrong," I say with every ounce of confidence. "Shanti will never marry you. She will never be yours."

"Oh yeah?" He shoves his hands in his pockets and cocks a brow. "And why is that?"

I can't help the smile that curves my lips. "She'd run away before walking down any aisle toward you. Even if she appeased her parents and went through with this antiquated bullshit, it wouldn't matter." Confidence ripples through my veins. "Shanti will *always* be mine. She always has been. And there's not a damn thing you or anyone else can do about it."

Giving him my back, I enter Dalton's, scan the crowd, and saunter across the room when I find Shanti. Without a word, I haul her into my arms, pin her to my chest, envelop her in love, and whisper reassurances as I kiss her hair. The music and people around us disappear as she clings to me, her muffled cries dampening my shirt.

"Love you," I whisper, my cheek pressed to her head.

Her cries turn to choked sobs.

"I've got you." I run a hand up and down her back. "I'll never let you fall."

"I don't deserve you," she says between hiccups.

Inching back, I press my lips to her forehead. "You deserve everything."

NINETEEN
I CAN DO IT WITH A BROKEN HEART
SHANTI

Just Over Five Years Ago

"Why did you open that?" My shrill voice bounces off the living room walls as my knuckles blanch at my sides. "Is your name on the envelope? No, it's not."

"Do not speak to me with such disrespect, young lady."

Scoffing, I roll my eyes at my father. "You want respect?" I point to the envelope and letter in his hand. "Then show me some. That was not for you."

My father glances down at the single piece of letterhead and matching envelope. When his dark gaze comes back to mine, there is nothing of value in his eyes. No adoration, no appreciation, no pride, no hope. All I see is annoyance, frustration, and displeasure.

Just once, I want to know what it is like to be loved and valued by my parents. To have them look at me with delight and admiration. To have them say they are grateful to call me their daughter.

But even once seems like too much for them.

"Everything you have is because your mother and I have provided for you. Your wardrobe, your lavish bedroom decor, that precious little dance school you care about too much, you have all

of that because of me and your mother." The paper in his hand crumples as he curls his fingers and takes a step in my direction. "Everything you own is because of us. The very least you could do is pretend you're grateful."

"Grateful?" My voice squeaks on the word.

"Yes," my father's voice booms, and my mother winces then composes herself. "You want to be treated with respect? Quit acting like a petulant child. Quit fighting your mother and me at every single turn. And do as you're told."

My hands tap the sides of my thighs over and over as restless energy floods my bloodstream. Pain shoots through my ears and into my head as I gnash my molars harder with each inhale. But the anxiety and throbbing are nothing compared to what I feel most. Because the sting behind my eyes and tightness in my chest stem from somewhere much deeper. A void only one person scratches the surface of... and it's no one in my family.

"Why am I here?" My voice shakes as the words leave my lips in a faint whisper.

With a deadpan expression, my father shakes his head. "What now?" he asks, exasperation evident in his tone.

That he sounds irritated rather than concerned should be answer enough. Obviously, I am a glutton for punishment because I continue to push.

"Why do I exist?" I rest a hand over my heart, my fingers digging into my chest in an attempt to settle my now-erratic pulse. "You don't want me."

"Don't be so dramatic," my father says at the same time my mother says, "Why would you say such a thing?"

I laugh without humor. "It's a legitimate question." I tip my head back, close my eyes, take a few steadying breaths, and then level my gaze. "Everything I do is substandard in your eyes." With each word, my confidence grows, as does my voice. "My schoolwork, my extracurriculars, what I want for my future. No matter what I do, no matter how hard I try, no matter how much I want to make you proud, it's never good enough. *I* am never good enough. So why *wouldn't* I ask such a thing?"

Not a twitch of sympathy or understanding crosses my father's expression. Although his lack of compassion or acknowledgment of my feelings saddens me, I'm not surprised.

"Is it wrong for us to want the best possible future for our child? We have done everything in our power to make sure that happens, to make sure you have the very best." A huff leaves my father's lips as he shakes his head in obvious frustration. "Do you know how many people would kill to be in your position? You practically have everything, and it's still not enough."

"I don't have everything," I scream, exhausted by the fact that he isn't grasping what I'm saying.

My father jabs the air with a finger in my direction. "Do not take that tone with me, Shanti."

"What is so wrong with me wanting to pursue dance as a career? Do my dreams, my passion, mean nothing?"

He waves the paper. "You were rejected, Shanti. Dance is a great hobby, but you need to aspire to be more. Something broader. Something that doesn't limit your options."

The first three words are a punch to the solar plexus, and they ring over and over in my head. *You were rejected.* The backs of my eyes burn as my vision blurs. But I blink back the tears.

Now is not the time to cry. Not in front of him.

"What I choose to do with my future is *my* choice."

Lips pursed, my father plants his hands on his hips and shakes his head. "While you live under this roof, everything about your life is *my and your mother's* choice."

"So, what? I'm a puppet without a voice. An extravagant prize to sell to your friend's son." My lip curls in disgust as I fold my arms across my chest. "Thanks for making me feel like I matter."

"Again with the theatrics." He tosses the letter and envelope onto the coffee table. "I've heard enough."

"Obviously not," I yell. "Because you still don't see me as a living, breathing person with my own mind, my own ideas, and my own wishes."

"Do not—"

I cut off his harsh tone with my own. "I will *not* be forced into a marriage I don't want. I will *not* be forced into a career I don't want." I shake my head vehemently. "I won't," I add, voice firm as I point harshly at the floor.

Nostrils flaring, my father narrows his eyes. Seconds feel like minutes as he stares me down in silence. But I hold my ground. I straighten my spine, square my shoulders, and go mentally toe to toe with him. If I don't, he will continue to subjugate my every action.

When he breaks the silence, he says the last thing I expect. "Then you should start looking for another place to live."

My jaw hits the floor. "Are you serious?"

His face is void of emotion. "Do I ever say anything I don't mean?"

My mother gasps but says nothing.

I've known my father to be ruthless in business and stern at home. But never in my life did I picture him giving me such a steep ultimatum. Who tells their child they must marry a specific person and go to a set school or move out before they're of age? Someone who sees their child as a material possession instead of a loved one.

"You would kick out your own child because I want to make my own decisions? Because I have my own voice?"

Crossing his arms over his chest, he arches a brow and glares at me as if I'm a nuisance. A chewed piece of gum on the heel of his precious, overpriced dress shoes.

I glance at my mother and silently beg for her understanding. Plead for her to say something to make my father see reason. But a breath after our eyes connect, a sadness colors her features. My stomach plummets as an array of conflicting emotions whirls in my chest.

To keep my father happy, she remains silent. Instead of standing up for her youngest daughter, their only child subjected to such harsh rules and expectations, she sides with my father.

I don't get it. Is she afraid of him? Does he hurt her behind closed doors? Or did she lose herself so long ago she doesn't know what it means to fight for others?

I can't take it anymore. The betrayal, the hurt, the soul-crushing heartbreak. At some point, I knew I'd feel these emotions. But I expected them to only come from boys who broke my heart, not my own flesh and blood.

Tears threaten to spill down my cheeks as I suck in a sharp breath, snatch the letter off the coffee table, and bolt from the room without a word. Speed walking to my room, I grab my dance bag, shove some extra clothes inside, sling the strap over my shoulder along with my purse, and make a beeline to the front door.

Within a couple minutes, I'm in my car and on the road. I drive through town faster than safe, but I don't care. I need to get away from them. I need time and space to think.

I need Jet.

Taking the next turn, I focus on my destination. The dance studio. Since graduation, Jet spends a lot of his free time there, dancing and coaching the younger students.

God, I hope no one else is there.

I let out a sigh of relief when I pull into the lot and only see Jet's car.

Cutting the engine, I tip my head back, close my eyes, and take several deep breaths. The last thing I want to do is walk through the door and make Jet panic. He already shoulders enough when it comes to me and my baggage.

After one last inhalation, I open my eyes, grab my bag from the passenger seat, and exit the car. With each step forward, some of the stress eases from my shoulders. Knowing I'll see Jet in seconds, an inkling of the hurt fades to the background.

When I step inside, Jet glances my way. And damn, the vibrant smile he flashes me is exactly what I need. It says I am wanted. I matter. I am loved.

Emotion swells in my throat as the first tear spills down my cheek. And it's like all the other tears were waiting for the first to give them permission to follow. My vision blurs as I stutter to a stop and silently cry.

In a heartbeat, Jet is in front of me, his hands framing my face. "What happened? Are you hurt? What can I do?"

My shoulders shake as my quiet cries morph into unruly sobs. With a loud *thump*, my duffel hits the floor.

Jet wraps me in his arms and holds me firmly to his chest, his lips pressed to my head. He sways side to side and tightens his grasp when I shake harder. "Shh. I'm here." He kisses my hair. "I've got you."

I have never been more thankful to have this incredible man in my life. If not for him, I'd have lost myself a long time ago.

For hour-long minutes, he simply holds and comforts me. He eases the shadows darkening my heart. When it feels like I've cried every possible tear, he inches back, brings his hands back to my face, and meets my gaze. So much love and devotion shine in his spellbinding gray eyes.

He presses his lips to my forehead and kisses me with so much reverence, affection, and tenderness. In his arms, under his touch, I feel like the most precious person in existence.

"Want to talk about it?"

Not really, but I know I should. Jet is aware of some of the nuances with my parents—especially the whole Rohan situation—but I haven't told him everything. He deserves to know.

"Can we sit?"

A corner of his mouth quirks up into one of my favorite smiles of his. "Of course." He takes a step back, wraps his hand around mine, and leads us to the back wall.

For the next half hour, I spill my heart out. Share my frustrations with all the demands my parents have put on me, but not my sister. Tell him about my father telling me to find another place to live if I don't want to abide by his absurd rules. I bleed every ounce of hurt I've been through at home, and Jet listens without interruption.

And god, is it a relief to get some of this out in the open, to get years' worth of hurt off my chest. Immediately, I feel lighter. Less burdened. I feel heard, seen. Important.

When I finish my story, Jet pulls me back into his arms and pins me to his chest. I close my eyes and bask in the sensation of being cocooned by him. Surrounded in love and warmth and a sense of security only he provides. I breathe in his clean, crisp scent mixed with something distinctly him and melt more into his embrace.

"I have something for you," he whispers after a moment.

My pulse soars in my chest. I have no clue what it is, but it doesn't matter. Anything Jet gifts me has meaning, purpose, love.

"You do?"

He nods and leans back, his arms unraveling from around me. Twisting, he reaches for his duffel and drags it closer. Riffling through the contents, he pauses then reveals a small jewelry box.

I straighten and look from the box to him, my brow furrowing. *That's an awfully small box.* Perspiration licks my skin as my pulse doubles. I swallow and ask, "What is it?"

His cheeks redden as a breathtaking smile stretches his face. "Something I've held on to for a while." Sensing my confusion, he clarifies, "I bought it for your sixteenth birthday, but things were a little hectic with my upcoming graduation and dance. I wanted to give it to you at my birthday-slash-graduation party, but..."

He doesn't need to say it. The reason he didn't give it to me was because I arrived with douchebag Rohan.

Holding it out to me, he whispers, "Happy birthday... for last year and this one."

I take the box and hold it as if the contents are priceless. With shaky fingers and so much care, I open the lid and peel back the delicate tissue paper inside. Nestled in a soft insert is a dainty, rose gold necklace with a small feather charm at the heart.

For an entirely different reason, tears well in my eyes. I brush a finger over the charm. "It's beautiful," I say, choking on the words. Swallowing, I lift my gaze to meet his. "Thank you."

His thumb swipes my cheek. "I'll never let you fall," he vows. "Because you're magnificent when you soar." The sentiment rolls off his tongue with such ease. As if promising to support my dreams, to support me, is the simplest, most natural thing in the world.

"I don't know what to say." I sniffle as I drop my gaze back down to the most precious thing I now own.

"You don't need to say anything." He reaches for and takes the box, removing the necklace. "May I put it on you?"

I nod vigorously. "Yes, please."

A notable hum dances under my skin as his fingertips brush the sides of my neck. I close my eyes and relish the simmer, the heat, the love I feel in his touch. He hooks the clasp, his fingers tracing the thin chain and the nape of my neck for what feels like hours.

My pulse whooshes in my ears as my breath catches in my throat. He trails his fingers along my shoulders and down my arms until his fingers lace with mine. Then he presses a kiss to the back of my neck where the chain rests. A shiver of pleasure rolls down my spine.

I came to the studio to be comforted. What I got was so much more.

Jet has loved me for years. He has been my pillar of strength, my best friend, my partner. He has been my everything. And god, how I wish I could give him as much love and courage as he has gifted me.

One day, I will.

For now, I will be thankful. I will give him what I can. Show him how much he means to me, the only way I know how.

Glancing over my shoulder, I meet his gaze. "Dance with me?"

He drops a kiss to my shoulder. "Always."

As we move together seamlessly on the dance floor, I pour every ounce of affection I have for this beautiful man into the routine. I tell him without words that I love him too.

If only I could be his as much as he is mine.

TWENTY

LIFT HER UP AND HOLD HER HIGH

JET

Five Years Ago

HAVE YOU EVER WATCHED THE LIGHT SLOWLY DISAPPEAR FROM someone's eyes? And no matter what you do, no matter what you say, the light continues to fade. A little each day, you internally weep as your favorite person turns into a shell of the one you once knew.

Witnessing Shanti turn more inward and withdraw breaks my damn heart.

Her parents exaggerate how important it is she gets accepted by one of three colleges—as if her life is meaningless without an Ivy League education and a degree she doesn't want. They force her to spend time with Rohan, a man who treats her like a shiny trinket with puppet strings rather than a young woman who deserves love and respect.

Since she opened up to me a few months ago, I've watched the woman I love go numb. And I don't know how to spark her soul back to life.

Unless I prompt conversation, she rarely speaks anymore. Most of her days are filled with schoolwork, which I've resumed helping her with. After the huge fight with her parents in the

summer, Shanti adjusted her schedule and decided to cancel all her extracurriculars and volunteer hours to do what she wanted—dance.

To say I am beyond grateful for the additional time together is an understatement.

I just wish I had the ability to take away her pain. All I want is her happiness, her smile, her light to shine like it did years ago.

"Damn it," Shanti grouses as she curls her hands into tight fists and stomps a foot on the floor. Stretching out her fingers, she plants her hands on her hips, tips her head back, and takes a deep, methodical breath. When she drops her chin, her jaw works back and forth as she begins to pace the room.

I want to tell her it's okay to miss a step. It happens to all of us every now and then. With the stress she is under, it would be a miracle for her to *not* miss her mark.

But I keep those thoughts to myself. All they would do is frustrate and upset her more.

Instead, I ask, "Should we start from the beginning?"

Dance has been Shanti's only outlet. Her one refuge while her life spins in a rapid, chaotic, aimless tornado. As best I can, I keep her grounded. Do whatever I can to encourage her to keep dancing. To keep searching for the positives, because eventually this dark period will pass.

Thump, thump, thump.

Shanti takes ten steps one way before spinning around and taking the same path back. The muscles in her jaw tighten then relax over and over. Her nostrils flare. Her knuckles blanch as she clutches her hips.

A minute passes, then another, before she stops and meets my gaze. Her shoulders relax the slightest bit. The action may seem small to some, but it is monumental for Shanti. Every muscle in my face twitches to react and give her a smile. Instead, I bite the inside of my cheek. Not because she isn't deserving of a smile or warm reaction, but because her head is a jumbled mess, and she may misconstrue *why* I'm smiling.

With a curt nod, she says, "From the beginning."

I move into position, grab the small remote tucked in the side pocket of my practice leggings, start the music over, and wait for my cue. Seconds turn into minutes as Shanti and I glide across the dance floor, lost in the melody, the routine, in each other. She pours her soul into the performance, expels her anger and grievances as she thrusts her arms and darts across the room on her toes.

When the song gentles, so do her movements. Her limbs soften and flutter. A sadness and sense of longing take over her expression. And when I step up behind her, the front of my body grazing the back of hers, she gasps then leans into my frame.

The almost indiscernible move makes my pulse soar. It tells me the Shanti I fell in love with is still in there. It tells me to keep trying. To never give up on her or the possibility of us. To keep lifting her up and holding her high, even when it seems difficult or impossible.

Every cell in my body screams to ask if she is ready for more. If she wants to take the leap with me. But I shove down the urge. Pack it away and seal it tight in the confines of my mind. Because I already know the answer.

Now is not our time.

But I'll wait. As I have for years, even when it hurts, I stay by her side and hold steady. For Shanti, for the chance to have her heart forever, every second is worth the wait.

When the song ends, we sit next to our bags, taking a moment to hydrate and eat a snack. Halfway through my granola bar, I realize I haven't shared my recent news with her yet.

Nudging her leg with my knee, I wait for her to look up. A beat passes before her golden-brown eyes level with mine. Even with her happiness absent, those gorgeous eyes always make me breathless. They always will.

"June and I are moving into the guesthouse." A soft chuckle leaves my lips. "We're *moving out*." I make air quotes around the last two words.

Shanti's brows twitch, a faint crease forming between them momentarily. But as quickly as it appeared, it vanishes. "Oh." She drops her gaze to her lap and fumbles with her protein bar wrapper. "That's... great."

Wanting to lighten the shift in her mood, I shoot for a joke. "I'm more excited about not being clawed to death by Rebel than anything else."

Her gaze darts to mine, the faintest hint of a smile tugging at the corner of her mouth. "That cat is feral and super territorial."

I snort. "And I have the scars to prove it."

Silence swallows the air between us as we sit here. As the next idea surfaces in my mind, my heart begins to thunder in my chest, my pulse whooshing in my ears. I inhale a slow, deep breath and reach for every ounce of courage I own. Before I lose the nerve, I swallow and trudge forward.

"There's space for you, too." My thumb taps my thigh again and again, and I shove my hands under my legs to sit on them. "If you need somewhere to go, there's room for you. No strings."

Shanti's gaze flies to mine, her eyes wide with surprise. Her beautiful stare holds me captive as the proposition sinks in more. "I can't—" She cuts herself off and pinches her eyes shut so tight it looks painful. Her chin drops to her chest as she rocks back and forth, shaking her head. "I wish..."

Alarm blooms in my chest, her unease gnawing at my heart. The fraction of space between us suddenly feels like a canyon, and it's too much. Without a second thought, I scoot across the floor and erase every millimeter of distance. Legs on either side of hers, I press my body to hers and wrap my arms around her chest.

I cocoon her in warmth and love and silently promise to always be there for her.

When she leans into me and sighs, the world wobbles a little less. The ground steadies beneath us. In this moment, it feels as though everything will work out.

So, I believe it will.

"Thank you," she whispers so softly I almost miss it.

I drop my chin to her shoulder and lean my head against her cheek. "Why are you thanking me?"

Slowly, she starts to rock us side to side. "Feels like I should never stop thanking you." Soft, dainty fingers gently curl around my forearm. "You're my rock." Her voice cracks on the last word, but she keeps going. "No matter what happens, you remain steady. Strong. Solid. You hold me up. Lift me up." She goes still, and her grip on my forearm tightens. "Without you, my life would be shit."

As badly as I want to argue with her, I say nothing. I have zero right to say I understand what she is going through—because I don't. Our parents are opposites in every possible way. Although I did grow up with structure and rules, they were very relaxed when compared to Shanti's upbringing.

"So, thank you." She turns her head slightly and gives me more of her weight, her lips a breath away from mine. "I owe you everything."

The only thing I want is your heart.

Closing my eyes, I strengthen my embrace and breathe in my favorite scent—orange blossom, honey, and her. "Whatever you need, whenever you need it, I will always be here for you."

Her body melts into my hold. That simple act says so much more than her words ever will.

In my arms, Shanti feels safe, wanted, loved, cherished. And there isn't a single word that expresses that level of emotion or comfort.

The bell on the front door tinkles and snaps us back to reality. We both stiffen as though we've forgotten where we are and why we are here.

Every instinct and desire in me begs to keep her in my arms. To hold her just a little bit longer. But when excited chatter filters into the room from the reception area, I loosen my hold on Shanti. Taking one last deep pull of her subtle fragrance, I press my lips to her temple, kiss her tenderly, then rise from the floor.

I swear she whimpers, but I don't have time to question it.

Two girls in pale-pink leotards enter the room, matching leg warmers covering their calves as they cross the dance floor. "Hi, Mr. Jet," one girl greets as the other waves eagerly.

"Good afternoon, ladies," I greet as I offer Shanti my hand, not that she needs help up. "You remember Ms. Shanti?"

Bright smiles plump their cheeks as they nod vigorously. The second girl steps close to Shanti, a twinkle in her eyes as she stares up at her. "I want to be as good as you when I get older, Ms. Shanti." The awe in her voice is undeniable.

Eyes glossy, Shanti blinks a few times. Swallowing, she offers the girl a shaky smile. "That's very sweet of you," she says, emotion evident in her voice.

Without another word, the girls scurry off to prepare for class. When they are out of earshot, I inch closer to Shanti and lower my voice.

"Will you stay?"

Shortly after graduation, Neesa and Aurelio offered me a position to teach the five-to-eight-year-old beginner class. Seeing as I had no plans to further my education at the moment, I said yes. The idea of passing down what I've learned, what I am passionate about, is the best reward for all my years of hard work and dedication.

Shanti nods. "No other place I'd rather be."

As if I've done it countless times, I reach up and clasp the pink ribbon in Shanti's hair. Once, twice, I rub the soft, silky fabric between my thumb and forefinger. When I let it go, I lightly trace my knuckles from her temple to her chin, my eyes following the action.

On my next breath, my gaze lifts to her lips. My heart bangs beneath my sternum, my pulse booming in my ears. Her lips part with a gasp, and the room disappears around us. Inch by painstakingly slow inch, I dip my chin and close the distance from my mouth to hers.

As my eyes roll closed, as her warm breath paints my lips, the bell over the door jingles again. My eyes fly open and lock with hers. Neither of us makes a move to step away or create distance.

For the first time in far too long, a spark dances in Shanti's eyes. It's almost imperceptible, but I see it. In that small glint, hope shines through.

I rest my forehead on hers and close my eyes. Bring my hands to her cheeks and stroke her soft skin with my thumbs. Warm fingers curl around my hips and anchor me to her further.

Right here, in this moment, everything feels perfect. Real. Whole.

"Love you, Shanti."

This time, there is no mistaking her whimper. She may not verbally reciprocate the sentiment, but I feel her love for me in every touch we share, every second we spend together, every time her eyes hold mine.

Breaking apart, I press a kiss to her forehead. "Let's grab food after."

Shanti nods. "Okay."

For the duration of the class, I *feel* more than see Shanti's eyes on me. When I'm able to glance her way, I soak in the sight of her as she watches me teach the next generation of Stone Bay dancers. I also don't miss the tinge of sadness mixed with what I'd interpret as love in her eyes.

Something about that look makes me fall harder for Shanti.

Her future may be up in the air, a jumbled, undesirable mess, but it doesn't matter. Through ups and downs, I will stay at her side. Until my final heartbeat, until my dying breath, I will be her extra backbone, her source of encouragement, her biggest fan, and the one person she can always count on. Even if I get nothing in return.

That is what you do when you love someone. You give them your all. You show up no matter how rocky the road gets or dark the day turns. Time after time, you lift them up and love them unconditionally.

It may not be our time yet, but I know the day will come.

When it does, everything will fall into place. The pain of the past will fade away and make room for love.

Whether it's a year or two or ten, I know with absolute certainty, I will wait for her. Even on the days when it hurts. And the times when she chooses someone else.

I can't help it.

I love her.

Shanti is worth the heartache, the occasional doubt, but more importantly, the wait. One day, her heart and soul will be mine. And when that day comes, it will be everything.

TWENTY-ONE
NEVER GOING BACK
SHANTI

Four Years Ago

A HYPNOTIC BEAT THUMPS THROUGH THE ROOM, THE WALLS, MY bones, and I close my eyes, throw my arms up high, and sway to the music. The din of conversations, laughter, and chants echoes around me as I dance without purpose. As I simply *feel* what it means to be young, alive, carefree.

Slender fingers wrap around my biceps, and my eyes pop open. Huge smile and shimmering, wide eyes greet me as Katy Reynolds bounces in place. I return the infectious sentiment immediately. Katy is one of a handful of friends I've made—and kept—in high school. My hectic schedule keeps us from hanging out as much as I'd like, but she understands and swears it doesn't detract from our friendship.

Aside from Jet, Katy is the only person I'd consider a best friend.

"Having fun, birthday girl?" Katy taps the sparkly plastic tiara on my head.

Throwing my arms over her shoulders, I haul her to my chest and deflate her lungs with a vigorous hug. "I've never had a party like this."

I release her, inch back, and take in the hint of sympathy in her expression. Before it has time to sink in, she blinks and resumes her chipper hostess appearance.

"Thanks for throwing me the best birthday bash ever. Don't know what I'd do without you, Katy."

With a wave of her hand, she playfully dismisses my gratitude. But deep down, I know she appreciates hearing the words. "Blah, blah," she teases, then takes my hand with hers and leads me through the crowd. "Time to *really* enjoy your birthday."

I've only been to Katy's house a few times. We had a joint history project earlier this year and needed a few in-person study sessions to complete it. My first impression of her house was how different it is from mine. It isn't the smaller floor plan or half-dead potted plants on the front porch that garnered my attention. It's the warmth you feel as soon as you walk through the front door. The dozens of candid photos throughout the house—on shelves and walls and mantels. The hint of cinnamon that drifts from the kitchen as if Katy's mom made something sweet every morning. And this inexplicable feeling of love that radiates from the walls like a heartbeat.

Every second I've existed in Katy's house—a real home—I absorbed what I could of that love and tucked it away for the times I'm alone.

There is only one other home I feel something similar, maybe even stronger. Jet's home.

But things have been... *different* between me and Jet. We are still us, but not really. I shoulder the blame for the change. Between senior year, my parents breathing down my neck at every possible moment, Rohan annoying the hell out of me, and feeling like I'm dying a slow, agonizing death, I've neglected my friendship with Jet. And ignored those regular I love yous he says with ease.

We move through the kitchen, a small group of people gathered around the small island at the heart. Everyone I pass wishes me a happy birthday and sounds genuine in the sentiment. The notion sparks an unfamiliar warmth in my chest.

Stopping in front of the fridge, Katy tugs the door open and sifts through the contents. "My parents agreed to let me throw you this party with a few conditions." She peeks around the door and gives me a wicked smile. "Don't let things get out of hand. No one drinks and drives."

My brows inch toward my hairline as my eyes widen.

Katy shrugs. "My parents aren't idiots. They know people will be drinking, even underage." She says it like it's no big deal. "As long as my friends are in a safe environment and not getting sloshed, my parents don't care."

"Wish my parents were so easygoing." Every party they've thrown me has never been *for* me. With no say in the guest list, the food, or the vibe, I learned early on that events at the Mahal house were for my parents.

Katy rests a hand on my arm, gives a gentle squeeze, then releases me. "We all want something different from what we have. But sometimes, different isn't always as great as you think." She gives a small shake of her head, as if to rid herself of the shadows creeping into our conversation. "Anyway, back to what I was saying." She ducks back into the fridge and comes out with a couple cans. "Mom said, and I quote, *'Shanti must have fun for her eighteenth birthday. Let loose a little.'*" She hands one of the colorful cans that could easily be mistaken for a fun, sparkling water.

It may be fruity and fizzy, but it is far from water.

Seconds pass as I stare down at the can, unsure what to do next. Years of strict upbringing, hard work, and rigorous schedules flash in my mind. All the time I've put in, all the blood, sweat, and tears I've given, all the dreams I've pictured time and again. None of it has gotten me anywhere except where I don't want to be.

I am so damn exhausted from being someone other than myself.

A hiss rings through the air as I pull back the tab and crack open the can. Lifting it to my nose, I sniff the drink my parents would have a coronary over me drinking.

"It's like fizzy fruit punch." Katy takes a sip of hers. "Only different."

How is it this one act feels like the most rebellious thing I've ever done? The singular thought makes me want to be more than defiant. I want to be wild and unbothered by the opinions of others. Mischievous and free to live in the moment.

Above all, I want to feel alive.

Bringing the can to my lips, I tip it back and take a hefty sip. Carbonation tickles my lips, my tongue, and my throat as I swallow. My tongue darts out to lick my lips as I hold out the can and read over it again. I expected to be repulsed by the taste, but I'm not. In fact, I'm the complete opposite.

I take a long pull from the can. Then another. It really does taste like fizzy fruit punch.

"Whoa there." Katy taps my shoulder. "Slow and steady, my friend. No need to drink so fast. A nice buzz is better than blacking out and forgetting the whole night."

Katy is right. Fun over fainting.

"Where would I be without you?" I wrap her in a hug. "Thanks for giving me the best birthday yet."

Her body shakes as a chuckle vibrates her chest. "What kind of friend would I be if I didn't?" She peels herself out of the hug and holds me at arm's length. "Now come on, let's go have fun."

Several songs later, my muscles are all soft and noodly. The music pulses in time with my heart as I swing my hips and arms to the rhythm. The room is wavy but not in a nauseating way. Still, I close my eyes and get lost in it all. Because nothing has ever felt so good, so normal, so freeing.

"Hey, birthday girl."

Lazy smile on my lips, I open my eyes and greet the third random guy to approach me with a flirtatious tone. "Hey."

He steps closer, the colors from the portable disco lights glimmering in his eyes and dancing over his skin. "I'm Ryan."

Reaching out, he curls his fingers around the curve of my waist. "Mind if I dance with you?"

I finish the last of my second drink and toss the can in one of many trash cans throughout the house. *Katy is so smart.* "Hi, Ryan. I'm Shanti. And I'd like that."

With a slow tug, Ryan hauls me flush to his chest, every inch of me pressed firmly to him. His body moves in a delicious, provocative way so different than what I'm used to. Heat sparks deep and low in my core. A spine-tingling hum has goose bumps blooming on my skin. And when he leans in and trails kisses up the length of my neck, I shiver in his grasp.

One song blends into another. Then, someone presses themselves to my backside. Ryan grins at whoever it is.

I peer over my shoulder and smile at the new guy. A little taller and thinner than Ryan, he gives me a devilish smile. I mirror his expression and give him a little of my weight as I turn back to face Ryan.

"Great party, birthday girl." Warmth tickles my ear as his fingers trail down my curves and stop on my ass.

With a hum, I press myself into his palms. Grind my hips. Drop my head back onto his shoulder.

"So damn pretty." He nips my earlobe, my neck, the curve of my shoulder. "If you haven't made your wish yet tonight, Ryan and I would be happy to help."

His words swim circles in my head, and I grow dizzy from what he means. *He and Ryan?* I lift my head and meet Ryan's lust-filled gaze. As tipsy as I feel, I am not so far gone I don't know what's happening. Apparently, I've fallen into Ryan and his buddy's little tag-team trap. Unfortunately for them, I have enough wits about me to say no.

As I open my mouth to respond, my eyes catch on someone over Ryan's shoulder across the room. *Jet.*

Pain etches deep lines between his brows. And I can't be sure, but he looks... jealous. Which is totally rational, considering he is in love with me.

Although I have zero desire to be the center of attention with two guys in a stranger's bed right now—hello, I'm inebriated, and that's an experience I want to be sober for—I'm tired of following societal rules. Tired of feeling held back from having a fun life because of what someone else wants me to do.

I love Jet, but not as he does me. It hurts to admit that I'm all wrong for him. But it doesn't make it any less true. I am broken. A disaster waiting to happen. And Jet needs more than I can give him.

Maybe one day, I will be worthy of him. But that time isn't now. And if I'm honest, that day may never come.

What *I* need is the chance to learn who I am, the chance to *be* me. I need to figure out how to love myself, really and truly love my life, before I attempt to love someone else. If I don't, none of it matters.

Jet deserves to be loved as madly and deeply as he loves. It shreds my heart to know I'm incapable of loving him fully.

I blink away from Jet's soulful stare and meet Ryan's hungry gaze. "Fun as that sounds, I'm going to pass." I glance over my shoulder at the other guy. "Maybe another time..."

"Pierce," he says then sticks out his bottom lip in the most adorable pout. "Bummer, but I understand." He presses a kiss to my shoulder. "Can I friend you online?"

This I can say yes to.

Nodding, I tell him my social media handle. Both guys promise to chat with me online. They wish me another happy birthday then disappear into the crowd.

Looking back to where Jet stood moments ago, he is gone. I scan the growing throng of people for him and come up empty. A voice in the back of my head says to go search for him, but I ignore it. Instead, I do something I should have done a while ago.

I try to let him go. I try to move on.

Needing another drink, I go in search of Katy. I ask several people if they have seen her, and they say I just missed her. When I enter the kitchen and still don't find her, I go to the fridge and shove aside sodas and sports drinks until I discover the hidden stash of the fizzy drinks. Taking one, I hide the rest and close the fridge.

From when I pop open the third until I drain the can, time seems nonexistent. When the floor wobbles and room spins, I stumble over to a couch and plop down.

"Looks like you're enjoying your birthday."

Turning to meet the voice's face, my vision teeters. I grip the couch cushion to steady myself, my knuckles strained but not painful. *Too fast.* When my sight becomes static, I loosen my hold and smile at the guy next to me on the couch.

"Best one ever," I proclaim as my gaze dips low to take him in. "Are you having f-fun?" I hiccup on the last word. The corners of his mouth curve up into the most irresistible smile, and I can't help but stare at his lips. His very plump, very kissable lips.

"Great music, good drinks"—he pauses and throws an arm over the back of the couch—"beautiful women. Of course I'm having fun." The tips of his fingers dance over the bare skin of my shoulder. "But today is all about you. Only your opinion matters."

"Is that so?" I arch a brow at him.

He leans closer, the move causing his fingers to graze the length of my shoulder to the back of my neck. The simple action makes me shiver then turn to face him more.

"Mm." His gaze drops to where his fingers toy with the loose hairs at the nape of my neck. "It's birthday rule number one." His eyes flit back to mine. "Whatever you want, it's yours."

God, if only that were true.

But… maybe for tonight, it can be. If my head stops spinning long enough, maybe I'll figure out what it is I want.

I lick then bite my bottom lip. "I'll have to put some thought into it."

His eyes lock on my mouth as if he wants to consume it. "Let me know if you need help." Amber eyes lift and meet mine. "Blaze."

My brows scrunch as I stare at him through narrow eyes. "Huh?"

The corner of his mouth quirks up as he scoots impossibly closer. His fingers drift up and tug at the ribbon covering the elastic of my ponytail. Heat dances over my skin as his lips move to my ear.

I stop breathing as my pulse pounds in my chest.

"My name, birthday girl. Blaze is my name."

His breath on my ear makes me swallow and fist the couch once more. Mint and something woodsy invade my nose a beat before he takes the lobe of my ear between his lips and sucks.

My insides dissolve into a puddle. An unfamiliar sensation throbs between my thighs. I suck in a sharp breath and close my eyes. Focus on the feel of his lips, his tongue, his heat on my skin. God, it feels like he is everywhere, yet I need more.

I've been turned on before, but not like this. Not to the point where my skin feels electric and my core all but begs for relief.

"Sh-Shanti," I stutter.

Blaze curls his fingers around the back of my neck, pins me in place, and takes the curve of my shoulder with his mouth. A hum vibrates from his lips and tongue, and it is a direct line to my aching core.

I whimper in his hold. Reach out and clutch his shirt. Tug him closer and tilt my head to give him more access.

On the next breath, he tears his lips away. My audible mewl makes him chuckle.

"You are divine, birthday girl." He inches back enough for our eyes to meet. "Always thought you would be."

My face scrunches in confusion.

Blaze spends the next two songs telling me about his time at Stone Bay High School. A year ahead of me, he just finished his freshman year of college. Home for the summer, he is ready for fun and relaxation. And then he talks about normal-life stuff. Being stressed out by his family, feeling like his all is never enough, and it is in that moment that I connect more with him.

When he finishes his story, I share things about my life. The bullshit that has gotten thicker in the past two years. The forced relationship by my parents. Expectations for school, extracurriculars, and more. I blather on without an ounce of care because Blaze hasn't averted his attention for a single second.

And damn does it feel amazing to be heard, to be seen, and still be wanted.

Maybe it's the alcohol swimming through my veins and impairing my judgment, but something about Blaze feels different than the other guys. Those small tidbits he shared about his life are relatable. Comforting. He gets what it is like to be under someone's thumb and feel the constant pressure of expectation. What it is like to give and give and give and then be told it will never be enough.

So when Blaze asks if I want to leave the party with him a little later, my answer is an immediate yes.

"Are you sure your friend won't be mad I'm stealing you for the rest of the night?"

Slowly, I scan the room, searching for any sign of Katy. When I come up empty, I turn back to Blaze and shrug. "Don't know where she went. She'll be fine." I rise from the couch on unsteady legs. "Come on, let's go."

Blaze takes my arms and braces me until I stabilize. "Good?"

I nod. "Yep."

Slipping his hand around mine, we weave through the crowd for the front door. His fingers woven with mine is a jolt to my heart. Sure, I've held hands with guys before. And I've done a lot more than that. But something about my physical connection with Blaze is different. Alive. Intense. More intoxicating than alcohol.

As we round the corner for the door, another hand wraps around my free arm. Without looking, I know who it is. Because anytime Jet touches me, a unique current vibrates under my skin.

"Shanti." My name rolls off his tongue like a caress. There is no hurt or anger in his tone.

My steps falter, halting Blaze in the process.

"What's wrong?" Blaze looks from me to Jet then back to me. "Do you know him?"

Stepping more in front of me, a muscle in Jet's jaw flexes. "Leaving your own party already?" He doesn't acknowledge Blaze at my side. "Didn't get the chance to wish you a happy birthday yet."

I open my mouth to answer, but Blaze inserts himself into the conversation.

"We're finishing her celebration elsewhere."

A soft groan rumbles in my throat as I glare toward Blaze. "Don't speak for me." Although the comment is aimed at Blaze, the demand is meant for them both. If Blaze riles him up, Jet will posture right back. And that is not how I want to spend my birthday. My attention back on Jet, I say, "You disappeared."

An uncomfortable smile tugs at Jet's lips. "You were... busy."

Without asking, I know he is talking about Ryan and Pierce. "Could've found me after." Why does that sound so weird? Like I'm the girl at the kissing booth with a line a people waiting for her.

"I grabbed a drink. By the time I came back, you'd disappeared."

Blaze tightens his hold on my hand, no doubt to remind me of his presence.

Ugh. Why are guys so territorial sometimes?

"Here I am," I say with a huff of annoyance.

Jet's gray eyes lock onto my golden browns, a silent storm swirling in his irises as a thick cloud of tension forms between us. He doesn't say a word, but he doesn't need to. When you've known someone as long as we've known each other, when you've had to hand over your trust to them completely, you don't need words to communicate.

In his eyes, I read every single question and thought in both his mind and heart.

Do you know this guy?

What about the other two?

Are you really going home with him?

Are you sure that's a good idea? You aren't sober.

Why him? What makes him so special?

Why is it never me?

I miss you.

I'm worried about you.

I love you.

The last one sobers me slightly, and I stand taller. To the best of my ability, I try to silently tell Jet I love him too. Just not the way he wishes I did.

As if he hears me, he purses his lips and gives a curt nod. "Happy birthday, Shanti. I…" He doesn't finish his thought aloud, but he doesn't need to. It's the final one. *I love you.*

"Thanks, Jet." The backs of my eyes sting, but I blink away the sensation. "Me too."

As Blaze and I take a step toward the door, Jet trails his fingers down my arm, grips my hand long enough to let me feel our unshakable connection, then releases me. The moment lasts for a breath, but I feel it until we reach Blaze's house.

Needing to shove all things Jet into a box in my mind, I press my lips to Blaze's mouth the second we step inside his apartment. In a matter of seconds, clothes are ripped off and tossed across the room. His tongue tangles with mine as he guides us to the bedroom and lowers me onto the mattress.

He tastes of mint and oak—a weird combination I choose to ignore. Instead, I focus on his hands. The way his grip is firmer than expected. Rough but in a good way. He palms my breast then pinches my nipple. It feels good. So damn good.

As he kisses his way down my body, as he worships me with his mouth and fingers, I shut my eyes and let my mind wander. Still quite tipsy, my thoughts come and go like the tide. But the pleasure… god, he is so good at giving me what I need.

For the briefest of seconds, I think the worst possible thing. Blaze could be anyone I want right now. In my inebriated state, I could imagine Ryan or Pierce over me, kissing me, trailing

their fingers up the inside of my thigh. I could even picture...
Jet.

The idea makes my skin heat and thighs wet.

It's wrong. So very wrong. But I don't care.

Instead of Blaze's mouth and fingers and hands on me, I imagine Jet is touching me. When he rips open a condom wrapper and rolls it down his length, I'm glad the lights are off. And when he fills me and pumps his hips over and over, grunting in my ear, I picture my lifelong best friend.

He finishes before I do, but I don't complain. I don't deserve to get off with one guy while thinking of another.

When he gets up to dispose of the condom, a sense of dread washes over me. Is he going to kick me out? Now that we've had sex, will Blaze throw me to the curb? I wouldn't blame him.

He returns from the bathroom with a warm washcloth. I clean myself up as he rummages through his dresser. When he comes back to the bed, he offers me one of his college T-shirts and takes the washcloth.

Not kicking me out. I breathe a sigh of relief and tug the shirt over my head.

A moment later, we slip under the covers. The air is thick with *what do we do now* vibes. But Blaze squashes the awkwardness when he drapes an arm over my waist and hauls me into his chest. I curl into his side and throw a leg over his hips.

His fingers gently comb through my hair. "So, birthday girl. Did you get everything you wanted?"

I hum. "I got enough."

His fingers drift down my back, brushing up and down my spine. "Enough?" he asks in disbelief. "That's not acceptable for such a monumental birthday." He presses his lips to the top of my head. "What else would you wish for, Shanti?"

God, where do I begin? The list of simple things I've always craved feels miles long, but one thing stands out more. It's the strangest thing to wish for, but it's what I want. Not sure how he'll react, I try to come off nonchalant.

"A place to stay until I graduate, maybe a little after." I shrug. "My parents are being impossible."

Blaze wraps me in a fierce embrace and breathes deeply. "You can stay here. But only if you want. No pressure."

I push up, jerk back, and look at him in disbelief. "Seriously? I was joking." I wasn't, but I'll keep that to myself.

"I'm not," he says. "You're an adult. Your parents make you uncomfortable." He reaches up and cups my face. "Look, I know we're basically strangers. I completely understand if the idea freaks you out. But think about it. If it doesn't feel right, say no. You won't hurt my feelings." He tucks a lock of hair behind my ear. "Either way, I'd like to keep seeing you."

In the cover of darkness, I hold his gaze a moment. Then another. Sinking back into the mattress, I make myself comfortable in his arms again. With a nod, I swallow past the knot of anxiety in my throat. "I'll think about it."

"Good." He hugs me closer and kisses my hair. "Sleep well, birthday girl."

For the first time in years, I sleep through the night.

In the morning, I do something spontaneous and out of character. I say yes to Blaze's proposal and start moving my stuff to his apartment.

And with each passing day, I turn into someone else. A stranger.

I go through the motions, complete my exams, and graduate high school. I move through the world but see no one and nothing. Not even Jet. And because I have lost all sense of self-direction, because I have no one to help guide me, I go numb. Become a shell of myself.

But it doesn't matter. Because at least I am free.

TWENTY-TWO
THE GHOST OF YOU
JET

Four Years Ago

I TEAR OFF A CORNER OF THE PAPER NAPKIN AND PLUCK SMALL BITS OF it away, one measly scrap at a time. As I have most days over the past five months, I zone out. Get lost in trivial, meaningless tasks.

Because everything feels off-balance without Shanti.

Since the night of her birthday party, when she left with *Blaze* —I don't even like thinking his name—Shanti has practically vanished from her regular life. Thankfully, she finished her exams and graduated. But she hasn't done much else, including dance.

Five months. It has been five months since Shanti met Blaze. In a single night, he managed to say all the right things to her. Lure her in. Keep her in a way I never could. Maybe it was her inebriated state. Maybe it was her desperation to get away from home. Or maybe he threatened her, manipulated her, hurt her in such a way she was too scared to say no.

None of it makes sense. No matter which way I spin it, I can't piece the puzzle together. I can't grasp this new reality. How did a few hours with him make her pack her most important possessions and move in with him? What had he promised her? What did he say or do to convince her?

Shanti changed her life overnight, moved in with a complete stranger, and faded away. She's shut out everyone who cares about her. She ignores calls, texts, and every possible form of communication.

On the days she shows up for dance, I almost don't recognize her. Skin dull and flaky, her leotard fits loosely on her curves. Her once immaculately styled bun sits messily atop her head. When she moves across the room, it's less elegant and more clumsy, stilted. But her eyes... pupils blown, gaze unfocused, and eyes so glassy you'd think she's on the verge of tears.

The one time I asked if she was okay, she turned volatile. Yelled at me in front of several people. Swore she was fine and told me to mind my own business. That what she did with her life was none of my concern.

I backed off. Inserted physical distance when she was in the room. But I will never stop worrying about her. It's impossible when every cell in my body screams Shanti isn't okay. That something major is wrong. And I'd be an idiot to ignore my instincts.

But what can I do?

Technically, Shanti isn't missing. Anyone looking for her knows she is staying with Blaze. Well, sort of. She is living at his place. Alone.

Last I heard, Blaze left about a month ago for college, fall semester. Wanting confirmation, I went on social media and scoured his most recent posts. From what I've seen, all the guy does is party, sleep around, and get high. And he isn't shy about sharing it publicly.

Does Shanti know he has been with three different people this week? And I don't mean just hanging out together. The photos he shares... let's just say I'm surprised his account hasn't been shut down.

Or is Shanti's relationship with him one of convenience? He gives her a place to stay, and she accepts he is with other people.

The thought makes me cringe and rage simultaneously.

"Hey, J."

I startle and look up to see June sliding onto the bench across the booth. Their brows tug together, a deep groove forming between them.

"What's wrong?"

Dropping my gaze to the now paper napkin heart in my hand, I shake my head. "Nothing new," I mutter then sigh.

June reaches across the table and rests a hand over both of mine. "Have you gone to see her?"

I lift my chin and meet June's kind eyes. Not an ounce of pity stares back, only love. Letting the paper heart fall to the table, I shake my head. "No." I roll my lips between my teeth. "I'm scared to."

Before June replies, the server steps up to the table and sets a pizza, plates, and napkins between us.

"Deluxe veggie with nondairy cheese." The server turns to June. "What can I get you to drink?"

"Cherry limeade, please."

"You got it." The server pivots and leaves.

I add a slice of pizza to a plate and hand it to June, then add two pieces to my plate.

The server returns with June's drink and says they will be back to check on us.

"Thank you." June takes a bite, their thinking face on full display.

My stomach churns. Twin intuition is a great hallmark most of the time. If one of us is hurt or upset, excited or giddy, we usually feel it. And that gift gives us the ability to help each other in a way no one else can. But of course, there is a downside. When those tough topics weigh either of us down, there is no escape from the emotional turmoil. June and I are two halves of the same soul in different bodies. When one of us is in pain, so is the other.

Wiping their hands on a napkin, June takes a sip of their drink. "Are you worried she'll be angry if you show up unannounced?" June didn't say her name, but I know they're referring to Shanti.

Needing more time to think, I shove too much pizza in my

mouth and chew for longer than necessary. I don't think one specific thing worries me most about Shanti. But the biggest of my concerns is losing her—as a friend, a person I love. When it comes to her life since her birthday, I'm clueless.

"Yes and no," I answer and wipe my mouth with a napkin. "She's been so distant. And when she's in the room, it doesn't feel like she's there." I squint then relax my features. "Does that make sense?"

June picks at the veggies on the pizza and nods. "Yeah. Like she's only there physically."

"Exactly." I inhale deeply, hold the breath for one, two, three, then exhale slowly. "I don't want her to think I'm being pushy or demanding like her parents."

June tilts their head and purses their lips. "Have you spoken to her sister? Maybe Reema is your way in."

"I haven't." I tear off bits of crust from my pizza. "Not sure how much she knows about what's going on with Shanti." Plus, Reema is fresh out of college and working her first degree-focused job at the high school. The last thing I want to do is worry her without knowing what's going on first.

"Maybe you need to tell her," June says, tone gentle, loving. "You aren't responsible for Shanti and her decisions. But if something bad happens to her, you will never forgive yourself."

I let those words sink in for a moment. "You're right."

"Of course I am."

I roll my eyes then laugh despite my mood. But it dies quickly as I sag in my seat. "Think I should call Reema before checking on Shanti?"

"What's your gut telling you?"

The question is simple because I already know the answer. Speaking with Reema, getting her on my side first, is the best way to reach Shanti. Either of us approaching her on our own probably won't stand a chance. But together, we may be able to reach her.

"Talk to Reema first," I finally answer.

June nods. "If the most important people in her life stand

united before her, there's a better chance." They sip their drink. "Do you know if Reema has talked to or seen Shanti recently?"

"No idea."

"Then tread lightly. Don't toss out assumptions. Just explain why you're concerned—her not coming to dance or replying to messages. If you mention the guy, be vague. You don't know what Reema knows about him."

Reaching across the table, I take June's hand and squeeze. "Thanks, J. You always say what I need to hear."

"Right back at ya. You know I'm always here for you, no matter what."

"Same."

My knee bounces as I stare at the typed, unsent message on the screen. Shifting from the send arrow to the delete button, an onlooker would think my thumb is having severe muscle spasms.

If only it were that simple.

Just hit send. It's the right thing to do.

Shoving every ounce of guilt aside, I press send. A soft *whoosh* sounds from my phone and my stomach immediately twists. I hate it has come to this, but I don't know what else to do. I can't keep sitting here, wondering as countless horrible scenarios run through my mind.

> Hey Reema, it's Jet. Have you heard from Shanti? She won't answer my texts or calls and I'm worried.

When the screen dims, I lock my phone. Reema probably has her hands full with rowdy teenagers wreaking havoc at the high school. It'll be hours before she has a moment to breathe, let alone reply.

Tossing my phone on the bed, I push to stand and go to my dresser. As I grab a pair of leggings from the drawer, my phone dings with an incoming text. In two swift strides, I drop the leggings and reach for my phone.

REEMA

Hi Jet. I have not. Sorry. I've been concerned about her too. She does answer when I reach out, but there's always an excuse to not talk.

It's shitty that her response gives me a hint of relief, but it does. At least it's not just me she's brushing off.

My fingers fly over the screen as I type out my next thought. I hit send.

I can't just sit here and do nothing anymore. I have a really bad feeling.

I've sat on the sidelines long enough. I've ignored the constant twinge in my gut, all so I didn't come across as a nag or nuisance friend. But I am done dismissing the blaring intuition siren in my head. Now is the time to act. Even if it makes Shanti hate me in the end.

Better to have her alive than feel the weight of regret for not stepping up when I should have.

It's been a while since she and I have spent time together. How about I reach out and pull the sister card and beg to see her. If she makes an excuse, I'll be ready. Somehow, I'll get her out of the apartment.

What can I do?

I nibble on my bottom lip, blocking out the sharp sting until I taste blood. I *need* to do something. Being idle while Reema tries to connect with Shanti… I feel like a ticking time bomb. Like I could blow any second, not knowing what is happening.

Shanti is not okay, this much I know. But I have no idea *what* is going on. And being in the dark about the *what* bothers me most.

How can I fix anything if I haven't the first clue what needs mending?

> Be patient. As hard as that sounds, please try. I'll call her and ask to have lunch or dinner and keep you updated.

Patient. Reema wants me to be patient. An impossible notion, but patient is all I have been for months. Hell, I've waited for Shanti in some form or another for years. Another day or two is nothing.

> Okay. Thanks, Reema.

> No need to thank me. Talk soon.

Time is a peculiar construct. The oddest way to measure life as it passes. A rhythmic tick. A hash mark to remind you another breath or heartbeat has come and gone. But the most bizarre part is when those metrical, consistent ticks slow. When they drag by as if time itself struggles to move forward.

That's what the past two days have felt like. A struggle with time.

As I teach a small group of five-year-olds their first ballet steps, I do my best not to look at the clock on the wall. I try to ignore the impulse to see how much time has passed and instead coach my newest students.

And damn is it difficult.

At this very moment, Reema is having lunch with Shanti. I have no idea where—Reema thought it best I didn't know. It was a smart move on her part. Had she told me where they were meeting, I'd have asked another instructor to take over. Then I'd linger outside the restaurant in the hopes of catching a glimpse of Shanti.

Reema's smart enough to know it would've been disastrous.

Instead, I wait—for time to pass, for Reema to reach out, for an abbreviated summary of how my best friend is doing.

The thirty-minute class finally ends, and I congratulate the newest Rhythm and Flow dancers on a job well done. Voices animated, they scurry to their bags, swap out their ballet flats for regular shoes, and collect their belongings.

"Bye, Mr. Jet," Joel says with an excited wave of his hand as he heads for the exit. "Today was so much fun."

"Glad you enjoyed it. See you next class." I return his wave and give him what I hope is a warm smile.

When the kids are gone, I dart for my duffel and dig out my phone. One text notification from Reema. I suck in a sharp breath, hold it, and tap the message.

REEMA

When you have a moment, call me.

My lungs burn as I stare down at the screen. Seconds feel like hours as I read the message again. *This can't be good.* Exhaling the breath I'd been holding, I tap Reema's name at the top of the screen and hit the phone icon.

She picks up on the first ring. "Jet, where are you? I'd rather speak in person."

Anxiety bubbles in my chest. I close my eyes, take a slow, deep breath, count to five, then exhale and open my eyes. "The dance studio."

"I'll be there in a few." Her words come out in a rush as I hear her car pick up speed.

Neither of us says anything, nor do we hang up. I tell myself Reema will be here any minute, and we will figure this out together. Another minute, maybe two, and she will share everything from her visit with Shanti.

Moving to the lobby, I check all the students have been picked up. The next class doesn't start for an hour, so we should be able to talk freely.

"I'm here," she says, then disconnects the call. Five breaths later, the bell over the door jingles and Reema enters the studio.

"Hey." I gesture to the couch and chairs in the waiting area. "Let's talk here."

Reema lets out an audible exhale as she takes a seat. "It's bad, Jet." The words are a blow to the solar plexus, but I appreciate Reema not sugarcoating the situation.

Leaning forward, I drop my elbows to my knees, my head in my hands, and fist my hair for one, two, three breaths before straightening to meet her gaze. "Define bad." I need clear, concise words. Otherwise, my mind will make up endless scenarios.

Reema hugs her purse to her chest, clutching the straps until her knuckles blanch. "She's lost an unhealthy amount of weight." Reema closes her eyes as pain etches her features. "God, she looks haunted. Pale, sweaty skin. Dark circles under her eyes. And she just kept scratching." On an inhale, she meets my gaze. Tears rim her brown irises as she starts to shake. "Jet, I think she was high. Not sure on what, but she wouldn't look me in the eye."

A sharp pang flares beneath my sternum. A niggling voice in the back of my mind says Reema means high from something other than marijuana. Because pot doesn't make people lose weight or obsessively scratch themselves.

I will make this better, Shanti. Whatever it takes.

I swallow past the thick ball of emotion in my throat and take another breath. Right now, we need to focus on next steps. Getting Shanti out of this situation and finding her help are what matter most.

"We need to separate her from Blaze and that apartment," I say.

"Agreed, but we can't go in without a plan. If we're impulsive and show up without a strategy, it'll go sideways fast."

Reema's right. Although I don't want to wait another second to extricate Shanti from Blaze and the nightmare he comes with, we will lose her completely if we go in ill-prepared. Because Shanti will fight for the freedom she has gained, even if this version is destroying her life.

"What do you have in mind?"

"An intervention. Initially, it should be only me and you. We're her strongest relationships. The people who love her most. The people she doesn't want to let down." Reema relays a few more details, saying we can hash out the finer details over the next week. "If we get her out of the apartment, I'll call it a partial victory. Then, I'll take her back to my place and we'll start the next step."

Reema doesn't say it, but the next step for Shanti is detox. For anything else to take root, Shanti needs to be sober first. It'll be rough, but she won't go through it alone.

One week. We will get Shanti back in one week. I only hope one week isn't too long.

TWENTY-THREE
BEAUTIFULLY TRAGIC
SHANTI

A MONSTER ROARS IN MY STOMACH, AND I PRESS THE HEEL OF MY hand to the grumbly beast. "Quit being so dramatic. You're not going to starve." Laughter falls from my lips as my hand falls to the side of the couch, the scratchy fabric slick under my palm.

Blaze will be pissed when he finds out I spilled a bowlful of buttered noodles on the couch, but I can't find a reason to care. He won't be back in town until Thanksgiving break. Maybe I'll clean it up before then.

Probably not.

Do I still have leftovers from lunch with Reema?

I muster the energy to get up from the couch and stumble toward the fridge. A pungent, nauseating odor smacks me in the face when I open the door. My throat spasms and burns as bile inches up, and I slap a hand over my mouth as I survey the fridge contents.

Skipping over the moldy cheese and lumpy milk, I reach for the take-out box then slam the fridge closed. After a breath of funk-free air, I set the box on the counter and open the lid. My stomach sours further when I see something fuzzy and green on my chicken pasta.

"Dammit," I yell, snapping the lid shut and shoving the box

across the counter. Irritation simmers under my skin that the only real food in the apartment is now garbage.

Ignoring the spoiled leftovers, I move to the cabinet and search for something more reliable. Crackers or cookies. A shelf-stable food loaded with enough preservatives to keep it good for years.

"Jackpot," I singsong when I find a box of cheese crackers.

As I tear into the salty snack, a knock sounds at the door. With a groan, I leave the box on the counter and shuffle toward the door. I'm not expecting anyone, but maybe Blaze forgot his key and is surprising me for the weekend.

I twist the dead bolt, turn the knob, and swing open the door. "Hey, you…" I squint at the two people at the door, my head a swirl of confusion. "You're not my boyfriend." I snort and everything starts spinning. I grip the doorframe.

"Whoa there." A warm hand grips my arm.

I try to shake it off, but my arm feels so heavy. "Go away. I'm fine." Taking a step back, I lose my footing and start to go down.

Whoever holds me takes more of my weight. "Let's sit you down a minute."

My butt hits a seat, and I blink up at the person in front of me. "Jet?" His name comes out slow and heavy on my tongue.

"Hey, Shanti."

A familiar cloud of bliss blankets me, and I close my eyes for a moment. "What are you doing here?"

"This place is atrocious," Reema mutters.

I turn in the direction of her voice and crack open my eyes. "Reema? You're here too?"

A soft hand cups my cheek then tilts my chin up. "Of course I am. Jet and I are getting you out of here."

Her declaration is a cold bucket of water over my head. My eyes fly open as I bolt up from the couch, stumbling slightly. "Like hell you are. I'm not going anywhere." I wave an arm around the room, almost hitting Jet. "This is where I live."

"Not anymore," Reema booms.

"I'm not a fucking child," I yell in her face. "You can't make me do shit."

A look I've never seen on my sister's face makes me wobble and fall back onto the couch.

"I will not watch you slowly die in this place," she says after a moment, emotion thick in her voice as she points to the floor. Reema wipes her cheeks. "Look at you, Shanti." She sniffles. "You're wasting away."

I scoff. "At least I'm free to choose how I live my life."

"I know life was tough with Mom and Dad. I get why you walked away from them. It wasn't about what they provided; it was about gaining your own voice." Tears spill down Reema's cheeks. "But is *this*"—she gestures to the filth everywhere— "worth dying for?" She steps closer to me, takes my face in her hands, and tips my head back until our gazes connect. "Is losing who you are, what you love, *who* you love, worth a fleeting high?"

Her words make my skin itch, and I squirm in her hold. "I'm fine, Reema." I reach for my elbow and scratch as my gaze flits around the room. "Just need to clean the apartment."

"You're not fine." Reema swats at my hand scratching the patch of dry skin. "So let's get your things and go."

Anger simmers in my chest, and I glare up at my sister. "I'm not going anywhere," I scream. "This is where I live. You just can't stand that I'm finally happy with my life."

"Happy?" she hollers before her humorless laughter echoes in my ears. "You live in literal filth, Shanti." Disgust curls her lip. "Popping pills and getting drunk every day is your definition of *happy*? Abandoning people who love you unconditionally makes you happy?" Her voice grows louder with each word. "Throwing your passion and ambition in the dumpster makes you happy?" She shakes her head. "Someone else might buy the lies you're selling, but not me."

I roll my eyes. "Don't try to guilt-trip me with your psychobabble bullshit, Reema. I'm not one of your students. I didn't ask for your opinion or guidance."

Reema erases all the space between us and comes nose to nose with me, her expression serious, stoic. "You don't think I know what it's like? The constant pressure. The burden of always trying to be the best at every single thing you do." She tilts her head. "To wonder if this deed or that award will finally make them proud."

"You don't—"

Holding up her hand, Reema cuts me off. "No, Shanti. It's my turn to talk." Hurt shines in her eyes. "I grew up in the same house as you. Dealt with the same strict parents as you." She pauses to inhale an audible breath. "Sure, I could've taken the same path you did. Rebelled. Got angry. Acted out. Left home as soon as I turned eighteen. But I didn't." She shakes her head. "No, I used all my pent-up frustration as fuel. Not to make them proud—I gave up on that a long time ago. I used it to build a better life for myself. One *I* am proud of. A life *I* control." She inches back slightly. "And I want that for you too."

"I am in control of my life," I tell her.

Reema shakes her head. "No, Shanti, you're not. Addiction controls your life. Blaze controls your life." She places a hand over her heart. "Me... I'm trying to *save* your life." A tear rolls down her cheek. "I'm trying to save you from tragedy. A fate you can't come back from if you keep walking the path you're on."

I purse my lips. "A bit theatrical, don't you think? I'm not dying, Reema."

"Listen to me." She moves until she is all I see. "Are you listening?"

A huff of air leaves my lips. "Yes, Reema," I say sarcastically, "I'm listening."

"I love you, Shanti."

Such simple words, but they feel massive and tender and profound coming from my sister's lips. My chest constricts. The backs of my eyes sting. A dull ache flourishes under my breastbone.

She cups one cheek then the other. Her thumbs slowly stroke my skin as she stares into my soul. "I love you." The words come out slower this time. Softer. More affectionately. "And I refuse to watch you die over something I can help you with."

Curling my fingers into fists, I close my eyes. Take a few steadying breaths. Work to not let a single tear fall. Because all I keep hearing is that I need help. That she is better than me and can fix me up.

"What if I don't want your help?" I open my eyes and glare at her. "I'm not a fucking charity case."

"No, you're not." She straightens and takes a step back. Glances toward Jet, who I forgot was even here. "You may not want our help, but you're getting it. Jet and I will do whatever it takes."

Eyes narrowed, I shift my attention to my best friend—if I am that to him anymore. "Still hung up on me, huh?"

The barb-coated words hit him, and he jerks back. Then he relaxes his expression, holds my gaze, and takes Reema's place in front of me. "Spit every cruel and vicious word at me, still won't change how much I love you." Jet drops down into a squat and takes my hands in his. "How much I will always love you." His thumbs brush lazy strokes over my knuckles. "Maybe I'm a fool to not let you go, but that's my choice. I love you, Shanti, and I am fighting for you. Both of us are." He squeezes my hands, and it makes my heart skip. "Please let us fight for the person we love."

My eyes burn, and I don't fight the tears that blur my vision. A tremble ripples through my limbs as I swallow down the pool of saliva in my mouth. "I won't go back to Mom and Dad."

Reema squats down next to Jet. "Never." She rests a hand on my leg. "You'll come to my place. Live with me."

Glancing around the room, I take in the absolute filth for the first time. Really see the squalor I've lived in for months and not cared about. Note the empty bottles and cans, take-out containers and moldy food, dead bugs and evidence of smoked joints and various pharmaceuticals taken.

A tear rolls down my cheek. "What about the apartment?"

Jet gives my hands another squeeze. "Let us worry about it."

The last thing I want is to fall back into another situation where I depend on someone else's approval to feel good about myself. I don't want to live a life of someone else's choosing. Blaze has his faults, but at least he let me decide what I wanted to do. He let me choose my future.

Yes, I deviated from what most consider normal. But I got to experience the world on my own terms.

I don't want to admit Reema and Jet are right, but I know they are. I can still live the life I choose, but I need to make more rational decisions. I need support without judgment.

For years, I've barely lived. Then I escaped the clutches of my parents and had a real chance at life. But if I'm truly honest with myself, these past five months, I've merely existed. And I can't do it anymore.

It's time to breathe. Time to let go of a past I cannot change. Time to find my wings and extend them fully.

"I'm scared," I admit, a breath above a whisper.

Reema reaches for me and wraps me in her arms. "I know." Her hand rubs slow, soothing circles on my back. "We are too. But we'll get through this." She releases me and drops back into a squat. "Together."

As I take my next breath, Jet hauls me into his arms. "Day or night, through thick and thin, I will always be here for you." He tightens his hold on me and buries his nose in the crook of my neck. "I love you. No matter what," he mumbles against my skin. "Forever."

A sob rips from my chest as tears pour down my cheeks. Jet pulls me flush to his chest, and I fist the back of his hoodie. I inhale the crisp cotton and a scent that has always been distinctly Jet. *God, I've missed his smell. Him.* The thought brings on a fresh wave of tears.

Jet simply strengthens his hold as if it's the most natural thing.

When the tears come less often, Jet relaxes his arms enough to lean back and meet my gaze. "We should pack your things and get going."

I nod. "There isn't much. It's all in the bedroom. I think."

"Okay." Reema steps around the couch and heads toward the alcove separating the bedroom and bathroom.

Pushing up from the couch, I follow her, Jet at my side. Sadness and shame swallow me whole as I move through the room gathering my things. Because for the first time in months, my eyes are open. I see the squalor I've lived in. See the life I thought less than an hour ago was incredible because it was my choice.

But it's all been a lie. Another version of hell disguised as freedom.

Lucky doesn't begin to describe what I am, but it's the only word that comes to mind. Because, without Reema or Jet, I'd have withered away in this place. Possibly taken my last breath.

Instead, their love has saved me.

With my bags packed, the three of us walk out the door and Reema drives us back to her place. The ride is silent, but I don't mind. When she puts the car in park minutes later, I glance out the windshield and sigh as I stare at my new home. My safe haven.

Thank you for saving me.

TWENTY-FOUR

ONE FOOT IN FRONT OF THE OTHER
JET

Three and a Half Years Ago

A LIGHT DUSTING OF SNOW BLANKETS THE GROUND AND COLORFUL lights decorate storefronts as I drive north on Granite Parkway. Bundled in coats and scarves, residents mill about on the sidewalk from one shop to the next in search of the perfect holiday gifts. Kids scoop up whatever snow they get their hands on, shape it into a ball, and toss it at their friend or loved one.

As I roll through the main part of Stone Bay, everything looks normal. Happy. Perfect.

And for the first time in too long, it feels as though my life is headed back in that direction. To a better place. A happier place.

Flipping on my blinker, I slow and turn onto Merlinite Way. In a matter of seconds, the shops disappear in my rearview as I pass tall evergreens and a mix of craftsman, bungalow, and cottage homes. My eyes scan the forest on the right and quaint neighborhood on the left after the library. Children play in front yards, creating art with snow. Older residents sit on porches with mugs while sharing conversation.

Life finally feels more stable. For the first time in almost a year, I breathe deeper without trouble. I can close my eyes at night and

sleep without nightmares. More importantly, when I smile, it's genuine. I feel purpose and hope again. And it's all because Shanti is back, safe, and on the path to healing.

I haven't seen her much since the day Reema and I picked her up from the apartment, but Reema texts me with updates. For now, that is enough. It has to be. Recovery isn't easy. Neither is getting your feet back under you after hardship or change. And I'd rather get the occasional snapshot of her life than lose her completely by overstepping.

With every heartbeat, I miss my best friend. I miss the woman I love. But this isn't about me or us right now, and I need to keep that front of mind.

After a right onto Obsidian Pass and a quick left, I pull into the parking lot for Rhythm and Flow. Cutting the engine, I grab my duffel and cross the lot on quick feet.

I spot Neesa in the office near the entrance as I step inside. Glasses perched on her nose and a stack of papers next to her laptop, the weary look on her face says everything. She is in spreadsheet hell. Can't say I blame her. Bookkeeping is probably the most exhausting and tedious part of owning a business.

"Morning, Jet," Neesa greets when she glances up.

I lift my hand and wave, giving her a kind smile. "Morning." I take a few steps in her direction. "Admin day?"

Neesa leans back in her chair and sighs. Taking off her glasses, she tosses them onto the desk before pinching the bridge of her nose. "Yeah. A necessary evil, unfortunately."

I don't have firsthand experience with the paperwork side of owning a business, but I've seen Mom and Dad hunched over a computer with the same drained expression enough times to know it was the opposite of fun.

"Wish I had words of encouragement," I offer.

Neesa chuckles. "Thanks. If I quit futzing around and get it done, I won't have to look at it for another month."

"Put in your earbuds and crank some upbeat music. Maybe it'll help."

"Why didn't I think of that?" Neesa brightens for the first time since I walked in. "Thanks, Jet. Have a great class today."

"Never knew how fun and reminiscent it'd be to teach beginners. They definitely keep me on my toes, pun kind of intended."

We both laugh. Then I give Neesa another wave and leave her to the boring stuff while I step into the studio and prep for today's class.

Setting my bag down along the back wall, I swap my shoes for my ballet slippers and grab my phone, connecting it to the wireless speakers in the room. Playlist selected, I close my eyes and get lost in the music as I warm up my muscles.

As I transition from lower to upper-body stretches, movement from the other side of the room steals my attention. The catch of my breath is immediate, my heart stuttering at the sight of Shanti as she crosses the room and sets her bag down next to mine. Fire scorches my lungs the longer I stare at her in the mirror, and I force myself to exhale then take in fresh air.

She's here. Thrill courses through my veins at the sight of her. But it's quickly replaced with concern.

Should she be here? Is it too soon?

A little more than two months have passed since Reema declared Shanti was coming to live with her. At the time, I didn't know the extent of what Shanti had been through while living with Blaze. Reema and I had our suspicions, but we didn't know anything for certain.

With each new update Reema sent, an invisible fist clutched my heart impossibly tighter. My soul ached and wept for my best friend, the woman I loved so desperately.

It had been more than booze, weed, and a pill here and there. From what Reema shared, Blaze basically kept Shanti high every waking minute the first month she lived with him. The moment he stopped feeding her newfound addiction for free, she had to figure out new ways to supply her habit. Since she didn't have an income, she got… resourceful.

I shake off the dark path of my thoughts. Redirect my attention back to the present. Focus on the positives.

Shanti is here. A hint of pink colors her once sallow cheeks. The dark crescents that encircled her eyes months ago are nowhere to be seen. Where bones protruded in an unhealthy manner, she now has more curvature and softness. But the biggest and most welcome change is the light and fire that has returned to her amber eyes.

Maybe it isn't too soon.

Maybe being here is exactly what she needs.

Ballet slippers on her feet, Shanti abandons her bag and walks toward me. Her gait is strong, stride elegant yet purposeful. Like she has every time on the dance floor, she exudes beauty and grace.

The corners of my mouth twitch, eager to give her my biggest smile, and I bite the inside of my cheek to cut off the action. Happy as I am to see her at the studio, I don't want to come off intense or overzealous. Or for her to think my smile is disingenuous. She has enough people tiptoeing around her with superficial expressions; I won't be one of them.

"Hey," I greet, rotating my shoulder joints. "Wasn't expecting you." I keep my tone light and easy.

Shanti steps up to the barre and starts her warm-up routine. A wince tugs at her mouth as she lowers into a hamstring stretch, but she turns her head to hide it. "I know." She inhales deeply and eases out of the stretch. "Hope I'm not intruding."

Impossible, I want to tell her. Instead, I settle for a more casual response. "Of course not."

With a slow nod, she transitions to her next stretch. "Mind if I join your class?"

My brows shoot for my hairline as I stare at her. When I don't respond after a moment, she glances up.

"If I'll be in the way, just tell me."

"It's not that." I can't resist the smirk curving my lips.

Shanti straightens and tilts her head, eyes curious. "Then what is it?"

With a lick of my lips, I step within arm's reach of her. "You want to join my beginner's class?" My tone is playful and light.

Shrugging, she brings her heel to her butt, grabs her foot, and extends her hip joint to get a deeper stretch of her quads. "I'm out of practice." Her gaze drops to the floor, and the loss of eye contact twists something inside my chest. "It'll do me some good." She nods. "Going back to the basics and being around a group of highly enthusiastic dancers."

For a beat, I absorb her words. Let them really sink in.

Teaching the next generation of dancers has been so refreshing and enlightening. Their endless excitement and relentless hunger to learn more reminds me of the passion I had for dance in the beginning. The way they cheer each other on and applaud accomplishments makes me fall in love with dance all over again.

Taking this job was one of the best decisions of my career.

Without thinking, I inch closer to her. Reach up and brush a stray lock of hair off her temple, tucking it behind her ear. Toy with the silky ribbon in her hair. "Okay, yeah. Sure." I meet her gaze, my body heating at the warmth in her golden-brown irises. "But I have a better idea."

She sucks in a sharp breath but doesn't move otherwise. "And what's that?"

I step close enough to feel the heat of her on my skin and take her hand. The last thing I want is for her to run. "Teach the class with me?"

Jerking back, her brows pinch together. "What? No."

My thumb paints the back of her hand with lazy strokes. "Yes."

Her features relax, but pain still lingers in her gaze. "Not sure it's a good idea."

I take her other hand and hold both with a firm yet tender grip. Do my best to comfort her with my touch. Anchor her to me while I expose what might be a painful wound. "Why?"

Tears rim her eyes, and she glances off to the side, swallowing. One deep breath, then another, and she faces me again. "Because I'm a mess." The admission floats through the air, emotion weighing each word. "Because I've barely worn my slippers or pointes in the past year," she says with a little more conviction. "What if I…" Her gaze drops to the floor as she wilts.

Anguish radiates off her like a venomous shadow-beast, and I hate it. I hate seeing her like this—insecure about her talent, doubting her abilities, dismissing her gifts. I want to slay every monster who stole a piece of her light and shattered her confidence. I want to take all her pain away, package it up, and label it *return to sender.*

The sudden urge to wrap her in my arms and assure her it doesn't matter she is out of practice nips at my heels. Somehow, I resist. So what if she is a mess. Who isn't nowadays? So what if she has made decisions she now regrets. Who hasn't?

No one is perfect. No one always has their life together. And I need her to recognize and understand that what she considers her flaws is what makes her beautiful and unique, brave and fierce, impressive and influential.

Whatever it takes, I need to make her see the good.

I lift a hand to her chin and tip her head until our eyes connect. Slowly, I brush her bottom lip with my thumb, the corner of my mouth curving the slightest bit when she shivers at the contact.

"What if what, Shanti?"

Inhaling a shaky breath, she blinks back the tears threatening to spill down her cheeks. Her bottom lip trembles a beat before she tucks it between her teeth for one, two, three heartbeats. "What if I can't do it anymore?" she asks, uncertainty lacing her whispered words.

Releasing her other hand, I bring both of mine to frame her face. My grays lock on her golden browns as I drop my forehead to rest on hers. "What if you can?" My thumbs stroke the apples of her cheeks softly, reverently. "What if you are exactly what these kids need?" The warmth of her breath paints my lips as I fight every instinct to kiss her. "*I believe in you, Shanti. I need you.*"

Her eyes close as she takes my hips, her fingers curled in a bruising grip. "I need you too," she confesses.

Back and forth, my thumbs slowly brush her cheeks. "For now, let that be enough." Inhaling deeply, I inch back then press my lips to her forehead. "Impossible as it sounds, remember that everything happens for a reason, and it will all work out in the end. Remember that we all stumble from time to time, but it's how we rise afterward that matters most."

Leaning back, I meet and hold her gaze once more, needing her to really hear what I say next.

"I will never let you fall, Shanti," I repeat the vow I told her almost two years ago. "Because all I want is to see you soar."

TWENTY-FIVE
THE PERFECT BALM
SHANTI

Three Years Ago

Boring. Over the past eight months, my life has slowly transitioned into a tame, monotonous existence. A life full of invariable routine and the same faces over and over.

And for the first time in years—perhaps, the first time in my life—I am happy with boring. Ridiculously delighted, in fact.

Many would balk at the repetitiveness in my life or the jam-packed itinerary I keep. Not me. I *crave* the structure that comes with my entire day being scheduled weeks ahead of time. I *covet* the certainty of knowing what will happen when I wake up, who I will see throughout the day, and how my day will end.

Every second doesn't need to be scripted, but knowing the foundation of my day has been laid soothes my soul.

Coffee and a hearty breakfast with Reema before she leaves for work. An unhurried, low-stress morning routine. Dance with my favorite person and a room full of eager children who admire me and my talents. The opportunity to work on my health and past trauma with compassionate doctors. Downtime—which I rarely had until now—to do whatever makes me happy. Lately, it's been reading, binge-watching shows, and exploring outdoors.

Most of my days end with dinner with Reema or Jet. On occasion, I have dinner alone, which I've found a new appreciation for.

Though she will never admit it, Reema loves cooking for me and chatting over egg bhurji, aloo gobhi, coconut chia pudding, or a fun new recipe she discovered and wanted to try. She doesn't love the act of preparing food or hovering over the stove, but I think having someone to cook for has softened her to it. Reema has never loved domesticity or chores, but she loves spending uninterrupted time together and getting to know her little sister better—something we weren't allowed to do as kids.

These past eight months haven't been easy—not that the years prior were effortless—but I love where I am now. The shape of my life. The comfort I've discovered. The future that's a little less fuzzy.

Had I not experienced those hiccups and challenges, I wouldn't appreciate this new version of my life or the peace it brings.

Glancing at the clock on my bedside table, my eyes widen. "Shit." I need to be out the door in five minutes. "Where are you?" I mumble to myself as I sift through the small jewelry box on the dresser.

Exhausted last night, I unknowingly deviated from my bedtime routine and set my necklace somewhere other than the dish next to the lamp on the nightstand. Now, I can't find it.

Closing the jewelry box lid, I shuffle toward the bed, drop to my knees, and run my hands over the rug for the third time. I do a final check of the bedding and dish by the lamp. Nothing. I jog out of the room and down the hall to the bathroom. The backs of my eyes sting as I scan the vanity and come up empty.

Shoulders caving forward, I blink back the tears blurring my vision. I inhale deeply, methodically, in through my nose and out between my lips.

Everything is okay. You will find it.

Yes, the necklace is a trinket, an inanimate object. I know this.

In the deepest parts of my soul, I know with one-hundred-percent certainty Jet won't be upset.

To me, though, the simple, dainty rose gold feather and chain are more than shaped metal and fashionable body decoration. That necklace is a symbol. A token. A promise. Jet chose the small charm with me in mind. He put time and energy and love into buying it. He waited until the perfect time to give it to me.

"Where are you?" I mutter, my voice shaky as panic sets in. My gaze flits to the blue-and-white vintage-patterned floral shower curtain. Hope soars in my chest. "Maybe…" Seems foolish to think the necklace fell off while I washed up, but it's one place I haven't looked yet.

I rip back the shower curtain and visually roam every inch of the tub. Aside from the pristine white surface, hair care, body-wash, and loofahs, the tub is empty. It's not in the drain catch, either.

A sharp pang flares beneath my breastbone, and I press the heel of my hand to the invisible wound. "No." The air leaves my lungs in a *whoosh* as my heart thrashes violently in my rib cage. The room spins, and I stumble forward, gripping the vanity a beat before I settle on the toilet seat lid.

Closing my eyes, I try to regulate my erratic breathing. I work backward on the mental list my therapist gave me for when I have panic attacks.

One thing I taste. *Spearmint mouthwash.*

Two things I smell. *Disinfectant wipes and the lingering smell of Reema's perfume.*

Three sounds I hear. *The thrumming of my pulse in my ears, the faint sound of water dripping from the leaky faucet, and trees rustling in the wind outside.*

Four textures or surfaces I feel. *My feet on the floor, my butt on the seat, the soft fabric of my cover-up, and the wood grain of the vanity.*

I open my eyes and name five things I see. *Window, subway tile, face cream, toilet paper, and—*

My eyes go wide as I stare down at the floor between the toilet and vanity. A sniffle echoes through the room as I blink back tears and reach for my necklace on the floor. Relief hits me like a tidal wave as I hold the delicate and most precious keepsake I own.

After a wipe of my cheeks, I latch the necklace at the nape of my neck, rise from the toilet, give myself a once-over in the mirror, and run back to my room for my bag.

"I'm late," I grumble, frustrated with myself. Reaching up, I graze the feather with my fingertips and sigh. "But it's worth it."

Driving seven over the limit and only slowing at stop signs gets me to the studio a couple minutes after my scheduled time. I hate being late, but at least it's not by much.

Lengthening my stride, I cross the lot on quick feet and push through the entrance. I wave to Flora, the young woman at the front desk, but don't stop to chat.

She gives me a kind smile and mirrors my gesture. "Have a great class today."

"Thanks. You too." The second the last words come out, I shake my head. *Bumbling fool.* "I mean, have a good day too."

Flora chuckles. "No worries. I do that all the time."

I scurry into the main room, all but run to where Jet's duffel already sits, drop my bag, and make quick work of swapping my shoes for my split-sole slippers. Tugging off my shirt and wide-leg yoga pants, I toss them in the bag, shuffle over to the barre, and start my warm-up routine.

"Everything alright?" Jet meets my gaze in the mirror, concern marring his brow.

The last thing I want to do is tell him I thought I lost my necklace. But I also don't want to lie to him, not after all the obstacles we have overcome.

"Yeah." I nod, take a deep breath, then transition into my next stretch on the exhale. "Just had a minor panic attack before I left home."

Jet straightens in my periphery. "Want to talk about it?" His posture says relaxed and open, but his voice trembles slightly and betrays his easygoing facade.

Seconds of silence pass in lifetimes as I mentally fumble over the right words. In hindsight, getting so upset over a necklace seems silly and unwarranted. It's just a necklace. A replaceable piece of jewelry. But then I remember what my therapist told me months ago.

"It's perfectly normal to feel things differently than others. It's okay to cry or be numb or want to break something. To love something you once hated and hate something you once loved. The way you feel about anything or anyone is not permanent. It's allowed to change, as are you. As you grow, as you find your authentic self, the way you process emotions will change. You have so many bricks to remove from the walls around your heart, and that's okay. Just remember that as those walls come down, you'll experience strong emotions. Things you've protected yourself from before will overwhelm you, but you need to let those feelings in. More importantly, you need to share what you feel."

I swallow past the thickness forming in my throat and dig for the courage I need to admit what happened. I remind myself this is Jet, the most understanding and empathetic person in my life. Although things haven't always been perfect between us, he has supported, lifted, and loved me through it all. Wish I could say I've been equally as kind and generous in return.

Jet deserves someone better than me. Someone who owns their feelings, who doesn't hold back. Someone who isn't scared to love him, who is worthy of his love in return.

I'll admit I love Jet. Fiercely. If I'm honest, I have loved him for as long as he has me.

My love for him over the years hasn't always been romantic. In the beginning, it was sweet, similar to the affection I had for my sister. Jet had been the first person other than Reema to let me in and welcome me as I am. Before him, I never experienced true, full acceptance from a peer.

As time passed, as our friendship flourished, what I felt for him morphed and bloomed. My love for Jet became my most prized possession. I was greedy for more. Craved his attention and affection on an unhealthy level. Did whatever I could to insert myself more into his life.

Before long, a niggling voice in the back of my mind told me Jet deserved more. It was loud, unavoidable, and I couldn't help but listen to it, believe it. I let that voice invade every crevice of my mind and rewire the way I felt.

That voice broke me. I didn't want it to break him too. So I put distance between us. I chose people I didn't care about hurting. Most of all, I avoided real affection. In doing so, I stopped loving myself.

But all of that is in the past.

Now, I'm on a path of self-compassion. Every day, I work harder than ever to shut down the voice of doubt and despair. Although it hasn't quieted completely, it has dimmed to background static. A low-level hum I only hear when alone in silence.

Until I can vanquish that voice, until I can love myself without uncertainty nipping at my heels, it isn't right for me to reciprocate Jet's affections. Even if I desperately want to.

Embarrassment climbs up my neck to my cheeks as I admit, "I thought I lost my necklace." Forehead pressed to my leg, I close my eyes and take a steadying breath. "And I just spiraled." I grip my foot tighter and drop deeper into the stretch on an exhale. "I panicked and couldn't breathe."

Heat blankets my side, and I open my eyes. Long, lean, muscular legs in black leggings fill my vision, his feet unintentionally in first position. I study the skintight black fabric on his thighs with excessive intensity. Transfixed by the solid lines of his quads, my mouth goes dry. My stomach flips.

God, how I wish I was those leggings.

I close my eyes and mentally shake off the thought.

"Shanti." Tenderness wraps around my name on his lips. "It would've been okay if you lost the necklace."

Swallowing, I straighten my spine and lower my leg from the

barre. Slowly, I meet his gaze. Lock on to his kind, gray eyes and shake my head. "No, it wouldn't."

He opens his mouth to say something, but I hold up a hand to cut him off.

"I know it's just a necklace. A *thing*." Reaching up, I take the feather between my finger and thumb, rub it gently and let it ground me. "But it's not."

It's so much more. A sense of security. A safety net. A symbol of his reverence.

Losing his necklace would feel like losing him.

His eyes dart between mine, searching, silently asking questions I'm not willing to answer. Not yet. Infinitesimally, he nods and shuffles closer. Unhurried, he lifts his hand and lays it over mine.

My breath catches in my throat as my pulse thrums faster, louder. He's so close. Too close. His scent envelops me like a thick, rapturous cloud, and I inhale deeply, greedy for more.

Neither of us speaks. We don't need to.

Jet has made his feelings for me abundantly clear. He loves me. More than anyone has. More than anyone ever will.

But am I as easy to read? It feels as though my love for him is a neon sign, flashing and enormous with the words *she loves you too*, a big arrow pointing at my face. And when he looks at me like he is right now, as if he sees every one of my secrets in a single glance, as if his soul knows the contours of my soul, I wonder if he is more aware than he lets on.

He must feel how intensely my heart hammers when he touches me. See how flushed my skin gets, feel how feverish my body gets when he holds me close. When he says those three words.

I won't say it. I won't risk everything. Not yet.

But does he already know?

His fingers spread across my collarbones, caressing back and forth with subtle strokes. "No, it's not." His reciprocity is a delicate, whispered acknowledgment as his gaze drops to my lips for a heartbeat. "It was always more." He licks his lips. "It will *always* be more."

God, I want to kiss him.

I want to drop the curtain on this charade and let him in completely.

If only I were ready.

"I know," I say, voice hoarse with emotion. "I wish I could give you more." The admission escapes without permission. And as much as I want to reverse time and take it back, as much as it hurts to tell him, it feels like the right thing to do.

Jet shouldn't waste days or weeks or months wondering if we will ever be more than what we are now. I'd like to think one day we'll take the next step, but I can't say yes with absolute certainty.

His hand drifts up my neck, his fingers lighting a fire under my skin. Thumb stroking the line of my jaw, he clutches the nape of my neck. Holds me like I'm precious, like I mean everything, like I'm his. He slowly drops his chin, lowers his mouth impossibly close to my lips. And just when I think he might kiss me, he rests his forehead on mine.

"One day, you will," he says as if it's fact. "When the time is right, I'll sew the final stitch of your tattered heart back together." With a stroke of his thumb, he gives a subtle nod. "Until then, I'll wait."

I open my mouth to ask why he would wait, but I don't get the chance. Chatter echoes through the studio as students file in for class. Reluctantly, I step out of Jet's hold.

I'll ask him after class.

"Dance with me?" I ask after the final student exits the studio.

"As if you need to ask." Jet trails his fingers down the length of my arm until his fingers twine with mine.

I guide us over to our bags, grab his phone, and scroll through his music library until I land on the song I want. Hitting play, I lock his phone and drop it back in his bag. The first chords of the melody float through the room as we cross to the center of the floor.

Without a word, he spins me until I face him and guides the contemporary dance we learned years ago. In perfect synchronicity, we coast through the room, one of his hands on my hip and the other cupping my cheek. With unparalleled fluidity, we perform a dance that once felt innocent and now feels anything but.

Pressing closer, I inhale his scent and sigh a beat before I turn, my back now precariously close to his front. His hands graze my sides slowly, purposefully, leaving fire in their wake. His touch delivers just enough pressure to let me know it's less about the dance and more about having his hands on my body. By the time he reaches the curve of my hips, my insides feel like warm honey. With exquisite strength, he curls his fingers around the flare of my hips. On the next breath, I'm in the air, weightless and blissful as I soar.

Lost in the moment, I miss the subtle shift in Jet's posture. And in one orchestrated move, he steals my breath.

As if he's done it countless times, he lowers me to the floor inch by excruciatingly slow inch. The solid, lean muscles of his torso graze my curves, and I inwardly groan. Closing my eyes, I send all my attention to every point of contact. Memorize the way his body frames mine, fits mine, cherishes mine.

The unmistakable chemistry we have always shared looms in the air. Only now, it sizzles. Crackles. Vibrates with anticipation and need and something so deeply primal. Something we both know exists, but I am too afraid to give into.

For a heady beat, I bask in the weight of it. The visceral intensity of what I feel for my best friend. The acute severity of the fire in my veins.

I want him. Crave him. And damn do I love him. Desperately. Hauntingly.

As my feet meet the floor, my eyes ease open. With a single

blink, the fantastical, lust-filled bubble we were in pops. All the what-ifs and maybes fade to the background as reality settles back in.

Sometimes—okay, most of the time—I really hate reality. But one day, I pray all those fantasies become my reality.

Silence filters in as the song ends, and I spin on my toes to face Jet. I suck in a sharp breath when my gaze locks on the thin ring of onyx encompassing his smoky-gray irises. With a single look, I read every emotion and thought in his captivating eyes. The way he covets and craves and pines for me.

A slow, delicious ache blooms low in my belly, and I clench my thighs. As badly as I want to step into him, push up on my toes, and press my lips to his, I compel myself to do the opposite.

One step back, then another. I inhale deeply, lick my lips, and swallow on the exhale. "Thanks." The single word is scratchy and thick on my tongue.

Soul-searing stare fixed on me, he strips the distance I put between us in one move. His crisp, clean scent fills my nose as he lifts a hand to cup my cheek. "You never need to thank me for that." Lazy and decadent, his thumb strokes my chin, the tip grazing the bottom of my lip.

I want to stay like this forever—lost in sensation, ensnared in his orbit.

If only now was the right time. If only I was ready.

With a subtle nod, I whisper, "I know, but I wanted to." Then I take a reluctant step out of his hold. A chill sweeps over me as his hand falls away, and I immediately miss his warmth and the feel of his skin on mine.

"Come on." As greedy for me as I am him, he reaches for and takes my hand. "Let's get out of here."

As we dress and swap our slippers for shoes, the overwhelming need for more time with him thrums beneath my breastbone. Before I realize what I'm doing, I open my mouth.

"Want to grab something to eat?"

Swiping up his bag, he shoulders it. A corner of his mouth

kicks up in a half smile I will undoubtedly dream about later. "I'd love to. I'll follow you."

We walk in silence to our cars, and I give a quiet *see you in a few* just before I slip into the driver's seat. With the start of the car, I crank the air conditioning, drop my head back on the rest, and audibly exhale.

This is it. Now is the time. Today is when I lay everything on the table. Tell him how deeply I feel for him, but also share how I'm not quite ready to explore the irrefutable attraction between us... yet.

I just need more time to work on myself. To truly love who I am, so I can love him the way he deserves.

Over a meal, I will ask him for a little more patience. I will ask him to wait.

Please let him be okay with waiting.

With the dance studio in my rearview mirror, I drive toward the only sushi restaurant in town, Let's Roll. We park a few spaces from each other, and I wait for Jet at the entrance. Considering it's the middle of the week, the place is packed.

A server leads us to a table near the sushi bar, hands us menus, and promises to return soon with waters.

My knee bounces under the table as I lift the menu and shield most of my face. I already know what I want. It's rare I deviate from my favorite foods. Still, I act as if I'm undecided to give myself a few more minutes to think.

We order way too much when the server returns.

"I'll be back with your appetizer soon." With a quick pivot, they scurry off to assist other patrons.

"So..." Jet takes a sip of water, sets the glass down, and spins it in place. "What's got you jittery?"

Of course, Jet sees more than I want him to. I should expect nothing less.

I wipe my hands down my thighs, squeezing just above my knees. "I wanted to talk to you about something."

When I don't elaborate, he leans in closer, drops his elbows on the table, rests his chin on his clasped hands, and raises his brows. I wait for him to ask me what I want to talk to him about, but he says nothing. He doesn't need to. His expression says it all.

Take your time. You can tell me anything.

Reaching for my water, I down half the glass. The cool liquid settles my nerves, but only for a moment. I just need to speak my mind. Just get it off my chest. *This is Jet*, I remind myself. I can tell him anything.

Tucking my chin to my chest, I take a deep breath and blurt out, "I love you." Every muscle in my body stiffens. The background music disappears and is replaced with the thunderous *whoosh, whoosh, whoosh* of my pulse in my ears. A sharp sting radiates from my palms, but I don't relax my fingers. The pain is a perfect distraction.

Jet's voice wiggles its way past my thrumming pulse. "Shanti."

I relax my fingers but don't look up from my lap. Nausea creeps up my throat, and I close my eyes and mentally shove the sensation down.

"Shanti," he repeats softer. "Please look at me."

Is it irrational to feel this worried about his reaction? Jet has expressed his love for me several times. For years, he has said those three words with so much feeling and not an ounce of reservation.

But this is different. This is *me* being the vulnerable one. I'm the one with my heart on the line and in his hands.

"Please," he whispers.

Swallowing, I lift my chin, open my eyes, and meet his waiting stare. The moment our eyes connect, the fear from seconds ago fizzles out.

Jet lays his arm across the table, palm up in silent request. As I slip my hand in his and our palms kiss, an inexplicable warmth radiates up my arm and through my chest until it cocoons my heart. The sensation is unlike anything else. An incomparable balm comprised of love and tenderness and a nameless emotion I've only ever experienced with him.

"Can I ask why you're scared?"

The soft timbre of his voice rouses me from my thoughts. My grip tightens, and he soothes me with a single stroke of his thumb.

"Because I can't give you more than the words right now," I confess as my stomach cramps.

His brows pinch then relax. Methodically, his thumb brushes my knuckles once, twice. "When it comes to you, I never want to assume anything." He gives an infinitesimal nod. "So I'm going to need you to elaborate."

I didn't need a crystal ball or telepathy to see that coming. When someone has loved you as long as Jet has loved me, of course he'd want to know why I can't give him more than the words. And he deserves to know my reasons.

"For years, you've owned the biggest piece of my heart. You've been my only constant. My guiding light and steady hand." I lift my glass, take a sip of water, and swallow past the sudden dryness in my throat. "And I'm so damn thankful to have you in my life."

"But..."

The server sidles up to the table and sets edamame and Japanese-style egg rolls on the table. "Would you like anything to drink besides water?"

We both shake our heads.

"Shouldn't be long for your meal." And then, they're gone again.

I dip an egg roll in sauce and savor it slower than necessary while granting myself one more minute. Jet pops edamame in his mouth, a cool air about him as he leans back in his seat. But he doesn't fool me. I know him better than anyone. I sense his anticipation, his eagerness for me to continue. Unflappable as ever, he still has his tells.

Wiping my mouth with a napkin, I meet his eyes and hope he sees every ounce of love I have for him in mine. "I need you to believe that I want to give you more."

His brows twitch for a split second. "Okay…" His simple response feels miles long.

My palms sweat as the next words dance over my tongue. "I love you." My stomach churns, and I press a hand to the restless organ. "But I'm not ready for anything more."

I see the words turning over and over in his mind as he tries to make them make sense. Faint lines mar his forehead as his eyes narrow a fraction. Then, his expression softens. "Define more."

I snicker. It's such a Jet response.

"Anything beyond friendship." I grab another egg roll, needing something to keep me from fidgeting, and dunk it repeatedly in the sauce. "So much has happened in the past year or so. I'm still trying to process it all." Shoving the egg roll in my mouth, I eat most of it in one bite.

"And you shouldn't rush it." He nods. "I may not know everything, but I've seen you under pressure. I've been there during the highs and lows. Stressing yourself will only cause more problems." He leans his leg against mine under the table, the heat of him an instant balm. "Invisible wounds leave different scars. Marks that stay with you forever. Sure, they heal with time. But it isn't the same. They never go away. Not fully."

I tilt my head and study his features. The sharp lines of his jaw and hint of stubble shadowing each angle. His slender nose that leads to the most perfect, kissable lips. The thick black strands that frame most of his face and add to his devastating beauty.

"What are you looking at?" A corner of his mouth curves up.

"Since when are you so wise?"

He takes some edamame, pops them in his mouth, and shrugs. "No clue what you're talking about."

I grab a few of the beans and chuck them at him. "Mm-hmm."

Mock horror colors his expression. "You didn't."

Tucking my lips between my teeth, I nod.

An exaggerated sigh leaves his lips. "I guess I forgive you." Then, he reaches across the table and takes my hand. Curls his warm fingers around mine and gives a gentle squeeze. His playful expression turns serious but still has a softness to it.

In a single breath, we shift back to the previous conversation.

"However long it takes."

What? I sift through the past however many minutes in my mind, but I can't pin down exactly what he is talking about. I *think* I know, but can't be sure.

Reading the confusion on my face, he clarifies, "You need time to heal, to learn to love yourself." He nods. "I'll be here. However long it takes, I'll wait for you."

"Jet..."

He lifts my hand to his lips and kisses my knuckles. "No matter what."

PART FOUR

PRESENT

ALL PATHS
LEAD TO YOU

TWENTY-SIX
THE PATIENCE OF A SAINT
JET

Every other breath, my eyes flit across the room to Shanti... and the guy clinging to her side. I bristle, my knuckles burning and nails biting my palms as he leans in for the umpteenth time and whispers something that makes her blush.

They are all the same—dark, broody, uninhibited, flirtatious—yet nothing alike. Intentions on their sleeve, they don't shy away from what they want from her. Still, not a single one gives her anything in return. At least, nothing of value. Nothing she will hold close or treasure later in life.

And it makes me wonder...

For years, I've made my feelings toward her abundantly clear. I've told her an infinite number of times I love her. Yes, I've said the damn words. But I've also articulated my affection in other ways. Every squeeze of her hand, every caress of her skin, every time I lock on to those rich, cognac irises, I wordlessly express the intense grip she has on my soul. Time after time, I continue to put myself out there. Expose my vulnerabilities. Lay my delicate, empathetic, reverent heart in her hands.

And year after year, I am dismissed. Overlooked. Cast aside for someone else. Someone unworthy of her.

Does she intentionally seek out guys with no depth? Guys she

can drop without any concern of fallout? Guys who will move on and not give a second thought at the loss of her? Guys she doesn't need to care about because they are temporary?

It sure as hell seems that way.

What about me is so damn unlovable?

On my next glimpse of her, the guy has his arm hooked in hers as they weave through the crowd toward the exit. Fire singes my veins as I track every step. But it dies a quick death when I take in her vacant expression.

When he isn't watching her, she drops all pretenses. For a brief moment, her indifference shows.

And it breaks my fucking heart.

Why?

Why does she repeat the cycle of misery over and over?

Why won't she let me love her the way she deserves?

I don't understand.

Years ago, during a rare blip in time, she let me in. She confessed her true feelings. Told me she loved me and asked for my patience.

And because all I have ever wanted is her, I promised to wait.

But was it the wrong move? Should I continue to put my life on hold for someone who only wants or needs me when it is convenient for them?

As Shanti exits the pub, artificial smile back in place, I accept it may be time to give up. To concede. To admit the truth and move on. Shanti may never reciprocate my love—not more than a friend —and that's okay. I can't change how she feels, nor would I want to. But I shouldn't have to live in limbo for eons while she decides.

"You okay?"

A heavy sigh deflates my chest as I turn toward June. "When do I say enough?"

June doesn't need to ask who I'm talking about. They know. Hell, I'm sure half of Stone Bay is aware of my unrequited love for Shanti.

Looping their arm with mine, June leans into my side, gives me some of their weight, and rests their head on my shoulder. "Only you know the answer, J." Their arm squeezes mine a little tighter. "But let me say this. Loving someone should be the highlight of your life. It should be euphoric and thrilling. A reason to get up each day. A reason to be silly and weird and laugh at inside jokes only you two understand. It should be individual and shared hopes and dreams you both support. More than anything, love is acceptance.

"Yes, love takes work. Nothing comes without its challenges." June lifts their head to meet my gaze. "But if all you're doing is working, and the effort is one-sided, is it really love? Or is it wishful thinking?"

Ugh. The logical part of my mind says to heed June's advice and do a mental deep dive. To take an immersive look into why I hold out hope. Simultaneously, my irrational heart spasms and aches and says to ignore my damn brain. I love her, and that should be answer enough.

I drop my chin to my chest and groan. "Thanks, J. I'll take that under advisement." Bringing my lips to their cheek, I give them a chaste kiss. "What would I do without you?"

"Odds are you'd perish." A mischievous smile tugs at the corners of their mouth. "I am exceptionally badass."

A hearty chuckle rumbles my chest, and it feels so good to laugh. "You're right." I unloop our arms and hook mine around their shoulders. "Come on. Let's enjoy the rest of our party."

Hailey's Fire plays in the background while June and I chat with family and loved ones. We eat and drink and forget about the stresses in our lives for a couple more hours. When the party crowd thins and the jukebox music plays in place of the band, the Fox family starts to clean up.

As I add glasses to a bus tub, Delilah steps between me and June and drapes an arm over each of us. "How's it feel to be so old?" She kisses my cheek then does the same to June.

"After twenty-one, birthdays are all the same." June tosses

napkins in a trash bag and shrugs. "I guess until dirty thirty, fuck-it forty, and fabulous fifty, there's not much else to get excited about."

"Fuck-it forty?" I peer around Delilah to look at June. "Haven't heard of that one?"

Pride curves their lips. "Because I just made it up." Their eyes go wide. "We should start a fuck-it list now. That way, in sixteen years, we'll have tons of crazy stuff to do."

Eyes slightly narrowed, I nod. "I can get behind this idea."

"I'll brainstorm later." June walks off toward the bar with the trash bag.

Delilah wipes down the table once I clear the last of the glasses. "Shanti left early. Everything okay between you two?"

The familiar pang I only experience with Shanti wiggles its way to the surface. I close my eyes for a single deep breath and swallow past the building uncertainty climbing up my throat.

"Yeah, we're good," I answer after a beat. "Her friend needed to leave." The deceit is sour on my tongue, but I make no attempt to tell her otherwise.

Delilah's gaze brands my profile like a hot iron, but I keep my eyes on the task at hand. Seconds mirror minutes as she stares at me with tenderness and so much damn love.

"Are *you* okay?" she finally asks.

I hate that my family feels this need to constantly check on my emotional well-being any time I spend time with Shanti. Our relationship may be precarious and somewhat unhealthy, but I am strong enough to distance myself when necessary.

Ignoring the mess on the next table, I step into Delilah, band an arm around her, and haul her into my chest. "Yes. I promise." I kiss the top of her head. "I'm with all my favorite people on the best day of the year. I'm better than okay."

I feel her smile against my chest a second before she nods. "Good." She inches back just enough to meet my gaze. "Promise you'll tell me if that changes? Even if only to listen, I'm always here."

Warmth and love bloom in my chest. I drop my lips to her head and press a kiss to her hair. "Best big sister anyone could ask for. Thanks for always looking out for me and June. I love you."

"Love you too, J. So much." Delilah eases out of the hug. "Now, let's wrap this thing up. I have a book on my nightstand calling my name."

A snort of laughter leaves my lips. "Monster romance?"

"Finished that one yesterday. Now on to a spicy poly romance."

"Keep me posted on how it is."

She winks. "You got it."

My family and I clean up the last vestiges of the party. After more than a dozen hugs, June and I say good night, exit the pub, and head for my car.

"Tonight was fun," June says as I turn onto the road that leads to the guesthouse we occupy.

"Every day I get with you is fun."

From the corner of my eye, I see June roll theirs. "A little heavy on the sibling love, don't you think?"

I park in front of the house and cut the engine. "Not if it's true."

"Okay." Sarcasm laces their tone as we exit the car. "Anyway, I'm going to wind down with some game time. Want in?"

I shake my head. "Another night."

June nudges my arm. "You know where I'm at if you change your mind."

In the house, June goes to their room while I head for mine. After I swap my clothes for a pair of basketball shorts, I fall back on the bed and stare up at the ceiling. Until my eyes grow heavy, I replay June's advice from earlier tonight. I question if exerting so much time and energy and effort in loving Shanti, in waiting for her, is worth it.

The hard truth is I should let her go. I should release Shanti from my heart and live my life to the fullest. Because right now, all I am doing is hanging on by a thread.

I should step back, pivot, and walk away.

But the frail thread just won't break. Because I know somewhere deep in my marrow, Shanti is worth the agony and heartache.

I love her.

When you love someone, you fight for them. And I'm willing to stay in the fight longer.

Her heart is worth it. *She* is worth it.

TWENTY-SEVEN
ALL FOR SHOW
SHANTI

LOOPING A SILKY, PINK RIBBON AROUND THE BASE OF MY BUN, I TIE IT into a neat bow at the front. Every pinch and whirl and flick of my fingers is pure muscle memory. The gentle tug of the fabric and twirl of the silk before securing it in place is second nature.

The first day I wore a ribbon in my hair, I met my best friend. I was so nervous, but he made me feel welcome and at home in my first pair of ballet slippers. I've rarely gone a day without a ribbon in my hair since. Either around my bun, the elastic of my ponytail, or at the end of a braid, the pale-pink silk became part of my signature.

I also remember the reason why I continued to wear them as a girl—Jet told me it was pretty. His kind eyes, big heart, and sweet words made *me* feel pretty.

A few times over the years, Jet tugged the ribbon from my hair and stowed it in his pocket or the waistband of his leggings. I've never told him, but I loved that he did it. He played it off as a game or tease, and I let him think I was annoyed. But I wasn't. I secretly loved that he had pieces of me with him.

I wear the dainty pink silk in my hair because I love it. But I also wear it because I know Jet loves it too.

After a final once-over in the mirror, I grab my dance bag from the bed, slip on my shoes, and head for the front door.

"Leaving for the studio," I shout to Reema as I exit the small hallway, unsure of her whereabouts.

"Love you," she shouts from her bedroom.

"Love you too," I holler back as I step outside.

Jogging to my car, I drop my bag in the passenger seat, crank the engine and air conditioning, and connect my phone. A moment later, an upbeat song blares from the speakers as I put the car in gear and drive toward the studio. Singing is not a talent I possess, but I belt out lyrics like a legendary pop star. I don't care who sees me or what they think; the energy boost is well worth the side-eye glances.

The playlist shuffles to a quieter, slower song. One I've heard several times and love. But something about hearing it now feels different. The lyrics nudge my subconscious and conjure abandoned thoughts to surface. As much as I want to shove them back down and bury them so deep they'll never resurface again, I let them resonate.

Per my therapist, the best thing to do when this happens is process my thoughts and feelings in the moment. Acknowledge the thoughts, feel the emotions, and breathe through each one as I unpack what they mean. Until I accept what is and what has been, I can't move forward.

So, I let the wayward thoughts in and soak up the way they make me feel.

I should give up on love.

The idea is a jab to the solar plexus. A self-inflicted, breath-stealing gut punch. A familiar frigidity winds itself around my spine, an unshakable bone-deep cold. I shiver but make no attempt to diffuse the sensation. Do I despise the way it makes me feel? One hundred percent, yes. But squashing the feeling, or the reason behind it, won't fix anything.

I detest my pessimism and loathe my sometimes-catatonic

heart, but the only way to change both, to grow, is to face it all head-on.

At a four-way stop, I inhale deeply, count to five, and exhale slowly. As my foot moves from the brake to the accelerator, I acknowledge and counter the thought. "You can't give up on something you haven't experienced. Not in the way you want or need."

The last guy—I think his name was Johan, but I honestly don't remember—was cute, funny, and flirty as hell. The night before Jet and June's birthday party, he stood behind me in the takeout line at Gigi's Italian. He asked what I ordered—chicken marsala—and shared how eager he was to try the pizza special —shrimp scampi with fresh mozzarella. Then he asked if I was eating alone, and I said yes. When my name was called for my order, he asked if I wanted to eat with him at the park. As I have with most guys, I said fuck it and told him I'd meet him there.

We ate and talked for hours, but I'd been enamored within minutes. He told me about his recent move to the area—he was from one town over—and how he tried to explore a new place at least twice a month. The ease of our conversation felt so natural. He ticked off so many boxes, but everything felt surface level.

So, I made a bold move and asked him to join me at Jet and June's party. I figured it was the easiest, quickest, and safest way to know if what I felt was right.

No surprise, my instincts were accurate as ever.

Johan's a nice guy, but he isn't a person I could spend more than a fun night with. And there is nothing wrong with that. There is nothing wrong with only wanting someone as a distraction for a limited time. Flings have their place, and I've had my share of them.

The guys I've recently been with, the public dates, they are all for show. A charade. A safety net to keep my true feelings masked.

But as time moves on, as I gain more perspective, I realize I need something more than a good time. I need someone who matters.

It's this precise moment that I pull into the studio parking lot and spot Jet's SUV. And as it has countless times, guilt gnaws at my soul.

I love Jet, and he is fully aware of this fact. But I've never given my love for him room to breathe or stretch its wings. I've never lain in bed, surrounded by silence, and let myself dig deep into what my love for him means. I've never fully let in what I feel for him because I'm scared of what I'll find.

Parking next to his SUV, I cut the engine, grab my bag, and cross the lot for the studio entrance. Peculiar, jagged music greets me when I open the door and step inside. The energy in the space is harsh and frantic and unnerving. I grip the strap of my bag tighter and clutch it closer to my chest as I tread lightly, slowly into the room Jet and I always use.

As the center of the room comes into view, I suck in a sharp breath as my gaze lands on him. In only a pair of muscle-hugging black shorts, Jet moves to the chaotic beat. Arms and legs bent in severe, unnatural angles, he contorts his body in ways I've never witnessed from him before. Warping and twisting, he skitters across the floor. Bends in half backward and stutters sideways in jagged bursts of movement. His body screams broken, possessed puppet. His energy shrieks darkness and pain. The dance is disturbing and evocative and… beautiful.

I can't take my eyes off him, nor do I want to.

When he pops upright, he spots me in the mirror. Eyes wide, he jolts in place, spins to face me, and looks momentarily panic-stricken. He jogs to his bag, grabs his phone, and cuts the music.

"Hey." The word comes out breathy and apprehensive as he drops the phone.

My brows inch up. "Hey?" I cross the room and set my bag next to his. "I walk in on the most… jarring and alluring dance I've seen you perform and all you have to say is *hey*?" I swap my shoes for my split soles. "What was that?"

Jet runs a hand through his now-shorter hair, and I can't help but watch the way his muscles flex and ripple at the action. Lips pinned between his teeth, he rocks his jaw back and forth once, twice. Then he releases those perfect, kissable lips and shrugs. "Just something I've been working on."

He says it so nonchalantly, like the choreography is no big deal. Normal.

It's a cloudy day. Mom's cat scratched me at dinner last night. I had scrambled eggs for breakfast. It's just something I've been working on.

Peeling off my shirt and yoga pants, I stuff them in my bag. "Any special reason?" I try my best to not come off as eager or nosy, but it's hard not to. There aren't many reasons to choreograph dance other than to perform. And to my knowledge, Jet doesn't have any stage time lined up.

He takes a hefty drink from his water bottle then shakes his head. "Watched a similar routine online and connected with it." Trading the water bottle for a towel, he drags the terry cloth down his chest.

Pulse whooshing in my ears, my eyes follow every single millimeter of the action. *Dear god, kill me now.* When my gaze returns to his face, there is no denying the scorching fire in his eyes.

I'd apologize, but I'm not sorry. Not in the least.

"Mm." The simple hum of acknowledgment is all I muster.

This curves his mouth into a salacious smirk. "I'll show you later, if you want. When it's just us."

"Yeah." I start toward the barre. "I'd like to see it."

Although he's already warmed up, Jet joins me at the barre. We fall into a trance as we move through stretches. The routine is monotonous and unremarkable yet soothing, like a cozy, warm blanket on a cold night or a hug from your favorite person.

Any time I think of dance or favorite people, Jet appears front and center. How can he not when he is both? But those aren't the only reasons he pops into my head nowadays. More and more, I get flashes of *him*.

How his lean, honed muscles flex and swell and bunch as he bows and twists his body. A thin layer of sweat on his skin highlighting and accentuating the peaks and valleys of his abdominals. The way every inch of him curves perfectly with every inch of me, as if his body was designed with me in mind.

But also how his tongue darts out to wet his lips. The slow bob of his Adam's apple when he swallows. How his long, dexterous fingers weave through his hair when he brushes it out of his face. The gentleness and fire and irrefutable need in his eyes when he meets my gaze. How he takes advantage of every opportunity to put his hands on me and ignite the embers under my skin.

The more time passes, the more intense and incendiary my feelings are for Jet.

And god, do I wish I was brave enough to do something about it.

But every time I gain an ounce of strength to take a step in the direction of more, the stupid voice in the back of my mind tells me I'll mess everything up. I've made countless stupid decisions, said plenty of hurtful things, and inserted doubt in every relationship —familial, friendship, and romantic. It's hard not to believe I won't screw things up with Jet too.

Letting Jet all the way in, reciprocating his affections openly, would be scary and soul fulfilling. If his love is potent now, it would be explosive and unstoppable were we together. Given permission to touch me or kiss me or whisper every single one of his greedy thoughts any time he wanted, Jet would turn ravenous. Feral. Relentless in the best, most delicious ways.

I shake off the thought and blink back to the present.

Not yet. Not until I'm ready. Not until I know I won't ruin us.

"Whatcha thinking about?" Jet singsongs.

Dropping my foot from the barre, I clasp the lacquered wood and kick my foot in front of me again and again. "Nothing." The lie comes out dry and squeaky.

He chuckles. "No, it's definitely something." Pointing at my chest, he circles his finger in the air. "You're all red and splotchy."

Maybe because I want to lick my way down your midline until I reach—

Nope. Not thinking about that right now.

I may have cut off the thought, but it's too late to hide it from Jet. The way his eyes flared a second ago as they roamed my face and neck... he definitely didn't miss the way my skin went from lightly flushed to on fire.

"Ooh." A devilish smirk plays on his face. "Now I really need to know."

Vehemently, I shake my head and look anywhere but at him. "Confidential." Lifting my hand to my mouth, I pinch my thumb and finger together, drag them across my lips, and pretend to throw away the key. "Sorry."

He stops his warm-up routine, drops the smirk, and moves until only inches separate us.

I gasp, my knuckles burning as I grip the barre for balance.

Infinitesimally, he lowers his lips to mine until only a breath exists between us. My heart thrashes in the confines of my rib cage, desperate to escape. Instinct whispers to close my eyes and push up on my toes. To close that last little bit of distance and taste him for the first time. But I can't take my eyes off his.

Hunger simmers in his steely grays, and I willingly let him devour me with a single glance.

If this is all I can give him right now, if this is all I will allow myself to have, then I will bask in every smoldering second.

"I see you," he confesses, breath warm and inviting as it paints my lips.

Anxiety bubbles in my chest as my pulse throbs in my neck, and I swallow. Jet has always been good at reading me, but I'm not ready for him to see *everything*.

Warm fingers graze my chin a beat before he lifts it, my lips skimming his just enough to light my soul on fire. Need ignites low in my belly, and I exhale a shaky breath.

"Your rosy skin and those tiny gasps..." His eyes roll closed for a heartbeat. "The way you lean into me and inch impossibly close…" His fingers drift along the line of my jaw and over my erratic pulse until they curl around the back of my neck and pin me in place. "You know it'd be good, don't you?"

I tremble in his hold but don't say a word. I don't need to. My answer is yes, and he knows it.

His lips caress mine for a fraction of a second that feels like a lifetime. Then his cheek kisses mine, his breath hot on my ear. "It's okay to admit how you feel, Shanti." He runs the tip of his nose along the angle of my jaw. "You're allowed to want me." A hum vibrates his chest as his grip tightens on my neck. "You're allowed to want more." The last word is a growl, an invitation, and a promise all rolled into one.

I press my palms to his chest and revel in the feel of his skin, the strong, vicious beat of his heart under my touch. I memorize his heat, the way his chest rises and falls faster and faster the longer my hands are on him. His reaction is a direct thunderbolt to my heart. A life-saving jolt to the soul. And before I can stop myself, I spill my confession.

"I do want you." My eyes close and pinch so hard, I see stars. Taking a deep, shaky breath, I meet his waiting stare. "I do want more."

His entire body comes alive. "Then have me, Shanti."

Tension tugs at my brows and my chin starts to quiver. "Not yet." The heartbreaking words are barely audible, but he hears them loud and clear.

Dropping his forehead to mine, his thumb strokes my jaw. "Why?" So much pain laces those three letters. Years and years of torment.

And it's all on my shoulders.

My hands slide down his body until I reach the start of those *V* muscles at his hips. I curl my fingers and anchor myself to him as if my life depends on it. Close my eyes and take a steadying breath. "Because I don't love myself." My rib cage cracks wide open, my heart tumbling to the floor. "How can I love you if I can't even love myself?"

"Open your eyes, Shanti," he whispers, his other hand cupping my cheek and framing my face.

Apprehension surges in my veins as nausea claws up my throat. I fear what I'll see in his eyes, but worry more over what I'll miss if I don't look. Slowly, cautiously, I peek up at him. The confidence and comfort I see in his gaze soothe the deepest scars on my heart.

"I know you love me," he says, voice gooey and warm and reassuring. "And I know you've been through a lot." His thumbs stroke twin lines of affection over my cheeks. "And I told you I'd wait."

I feel a *but* coming.

Of course, with Jet, there is no *but*.

"You're worth a lifetime of waiting, Shanti." His lips move back to my ear. "Never said I'd make it easy on you, though."

Scoffing, I lift my hands to cover his. "Please don't."

He inches back enough to roam my eyes, my nose, my lips with his fiery gaze. And then his lips are so close to mine, I practically taste him. "You have no idea what you just asked for."

TWENTY-EIGHT
INVITATION OF A LIFETIME
JET

PUTTING THE FINAL TOUCHES ON NEXT WEEK'S CURRICULUM, MY entire body sighs with relief as I set the pencil down. I love my job. I am more than grateful to do what feeds my soul every day. But the paperwork... zero tears would be shed if it magically disappeared.

I close the binder and set it next to my bag. Take a steadying breath and center my mind. Shift out of teacher mode and into my creative headspace.

Teaching the next generation has been a gift. A valuable reminder of why I love dance. Of why I slide on slippers or pointes and give myself over to the music. Dance isn't just something I do because it's fun or creative. For me, dance is vital. Monumental. Significant. It's in my bones, my soul—as essential and fundamental as breathing.

Since taking on this new role, I've seen a completely different side of the industry. The boring side. No wonder Neesa chooses one or two specific days a month to do the admin tasks. Paperwork sucks the joy out of everything.

Thankfully, I'm done with penning curricula for the next two weeks. Now, on to my favorite part and why I am here in the first place.

Digging my phone out of my bag, I open the music app and scroll through playlists. My thumb hovers over two, undecided which routine I want to run through first. With the studio closed today, I have free rein over the space and plan to take advantage.

Recently, I've used most of my free time to create new dances or simply vibe with a song or album I discovered and connected with. It's been my favorite new form of therapy. It's no secret I dance when I need an escape or clarity.

Until a couple months ago, I had always performed someone else's inspiration or choreography. As impactful as it has been, it's not the same as orchestrating the entire routine myself. What I do now is one-hundred-percent me, and it fulfills me in a way I never anticipated. If anything, my passion, ambition, and need to slip on dance shoes have grown tenfold.

Settling on a playlist, I set my phone down but wait to hit play. I slip on my pointes, secure the elastics, and wrap the ribbons around my ankles.

"Warm-up time," I mutter as I rise from the floor.

Over the next several minutes, I zone out as I stretch and warm my muscles. I move through the routine I've done for years with ease. And as it often does, my mind drifts to my favorite person. Shanti.

Her early appearance in the studio while I worked on a darker contemporary number last week took me by surprise. I'd been so lost in my head, so fixated on the beat and piece, I didn't hear her come in. When I met her curious gaze in the mirror, my heart spasmed then soared.

It hadn't been my intention to hide what had me spending extra hours in the studio. The plan was to show her the edgy dance when it felt done. For the most part, it is done. I'm working out a few kinks, which is a bit of a challenge when there's only one of me and the choreography is made with a group in mind. But like other dances I've composed, it's still a work in progress.

Muscles warm and ready, I reach for my phone, tap the first song on the playlist, set my phone down, and scurry across the floor. I reach the center a few seconds in and slip into the arrangement with ease. Move with the music and allow myself to deviate from the sketch I've created.

One of my favorite parts of the choreography process is I get to change whatever I want, whenever I want. If the routine doesn't flow, if it feels clunky, or if I simply don't like it, I have the final say. I can swap a move for another or remove it altogether. It's empowering.

Art is subjective and thought-provoking. What one person loves about a piece, another may despise—a normal, human reaction. Either way, art should be emotive. Titillating. Immersive. Art should speak to your soul. It doesn't always need to be profound, but it should make you feel *something*.

That I am in control of someone's reaction to my art is powerful. That I have license to tweak the emotional scale is monumental.

Free time in the studio has been an opportunity to experience my passion with new perspective. I'm fortunate to have such wonderful mentors and bosses who encourage my creativity. Who encourage me to feed my soul on the dance floor. Without Neesa and Aurelio's praise and support, I wouldn't be who or where I am today.

One with the music, I circle the floor in a series of widespread leaps. When I reach my next mark, my feet shift into second position just before I hinge my hips and bow forward. Chest inches from my thighs, I sway left then right, my arms rippling like gentle waves. As I roll up out of the move, the song shifts, turns harsh.

As the last of my spine straightens, I pop up on my toes. Snap my arms out wide. Bring my feet together and cross the room in a series of rapid, tight steps. I thrust my torso forward and back, my arms ebbing and flowing with each move.

And as it does most times when I dance en pointe, my mind drifts to Shanti. When I slip on these shoes, when I make power and strength look ethereal and graceful, when the muscles of my ankles burn slightly and toes sting, I picture her. Poised and agile. Formidable and exquisite. It's the vision of her that pushes me harder. How she makes something so demanding on the body appear elegant and willowy.

Then my thoughts transition—still on Shanti, but in a different context.

In this illusion, she is in my arms. Warm and soft. Curves and limbs molded perfectly to mine. It starts as a familiar dance but quickly morphs into something else. Something more… provocative.

Hands and lips on skin, kissing and bruising. Fabric dragged down curves and slowly, delicately peeled off bodies. Pebbled nipples and breathy sighs as teeth mark flesh and tongues taste.

"Fuck," I groan as I halt, my heels dropping to the floor. Hard as stone, I reach down and attempt to adjust myself in my dance belt. Of course, it's pointless.

So, while I wait for my body to calm down, I shift my focus. Shanti remains front and center, but the momentary pause has me thinking of her in a new light.

Can't quite put my finger on it, but something about Shanti is different. The shift was subtle, gradual. Covetous glances she shied away from less often when caught. Amorous touches she leaned into more than before. For a time, I thought my mind was playing tricks. That I projected my desires to a marginally intimate moment.

Until the day she surprised me with her quiet voyeurism.

On that specific day, a whisper of yearning scratched the surface of her gaze. Desire simmered beneath her skin. Each point of contact sparked with more fire.

Disregarding the insatiable chemistry pulsing between us is futile. My feeble attempts to resist Shanti and the future I want with her have become harder to ignore.

So, I made a bold move. I invaded her space, threw caution to the wind, and put everything on the line.

Her reaction... gods, it was everything I needed yet still not enough.

Patience. Just a little more patience.

In the end, the future I envision with Shanti is worth every setback, every fiery exchange, every ache. Because she loves me too. Honestly, I think she has loved me longer than she will admit —to me or herself.

The invisible tether I felt early in our friendship has been through countless trials. Tugged at viciously. Dragged through proverbial mud. Frayed and worn so significantly, I questioned how much it would withstand. Frequently, I feared it would snap. I worried I would lose Shanti for good.

But with each chafe of our bond came a wave of healing energy. A new opportunity to grow and move forward.

Many call me foolish for the amount of time and energy I've given Shanti. They say I'm naive. Stuck in a distorted fantasy. And maybe they're right. Maybe I've been fixated on this dream existence with Shanti so long, I've lost sight of reality.

But what if they are wrong?

What if I've been exactly what Shanti needs when she needs it?

What if all our trials have been a test? What if we are still being tested? In the end, isn't the endurance and flexibility of our bond what matters most? Isn't it significant to know anything can be thrown at us and we'll come back stronger?

In some regards, I may be a fool. A lovestruck idiot who only sees Shanti through rose-colored glasses. But I'd rather be smitten and hopeful than indifferent or pessimistic. That's just how my heart works.

A song I hadn't noticed started ends. I cross the room, pick up my phone, and tap on a random playlist. Rather than practice choreographed routines, I opt for freestyle and escapism.

Hitting play on the first song, I lock my phone and drop it in my bag. Then, I let the music guide me. Let the occasional deep thump of bass rattle my bones. Let the distinct trill of a string instrument zip through my bloodstream. Every thud becomes a stomp. Every zing makes me twirl or kick or fly.

As one song fades into the next, I pause long enough to connect with the beat. Then, I soar. I detach from reality and assimilate with the music. Over and over, I get lost in a new fantasy. Allow my mind to create a new world from the melody and how my body reacts to it.

More than a dozen songs play before the tinkling of the bell on the studio door hits my ears. For a beat, I redirect my attention. Listen beyond the music for familiar sounds. When I rise up on my toes, the first recognizable taps filter past the song. A smile tugs at the corners of my mouth, and I don't fight it. As I slowly lift a leg, toes headed straight for the ceiling, Shanti enters the room. I have yet to look her way in the mirror, but I know it's her.

I always know when she exists in the same space. I always will.

Over the next forty-seven seconds, I resist the urge to stop dancing before the song ends and go to her. Instead, I make each move count. Thrust every ounce of energy into each step.

When the song fades, I relax into first position, take a deep breath, and glance at her reflection. Distracted by her phone, she fails to notice I've stopped dancing to take her in. These precious seconds are rare, so I take full advantage of them.

While she scrolls, I roam the captivating lines of her profile. The delicate slope of her nose and soft pillow of her lips. *Gods, I could kiss that mouth forever.* Swallowing, my gaze drifts down, down, down until I reach her supple curves. Irresistible curves I want to memorize with my fingers and lips and tongue.

As my gaze dips lower, her body stiffens. My eyes immediately fly to hers as unease stirs in my belly. When I find her eyes still fixed on her phone, relief soothes my anxiety. But it doesn't last long.

Knuckles blanched, her fingers painfully clutch the phone. I have no idea what has her upset, but I want to rip the phone from her hands and tell whoever to fuck off.

Instead, I play it cool. One foot in front of the other, I cross the room, inhale a slow, methodical breath, and stop within inches of her. "Wasn't expecting to see you today?"

That came off unruffled, right?

Two drawn-out heartbeats pass before she gives a single shake of her head and looks up. "Hey." Her brows pinch then relax. "Yeah, I know." Another shake of her head. "Sorry if I interrupted."

Bending, I grab my water bottle and towel. "Not at all," I say, dragging the towel over my face and down my torso. I nod toward her phone. "Everything okay?"

On an audible exhale, she locks her phone and shoves it in her bag. "Just strangers being shitty online. Nothing I should let bother me." After what feels like hours, her gaze clicks with mine. She swallows, and I love the instant satisfaction that floods my body with the single action.

Downing a third of my water, I drop my towel, cap the bottle, and return it to my bag. "I ignore the comments section most of the time. It's the only way to maintain my peace."

"Wish I had your self-control."

I bite the inside of my cheek to not laugh. She has no idea how much self-control I have. The day I lose it…

"Are you sure I'm not intruding on your time?" Worry dances in her golden-brown eyes.

Invading her personal space, I pinch her chin between my thumb and finger and lift until I'm all she sees. "The only intrusion you are is a welcome one." I skate my fingers down the side of her neck, pausing on her collarbone. "A very welcome one."

Last week, I told her I wouldn't make this waiting game we've gotten ourselves into easy for her. And she literally told me not to.

So here we are. Toe to toe. Her shaky, warm breath painting my lips. A thick, pulsing fog of tension and need closing in on us. Me edging us closer and closer to what we both want.

I must admit, I never expected to enjoy this. But tempting Shanti, gently coaxing her, softly and slowly seducing her… It's the most beautiful brand of torture. One I've taken immense pleasure in.

A shiver ripples through her a beat before goose bumps prickle her skin. "Okay," she says barely above a whisper. "I..." Her brows pinch then relax. "I just need to dance."

Dropping my gaze, I follow the path my fingers take along her collarbone. "Mm, I get that." Inch by painstaking inch, I drag my fingers back to her throat, up the length of her neck, curling them around the back as I cup her cheek with my palm. "Want to be alone?"

Say no.

With a slow shake of her head, she whispers, "Never."

I open my mouth to ask what she means by never but am cut off by the click of heels coming from outside the room. Dropping my hand, I straighten and put a modicum of distance between us, but I don't step back.

"Oh, good," Neesa says. "You're both here."

Shanti blinks and the fog around us evaporates. Against every deeply rooted desire in my bones, I take a step back and turn to face Neesa, only she is not alone.

Every muscle in my body locks. A chill blankets my skin. And no matter how much I assure myself everything is okay, my stomach groans and twists, nausea rioting to escape.

A painful beat passes before Shanti moves to stand in front of me, fierce and protective. Straightening her spine and squaring her shoulders, Shanti lifts her chin and makes herself tall and formidable.

It makes me love her more.

Oblivious to my discomfort, Neesa scurries forward, stopping an arm's length from Shanti. Neesa brings her hands into prayer at her lips, a giddy smile tugging at the corners of her mouth. "I found out the other day but waited to tell you." She practically vibrates with excitement. "I wanted it to be a surprise."

Considering Vivienne Bellecourt is here when her name hasn't appeared on any class itineraries, I am most definitely shocked by her appearance.

"Wanted *what* to be a surprise?" Shanti asks, an edge to her words.

Neesa glances over her shoulder, and I follow her line of sight. Aurelio stares at his wife, a monumental smile stretching his face and pride shimmering in his eyes. He gives her a swift nod, and she turns back to face us.

Vivienne has yet to utter a word, and I don't know why, but that bothers me more.

Neesa bounces on her toes. "You've been invited to this year's West Coast Ballet Competition." Her entire body is a beacon of joy.

Were I Neesa, I'd feel the same. Having any of your dancers invited to one of the biggest, most prestigious ballet competitions in the United States is a prodigious triumph. She has every right to be proud and thrilled.

Not to be rude, but I need to know. "Why us?"

Most wouldn't question why they were invited. They'd simply accept, practice until their toenails cracked and bled, and perform on stage as if they were the best.

The only problem is Shanti and I haven't graced a stage in years. We haven't put ourselves out there to be seen by the committee members who invite dancers. For years, we've been on our own and teaching future ballet dancers.

Us being invited makes no sense. It'd be odd for us *not* to question it.

Neesa drops her hands as confusion wrinkles her forehead. "I'm sorry?" She tilts her head and narrows her eyes.

Keeping my eyes aimed at Neesa and Aurelio, I gain back some of my strength and find my voice. "Why us? As enormous as this honor is, our being chosen isn't logical."

Shanti reaches back, takes my hand, and gives it a squeeze. A subtle form of encouragement and silent message of agreement.

"We haven't performed on stage or in the studio for anyone in years." My gut clenches in preparation for my next words. "Please don't take this the wrong way, but it makes me suspicious." I finally bolster the confidence to look at Vivienne. "And if I'm honest, it also makes me very uncomfortable."

"Jet…" Neesa's confusion immediately morphs into concern.

I hate it. More than anything.

Years ago, I promised Shanti I'd find a way to tell my parents, Neesa, and Aurelio how I felt when Vivienne visited the studio. How her proximity, her inspection, her physical contact made me unsettled and nauseous.

But I never came up with the right words. I never garnered the confidence. Never made the time. And when Vivienne didn't return the following year, or the one after that, I let the subject go. As more time passed, I dismissed all thoughts of Vivienne Bellecourt.

Obviously, I made a mistake.

Because now I see a long list of questions forming in Neesa's eyes. Questions I will no longer be able to avoid answering.

The first question Neesa offers is silent, but I hear her loud and clear. *Can we talk after this?*

I give her a single, almost imperceptible nod, and she does the same.

Neesa's shoulders rise with a deep inhale. "I understand your hesitancy and skepticism." Her frame relaxes, but not fully. "But when the committee reached out, they were curious why two of our star pupils from years ago simply disappeared."

Okay, *that* seems legitimate. It's rare for dancers like me or Shanti to not move forward with a top-tier ballet company. It's a natural transition for dancers with our skill set. Although we are far from the best, our talent is irrefutable. Our chemistry on stage is pure magic. So, it's plausible for previous generations to wonder where industry prospects went.

As long as the inquiry isn't from Vivienne Bellecourt.

"We told them you are still dancing, but spend more time teaching in the studio now," Neesa says. "They were delighted to hear your talents hadn't gone to waste and extended an invitation for you both to attend the event."

Neesa laces her fingers in front of her, the epitome of calm. But her gratitude and exhilaration for this opportunity radiate off her aura in orange and yellow waves. To have your students selected is an honor and privilege. Whether or not we accept, Neesa will be proud her pupils were chosen.

"If you say yes, it's a ten-day, all-expenses-paid trip." Her eyes widen as her brows shoot up. "You're not required to perform, but they'd be honored to see you on stage. A few committee members asked you to judge the competitions."

Attend? It's an opportunity of a lifetime. Hell yes, I want to go. Although neither of us is with a company, it'd be incredible to connect with others in the industry. Network with nearby schools and companies. Build a rapport with others for when dancers from Rhythm and Flow are ready to take the next step.

Dance? Maybe. If we both say yes, Shanti and I will need to sit down and discuss it. I have no issue dancing for a crowd. But do I want to perform as a contestant? I don't know.

Judge? I'll admit, the idea sparks interest. I need more details to decide, though.

"Do we have time to think about it?" Shanti runs her thumb over my fingers.

Neesa glances over one shoulder at Vivienne, then shifts her attention to Aurelio. Neither gives anything away. When Neesa turns back to us, her sympathetic wince is answer enough. "Unfortunately, we need an answer today."

Why does it feel like *we need an answer now* is more accurate?

Eyes forward, body still shielding me from Vivienne, Shanti nods. "Will you give us a moment alone?"

Neesa reaches for and takes Shanti's free hand with both of hers. "Of course." She jerks her head toward the door. "We'll wait in the office. When you've decided, come find us." Neesa steps closer to Shanti and lowers her voice. "If you don't want to go, that's perfectly acceptable. Please don't think we're pressuring either of you." Her eyes dart to mine as she mouths, "Later."

I nod.

Pivoting on her heel, Neesa walks off, hooks her arm with Aurelio's, and leads them out of the room, closing the door behind them.

For the first time since I noticed Vivienne in the room, I take a deep breath. As I release it, fire roars in my veins. After all these years, it pisses me off that this woman still gets under my skin. It pisses me off that she keeps showing up.

Why the hell can't she stay away?

Releasing me, Shanti spins around, takes both my hands, and lowers us to sit. "You never told them about Vivienne, did you?" Not an ounce of frustration or accusation colors her tone. She simply wants to know so she doesn't say the wrong thing.

"No." I shake my head. "I kept putting it off. Then, she hadn't been here in a while." I shrug. "Guess I thought she wasn't coming back, so I dropped it."

Shanti rubs soothing strokes over my knuckles with her thumbs. "Makes sense." She gives both hands a gentle squeeze. "But you're going to tell them now, right?"

As much as I don't want to, I need to tell Neesa and Aurelio everything. The last thing I want is for any of the children under my care to experience what I did. Vivienne's actions were subtle and didn't blur the lines enough for me to confidently think an adult would believe such a heavy accusation without solid proof. But as I've gotten older, as I've gained perspective, I now know what she did and how she made me feel was wrong. Very wrong.

I won't let it happen again.

"Yes." My heart rattles my rib cage as my breaths come quicker. "When she leaves, I'll talk with Neesa and Aurelio." I swallow past the sudden dryness in my throat. "And I'm going to ask them to not allow her back in the studio."

"Good." Shanti leans into me, drops her forehead to mine, and takes me by surprise. "You deserve to feel safe here. You deserve to always love this place. I won't let her taint it for you."

Warmth and affection bloom in my chest. The panic from seconds ago fizzles out. "Thank you."

"You don't need to thank me, Jet. You'd do the same for me in a heartbeat."

Without a doubt.

"Now, about the invitation." She leans back to sit up, and I miss the intimate contact immediately. "Do you want to go?"

Lifting my gaze to hers, I twist my lips and narrow my eyes. "Yes," I answer, dragging out the word and drowning it with indecision. I sigh. "Saying no feels foolish. Who knows if we'll ever have the chance again. I'd hate for either of us to miss out."

"But do you *want* to go?"

I roll the question around in my head. Really think on it. After only a few minutes, I know without a doubt I want to go. Vivienne may be part of the reason we were invited, but I won't let her ruin this for either of us. I won't let her win.

"Yes," I say with nothing but confidence. "I want to go."

Shanti squeezes my hands. "Then I guess we better pack."

TWENTY-NINE

ROAD TRIPS ARE FUN... AREN'T THEY?

SHANTI

"Jesus. Do you plan on staying forever?"

The suitcase wheel catches on an uneven floorboard, and I stumble then quickly correct before going face-first toward the floor. Pausing and collecting myself, I meet Reema's gaze and arch a brow. "Maybe I should."

Reema waves a dramatic hand at the large suitcase, carry-on, overstuffed duffel, hanging garment bag, backpack, and cross-body bag now piled by the front door. "You're definitely taking enough."

Making a show of looking at the luggage, I hum. "Am I, though?" I tap my lips with a finger. "I ditched several things on the packing list." My eyes meet hers again. "Hope I don't need them."

A snort of laughter floats through the room. "Even if you do, could you possibly fit more in Jet's SUV? He needs space for his stuff, too."

"Ha ha." I roll my eyes. "There's enough room for at least three times this with the back seats down."

As Reema opens her mouth to poke more fun at me, a knock at the door cuts her off. *Thank goodness.*

Stepping around the luggage, I fling the door open and smile.

"Perfect… timing." My mouth goes dry at the sight of Jet, and I swallow.

The man makes a T-shirt and jogger shorts lethal. And that's saying something since I've seen every single one of his…curves in the second-skin attire he wears at dance.

"Morning." A corner of his mouth quirks up in a roguish half smile. "Ready to go?"

"God, I hope so," Reema needles.

Jet turns to Reema and gives her his full, radiant smile. "Hey, Reema."

"Hi, Jet. Excited for the trip?"

"Definitely." He stuffs his hands in his pockets. "We haven't decided if we're dancing yet. But it'll be nice to connect with others in the industry face to face."

"Sounds dull."

Jet laughs. "No doubt. But it opens up more opportunities for us and the studio."

"Well"—Reema gestures to my mini mountain of travel gear—"good luck and have fun."

Jet takes my backpack and duffel and loops them over a shoulder before grabbing the handle of the big suitcase. "Is there more in your room?" It's an honest question with zero ridicule.

"This is it." I peer at Reema and flash her my sassiest *fuck you* smile. "But *someone* seems to think I packed too much."

Gaze darting between us, Jet snickers. "Nah. I have just as much, and my stuff folds up smaller."

Like a child, I stick my tongue out at my sister. "See. This is barely scratching the surface."

With a roll of her eyes, she says, "Whatever." She follows us to Jet's SUV and hovers like the true mother-figure I never had. "Don't forget to check in."

My chest warms. "I will."

When Jet takes the carry-on from me, Reema hauls me into a breath-stealing hug. "Tonight, tomorrow, and throughout your trip."

I hug her back with equal strength. "Promise."

"Take lots of pictures. I want to see and hear about everything."

Loosening my hold, I try to wiggle out of her arms. "So many pictures you'll be sick of looking at them."

"And have fun. Enjoy yourself. Experience the city." She finally releases me but keeps me at arm's length. "I love you."

The backs of my eyes sting as I nod. "Love you, too." I tip my head toward the car. "We should get on the road."

With a nod, Reema drops her hands and folds her arms over her chest. "Drive safe."

"Always," Jet vows as we head for either side of the car.

Buckled in, we give one last wave to Reema and drive away. A few minutes later, Jet turns onto a very quiet Granite Parkway. I roll down the window and breathe in the crisp morning air. Prop my arm on the door, my chin on my forearm, and close my eyes as the breeze rolls over my skin. One breath after another, I soak up the sudden sense of peace I feel.

And it's not until this very moment that I realize how much I need this. Time away from life.

When I open my eyes, we're a block from the only traffic light in town. The sun has barely crested the horizon. We've passed more pedestrians than cars, and even that hasn't been many.

"If you're good with it, I thought we'd get breakfast when we stop for gas in an hour or so."

Turning, I rest my cheek on my arm and stare at Jet. One hand on the bottom of the steering wheel, the other on his thigh, he leans back into the seat, completely at ease with himself. Then again, Jet has always been like this. Mellow. Comfortable in his own skin. Patient yet ready for anything.

He peeks over at me and smiles. "What?"

Instead of telling him how incredible he is, I shake my head. "Nothing. And breakfast after gas is perfect."

Minutes later, we pass the *Now leaving Stone Bay* sign, and this weight I didn't know I was carrying lifts off my shoulders. For the first time in too long, I breathe easier. Feel freer.

We may have gotten this opportunity at the suggestion of a horrid woman, but I'm happy, nonetheless. I can't think of a better person to take this trip with, to see and explore a new place with.

In Northern Portland, we stop for gas. Jet asks me to search for restaurants nearby while he fills the tank then grabs us water from the store. Back in the car, I give him the address for a breakfast place people rave about.

Less than ten minutes later, the scent of maple syrup, bacon, and buttery pancakes hit my nose. "Oh my god," I moan out. "I haven't even seen the menu and I want one of everything."

Jet chuckles as we approach the host. He holds up two fingers. On the next breath, we're weaving between tables for a booth in the corner. The fast-paced energy in the small restaurant steals the last of my morning grogginess.

"I'm ordering extra," I say as my eyes scan the menu. "I'll eat leftovers for lunch on the road."

"I like this plan."

We place our order, and the server looks at us like we've lost our minds. Maybe we have, but who cares?

When the plates hit the table, we share and eat a little of everything before boxing up the rest. As quickly as we arrived, we walk out the door with three boxes and two to-go cups of iced caffeine.

With a groan, I rub my belly as Jet pulls onto the highway. "We need to go there again someday."

In my periphery, a smile stretches wide on his face. "Yeah?"

"Mm-hmm." I twist in my seat to face him. "We need to splurge every now and then. Treat ourselves."

Wouldn't think it's possible, but his smile brightens further. He glances at me for a split second then returns his eyes to the road. "Another excellent idea."

The hand on his thigh moves up and down, over and over, and I'm momentarily distracted. Lost in the way his fingers curl and stroke his quads.

What else can he do with those hands?

"Shanti," he singsongs as if this isn't the first time he's said my name.

"Huh?" I flick my gaze to his and note his devious smirk.

"I said you should make a running list of places we see but don't stop at. That way we don't forget about them." He chuckles under his breath.

My cheeks heat, but I don't look away from him. Don't shy away from my embarrassment. It's pointless.

Digging my phone out of my cross-body bag, I open the notes app and tap to create a new one. Fingers flying over the screen, I title the note: Road Trip Must-See List.

"Done." I lock my phone and stow it in the interior door handle. Tucking a foot under my butt and bending the other in half, I lace my fingers and hug my leg to my chest.

Music plays in the background as the miles disappear. My eyes dart right to left and back again, taking in the sights and soaking up this new-to-me place on our trip. Every once in a while, I snap a picture or add a place to our list.

I've visited big cities before, years ago, with my parents, but I was either too young to remember or didn't do anything that made the trips memorable. Most of those trips were work-related. The only reason Reema and I went was because our parents couldn't find someone to watch us at home. There was no excitement. No lists of restaurants or tourist traps to see. No wandering the streets or marveling at how different the city was from our small town.

Until now, every trip I've taken has been drab and insignificant. Uneventful and unremarkable.

I'm glad my first real expedition is with Jet. He makes everything better. Extraordinary. Cherished.

Jet taps the volume button on the steering wheel and lowers the music. "Anything specific on your must-see list in San Francisco?"

A smile tugs at the corners of my mouth as I turn to look at him. I haven't made an official list, but I did look at a few things online. "Touristy places, of course. Golden Gate Bridge, Alcatraz, Lombard Street. The pier has lots of shops and restaurants, but I didn't research much on those." Thrill courses through my veins as I think about the buzz of city life, the bright lights, and all the places to see. "What about you?"

He chuckles. "A lot of the same. But I also want to hike a couple trails. Explore with no destination in mind. Maybe visit a museum. Eat at a restaurant that's only in the city."

I like his list.

"I love Stone Bay," he says. "So many good things have happened to me there."

I wilt slightly in my seat, wishing I had as many happy memories of Stone Bay as he does. As if he senses my dejection, Jet reaches over the console and lays his hand on my thigh. My body heats. Tingles prickle where his fingers slowly stroke and squeeze. Perspiration licks my skin, my pulse throbbing wildly in my ears.

With a single touch, he soothes the ache and drives me wild.

A quick glance in my direction, he says, "Stone Bay is where I found you. How can I not love it there?"

We've only been gone hours, and I'm already putty in his hands. *Fuck*. By the end of the trip, who knows what state I'll be in.

Needing a moment to cool down, I ask a question I should already know the answer to, but don't. "Have you traveled before?"

He licks his lips, the corner of his mouth fighting a smile. Damn him for knowing exactly what I'm doing.

"Not much, but yes." His chest shakes with a soft laugh. "Mom was invited to a metaphysical conference slash retreat in the middle of nowhere, Colorado. The organizers didn't say you couldn't bring anyone, so we all went. Five days of chakra healing, aura reading, crystal work, and more." He titters as he shakes his head. "Was definitely an experience."

"I bet."

"That was our biggest trip. We did some long weekends at amusement parks and national forests. Mom was big on getting us away from screens and staying in touch with nature."

Without thinking, I shift my leg, and his hand slides higher up my thigh. Not wanting to draw attention or make things weird, I don't move again. But I want to. And not to shift his hand back where it was.

I swallow in an attempt to wet my suddenly dry mouth. "I love your mom."

His thumb swipes back and forth, over and over, stoking the fire he lit. "She loves you too, you know."

A different warmth floods my chest. An affection I've only experienced with Reema, Jet, and the Fox family. "I do." The backs of my eyes sting and nose burns. "I'm grateful I have you... all."

"Goes both ways." His fingers flex slightly, enough to make me stop breathing for one, two, three heartbeats. "I'm glad this trip came up."

Oh, thank goodness. A topic change. "Me too."

His thumb strokes lazily on my thigh, up and down, again and again. For a blip, he peeks at me out of the corner of his eye. "What better way to explore a new place and experience new things than with you?"

It hasn't been half a day and I'm on the cusp of jumping him in the driver's seat.

Yeah, I'm fucked.

Hours later, the map guides us off the highway toward the hotel. My eyes dart from one building to the next, soaking up the sights. Chain coffee shops and grocery stores. Every possible type of fast-food place I've seen more commercials for than stepped inside of. A variety of pubs, breweries, and nightlife entertainment. Locals and visitors wander the sidewalks on their way to dinner or a night out. More cars on the road than I usually see in a day in Stone Bay.

It's a lot to take in and a bit daunting, but I love it.

I can't wait to see more.

Before long, Jet turns into the lot for the hotel. Two stories, the exterior is plain and ordinary, but clean and recently painted. Every other window on the first floor, shrubs break up the parking lot from the sidewalk of the guest rooms. It's far from luxurious, but perfect for what we need—a place to rest our heads for the night.

Stopping under the canopy by the office, Jet puts the SUV in park but leaves it running. "Be right back."

While he checks us in, I glance across the street at the restaurants and mega grocery store I've only heard about but never been in. We're only in Medford for the night, but part of me is twitchy to explore, even if only a few blocks. I want to absorb as much of this small city as time will allow.

Before I forget, I send Reema a quick text to let her know we arrived at the hotel.

Slipping into the driver's seat, Jet hands me the room keys as he buckles his seat belt. "We're near the end on the first floor."

At least we'll have one less neighbor and a better chance at decent sleep.

Backing into the parking space in front of the room, we grab what we need for the night. After almost a full day of driving, all I want is a hot shower, dinner, and to fall asleep watching random television with my favorite person.

"Anything you want for—" The question dies on my tongue as Jet pushes the door open and we're greeted by one bed in the cramped space. I swallow past the sudden dryness in my mouth.

At least it's a king. As if the bed being large will keep us apart.

Jet steps inside and holds the door open. Muscles relaxed and demeanor easygoing, he is the epitome of calm. But I don't miss the faint twitch of his lips. The momentary hint of a smirk.

Did he know? When he checked in at the front desk, did they tell him there was only one bed in the room?

I clutch the strap of my bag tighter, narrow my eyes and give him my most menacing glare as I walk past him.

Under his breath, he laughs.

Troublemaker.

Ignoring the bed, I set my bags down by the small table and chairs. After we take turns in the bathroom, I pace the room, pull out my phone, and check out the food options. "Any thoughts on dinner?"

"Whatever looks good." A faint *whoosh* filters through the air, and I know without lifting my gaze that he's on the bed. "Maybe something we can order ahead and bring back to the room. Don't feel like sitting in a restaurant."

Yeah, I get it. After a day in the car, neither of us wants to be in a busy restaurant. The main reason I'm pacing is to move. My body isn't usually so sedentary.

Sifting through options, I land on a place with potential. "What about Asian fusion?"

"Perfect." Jet pats the bed.

I pause midstride and turn to face him. His cheekiness from earlier is gone. In its place, exhaustion. Faint shadows dust the underside of his eyes. Propped on the pillows, he is so relaxed he could fall asleep any moment. And it's seeing him so spent that has me climbing up on the bed and sitting within inches of him.

We take a few minutes to browse the menu. After we put in our order for pickup, Jet swings his legs off the bed, slips on flip-flops, and tells me to wind down while he grabs our dinner.

The moment his SUV pulls out of the space, I riffle through my bag, grab my toiletries and pajamas, and head for the shower. As desperate as I am to stand under the hot spray for an hour, I make quick work of washing head to toe. Once we reach San Francisco, I'll indulge in a longer shower or soak in the tub if there is one.

Dressed in sleep shorts and a tank top, I'm working my damp hair into a messy bun when the door opens and Jet steps in, a brown bag and two water bottles in his hands. I don't miss the stutter in his stride when he locks on to me in different clothes.

He swallows, crosses to the bed in two lengthy strides, and sets the food and drinks down. Without a word, he moves to his duffel and pulls out a small bag and a change of clothes. Bundled in the crook of his elbow, he rounds the bed and heads for the bathroom, pausing at my side. Heat radiates off him like a cozy fire I want to lean closer to.

"Start without me. I won't be long."

Before I respond, he slips into the bathroom and shuts the door. Within seconds, the rush of water from the shower echoes through the walls.

I exhale the breath I was holding, my entire body sighing.

"Get your shit together," I berate myself as I climb onto the bed, grab the bag of food and empty it. "He's your best friend, for crying out loud."

Jet has seen me in next to no clothes that hug every curve of my body, and vice versa. But the way his eyes roamed my body in basic pajamas... It felt like he was peeling each layer off and slowly devouring me.

Slipping under the covers, I sit up in bed, lean against the pillows, and tug the fabric to my waist. Arrange the food, crack open the containers, and distribute the napkins and cutlery. As the shower cuts off, I reach for the television remote and surf the channels for a worthy distraction while we eat.

When *Legally Blonde* fills the screen, I thank the heavens. A light and funny movie to break up the sexual tension lingering in the room is exactly what we need.

Loading my fork with noodles and vegetables, I bring it to my lips as the bathroom door opens. Mouth agape, my eyes fix on Jet and the dangerously low way his sweatpants hang off his hips. A hint of a tattoo peeks out of the waistband. And of course, he's shirtless. Random dots of water emphasize the defined muscles of his abs, flexing and bunching as he dries each delicious inch of skin.

Thoroughly distracted, the food slides off my fork with a *plop* and splatters sauce on the covers. "Shit." I drop my fork and grab a napkin.

Jet chuckles as he runs the towel over his hair. "Slippery." His tone is teasing as he tosses the towel aside, pulls back the covers, and slides into the bed.

"Shut up," I say, trying and failing to sound annoyed.

He offers me more napkins, and I shove his hand away. It only makes him laugh harder. "Just trying to help."

"Mm-hmm. Sure you are." I ball up the dirty napkin and toss it at him.

Eyes narrowing, a mischievous smile tugs at his lips. "Do that again and there will be a lot more to clean off this bed."

I stop breathing at his insinuation. Go utterly still and silent. His comment may be completely innocent, but a quiet voice in the back of my head says it isn't. Not with all the delicious torture he has been delivering as of recent.

Rather than fumble over a response, I tuck my lips between my teeth, nod, and turn my attention back to my food. I pour every ounce of attention into securing my food on my fork so as not to have another incident.

Dinner passes with the occasional laugh at the movie and a few crumbs on the bed from the spring rolls. When we finish, Jet gathers our trash, stuffs it in the brown bag, and sets it next to the small trash can. After a quick wave of the covers to knock the crumbs off, he slips back into the bed and stretches out next to me.

With each passing minute, I become more and more *aware* of Jet.

A light sheen of sweat paints my skin as the temperature beneath the blanket gets hotter and hotter. My pulse beats harder, louder as an ache builds between my thighs. The movie carries on, but I miss every second. Hyperfocused on the man next to me, the occasional shift of his leg or arm, it feels like he is too close yet not close enough.

Although he's seen me in far less and the blanket is tugged up to my neck, I feel exposed. Bare. Naked. In the same breath, I want to tear off my clothes and crawl on top of him. Take his mouth with mine. Tear the sweats down his thighs. Show him with my lips and tongue and hands and body another way I love him.

Balling my fingers into fists, I pinch my eyes closed and take the quietest, deepest breath possible. Mentally shake off my wandering thoughts.

This is not the time. A mediocre hotel room is not the place to explore your feelings or cave to your hormones.

Jet deserves more than a spur-of-the-moment tryst on a bed hundreds of people have slept in. He deserves the perfect buildup to a monumental moment—the sweep of gentle fingers over every inch of his body, kisses that go from soft and sweet to harsh and combustible, whispered words that are equally as arousing as any physical act. Hours of foreplay until one or both of us are ready to detonate.

The longer I sit with this thought, the more I cool off.

Don't get me wrong, I still want him. I still want to mount him and kiss him until my lips and tongue are numb. Get lost in him and forget about the world as we discover a new side to *us*.

But tonight is not that night.

So, I turn my attention back to the screen and focus on the movie.

I startle when the room goes quiet, and a hand runs up and down my back in slow, gentle strokes.

"Shh." He presses his lips to the top of my head. "You're okay." More soothing strokes. "You fell asleep. The movie just ended."

"I fell asleep," I mumble, thoughts foggy.

"Yes." Jet shifts slightly, then the room goes black. "Go back to sleep."

Subtly, I nod and close my eyes. "'Kay."

As I start to drift off again, my mind suddenly registers that I'm lying *on* Jet. At some point after I dozed off, I got extra cozy, curled up to him, and rested my cheek on his shoulder. The realization erases my exhaustion and has my mind reeling.

Beneath me, Jet relaxes more. His breaths turn quiet, shallow. But he doesn't release his hold on me. If anything, he strengthens it. Secures me to him.

Minutes feel like hours as they pass, and my mind just won't shut up.

So, instead of fighting what I feel, instead of resisting what I want, I give in… to a degree. For tonight, I let go and simply *feel*. I relish the hard lines of his body. Revel in the way he pins me to him, needing me close even in sleep. Bask in his warmth and gentleness. Savor the peace and love I feel only with him.

And with that final thought, I drift off.

THIRTY
I WANT TO HOLD YOUR HAND

JET

A HINT OF DAWN PEEKS THROUGH THE SPLIT IN THE CURTAINS AS I open my eyes. For a moment, I stare at that sliver of light. The way it cuts through the room and makes the dust particles in the air sparkle like specks of glitter. The sight is ethereal and peaceful, but nowhere near as magical and comforting as my current situation.

Sweeping my gaze back to the bed, bone-deep solace floods and warms me as I stare down at Shanti. Curled into my side, her gentle breaths warm on my chest. Arm draped over my stomach, her hand is tucked between my rib cage and the mattress, anchoring her to me.

My fingers itch to reach up and brush the fallen strands of hair from her cheek. Caress from her temple to her chin. But I stop myself.

Rather than disrupt her sleep and lose this moment, I visually trace her features while she sleeps. Roam the softness of her light-brown skin. Take in this rare glimpse of her repose. Every few breaths, her dark lashes flutter, and I can't help but wonder if she is dreaming about me or us. My gaze drops to her slightly parted lips—two full, soft, pillowy lips I've wanted pressed to mine for years.

Closing my eyes, images flash behind my lids. Fantasies I've had countless times, but have done little to make a reality. But the start of almost every one of these wishful moments is me framing Shanti's face with my hands and getting lost in the feel and taste of her mouth.

On a slow, deep inhale, I open my eyes and come back to the present. To reality.

For now, I will settle for this. Shanti in my arms and clinging to me like a life vest. Until she is ready to take the next step, I am content with these small progressions.

Shanti loves me, but she needs time to love herself, to be happy on her own, to feel confident in her choices. Most of her life, she wasn't gifted the opportunity. I refuse to be the person who takes anything else from her. I won't rush her. Everyone deserves the chance to grow or improve without additional pressure or stress. Finding the light after being in the dark so long is hard enough; the last thing she needs is to be hounded to do it quicker.

"My beloved Shanti," I whisper so softly I barely hear myself.

When I turned off the television last night and she stirred from sleep, I silently pled with the universe for her to not pull away and move to the other side of the bed. And by some miracle, she stayed.

Those hour-long minutes between when I switched off the lamp and fell asleep, my heart thrashed in my chest. I did everything within my power to calm the wild, unruly organ. Meditative breathing. Recalling hikes and landscapes that brought me peace. But the one thing that finally made it settle was that Shanti didn't leave my side. Before I drifted off, I'd swear she burrowed deeper. In that singular moment, I felt more whole and balanced than ever.

And with her cheek still on my chest, with her body practically wrapped around mine, I can't help but return to my fantasy world. The place where I curve my hand around hers and she strengthens the hold. The place where we dance in the streets, where we kiss in the rain, where we tease each other and laugh often. The place where I tell her I love her, and she returns the sentiment without any sense of obligation. In this place, she tells me she loves me with ease and equal affection.

One day, this won't be all in my head. One day, Shanti and I will love freely for all to see.

Against every fiber of my soul, I shift in the bed. Just enough to disturb Shanti's limbs. Enough to make her groan the most adorable sound I've heard.

I love that she doesn't want to get up. That she doesn't want to peel herself off me. That she wants to stay like this longer.

Finally, I have the perfect reason to touch her. I bring a hand to her face and brush the hair from her cheek, gently tucking it behind her ear. I lightly sweep the back of my fingers along her jaw to her chin. Every molecule of my makeup comes alive at the feel of her.

Perfect. She is absolutely perfect.

Dropping my lips to her hair, I breathe her in then whisper, "Time to wake up."

She groans louder, and I smile.

I have no qualms about staying exactly like this. But the moment she wakes fully, the second reality hits her, she'll turn self-conscious. She'll apologize profusely for cuddling. She'll fumble over lame excuses as to why we should've been up and on the road already.

And I'll let her get it off her chest. I'll give her space to rush around. Then I'll assure her we are on schedule—not that we need to be in San Francisco by a specific time tonight.

I press another kiss to her head. "Someone's a sleepyhead."

"Mm," she moans.

"Can I tempt you with pastries, bacon, sausage, or caffeine?"

Twisting, she buries her nose in the crook of my neck and complains against my skin. But I don't hear a word.

All I can think about is her lips on my body. All I can focus on is how good it feels—her heat, her softness, her body perfectly curved with mine. My pulse soars. My chest rises and falls faster. And because I want more, so much more, all the blood rushes to my cock.

Before my next breath, my erection pitches the bedding. I could fight it, I could think of dozens of boner killers, but I don't want to. Shanti does this to me. She makes me feel. And for a moment, I want to live in this bubble of love and lust.

She wiggles away enough to push up on her elbow and meet my gaze. "You never fight fair." A lock of hair falls in her face, and she pushes out her bottom lip and blows it away. Only, it falls right back in her face.

Fucking adorable.

I swallow down the desire to fist her hips, flip her onto her back, and press my hard length between her thighs. "Nope." The single word comes out gruff and needy. "And that's not changing anytime soon."

Shifting her weight, she scoots up into a seated position. Although the room is still somewhat dark, her vision has adjusted enough to see *everything*. Her momentary pause speaks louder than words. She may not be looking directly at my groin, but she is fully aware of my need for her right now.

Ducking her chin, she swallows and inches away. "Sorry."

My hand finds her thigh under the covers, my fingers curling to anchor her in place. "Don't apologize."

Silence engulfs the room for one, two, three painfully long seconds before she nods and meets my waiting gaze. "Okay." Another nod. "Should probably get ready."

I soften my hold on her leg and give her warm skin one last stroke before pulling back. "Yeah." I sit up. "Let's get out of here."

Bags in the car, we stop at an artisan bakery not far from the hotel. Loading up with a couple breakfast sandwiches, a box full of pastries, and lattes of choice, I plug in the address for our next destination and head for the highway.

We eat in relative silence, occasionally sipping on our caffeinated beverages and slowly waking up. But I can't help but question the awkward silence that follows after we've crumpled our sandwich wrappers. Usually, I welcome the quiet with Shanti. Usually, it's easy, almost therapeutic.

But this is not that. And I don't like it.

"Should we play a game?" I blurt, needing some form of human interaction.

She turns her head just enough to take in my profile. "Huh?"

"A game."

Her relentless stare heats my face as another mile passes. Still, she says nothing. Then another mile.

I open my mouth to tell her to forget it, but she cuts me off.

"I've never played games in the car."

Sadly, this doesn't surprise me. Shanti's parents weren't the type of people to engage in frivolous fun or games to pass time.

Reaching over the console, I rest my hand on her exposed thigh. "Lucky for you, I have." I spend the next few minutes sharing the road trip games I played as a kid. Not wanting to overwhelm her, I elect to start with the easiest game. "Pick a car color."

Shanti twists more fully in her seat to face me. "Hmm. Gray."

Popular. That should make things interesting. "Okay. Now, pick a car brand."

She brings a finger to her lips and taps a few times as if this decision could alter her life. After a moment, she says, "Subaru."

I bite the inside of my cheek to fight a smile. She literally just picked *my* car. No matter.

"Okay, here's how it works." I peer at her for a split second then return my eyes to the road. "Every time you see a gray Subaru—doesn't matter what shade of gray or what type of Subaru—you shout *gray Subaru*. Whoever says it first and is right gets a point."

"How many points do we need to win?"

I shrug. "We can pick a number, but it should be high. It's a long trip."

In my periphery, she nods. "What about fifty? Or is that too low?"

"Fifty is a good start." I lift a finger from her leg and point to where her phone is stashed. "Should probably keep a tally in your notes or something."

"Good idea." She grabs her phone and taps the screen several times before locking it. "Ready," she declares.

Now, I set my smile free as I shout, "Gray Subaru."

Her eyes dart everywhere, scanning the handful of cars nearby. "Where?"

I give her thigh a gentle squeeze. "You're sitting in it."

She playfully swats at my arm. "No fair. Your car shouldn't count."

"Hey, I don't make the rules."

"Mm-hmm," she hums, tone sardonic. "Sure."

The next couple of hours pass a little faster. We both call out and point at gray cars on the highway, some of them the correct make, others not. After I rib Shanti profusely for calling it on several wrong cars, I jokingly say points should be deducted for saying it for other cars. This leads to Shanti giving me endless shit about every mistake I've ever made.

Keeping my mouth shut, I smile so wide my cheeks sting.

After a quick rest area stop, we dig through the box of pastries and snack until we figure out where to stop for lunch. While Shanti searches the map on her phone for restaurants, her knee begins to bounce. When I glance her way, she has her bottom lip trapped between her teeth.

I strum my thumb back and forth on her thigh. "Everything okay?"

Her lip pops free as she turns to glance at me. Her slight hesitation says a lot, but I wait her out.

"So, I've been thinking…"

When she doesn't continue after a moment, I prompt, "About?"

She audibly inhales, holds the breath for a beat, then exhales. "I think it's time to move out of Reema's." It all comes out in a rush, but I hear every word.

I get the sense this puts her on edge. "Is everything good between you two?"

"Yeah." She nods. "Of course."

"Okay." My thumb strokes her skin, back and forth, again and again. "I only ask because you sound nervous at the idea."

"Oh." She clamps her lips between her teeth and rocks her jaw side to side a few times. "Well, I am a little nervous. It's a big step. One I haven't taken before."

I peek over at her just as she winces.

"Let me rephrase," she says. "It's a big step I haven't taken after putting a lot of thought into it." She toys with the bottom hem of her shirt. "I don't like to think about… before."

Without saying his name, I know she means the situation with Blaze. He lured her in, tempted her with all the right promises, and essentially fucked up her life.

I'm not the type of person to usually say horrible things about others, but Blaze was a piece of shit.

Not wanting to make her more uncomfortable, I skirt the subject of *before*. "In a way, I get it. Not fully, considering I live in a guesthouse on my family's property. I guess what I mean is it's always tough making these types of decisions. Whatever you choose impacts so much in your life."

She wilts a fraction. "Yeah," she mutters, somber.

"Hey." I wait until I feel her eyes on my profile before I continue. "If you're not ready, then stay with Reema until you are."

From the corner of my eye, I see her nod.

"If you still want to move out"—I swallow past the nervous

lump building in my throat—"there are... other options." *Just spit it out already.* "You can always move in with me." On those last four words, my heart jolts then thunders in my chest. "Unless you don't want to." My nerves are fried, and I can't seem to stop talking. "No pressure. I just thought—"

Shut. Up. You goddamn idiot.

Holy. Fucking. Shit. I basically asked Shanti to live together.

What the hell was I thinking?

I wasn't. That's the problem. Every time I'm around Shanti, all the rational parts of my brain malfunction, and I blurt out the first thought I have. It's usually this undeniable impulse to do whatever it takes to make her happy. To make her life better.

But is it the right thing to do? How the hell would I know? I'm just going off what I feel. And with Shanti in my orbit, those emotions surge off the charts.

The car feels several degrees hotter. The air thick and suffocating. Like I'm in some dark, eerily silent, severely low-oxygen, humidified version of a deprivation chamber.

It fucking sucks.

And then, she surprises me.

"What about June?"

I try my damnedest to hide the shock from my expression. Because that was nowhere near what I expected her to say.

"They recently moved out." *Breathe, Jet.* "The weekend after our birthday, they moved in with their girlfriend."

Shanti abruptly twists in her seat, and my hand slides dangerously high up her thigh. I should move it, but every cell in my body screams to keep it right where it is. But if she moves my hand, I will respect her wishes. If she asks me to move it, I will without complaint... out loud.

"Since when does June have a girlfriend? Let alone one they've been with long enough to move in with?" Bewilderment and a hint of sadness lace her voice.

I try to soothe her with a gentle squeeze to her inner thigh.

"June's pretty private. The only people who know about their girl-friend are family. I guess more people know now that they're living together. But they've been dating about two years."

"Wow." The touch of melancholy from a moment ago is gone. "Two years." Shanti shakes her head. "I had no clue."

"You're not alone." I tap the brakes as we approach heavy traffic. "Think about what I said. But seriously, no pressure. I won't be upset if you say no." Bummed but not upset.

"I will." Shanti turns slightly and surveys the traffic. "Should we exit and eat? Maybe the roads will be better in an hour or so."

Master of changing the subject. Not that I fault her.

"Good idea. If the next exit looks promising, we'll take it."

Not far from the hotel, I steer us off the highway and wind through the city. We stop at a bistro with an array of options. In no rush to get stuck in traffic, we take our time and chat with the server about places to see while here. The whole experience is a perfect introduction to the area.

By the time we leave, traffic has thinned considerably. We make it to the hotel in under a half hour and pull up to the valet. Glittering lights and shiny fixtures snare my attention immediately. From the spotless marble floors to the perfectly manicured plants and floral arrangements to the art on the walls, this place reeks of prestige and wealth.

It makes my skin crawl.

After a quick stop at the concierge desk, we obtain our keys and take the elevator to our floor. As we step out of the elevator, I gesture for Shanti to walk ahead while I push the luggage cart. Halfway down the long hall, she stops in front of our door, holds the key card to the reader, and unlocks it.

The room is dimly lit as we head in, but from what I can see from the foyer, it's extravagant. More than just a room to sleep in, it appears to have a kitchenette and a small living room. It's more space than we need, but I won't complain since I'm not footing the bill.

I wheel the cart into the main part of the room and freeze. My nervous system flies into overdrive. My pulse all but screams in my neck.

For the next week, Shanti and I will share a bed. Again.

And I couldn't be fucking happier.

DID I REALLY DO THAT?

SHANTI

"Be right back." Pajamas and toiletry bag clutched to my chest, I slip into the bathroom and shut the door. As soon as the latch clicks, I sag against the door, tip my head back, and audibly sigh. Closing my eyes, I silently ask the universe if it's trying to torture me… in the best possible way.

This is going to be the longest week of my life.

And I have yet to decide if that is a good thing.

On a deep inhale, I open my eyes and drop my chin. Then I push off the door and cross to the vanity. Set my bag and clothes beside the sink, plant my hands on the counter, and lean in toward the mirror.

"You can do this," I tell myself. As if a pep talk is what I need. As if a pep talk will actually help.

I give myself another moment to sit in this dizzying swirl of emotion. Then I lift my hands from the counter, grab my pajamas, and go about my nightly routine.

Hair in a messy bun, face cleaned and moisturized, I gather my dirty clothes and exit the bathroom. "Wonder how much it—"

All the air is sucked from my lungs as I take in Jet on the bed. Dressed in low-hung sweatpants and nothing else, my brain short-circuits as I stare and stare and stare.

"What?" He peers up from the paper in his hands. As his soft-gray eyes roam my face, a corner of his mouth kicks up in the half smile that makes my heart all fluttery and wild.

Swallowing, I blink out of my Jet-induced haze and force my feet to move toward my luggage. "Wonder how much it costs to do laundry in this fancy hotel."

Paper crinkles as Jet hums. "According to this long list of amenities, if we have the hotel do it for us, it's three times as much if we do it ourselves."

"Triple?" I stuff my clothes in the luggage laundry bag and turn to look at Jet.

Waving the paper in his hand, he nods. "Mm-hmm. Everything on this list is at least triple normal prices."

With my eyes on his—because I don't trust myself to look at any other part of him right now—I cross to the bed and crawl onto the opposite side, keeping a couple feet between us. "I'll do it myself, thank you very much."

Jet shrugs. "If you have the hotel do it, the fee gets charged to the room."

What he doesn't add is charging it to the room means we don't have to pay. Since our presence was requested, we were promised a free trip. Of course, anything not in our prearranged budget for meals and fuel is on us. As is any exploring we do in our free time. But all normal costs associated with our stay are covered, including laundry.

I grumble under my breath. "I don't know." My nose and lips scrunch. "It's weird to have a stranger do my laundry."

He hums. "I get it. Wouldn't want some rando touching my panties."

Temporarily invading his space, I playfully slap his arm. "Now I'm definitely doing my own laundry."

Bottom lip pushed out in the fakest pout I've ever seen, Jet rubs where I hit him. "Always slapping me around."

I roll my eyes a beat before I extend an arm to shove him. But I never make contact.

Reflexes quick, he grabs my forearm and tugs me forward… into him. One second, I'm on my side of the bed. The next, I'm halfway in his lap.

Yep, I am definitely not going to make it a whole week.

The rims of his gray irises darken as he holds me close. So close, his warm, minty breath paints my lips.

God, I want him. My lips on his. His fingers memorizing my body. His weight over me, pressing into me, consuming me. Or him under me, my mouth and hands and body staking their claim on him.

His eyes dart between mine, asking hundreds of silent questions. And for a single, wild beat of my heart, I think he can read every thought I have. That he *knows* I want him so fucking desperately I can barely breathe.

Undiluted need pools between my thighs as the pad of his thumb strokes my bottom lip.

"One day, I'm going to bite this lip. Suck it so hard, you'll feel me for days."

I love and loathe the way his words make me whimper. The way my entire body ignites under his touch. The way a deep ache burns low in my belly and dampens my panties.

The corner of his mouth kicks up in a devious half smile. "But not tonight." Taking my chin between his fingers, he shifts to press his lips to my forehead. "Tonight, we're ordering dessert from room service." He releases me and inches back, and I immediately hate the added distance. "We'll need it to review our itinerary."

Right. The competition. The reason we are here to begin with.

I scoot back, sit a little straighter, and do my best to not think about the needy throb between my legs. "What's on the menu?"

Jet twists, grabs a small binder from the nightstand, and hands it over. "There's an entire section of desserts."

Opening the binder, my eyes widen at the number of tabs. I've never seen so many menu sections in my life. A tad overwhelmed,

I flip through several tabs at a time until I reach the one labeled *dessert*.

"Uh…" My vision blurs as I read the selection. Confections I've never heard of or can't pronounce. But what really makes me dizzy is the price. "Maybe we should order something through a food delivery app. This is…" A rip-off. Obscene. Mind-boggling.

"Ridiculous?"

I nod. "That's one word for it." I jab a finger at the cheapest dessert. "A scoop of vanilla bean ice cream is ten freaking dollars." My brows shoot to my hairline. "And if you want toppings, each one is an additional two."

"Shall I choose?" Jet holds out his hand.

Unable to decide, I happily forfeit the task. "Please. And next time, just give me the options without the prices."

Jet chuckles. "If that's what you want."

"It is."

Jet scans the dessert menu one last time. Hopping off the bed, he goes to the phone on the desk and dials the number for room service. Voice low, he talks far too long to order one thing. It feels like minutes before he hangs up and walks back to the bed.

"Did you order every dessert?" I tease with a laugh.

"Nah." He resumes his seat but leans back on the pillows. "But I did order a few things, just to see what they are."

He probably spent fifty dollars on freaking dessert.

Quit worrying about it. If they don't want us ordering room service, the company should've been clearer in their allowances for the trip.

Mirroring Jet's position, I work to forget about the things I cannot control and focus on the present.

We are in San Francisco. Just me and him. No nosy townsfolk to snoop and blather baseless, fictional stories about us. No family members to *check in* and ask not-so-inconspicuous questions about what we're up to. For the first time, it's me and Jet and the endless possibilities we've danced around for years.

I'm equal parts thrilled and terrified. On this trip, everything could change.

A knock at the door startles me from my introspection. Jet shoots up from the bed, grabs a shirt off the chair I hadn't noticed, and tugs it over his head as he goes to answer the door. Seconds later, he comes around the corner with a loaded tray in his hands.

"Oh my god." I bolt up on the bed and cross my legs. "That's enough sugar for days."

Chuckling, Jet sets the tray down and slides back into the bed. "Yeah, maybe I went overboard." He shrugs. "But they all sounded good, and it was hard to decide." He grabs the spoons and hands me one. "We'll order less next time."

Next time. By the time we leave, I have no doubt we'll have tried the entire menu.

While we read over the company's itinerary for the week, we devour thick, creamy custard with chocolate-covered fruit in the center, a mini pistachio-rose bundt cake with the freshest whipped cream, sprinkled pistachios and dried rose petals, and chocolate drizzle, and a puffed pastry stuffed with bananas, berries, and mousse that is a literal work of art. At least eating dessert makes reading about the boring parts of our trip easier.

Now that we have the official schedule and know when we're needed during the competition, we can plan our free time. I grab the hotel pen and notepad from the desk and hand them to Jet. As we finish dessert, he scribbles down which outing we'll do during each break. By the time he takes the tray to set in the hall, we've mapped out the *must-see* items.

"Channel surf?" Jet peels his shirt off and tosses it on the chair before coming back to the bed.

I can't tell you how many times I've seen Jet shirtless over the years. Hundreds of times. Possibly a thousand or more. Until recently, it's never affected me so wholly. Until now, I've never dreamed of every possible way to trace the lines shaping his muscles. With my fingers and nails. With my lips and tongue.

God, just the sight of him, the flex of his lean muscles as he walks, the dexterous way his fingers fumble at his sides... the ache between my legs from earlier flares back to life.

I need help.

"Yeah," I croak out then swallow. "Sounds great."

He doesn't hide his smirk as he swipes the remote off the nightstand. Rather than swatting him again and possibly creating another situation where we're a breath from kissing, I wiggle under the covers and scoot closer to him. Jet clicks through several channels before stopping on *The Golden Girls.*

Peeking up at him, I arch a brow. "Really?"

Don't get me wrong. I love *The Golden Girls.* Who doesn't? Four women speaking their minds and living life to the fullest. I can only hope I'm half as incredible, hilarious, determined, and brave when I reach that age.

Jet returns the remote to the nightstand and hums. "Blanche is a firecracker." He dips his chin toward me and waggles his brows.

The loudest snort-laugh rips from my chest as I shake my head. "True." When my laughter fades, I turn on my side, tuck my hands under my cheek, and stare up at him. "But we all know Sophia is the real gem. Bossy. Candid. Witty. Gives no fucks about people's opinions of her."

Without warning, Jet reaches over, wraps an arm around me, and hauls me into his side. "So you want to be sassy and domineering in your golden years?"

I yank a hand out from under my head and smack him midchest.

Wrong. Freaking. Move.

Jet captures my wrist before I'm able to pull my hand away. In a blink, I become hyperaware of my surroundings. The fire in his gaze as he stares down at me. The thin layer of bedding pinned between us all but vanishes. The television volume turns to white noise. Every single point of contact, every place our bodies connect, sparks and heats and pulses. Need and ache build and bloom low in my belly.

He lays my hand on his chest just above where I slapped him and sets his hand atop mine, effectively pinning it. One breath, then another, and another pass before he breaks eye contact and looks up at the television.

I close my eyes and count my breaths. Will my body to cool down. Beg my hormones to fucking relax. And once they level out a little, I open my eyes and look at the television. Focus on four sassy women and *not* where my body touches his.

"You know," he says as he shifts and gets more comfortable. "This week could be a test run."

My eyes refuse to meet his. "For what?"

"Living together." The two words roll off his tongue so easily, so casually. As if living together is no big deal.

Maybe to him, it isn't.

But for me, it's monumental.

"Oh." My quiet response lacks enthusiasm, but not for the reasons he may think. Believe me, I would love an easy, happy, simple life with Jet. A life filled with love and memories, laughter and dreams, adventure and the good kind of chaos.

I have no doubt a future with Jet would be extraordinary. Unforgettable. Sublime.

But am I ready? Before I say yes, I need to be sure.

Because I refuse to lose him. And if I mess us up, if I do something idiotic or reprehensible, I will break us forever.

"This isn't me trying to pressure you." Back and forth, ever so slowly, his thumb caresses the back of my hand. "I guess what I'm saying is we've been forced to live in close quarters for a week. It's long enough to get a glimpse of what it may be like to coexist in the same space."

"So this is my chance to see how messy you really are," I say, needing to lighten the conversation.

Jet scoffs. "Yeah. Not that you'll be surprised by the result."

He may not be a perfectionist, but I know with absolute certainty he is tidy. Organized. The type of person who only keeps trinkets or notes, or memorabilia if it holds meaning for him.

"Hmm, you're probably right." I tilt my head and wait until his gaze locks with mine. "But I've heard horror stories about friendships dying a painful death once they became roommates." I swallow past the sudden swell of emotion in my throat. "And I don't want that to happen to us."

"I wouldn't let it." Conviction weighs his declaration.

God, I wish it was that easy. "How?"

"Shanti, you mean *everything* to me. If romance isn't in the stars for us, I'll accept it. Eventually." His hand on my back shifts to the curve of my waist. "I want you in my life. Always. But if we figure out we're only meant to be friends, so be it." He rolls his lips. "You know I want more. I want all of you. But I won't lose you for selfish reasons." Lifting his hand from atop mine, he cups my cheek. "I love you. So fucking much. But my feelings shouldn't dictate yours. Okay?"

Utterly speechless, emotion pools in my mouth. The backs of my eyes sting. All I can do is nod.

With unparalleled tenderness, his thumb brushes my lip. Then he leans in and drops a kiss to my forehead. When he pulls away, a soft smile curves his mouth.

"Funny story about roommates..." He chuckles under his breath. "June and I have always been in sync. Literally. Science would say it's a twin thing." Pausing, a contemplative look crosses his face. "But when it was just the two of us in the guest-house, it was different."

My brows pinch together. "How so?"

"The littlest things would bug me, and vice versa. Until it was only us, I never paid attention to how they did mundane tasks or chores." His chest rises and stays for a moment. "When you like things a certain way, it's easy to get frustrated when someone in your space does them another way." He shrugs. "I'm pretty easygoing, but I'm not immune to exasperation. As far as first roommates go, June was probably the best one for me. I'm sure they'd say the same. We taught each other how to be more patient and compassionate. That you can be irritated with those you love and still resolve the issues if you talk them out."

Curling deeper into his side, I rest my head on his shoulder. "I bet nothing you do would bother me." It comes out in a whisper but sounds like I'm yelling it from the tallest mountain peak for all to hear.

And then, my hand on his chest drifts lower. Before I over-think what's happening, I trace down, down, down the midline of his abdomen until I reach the waistband of his sweatpants.

A hiss echoes through the room as Jet sucks in a sharp breath.

Slowly, I inch toward his hip, the ink I have yet to see peeking out and tickling my curiosity. But before my fingers trail over the tattoo, he takes my hand in his.

"What are you doing, Shanti?" His voice is thick and gravelly. Deep. Carnal.

The air crackles as I tip my head back and meet his gaze. The usual softness of his gray irises is nowhere to be seen. In its place is molten steel rimmed with fiery pewter. And god, I want to see just how hot I can make them blaze.

After years of pent-up frustration, after countless what-ifs, I want to feel my lips pressed to his. I want to taste him. Want to hear what sounds he makes as I deepen the kiss. Want to memo-rize the way his hands roam and fingers bruise as he hauls me closer and wordlessly begs for more.

Undeniable, potent need pulses between us as I lift my head from his shoulder and push up on my elbow. Inch by painfully slow inch, I close the distance from my mouth to his. Give him every chance to stop me. To push me away. To say now isn't the time, that this isn't the place.

Chest rising and falling faster with each breath, he doesn't move. Doesn't say a word. He simply watches me and waits.

As his breath paints my lips, as his heat warms every inch of my skin, I ignore the voice of doubt. Closing my eyes, I erase the final shred of distance between us and press my lips to his.

Warm and soft, Jet moans as he kisses me with confidence. The perfect amount of pressure, his lips move in time with mine. Slow. Sure. Capable. He tilts his head the other way. Takes my mouth at a different angle. Kisses me with unrivaled tenderness. Love. Devotion.

I melt into him. Get lost in how perfect this is. How perfect *he* is. His lips, his hands, the soft moan he made when our mouths first met.

He tilts his head again, his hands coming to my cheeks and cupping my jaw. Years of want and hunger boil to the surface. We both move faster as greed surges.

Beneath my thigh, he's hard.

I want to reach for his sweats and wrap my fingers around his length. Feel how thick and hard and big he is. Memorize his reaction to my kiss, my touch, my need for him.

But I don't.

As Jet's lips part, as his tongue darts out and licks the seam of my lips, I gasp and inch back. Against every desperate, ravenous cell in my body, I break the kiss.

"Sorry," he mutters between ragged breaths.

I shake my head. "Don't apologize." I fist the sheet. "You did everything right."

His thumbs stroke my cheeks. "Open your eyes, Shanti."

Swallowing, I do as he says. And when I lock on to soft-gray irises—not molten steel—my pulse soars anew.

Did I just fuck this up?

A moment ago, he wanted me. I saw it in the fire in his eyes.

But now, those same eyes are gentle. Tentative. Maybe a little concerned. Like I'm a scared animal who needs to be approached slowly and with caution.

I shove away from him, spin around, and bolt from the bed for the bathroom. He says something, but I don't hear him as the door closes and I flip the light and fan on.

Covering my face with my hands, I curse myself. "What the hell did I just do?"

Hour-long minutes pass as I edge near a panic attack in the

bathroom. After several deep breaths, I make it to the sink and splash my face with cold water. Once I've settled enough to go out and face my foolish decision, I give myself yet another pep talk.

Straightening my spine with more confidence than I feel, I turn off the light and exit the bathroom. I don't look directly at Jet as I move through the room, but I feel his eyes on me. Staring. Waiting.

Covers pulled back, I slip into bed and maintain an obscene amount of distance between us. Jet still hasn't said anything, but his stare heats my profile.

Needing to say something, I blurt out, "We have a busy day tomorrow. Should probably get some sleep."

Ugh, what is wrong *with me?*

"Yeah." He nods in my periphery. "Okay." He inhales audibly. "Good night."

The backs of my eyes sting, and I work to keep the emotion out of my voice. "Good night."

This feels wrong. So wrong.

Why can't I be normal for once? Why can't I let myself have who I want?

Jet turns off the television then the lamp. Shifting the pillows, he settles near the middle of the bed, not hugging the edge like me. Because, unlike me, Jet isn't scared to take the next step. He isn't afraid of his feelings.

Irritated with myself, I tuck the covers tighter around my neck and stare at the ceiling, dimly lit by the bathroom nightlight. Inspect the slight texture of the plaster as I count the number of dimples in the stucco. When I reach forty-seven, Jet's breathing changes. Turns softer. Quieter.

He's asleep.

For the first time since I broke the kiss, I breathe easier. Because if Jet was upset with me, he'd still be awake. He'd toss and turn all night. He'd try to talk and figure out how to make things better.

But he's asleep, which can only mean one thing. He may not know why I freaked out, but he isn't upset.

He still loves me.

With that thought, I ease across the bed and curl into his side. Nestle in the crook of his neck and breathe him in. And just as I drift off, he wraps an arm around me and whispers against my hair.

"Love you."

THIRTY-TWO
ESCAPE SEEMS IMPOSSIBLE
JET

WITH YESTERDAY BEING A HOLIDAY, OUR FIRST OFFICIAL DAY AT THE competition was a meet and greet and tour of the facility. Were it any other event, I'd likely have been bored. But not at the West Coast Ballet Competition.

To say this is an opportunity of a lifetime is an understatement. Yesterday, I shook hands and spoke with some of the biggest names of my generation in our industry. Although I consider them elite, world-class athletes in ballet, they interacted with me and Shanti as equals. Being in their presence was an honor, and they treated us with the same respect.

Coordinators of the competition sat down with us and reviewed our itinerary one more time. Thank goodness they did. Shanti and I are slated to judge several events, but not as many as we assumed. This gives us more free time and alleviates some stress. And after agreeing to go on stage, the committee shared a video of the routine they'd like us to perform the evening before our last day. They also gave us free rein to adjust it to our personal style.

Let's just say the title of the routine feels a little too fitting right now.

Midnight Lovers.

Since our kiss two nights ago, things between me and Shanti have been... different—in a good way. She seems less guarded when I move in closer or take her hand, or flirt with her. To some, her reaction would be no big deal. Insignificant, perhaps. To me, though, the subtle change means everything.

I have waited what feels like an eternity for this moment. The day when the planets align and the stars shine brighter. The moment when Shanti gifts me a bigger piece of her heart and lets me in further.

"Am I making us late?" Shanti calls from the bathroom, a hint of panic in her voice.

I glance from the muted television to the clock on the nightstand. If we leave the room in the next five minutes, we'll still have time to mingle before the first dancer takes the stage.

"We're still good, but should head out in a few."

Her sigh echoes through the room. "Swear I'm almost done." She steps out of the bathroom, her fingers weaving her ponytail into a braid. "I overheard the artistic director tell the photography crew they wanted lots of pictures. Of the dancers, the instructors, the judges. Everyone." She pauses between me and the bed and ties off her braid. "I just want to be perfect."

The last word has me shooting up off the bed. In two quick, lengthy strides, I'm within inches of her. Lifting her chin with a finger, I bring her amber gaze to mine and wait until I have her full attention.

"You are perfect."

She opens her mouth, undoubtedly to argue, but I cut her off with a shake of my head.

"Nah-ah." I lean in closer, the tip of my nose grazing hers. "We all have what we consider to be imperfections. But when I look at you, Shanti, all I see is perfection." I drop my mouth to hers and steal a chaste kiss. "You are perfect," I repeat with every ounce of reverence and affection I feel for this woman. "Perfect."

Shanti melts in front of me, her shoulders relaxing as she leans impossibly closer. "What would I do without you?"

I stroke her chin with my thumb. "Let's never find out."

With a subtle nod, she steps back. "We should go. I may not be the most punctual person, but I'll be damned if I make us late to this."

After I turn off the television and lights, we double-check we have our room keys, phones, and other necessities. Less than a minute later, we're in the elevator and descending to the ballroom floor. When the door opens, chaos hits us.

Hundreds of people fill the grand foyer. A cacophony of chatter and music floods my hearing. Dancers and instructors scurry from here to there, photographers hot on their heels to capture behind-the-scenes candids. Chairpersons and judges stand off to the right, clipboards in hand, huddled together and chatting as they survey the scene.

I take Shanti's hand and guide us toward the huddle. "Over here."

"This is"—she tightens her grip on my hand—"pure mayhem."

She isn't wrong.

As much as I love dance, a small part of me is glad I never went on to compete. Not that there is anything wrong with a little dance rivalry. It's just not my thing.

I didn't choose dance; it chose me. So when I put on slippers or pointes, what I do in those shoes is more about beauty and art over accolades and applause. When I'm on the dance floor, I feel alive. Whole. Free.

For me, that feeling is enough.

Weaving through the crowd, we reach our group. Greetings are exchanged, then Shanti and I are handed clipboards and instructed which room we'll be judging in today. Not a minute later, a voice calls through the foyer, alerting everyone to get to their destination.

In a blink, the crowd disperses and the foyer empties. From calamity to peace in under a minute.

"Feels like I should be impressed at how quickly that happened," Shanti says only loud enough for me to hear.

I lean into her. "Agreed."

My eyes survey the room as we step inside. To the right, a makeshift stage has been erected with curtains and lights and a black backdrop to separate the backstage area. On the left, dozens of chairs mimic theater seating, likely for coaches or family of the dancers. In the middle, a grand table with chairs, water, microphones, and name placards sits waiting for the judges.

The untrained eye would have no idea this setup is temporary. The hotel and crew did an incredible job mirroring a theater setting.

"Jet. Shanti." Whitney, one of the judges, waves us over. "Have you met everyone?" She gestures to the small group at the table.

"Not everyone." Shanti hugs her clipboard to her chest.

Whitney makes brief introductions, pointing to each person as she does. "Jude, Ira, Taylor, this is Shanti and Jet. They're joining us from Rhythm and Flow in Stone Bay, Washington."

Ira rests a hand over their heart. "Neesa and Aurelio are truly wonderful. It's been too long since I've seen them."

Before either of us responds, the overhead lights flicker, signaling a minute until the first performance.

"Let's chat over lunch," I offer to the table, and everyone nods.

Then the lights dim, and we critique our first ballet competition.

———

"You didn't feel awkward?" Shanti pops up on her toes, hands trailing up her body as I step up behind her. "Not even a little weird or jealous?"

I clutch her hips as she raises her arms above her head. "Not really."

She peers at me over her shoulder, rolling her body against the length of mine. "Seriously?"

My hands dip down the outside of her thighs then glide up, slowly, hungrily, until my fingers curl around her waist. "Yes." I duck my chin to hover within an inch of her shoulder and trace the curve of her neck with my nose until I reach her ear. "Seriously."

Shanti lifts her left foot from the floor, bends it at the knee, and brings her toes to the opposite knee. Slowly, I spin her in place. When she faces forward again, she kicks out her leg and creates a wave motion with the limb.

"Did it make you uncomfortable?" I prod as we transition to the next move.

Likely lost in thought, Shanti goes silent as we practice the choreography for our *Midnight Lovers* performance. I give her whatever time she needs to process her thoughts. When she's ready, she will answer.

In the final act, when the routine has us face to face, her chest pressed to mine, she speaks up. "Yeah. It did."

I trace the length of her spine, cupping the back of her neck as I dip precariously close to her mouth. "Want to tell me why?"

Uncertainty colors her expression as she swallows. "It's just hard."

"How so?"

We dance as if we've performed this routine countless times, but neither of us is fully invested. Not while she opens up and makes herself increasingly more vulnerable.

With an audible exhale, she spills her thoughts. "Seeing them on stage, so focused, so determined, dancing so flawlessly... I'm honored to critique them, but it makes me sad." She drops down on her feet, her hands slapping her sides. "Seeing them reach for their dreams, seeing a company name next to theirs on the roster... it reminds me of what I missed out on."

For years, Juilliard had been Shanti's dream. She was eager to walk the halls and follow the path of alumni she revered. Excited to brag about getting accepted. But more than anything, her dream was to become a prima ballerina under their tutelage.

So, she didn't apply anywhere else. She limited her options, all while battling with her parents about applications to traditional colleges.

Then, her heart broke when she saw the mail. A single, thin, small envelope with a letter she didn't get to read. One piece of paper and her dreams were crushed. Without a doubt, that moment started her downward spiral.

I hated every second of those dark days and did everything within my power to brighten them.

"It also reminded me of what *you* gave up on. Because of me."

This garners my full attention. "What?"

She takes a step back and props her hands on her hips. "Don't play coy." She walks in circles, her gaze focused off in the distance. "You gave up Juilliard for me." Her eyes meet mine, a deep groove between her brows. "How many schools and companies did you give up to stay with me?"

The answer is a time bomb on my tongue, waiting to detonate, but I will not light the fuse.

Her amber eyes turn glassy. "It's *my* fault you stayed." Her chin quivers. "It's *my* fault you're not on stage, competing with the best."

Nope. She will *not* burden herself with my decisions.

Yes, I stayed to be near her. I stayed *for* her. But *I* chose that. And I don't regret the decision. Not for a damn second.

Of course, I dreamed of being on stage, eager to share my art with the world. But the choice I made, being a dance teacher, is just as rewarding. Being with my best friend every day is irreplaceable. Enjoying and sharing my art, seeing the smiles and excitement from my students, not carrying a mountain of stress on my shoulders to be the best, is more than I could have ever thought possible.

I wouldn't have what I do now if I hadn't stayed for her.

She made this beautiful life possible. She gave me more than imaginable.

Shanti gave me this, and I am so grateful for her.

I invade her space and frame her face with my hands. "*I* made a choice. *I* chose to stay." My thumbs stroke the apples of her cheeks. "You know why?"

Sniffling, she shakes her head. "Because you're an idiot."

Laughter rips from my chest. "Probably." I shrug. "But I embrace my idiocy." Leaning in, I drop my forehead to hers. Hold her gaze for one, two, three breaths. Let her see how serious I am before I confess what I've held in for far too long. "I stayed because I am no one without you."

Her face twists in confusion.

I run the tip of my nose along the length of hers. "Shanti, when we're on the dance floor, you are all anyone sees." I kiss her left cheek, then the right. "My gorgeous, talented, tenacious woman. I am your support. The guy who lifts you up, holds you steady, and makes sure you shine so bright you're all anyone wants to see."

"Jet…" She reaches up and clutches my forearms. "You are so much more than that." Her eyes dart between mine. "You are everything." She inhales a shaky breath. "You are *my* everything."

A loud *whoosh* echoes through my ears as my pulse thunders in my chest. I inch back just enough to drop my gaze to her mouth. Lips I desperately want to taste again. But as I lean back in to press my lips to hers, she pulls away.

"We should probably get back to rehearsal."

Somehow, I resist the urge to say, *fuck rehearsal*. Instead, I nod. "Yeah. Sure."

We start the routine for what feels like the hundredth time when a creak echoes through the otherwise empty ballroom. As we turn to face whoever walked in, every muscle in my body locks up.

What. The. Fuck.

Before Shanti and I agreed to this trip, I sat down with Neesa and Aurelio. Spilled every interaction I had with Vivienne Bellecourt. The way she ogled me, even as a boy. Where she rested her hands on my body, leaving them there for longer than necessary. How she always seemed to favor me over every other person at the studio, but not because of my skills. How she always seemed to find a way to interact with me more. I told Neesa and Aurelio about additional solo training she offered that I declined. I shared every excruciating, dreadful moment and how I tried to avoid her as much as possible.

Vivienne Bellecourt toed the line when she existed in my space. She studied me not as a pupil but as a person of interest. Someone she cherished more than a teacher should a student. But every word she said, every physical touch, every smile and glance, stayed in a gray zone. As if she'd done it before. As if she knew exactly where to step until she leaped.

She may not have escalated things with me, but how many dancers had she crossed the line with? How many has she taken advantage of? As much as I want the answer, I will never ask.

One stipulation of me and Shanti agreeing to come here was that Vivienne Bellecourt is to keep her distance; neither of us wants to be in the same room as her at any time.

And I am fucking exhausted by this woman not listening. Tired of it not getting through her manipulative, disgusting, immoral brain that she needs to stay away from me. Pissed that she refuses to respect my boundaries.

She needs fucking help.

"You've almost got it down," Vivienne purrs, her eyes roaming my face. "Keep up the good work."

Shanti steps in front of me, blocking as much of my body as possible with hers. My fierce protector. She jabs a finger toward the door. "Get the fuck out."

"Now, now," Vivienne coos, coming too close for my liking. "There's no need for rude vulgarities."

Shanti shifts her weight as Vivienne tries to come closer from the side. I clutch her waist and take a step back, then another, bringing Shanti with me.

"Allow me to rephrase." Venom coats Shanti's voice, and it

makes me love her more. "Get the fuck out before I report you to the committee."

Vivienne throws her head back and laughs. "No one will believe a word you say." Brow arched and lip curled, Vivienne drags a nasty glare down and up Shanti's body.

I've never wanted to hit a woman the way I want to hit Vivienne Bellecourt. She is human trash.

Shanti scoffs then shakes her head. "That's where you're wrong." Resting her hands over mine, Shanti anchors me to her with a gentle, reassuring squeeze. "One move, and I can have your entire career and reputation ruined."

Vivienne points a finger at Shanti. "That fire is your only redeeming quality. Without it"—she leans in way too close—"you are nothing. A nobody. A washed-up girl who never had a chance at the big stage."

Done. I am so fucking done.

This ends. Now.

"Enough," I bellow, my fingers bruising Shanti's hips. "Get the fuck out. Do not come looking for us. Do not come near us. And if I see you in the same room as us again, it won't just be Shanti you need to worry about."

Vivienne has the nerve to cluck her tongue like she is disappointed by my reaction.

I am so sick of this woman and her bullshit. Too nice for my own good, I've given her chance after chance to leave me alone. Either she isn't used to defeat, or she's so fucked in the head she thinks I'll cave if she continues to push.

But this is it. Her final chance.

Next time, I won't be nice. Next time, she will wish she never visited Stone Bay. She'll wish she never met me.

With a finger wave over her shoulder and a smug smile on her lips, she ambles toward the door, a purposeful sway to her hips. "All the best, Jet, Shanti," she says, voice saccharine and sentiment pure artifice. "See you soon."

Now that, I believe. Because Vivienne doesn't comprehend limits, personal space, or respect.

But next time I see her, she will wish she'd listened. She will curse herself for not backing off.

I may be this sweet, fun-loving person, but when I've reached my limit, I flip. When my restraint goes, so does my benevolence and civility.

And Vivienne fucking Bellecourt is about to get a front-row seat to the show.

THIRTY-THREE
THE PERFECT DAY EXISTS... UNTIL IT DOESN'T
SHANTI

A smile curves my lips before my eyes open. Warmth and comfort curl around my chest. Swathe me in tender devotion. Fierce protection. Undeniable and incomparable love.

The sensation is truly divine. Rare and beautiful. Sublime.

And I want to live in this euphoric bubble forever.

Five.

For the past five nights, I've fallen asleep curled up to Jet. My hand on his chest and leg draped over both of his, I fell asleep to the steady rise and fall of his chest. To the rhythmic beat of his heart under my palm.

And each morning after, I've woken up with a smile on my face. A level of peace I'll only ever get from Jet. A steady and strengthening sense of purpose and hope and... intimacy.

Because of him, life is more than monotone snapshots of random memories. He fills my world with bright, vibrant color. He makes every moment better, every memory greater. With Jet, I'm not just moving through life. I am experiencing and feeling and opening myself up to new possibilities.

With him, I am alive. Carefree. Home.

The Jet effect. That's what I'm calling this feeling.

A hand trails from my hip to my shoulder as his other reaches

over to wrap around my waist and haul me closer. I slide my hand up his chest and around his neck as he presses his lips to the top of my head.

"Mm." His hold on me tightens as he breathes me in. "Good morning."

My insides melt at the gravelly sound of his morning voice, and I bury my nose in the crook of his shoulder. "Good morning," I murmur against his warm skin.

At the start of this trip, I was hesitant to coexist in the same confined space as Jet. Not because he made me uneasy. Quite the opposite, actually. I've been very aware of my feelings for Jet for a while but not ready to act on them.

With each passing day, with each taunt, each touch, each second in his arms, I grow more and more ready to take the next step. To shove all my insecurities aside, all my doubts, and take the leap.

After years of keeping Jet at arm's length romantically, I'm ready for more. To return his love with equal fervor.

"Excited to explore today?" Another kiss to my crown, then he inches back to meet my gaze. "We have a lot to check off our list."

After three jam-packed days, we finally have the entire day to ourselves. Twenty-four hours of me and him and countless places to see and get lost. A day full of fun exploration. A day to make irreplaceable memories to reminisce over in the future.

Warmth blooms in my chest, my heart fluttering at the idea of being with him out in the open, our hands linked as we wander and sightsee. Anticipation swirls in my belly, my nerves shaky at what else the day could bring. Either way, I'm ready. To smile with him, be awestruck with him, to go on an adventure with him, to love him.

I can't help but thank the universe for this moment. For letting me experience this place with him.

My cheeks sting with a wide smile as I nod. "What should we do first?"

Hand on my cheek, he brushes the hair from my face and

tucks it behind my ear. "After breakfast, I thought we'd hike before it gets too hot."

"Good idea." Last thing we need is to overheat in the middle of nowhere.

Slow and gentle, his fingertips travel my jawline toward my chin. His gaze drops to my lips as his thumb strokes my bottom one. He doesn't have to say a word for me to know what he's thinking.

He wants to kiss me again.

I want that too. God, do I ever.

Because I broke our kiss, since I continue to pull away whenever we're a breath from the next kiss, there is no chance Jet will initiate. Regardless of how much he wants to kiss me again, he won't make a move. With a staggering level of restraint and patience, Jet waits for me to take the lead. To give him permission. To tell him I'm ready for more.

His gaze lifts to mine a beat before he presses his lips to my forehead. "I'd love to stay in this bed with you all day, but we have a million things to see." His hand drops to my hip, gives it a squeeze, then he playfully shoves me off him and bolts from the bed. "Come on, lazy butt. Let's do this."

"Hey," I holler as I scramble beneath the tangled sheet and blanket. "Who are you calling a lazy butt? I was up at least fifteen minutes before you, Mr. I Sleep like a Hibernating Bear."

A hearty laugh echoes through the room as I swing my legs off the bed and sit up, putting myself eye level with his abs. And like the smitten woman I am, I gawk every fucking inch.

On the next breath, my chin is pinched between his thumb and finger. With a quick jerk up, my gaze is locked on his smoldering grays.

I swallow. Hard.

"Keep eye-fucking me like that and we're not leaving the room."

I clench my thighs and fist the edge of the mattress. It's on the tip of my tongue to say fuck it. To tell him I'm fine with us not leaving the room—or the bed. But I stop myself.

The way I crave Jet is tumultuous. Unrestrained and fierce. I want to feel him over me, under me, his hands and lips on my skin as he moves inside me. I want him to mark me, to moan in my ear as he takes me deeper, to growl my name when he comes. I want him wild, mad with lust and love as he takes me again and again, making it so neither of us can walk straight.

What I don't want is our first time to be on a whim. A spur-of-the-moment decision made in a wanton haze.

We've had years of foreplay. What's a little longer?

Tongue darting out, I lick my lips and nod. "Noted." I reach up, take his wrist, and slowly pull his hand away. "Now"—I rise from the bed, my breasts brushing his chest through my thin top —"if you don't mind, I need to get ready."

His body rumbles with a groan as I press into him further, purposely running my fingertips along the waistband of his sweats, then pass him for the bathroom.

God, I love how feral he gets when I touch him.

———

Opting to save time and money, we eat breakfast in one of the hotel restaurants. My eyes widen as I roam the menu. The most basic breakfast listed—two eggs, potatoes, toast, and choice of meat—is twenty freaking dollars.

Again, I'm glad we aren't footing the bill for our stay. Geez.

Loaded up on protein and carbs, hiking packs slung over our shoulders, Jet fetches the car from valet. In a matter of minutes, we are on the road and headed north. Once we're through the heaviest of the traffic, the city slowly disappears. The neighborhoods grow farther apart and give way to more and more trees.

I roll down the window, rest my arm on the door, and lean out to feel the crisp morning air on my face. Closing my eyes, I fill my lungs with the deepest inhale. Bask in the warmth of the early sun on my skin. Revel in the energy shift, the peace, the utter stillness of being away from the crowds and noise.

The road twists and turns as we head north. Colossal redwoods line either side of the street, the sun fading from above as the canopy grows thicker, wider overhead. We wind through the vast forest another mile or two before the road curves and opens to parking.

Jet slows as we approach a park employee. After showing them our parking reservation, they direct us where to go. Jet guides the SUV through the lot until he finds a spot. With the car in park, he grabs his phone and unlocks it, scanning something on the screen.

"Everything okay?"

He nods. "All good. Just wanted to double-check I had our tickets up."

Parking reservations and prepaid tickets? Glad he researched things ahead of time.

"Bring your phone for pictures," he says as he shoves his phone in his pocket. "But there's no reception anywhere in the park, according to the website."

The idea of no phone, no internet, no notifications for hours scares me as much as it thrills me. If I'm honest, I love that the only distractions I'll have here are Jet and nature.

We check in and receive a park brochure with trail maps. After a quick scan, we decide to do the full paved trail and wait to see what the extended, unpaved trails look like when we reach them. Looping his arm with mine, Jet guides us to the start of the trail and we begin our adventure.

Time and life and every ounce of stress fall away as we stroll along the path. We've barely made a dent in our excursion, yet I already feel at peace. Buoyant. Refreshed. Happy.

Oddly, it's the last that gives me pause.

I've experienced happiness before. Fragments of joy. Minor blips when I thought nothing or no one could rob me of my smile.

But as depressing as it sounds, I don't think I've ever been *happy*. Truly happy. Not like this.

And it's all thanks to the man at my side.

We stop at the Pinchot Tree, stand in front of the boulder with the dedication plaque, and simply stare up, up, up. The longer we gaze at the monumental redwood, the smaller I feel. Like an ant. Like this tree could stomp me into the earth and carry on without a care.

Had I come here years ago, I would've dropped my gaze within seconds, bored or uninterested. Years ago, I wouldn't have appreciated standing in the presence of a tree that's been on this earth more than eight human lifetimes.

In this place, where life has existed more than a millennium, where these mammoth trees have survived countless natural disasters and just as much human destruction, my problems and insecurities feel minuscule. Trivial. Not worth my time or energy.

In this place with Jet, I question why I continue to drag out the inevitable. I ask myself why I won't give into my feelings for him. And why I continue to punish both of us, but mostly myself, by not listening to my heart.

Finally, I'm ready—to be what Jet needs, to love him as he deserves, to open myself fully.

As we step away from the Pinchot Tree, Jet takes my hand and laces our fingers. He does it with such ease. Absolute surety. As if he's privy to my innermost thoughts. As if the tether linking my heart to his anchored itself permanently and signaled to him it's time.

Leaning into his side, I strengthen my grip on his hand. Clutch his biceps with my other hand. Press my lips to his shoulder for one, two, three steps before I return my gaze to the path.

Neither of us speaks, but our actions say everything our voices don't.

After this trip, our lives will be forever changed.

The rest of our hike is much the same. Quiet. Significant. Precious. We traverse the trails and groves, and at one point ask a couple if they mind taking our picture. We explore several of the extended, unpaved trails, our pace steady and unrushed. The deeper we go into the forest, the more I never want to leave.

Before today, I never thought anything other than Jet could soothe my soul. Today, I learned otherwise. More than trees and wildlife exist here. There is also wonder and hope and magic.

I squint and shield my eyes with a hand as we exit the trail. In a blink, the busy world rushes back in. People mill about the lot, children tugging on the arms of their adult companions to hurry them along. Outside the forest, the world is infinitely louder.

I want to turn around and go back.

"Gift shop?" Jet asks, drawing my attention back to him.

I meet his waiting gaze and nod. "Yeah. I'd like a keepsake." A token or memento to remind me of this place, not that it isn't permanently etched in my bones now.

After three full circuits of the gift shop interior, I leave with a shirt, key chain, and stickers. We load into Jet's SUV and wind our way back to civilization.

Before we reach the Golden Gate Bridge, Jet turns and winds along another road, up an incline. A few minutes later, he parks the car and hops out.

"Figured it's a good time to view the bridge since the fog burned off."

I step up to the guardrail, rest my arms on it, and stare at the iconic bridge. "Not sure anything will top Muir Woods, but this is another unforgettable moment."

"Glad you loved the trail. Wasn't sure how you'd feel."

I turn to meet his gaze, and it's in that moment I realize just how close we are. "Honestly, I wasn't sure either." I roll my lips between my teeth. "But I hope we visit again."

Jet leans closer. Lifts his hand and brushes his fingers down the length of my arm. So gentle, so intimate. "We will." There's a promise chiseled in those words. A solemn vow. Then he seals it with another. "I want to explore the world with you." His hand moves to my ponytail, his fingers wrapping around it and sliding down until he tugs the end. "You make everything more beautiful."

A ball of emotion swells in my throat, and I swallow. Move closer. Drop my gaze to his lips.

He erases the last shred of distance between us and crushes my mouth with his. I pivot and step into him fully. His hands cup my cheeks, his fingers curling around the back of my neck.

I've never been big on public displays of affection. But right now, I want to claim this man in front of the world. I want everyone to know he is mine.

Tongue darting out, he licks the seam of my lips in silent request. And this time, I give him permission. This time, I open for him and sweep my tongue along his.

His moan matches mine. Desperate. Insatiable. Savage. He tilts his head and deepens the kiss, his mouth insistent as it devours.

I fist his shirt. Haul him impossibly closer. Crush as much of my body to the length of his. Groan when his hardening cock presses to my lower belly.

God, I never want to exist outside of this feeling. Love and lust and the constant need for more.

The kiss turns soft, slow, far more tender. Jet caresses my cheeks with his thumbs. Presses a chaste kiss to my lips. Then another. And then he breaks the kiss altogether and drops his forehead to mine.

"Didn't think it was possible," he whispers.

I lean in for another chaste kiss. "What?"

"That I could love you more than I already do."

My heart catapults in my chest, hammering against my rib cage over and over. "I love you, too." I will never love anyone the way I do Jet. He has my whole heart, every thread of my soul, every second of my future.

Another kiss to my lips and he draws back. "Come on, beautiful. Let's do the touristy thing and take some pictures. Then we'll check some other items off our list."

I open my mouth to argue. As if he hears it coming, he holds up a hand.

"If I don't stop kissing you now, we'll never leave this lookout."

A smirk curves my lips. "And that's a problem because…"

He chuckles. "We have plenty of time to continue this later. The city, however"—he gestures toward the bridge and beyond—"is on borrowed time for us."

I tip my head back, roll my eyes, and grumble under my breath. "Fine. Let's go."

He laughs harder. "Pictures first."

***

After a full day of exploring and kissing and the most incredible dinner since we've arrived, Jet pulls up to the valet at the hotel. We hop out, he hands over the fob to the attendant and gets a ticket, and then he takes my hand in his.

It's been like this all day—holding hands, leaning closer, needing as much physical contact as humanly possible. And all I want is more.

Until now, I shied away from intimate affection. Hell, I repelled it like a magnet flipped the wrong way. Cold as it sounds, I gave very little of myself to the guys in my past. Intentionally. Was it fair to them? Of course not, but I didn't care. It was all I knew.

As a child, I was taught love was a tool, a weapon. My parents only ever used love as a reward. If I did something that pleased them, I was doted on. Words of praise, a gentle pat on the hand, arm or shoulder, a well-practiced smile. On rare occasions, I got a hug. Hearing the actual word *love* was almost unheard of.

One of the reasons I waited to pursue more with Jet was because I had to know I was capable of love. I had to know my parents hadn't permanently stripped away my softness, my humanity, my soul.

Were it not for Jet, I'm not sure I'd know love. Real, pure, bewitching and arresting love.

And now, I'm ready for what happens next. I'm ready to give myself fully to him.

The *whoosh, whoosh, whoosh* of my heart thrums in my ears as we cross the hotel lobby for the elevators. I dizzy, grow light-headed at the idea of what might happen when we enter our room. Leaning into Jet, I clutch his bicep with my free hand, needing his steady strength and support.

After a push of the elevator call button, he twists and presses his lips to my forehead. "Love you."

Goose bumps dance over my skin as a pleasurable shiver rolls up my spine. From his lips, those words are warmth and devotion. The ultimate vow. I want them often and forever.

"Love you, too."

The elevator doors swish open with a ding. As we go to step inside, a grating voice stops us.

"Well, look at you two. All cozied up."

We turn to see Vivienne Bellecourt within arm's reach.

Instinctually, I tighten my hold on Jet.

This lady needs more than professional help. She needs time behind bars.

Jet shakes his head. "You have got to be fucking kidding me right now." Anger vibrates off his aura.

"Oh, come now—"

"No," Jet shouts, cutting her off.

Several patrons stop and look in our direction. Good. Maybe what Vivienne needs is to be called out in front of witnesses. Maybe it will finally make her stay away.

Skin heating and face reddening, Jet bristles at my side. "I warned you." Cold, humorless laughter falls from his lips. "But as always, you think nothing applies to you. You think you're above it all." Jet's expression darkens in a way I've never witnessed. "Well, *Vivienne*"—her name is acidic on his tongue—"I hope you're prepared for your tragic and very public demise."

In a move neither of us anticipated, Vivienne steps closer and reaches around me to touch Jet. "How dare—"

Jet flings her hand off him. "How dare I what?" he booms.

Onlookers crowd us. More people stop to see what the commotion is about.

Red colors Vivienne's cheeks and neck as she clenches her jaw. She opens her mouth to say more, but Jet cuts her off again.

"How dare I want distance from a predator?"

Gasps echo through the hotel lobby.

"How dare I ask a woman almost twice my age, who has made me extremely uncomfortable since I was a *child*, to leave me the hell alone?"

Composure weakening, Vivienne's gaze darts around the room. Dozens of people stare her down, disgust written all over their faces.

She could have avoided this. She was handed the opportunity to walk away again and again. But she just wouldn't leave Jet alone.

Now, the consequences of her actions are here.

Now, she will lose everything.

"What happens next is all your doing, Vivienne."

Jet smashes the button for the elevator, his eyes never leaving Vivienne as she takes a step back, then another. Head high, she slithers away, disappearing around the corner.

When the elevator arrives, we bolt inside. Jet presses our floor number and the doors close.

The moment we're alone, I release his hand, step in front of him, and frame his face. "Breathe." Gaze locked on his, I stroke his cheeks with my thumbs. "We will handle this." I nod. "But right now, I need you to breathe."

Reaching up, Jet covers my hands with his and takes a deep, slow, calming breath.

"Again."

He repeats the process. In a matter of seconds, his cheeks cool as the red fades.

"Better?" This won't just fizzle out and go away, but I need my calm, levelheaded Jet back.

Giving my hands a gentle squeeze, he nods. "Yes. Thank you."

The elevator slows, the doors sliding open a moment later.

Taking Jet's hand, I lead us out and down the hall to our room. The moment we're in the safety of our own space, I wrap him in my arms.

"Tell me what you need."

Warmth cocoons me as Jet pins me to his chest. "This. Right now, all I need is this."

So, until he releases me, I hold him, comfort him, love him.

THIRTY-FOUR
I REALLY NEED YOU TONIGHT

JET

ORANGE BLOSSOM AND HONEY. SOFT SKIN AND SUPPLE CURVES. THE soothing rhythm of her heart and rise and fall of her chest. Her quiet strength and fierce tenacity.

Her.

Shanti.

Home. Shanti is my home. *My home.*

Arms around me, hands fisting my shirt, body pressed to mine, she grounds me in a way nothing or no one else can. With one simple embrace, Shanti guides me away from the dark path my mind had wandered down and leads me back to a place of peace.

Inhaling another deep pull of her sweet scent, I loosen my hold and draw back enough to meet her warm, rich, amber irises. "Thank you."

Reaching up, she combs her fingers through my hair before cupping my cheek. "I would do anything for you." It may have come out a whisper, but the meaning behind her sentiment is a roaring thunderclap.

I lean into her touch. Turn and kiss the heart of her palm. "Ditto."

Slowly, she walks backward and leads us to the bed. Dropping

to sit on the edge, she pats the spot beside her. "Is it okay if we talk about it?"

Love and anxiety ripple and writhe in my chest. Adrenaline and oxytocin flood my veins and fight for dominance. My stomach pitches, and I swallow past the sudden urge to throw up.

Shanti is a safe space. She is my person.

My home.

Closing my eyes, I take a deep breath, then another. I repeat the thought again and again. Let it sink in and calm my racing heart. Soothe my cramped stomach. Settle my frazzled nerves.

And when the discomfort eases enough, I meet Shanti's waiting gaze. "Yeah." I take her hand in both of mine, cradle it in my lap, and hold it like it's the most precious thing I own. "We should."

Arm pressed to my side, she gives me her weight. Silent reassurance. Endless support. And time. She gives me all the time I need to say what's on my mind, to get this gnarly anger and frustration out in a healthy way.

She may not know it, but she has done this often over the years. In her own way, she has been as much my support system and sounding board as I have been hers.

Shanti is exactly who I need, in the beautiful moments as well as the chaos.

"Please don't hate me," she whispers, dropping her eyes to our joined hands. "But I have to ask…"

I reach up and take her chin, lifting until our eyes lock. "I could never hate you." I release her chin and rest my hand over my heart, tapping twice. "You and I, we are two halves of the same beating heart. When one of us is broken or hurt or not at full strength, we both feel it."

And maybe for the first time, she is on the opposite side of the spectrum. For the first time, she has to be the strong one. The pillar. The framework. The bones.

Shanti has never not been strong. With what she has been through, all the emotional and psychological trauma, how could she not be? But holding yourself together and battling your own demons isn't quite the same as supporting and lifting up someone you love. Can she do it? I have zero doubts. Will she question herself along the way? More than likely.

Her amber irises glass over as tears rim her eyes. "Did Vivienne—" Brows pinched together, she swallows past the scratch in her voice. "Did she... do anything else? Anything you haven't told me or anyone?"

I get why she pled with me a moment ago. Why she asked me to not hate her. Some would be angry with this line of questioning.

Twisting to face her fully, I take both her hands in mine. Let their warmth and strength fill me up. Anchor me to her. Keep me whole.

"Everything I've said is true, but I didn't go into great detail with Neesa and Aurelio. And... I'm waiting until we get back to tell my parents."

Her thumbs rub slowly, gently across my knuckles over and over. "Is there a reason you held back?"

There are several reasons, but the biggest one is that it's hard enough to get people to believe boys or men get physically and/or sexually assaulted, especially by a woman. Tragically, most people don't believe girls or women when they speak their truth about assault. So why would they believe me, a grown man?

My family will believe me when I tell them, they will fight for me. I know this truth deep in my bones. Neesa and Aurelio said they would take action, and I believe them.

Still, I worry how others will look at me once the truth comes out. I worry dancers in the community who love and praise Vivienne will retaliate when they find out I'm the one who shined a light on her abuse of power.

"I held back because I didn't want to witness their pain. I didn't want them to blame themselves. I didn't want Neesa or Aurelio to be hostile if the situation was manageable. At least until I figure out what to do." My eyes dart between hers. "Does that make sense?"

The corners of her mouth bend into a frown. "Yes." She winces. "No."

I reach up and swipe at her bottom lip, smoothing her grimace. "If you haven't noticed, I don't like confrontation or stressful situations." I laugh without humor. "Will I insert myself into a hostile situation if necessary? Absolutely. Especially for those I love." I shift my hand to cup her cheek. "But I work hard to keep the peace."

Laying her hand over mine, she nods. "You do." She leans into my palm and closes her eyes. "And I love you so much for that." Her eyes ease open. "But if we're doing this, if we're giving a relationship a chance, I need all your scars too. Every hurt, every heartache, every painful thing you've masked to make sure everyone else is happy." She leans forward and presses her cheek to mine. "I love you, Jet. Please… let me love you the way you deserve."

Her words crack open the lock on my pent-up emotions. One line from her lips and everything comes tumbling out. For the first time in my life, I share without restraint. I spill my truth.

I tell her about my years of masked anxiety because I kept everything Vivienne had done to myself. How even the thought of her in the same room makes my skin crawl, makes me nauseous. Vivienne may have only scratched the surface of what she is capable of, but she used her position to violate me. She stole part of my innocence, my trust in others, and my soul.

What Vivienne did is unforgivable. Unforgettable. And I am done being quiet about it.

Moving past everything with Vivienne, I tell Shanti how much it hurt to watch her pick other guys over me—shitty guys—again and again and again. How it chipped at my heart. How I tried to move on with other people, but it never worked in my favor, which made me question my worth. How the messed-up cycle we kept repeating made me question my sanity because I stayed and helped pick up the pieces when things went wrong. How I hoped over and over that *finally* she would choose me, but she never did.

Until now.

It is the most effervescent feeling, knowing I am finally hers. Knowing I have her heart, and she has mine.

I tell her how dance and being her partner have been my saving grace. A way to add a ray of sunshine to my occasional cloudy day.

Loving her has been the best experience of my life.

When I reach the end of my ramble-fest, Shanti lunges forward, bands her arms around my neck, crawls into my lap, and doesn't say a word. Her sniffle on every other breath says more than enough.

Hour-long minutes tick by as we sit like a human double pretzel. As we linger in my confessions. As we start the process of healing from the past so we can have a better future.

"Can we order dessert?" she asks between sniffles.

I loosen my grip and lean back enough to cup her cheek. "Is that a serious question?" I wipe the tears from her cheek. "We're ordering all the desserts."

Like the sun coming out after the rain, she delivers a beaming smile. One I know she only gives me. And with the single action, another weight lifts from my shoulders.

Damn, I love her.

As promised, I order one of each dessert from room service. With another episode of *The Golden Girls* playing, we stuff our faces until our stomachs hurt. And after I set the tray out in the hall and slide back into bed, Shanti scoots over until her body is pressed to mine.

Clinging to me like a koala, Shanti falls asleep in my arms. As I stare down at her profile illuminated by the television, one thought runs on repeat.

I want this every night. Her in my arms is all I need in this life.

THIRTY-FIVE
MATCH LIT AND READY TO BURN
SHANTI

After the run-in with Vivienne at the elevator two nights ago, Jet and I elected to stay in our room yesterday. With the exception of when we were needed downstairs to judge, we stayed in our pajamas. Shoving the chairs and table to the wall, we practiced our routine for hours.

We also lounged in bed more than usual. Cuddled for hours. Kissed more often. Ordered room service when we were hungry and watched meaningless television just because.

Also in our downtime, we discussed what Jet wants to do about the whole Vivienne situation. We agree something needs to be done, but neither of us wants to be hasty. If we rush things, we'll likely miss pertinent details, and Vivienne will walk away with an inflated ego and a wicked grin. She'll move on to someone else and repeat her abhorrent behavior. And that cannot happen.

We need to approach the committee with concrete proof. Irrefutable evidence. Jet's voice and story are both, but it'll work in our favor if we have more. Another dancer who's had a similar experience. We've considered the possibility that Jet may be the only one, but our instincts say otherwise.

The most difficult part is finding the right way to bring the

subject up with dancers without invading their privacy while also keeping Jet's. It's a double-edged sword.

Regardless of what or who we find, Jet gets the final say in what happens. Having been on the receiving end of this entire ordeal, his voice, his choice, matters most. He has been hurt in incomprehensible ways for years. Violated in a way I will never fully grasp. He should have a say in what happens to Vivienne. His declaration needs to be heard. He needs to deliver the final blow.

Through it all, I will stay by his side. I will hold his hand and be his strength. Lift him up as he has me countless times. That's what you do for the people you love.

Goose bumps dot my skin, a delicious shiver rolling up my spine as Jet's fingers drift down, caressing and kneading my curves. I hug my leg, hooked over his hips, tighter. Draw him impossibly closer. Slide my hand up his bare chest, along the length of his neck, and into his hair, fisting the thick locks.

His chest vibrates with a low, throaty hum. "Keep it up," he warns. It's the same warning I've heard several times this week. He never finishes the thought. Never says anything further. He doesn't need to.

Keep it up, and we won't leave this bed.

Keep it up, and I'll show you what happens next.

Keep it up, and you'll see just how unrestrained I can be.

Keep it up, and I'll take you like I've wanted to for years.

Undeterred, I tug his hair, his chin jutting toward the ceiling as I trail my nose up the column of his throat. "What if I do?" I whisper when I reach his ear, taunting him. "What if I want you to follow through?"

Tightening his grip around my waist, he hauls me on top of his body. Drags me up, up, up until we are eye level. Until every hard inch of him is pressed to every single inch of me. Then his hands drift down. Grip the swell of my hips. Knead the fleshy curves with a bruising squeeze.

Then, with his fiery gray eyes locked on mine, his hands

wander lower. Glide over the cotton of my sleep shorts until he grazes the bare skin along the hem. His fingers sweep under the curves of my ass. Coast the length of where my ass meets my thighs. Flex then grip, hard, pinning me in place.

"You sure about that?" He rolls his hips and thrusts his very-hard, very-thick cock against my center.

I gasp, my nails biting my palms as I fist his hair with brutal strength. "Yes." The word is a whispered plea and bold demand for more.

Craning his neck, he takes my mouth with his. Presses his lips firmly to mine once, twice, before trailing his tongue along the seam. My lips part for him, and his tongue dives in. Sweeps along the length of mine. Tastes and devours again and again.

Carnal need simmers in my veins. Primal urge demands to take over.

I deepen the kiss. Wrap my lips around his tongue and suck. Hard. As I reach the tip, I ease the pressure. Give him a momentary reprieve. When I take him again, I all but devour him.

His guttural moan vibrates my chest and fuels the ache in my core.

I circle my hips. Grind my center up and down his hard length. Moan as it adds the perfect amount of pressure to my aching clit.

And then, I'm on my back, our kiss never breaking. Jet settles into the cradle of my hips, his fingers weaving through my hair. Fisting. Tugging. My scalp stings in the most delicious way. Over and over, he rocks his hips. Strokes my clit with precision. Drives me higher. Edges me closer.

Faster. His body moves faster. Almost frantic. Desperate. Uncontrollable.

Circling his hips with my legs, I hook my feet over his ass. I trail my hands up either side of his spine and sink my nails in when I reach his shoulders.

A sharp hiss echoes through the room a beat before he yanks

my hair and exposes my neck. He drops his mouth to my throat, sucking, but not enough to leave a mark.

Were we not performing tonight, I'd brand his back with my nails, and he'd openly claim me with dark love bites on my neck for everyone to see.

After tonight, I will mark him. After tonight, everyone will know he is mine.

Digging my heels into his ass, I silently beg him for more. When he delivers, I gasp. Sink my nails deeper as my breaths come faster, louder. And then my hands are in his hair, seizing his dark strands, yanking harder and harder.

"Oh god…" Fire and pressure bloom low in my belly. Expanding. Intensifying. Begging for release.

Trailing open-mouth kisses up my neck, he nips my chin and hovers inches from my mouth. "That's it, baby." He sucks my bottom lip between his. "Show me how pretty you are when you come undone."

With a fierce, heady rock of his hips, then another, I detonate.

A heatwave ignites every cell in my body as perspiration licks my skin. Light dances in my vision as I work to catch my breath. I release my grip on his hair and band my arms around his chest. Squeeze him with inconceivable strength as I come down from the most intense orgasm of my life.

Jet presses a chaste kiss to my lips. Then another. And another. "So damn perfect."

A wobbly smile lifts the corners of my mouth as I meet his carnal gaze. "Mm. Think you got—" Before I finish the thought, another pops in my head.

Concern flashes in his eyes. "What's wrong?"

"Did you?"

A corner of his mouth lifts, every ounce of worry vanishing from his face. "No."

I loosen my hold on him and reach between us. But he moves faster, gripping my wrist to stop me.

Jet shakes his head. "Later." He lowers his lips to mine and kisses me softly, reverently. "Right now isn't about me." He peppers kisses along my jaw to my ear. "It's about making *you* feel good."

My eyes roll back and close as my breathing turns jagged once more. "What if making you feel good is what *I* need?"

His chest vibrates with a deep, prolonged hum. "Then it'll be even better when it happens." He nips my earlobe. "Patience, baby."

I groan, and he laughs. Next thing I know, his fingers are digging into the sides of my rib cage. His mouth is on my skin, blowing raspberries. In a matter of seconds, we're rolling in the sheets, both of us laughing for different reasons.

"Stop," I beg. "I need to…" I wheeze. "Pee. I need to pee." And I need to deal with the dampness soaking my thighs.

"Fine," he relents and rolls off me.

I scoot to the edge of the bed and push to stand.

Jet smacks my ass. "I'm ordering breakfast. Any requests?"

On performance days, I usually eat oatmeal, fruit, and eggs. Today, I want to step out of the ordinary.

Before I slip inside the bathroom, I glance over my shoulder and smile. "Stuffed French toast with bacon."

Jet matches my smile. "Perfect."

After we indulge with breakfast, Jet suggests a little more downtime. I don't argue. For the two hours following, we kick back and bum out. I spend most of the time trying not to think about or resurrect what happened before breakfast.

Later.

Tracing a finger over the ink peeking out of his waistband, I tip my head to look up at him. "Will you show me your tattoo?"

Pink tinges his cheeks as his eyes dart between mine. Then he swallows.

Whatever he permanently imprinted on his skin means a lot. Maybe that's why he's kept it hidden so long.

Shifting, he inches his sweats lower on his right hip. Beneath the downward curve of his obliques, the thin, dark veins of a feather come into view. His pants dip lower, and my pulse catapults when I spot a thin dusting of dark curls.

I open my mouth to ask how big the tattoo is, but he stops before I get the chance.

Spanning from his back to the top center of his quads, an elaborate feather decorates the skin along his hip bone. Beneath the feather, in a delicate, handwritten font, is a quote.

I reach for him, tracing my fingertips over the letters as I read, "Never let her fall."

My gaze flies to his, the backs of my eyes stinging as my vision blurs. Dozens of questions flit through my mind, but the one that stands out most is if he got this for *me*.

Taking my chin in his hand, he sits up until the tip of his nose grazes mine. "Yes," he says as if he can read my mind. He kisses me chastely, presses his forehead to mine, and nods. "I will never let you fall. In any sense of the word."

My heart hammers for a completely different reason. Even at my lowest point, Jet didn't give up. He did everything within his power to help, to lift me up, to bring me back to him.

Will I ever fully comprehend how deeply this man loves me?

Am I worthy of his love?

He tugs his pants back up, hauls me into his arms, and leans back into the pillows. "I have no idea what's going through that pretty head of yours, but if you're questioning anything, please stop." He presses his lips to my hair. "I love you, Shanti. I have loved you a long time." He shifts us so I'm looking up at him. "And I will love you until my last breath."

What do I say to that? I honestly have no idea. I want to ask when he got the tattoo, but I stop myself. It's been years, that much I know, because I've seen hints of the ink for at least a few.

Instead of saying something foolish or awkward, I snuggle deeper into him. Close my eyes and breathe him in. Hug him closer and revel in his love and comfort.

When we reach the end of sloth time, I slink off the bed with a groan. Jet simply laughs.

We order fresh fruit and nutrient-dense salads for lunch and eat in the room. Then we warm up our muscles and do one last run-through of the routine.

This is it. Tonight is the night.

And we are going to show this community our best.

———

A surge of energy courses through my veins as the theater lights dim. A voice announces there will be a brief intermission. Dancers from the previous performance scurry off stage, congratulating each other on a great show. A few flash me a genuine smile as they pass.

"Merde," a dancer says as she enters the wing. The loose translation to English is shit. But like actors say *break a leg* because of superstition, dancers say *merde* to wish each other luck.

"Thank you." I dip my chin. "You were incredible."

She pauses and bows and offers thanks. Then she jogs off to catch up with the other dancers.

I glance across the stage where Jet stands poised, confident. We're ready to put on the performance of our lives. His gaze catches mine, and he winks. The simple, small action warms me bun to pointe and unravels the knot beneath my diaphragm.

All week, Jet and I have practiced this routine. Too many times to count. We know it backward and forward.

What Jet doesn't know is I have other plans once we're on stage.

The lights blink, signaling intermission will end in a minute.

Ducking my chin to my chest, I roll my shoulders, stretch my ankles, then take a deep breath. On the exhale, I lift my chin and hold it high. Square my shoulders and prepare for the biggest night of my dancing career.

A woman with a headset sidles up to me. "Fifteen seconds."

I nod and start counting down in my head as I move just out of the wings to get in position.

Fourteen. Thirteen.

When I started dancing, it wasn't by choice.

Twelve. Eleven. Ten.

Every time I've been made to feel small or insignificant, I've proved the cynics wrong.

Nine. Eight. Seven.

Tonight is no different.

Six. Five. Four.

Tonight, I will show some of the biggest names in this profession what I'm capable of. That I am worthy of the stage.

Three. Two.

They will remember my name.

One.

The curtain lifts as soft, colorful lights shine down from above. The first note of the song plays, and I rise up on to my toes. My arms glide through the air as I dip my chin and pas de bourrée couru to center stage. When I hit my mark, I look longingly to my left, then repeat the glance toward the right.

Each move is delicate, graceful, beautiful. Exactly as it was choreographed.

Midnight Lovers.

And if I've learned anything about lovers over the past week with Jet, it's that two people sneaking around would be anything but delicate or graceful.

So when Jet comes up behind me and takes my hips in his hands, instead of elongating my arms to either side as I have every practice, I drop my hands over his and anchor him to me.

Positioned where no one can see his mouth, he mutters, "What are you doing?"

Rather than answer him, I show him. Every angle and bend of my body is sharper. Every move of the routine is more punctuated and powerful.

It takes mere seconds for Jet to pick up on my energy. To seamlessly adjust and match my mood. In half a minute, the original choreography turns provocative. Bewitching. Risqué.

Every touch is seductive. Tempting. Impactful. In the moments when we should almost kiss, he presses his lips to mine. When he should hold me close, tenderly, I erase the space between us. Soak up his heat. Get lost in the fire in his eyes.

The song morphs, turns more dramatic. Jet cinches his hands around my waist and hoists me up as he crosses the stage. The move is meant to signify his character rescuing mine as our families try to tear us apart. In the original choreography, this scene makes me appear feeble and incapable while Jet comes off as courageous.

But I am not frail. I am not weak. And I damn sure am not helpless.

Did I have support throughout my journey? Yes, but that doesn't make me soft or inadequate. If anything, accepting help makes me stronger, formidable. Jet just happens to be the best person to have at my side.

Rather than float down when we *escape* our families, I press my back to Jet's front. Purposefully form my curves to the length of his body. Propel my hips back and grind against him.

A groan vibrates his chest as his fingers bruise my waist. "Tease."

I don't fight my smile.

As the song winds down, as we take our final steps, pride wraps me in its proverbial arms. We hit our mark. We danced as if this was our last performance. And we took a beautiful routine, added our touch, and made it unforgettable.

No matter what happens after tonight, this memory will be with me forever.

With Jet's arms around my waist, my hands locked behind his neck, and our lips a breath apart, the stage lights fade and the song ends. Deafening silence pulses in my ears. Seconds feel like hours as the backs of my eyes start to sting.

Then, the audience roars with applause, and tears roll down my cheeks for a wholly different reason.

Jet and I unclasp our arms. Then he takes my hand and guides us toward the front of the stage. He stops a step before me and gestures in my direction.

People are out of their seats, applause and cheers and whistles echoing off the walls.

Foot swept back, I flourish my arms outward and dip into a low bow. When I rise, I reach behind me and wait for Jet to take my hand. Then I haul him to my side, and we take a bow together.

The audience continues to clap and cheer.

Exhilaration and gratitude encompass every cell in my body. Under the house lights, I come to life. Next to Jet on this stage, I feel more alive than ever.

A single standing ovation is all it takes to eradicate every negative comment I've received regarding my dance career. All the tears, all the sleepless nights, all the hurt... I may not have danced the path I dreamed of, but my journey led me here. To this place. To this moment.

As difficult as it's been, I love where I am now. I love who I'm with and the person I've become.

After a final bow, the curtain falls. Jet sweeps me into his arms and spins me in dizzying circles.

"Fuck, I love you." His mouth crashes down on mine in a severe but welcome kiss.

Breaking the kiss, I open my mouth to tell him I love him too. But I don't get the chance.

Instructors and dancers crowd the stage, congratulating us on our performance. As I shake the hand of the owner of Pirouette School of Ballet in a small town outside Bend, Oregon, I spot Vivienne. I cut the conversation short, apologize and excuse myself, seek out Jet, and pull him aside.

"She's here." I don't need to elaborate. There is only one person I'd be referring to here.

"Where?"

As inconspicuous as possible, I gesture to where she mingles with other instructors. Jet gives my hand a sharp squeeze the moment he sees her.

"Over here." He weaves us through the crowd, smiling as people praise our performance. But he doesn't stop, not until we reach a small group. A very specific group.

The committee.

And until the crowd disperses, until Vivienne disappears, until we feel comfortable exiting the room, we make small talk with the very same people who will likely end Vivienne's career.

All it takes is one match, one purposeful strike, and the perfect amount of pressure to burn it all to the ground. And Vivienne Bellecourt is about to burn.

THIRTY-SIX
LOVE IS ALL YOU NEED
JET

Our last day in San Francisco starts out much the same.

I wake with Shanti pressed to my side, her limbs hooked over my hips and chest. Cuddling until one of us absolutely needs to get up, we talk about how we should spend our time today. When Shanti heads for the bathroom, I order breakfast. By the time room service knocks on the door, we're both dressed and ready to devour every bite.

"We're just wandering?" Shanti asks then pops a piece of melon in her mouth.

I load my fork with scrambled eggs. "For a little bit. Maybe we'll stumble upon the perfect shop or restaurant." I nudge her arm with mine. "I'll get you a souvenir."

"Like a magnet or shot glass?" She arches a brow, her lips doing some cute pucker thing.

I want to kiss the look off her face.

"Is that what you want? A mini version of the Golden Gate Bridge to stick on the fridge."

She pierces the berry on her plate. "Not really."

"That's what I thought." I bite the corner of my toast then give her what I know is a buttery, crumby smile. "Not to worry. I'll know the right gift when I see it." I wink at her.

We finish the last of our breakfast in silence, but Shanti's constant smile doesn't go unnoticed. I love that I put it there. That she smiles more often and easily now.

After I set the dishes in the hall, we brush our teeth and gather what we need for the day. Shanti secures her hair in a high pony-tail and braids the length. Then she slips on a small cross-body bag and says she is ready.

We spend hours roaming the city on foot. Visit cute and quirky stores. Explore a fun museum. Wander through the aquarium. Snack on salty and sweet treats. Stop for lunch and moan over the most amazing savory crepes.

When we finish lunch, I lead us toward a jewelry store on the pier. As we get closer, I feel her eyes on my profile.

"Why are we going to the jewelry store?" Suspicion laces her tone. She should be curious and a tad skeptical.

Shanti doesn't know it yet, but I have no plans of walking out of the store without buying her a keepsake for our trip.

It's rare for me to spend excessive amounts of money. My grandparents worked hard to make sure my dad and the rest of the Fox family understood what it meant to *earn* every dollar. Yes, our family is loaded. But it's generational wealth. Money we rarely touch. It mostly collects dust and interest. When we do make the occasional withdrawal, it's for necessities, special occasions, or to help others.

This trip qualifies as a special occasion, and I plan to treat my girl.

I peek over at her, a hint of a smile teasing my lips. "Souvenir shopping."

"What?" she shrieks and comes to a halt. "Jet, no."

Turning to face her, I cup her cheeks. "Yes." I lower my lips to hers. "Whether you go in or not, I'm buying you something." My thumbs stroke her cheeks. "I'd rather you choose what you like."

With a heavy sigh, she says, "Fine."

We wander the store for several minutes before I spot the perfect memento—an adjustable rose gold bracelet with several small diamonds and a shimmering pearl at the heart. Stunning, simple, and matches perfectly with the necklace I gifted her years ago.

Shanti argues with me over the price almost as long as it took for me to find it. When she figures out just how insistent I am, she relents then wanders off to look at another case while I pay. And while she isn't looking, I add a matching pendant and ring to the order... for later.

Bag dangling from my arm, we make our way back to the hotel hand in hand. After a full day of sightseeing, I want to take Shanti out. Spoil her further with a nice dinner. And set the tone for... more.

———————

After the most decadent five-star meal, we order dessert to share. At a candlelit table for two, I feed Shanti succulent bites of sponge cake, champagne-macerated strawberries, and dollops of thick, sweet cream.

Watching her lips wrap around the fork is borderline orgasmic, and far too often, I have to look away. Last thing I need is the wait staff taking notice of my hard-on.

"Anything else you want to see before we head back?" I ask as she swallows the last bite.

Wiping her mouth with the napkin, she shakes her head. "Today has been exceptional." She reaches up and clasps the feather on her necklace. "More extraordinary than I imagined our last day here would be." She reaches across the table, and I take her hand. "And this place is the perfect end to a memorable trip."

Before this week, I've pictured countless futures with Shanti. But somehow, I never envisioned them like this. So effortless and significant. Fierce and profound.

Early on, I knew Shanti was meant to be mine. I felt it in my bones. In each thumping beat of my heart, our connection pulsed through every fiber of my makeup. We are two pieces of the same soul, and the tether binding us is finally stitching us back together.

Once I settle the bill, I pull out Shanti's chair, hook her arm with mine when she stands, and head for the exit. The way she leans in and gives me her weight is an incomparable balm. Therapy for my soul.

In the car, I take her hand and weave my fingers with hers. Caress her knuckles with my thumb. Stoke the embers of the fire that has been building since we drove out of Stone Bay. The fire that grows hotter and hotter with time.

Handing over the fob to the hotel valet, Shanti and I wander to the lobby elevators for the final time. Press the call button and wait to ascend to our floor, to the room where each day we have evolved into a new, better us.

With a ding, we step into the elevator. When the doors close and the world disappears, the air crackles around us. Rather than ignore the steady hum of electricity, I pivot and step into Shanti. Press her flush to the wall. Take her chin between my thumb and forefinger and drop my mouth to hers.

She instantly opens for me. Fire ignites in the center of my chest, under every inch of my skin, low in my groin as her tongue dives in and sweeps the length of mine. Sweet and divine and downright insatiable, I take her deeper. Devour her. Moan as her taste dances over my tongue. Grind my hardening cock over her center.

My dress shirt goes taut as she fists the fabric and crushes me to her chest. Then her leg hooks my hip, her heel digging into my ass as she secures me to her.

All too soon, the elevator signals we have reached our floor.

I break the kiss, ease out of her hold, and take her hand. With the sting of her kiss still on my lips, I take long, purposeful strides toward our room. Dig the key card from my pocket two doors down. Tap the key to the reader and shove the door open when we reach it.

Putting the *Do Not Disturb* sign on the handle, I shut the door and engage the locks. When I turn to face Shanti, she has her heels off and is letting down her hair.

Without an ounce of hesitation, I cross the room to her. Erase the distance between my body and hers. Capture the nape of her neck with my hand and whirl her around to take her once more.

Again, she opens for me immediately. Ravishes me with purposeful strokes of her tongue. Feasts on me as if I'm her last meal.

And I need more.

Mouth sealed to hers, I bring my hands to her hips and take slow, steady, backward steps in the general direction of the bed. Shanti follows without an ounce of hesitation. A beat later, my legs hit the mattress.

I clutch her hips with bruising strength. Tear my lips from hers to pepper kisses along her jaw to her ear. "I want you."

Her groan in response only makes me harder.

"Please, Shanti." I rock my hips forward and thrust my aching cock over her lower belly. "Can I have you? All of you?"

Head tipped back, she gasps as I suck her pulse point. "Yes." The three-letter word comes out breathy and needy as she tugs at my shirt.

Needing clarity, needing to know with absolute certainty what she is consenting to, I ask, "Is that a *yes* as in this feels good? Or *yes* I can have you?"

She rears back, frames my face with her hands, and levels me with a gaze so combustible I may come in my pants. "Yes, it feels good. Yes, I want you inside me. And yes, I'm going to hurt you if you keep dragging this out."

There is no fighting the grin pulling at my lips. But it only lasts a second. On the next breath, our mouths are fused together. Urgent. Hungry. Obsessed.

Shanti yanks my dress shirt from my pants. Her fingers fly to the buttons, popping them free one by one.

My hands drift to the back of her dress. To the tab resting over her spine between her shoulder blades. Wanting to savor every moment, I slowly drag the zipper down the teeth until I reach the curve of her ass. Material parted and exposing her light-brown skin, I skim the length of her spine from her tailbone to the nape of her neck. So soft. So delicate. So unbelievably perfect.

Goose bumps dance over her skin as she shivers under my touch.

With measured precision and the lightest of contact, I caress her warm skin and slowly peel her dress from her shoulders. Drop my lips to the crook of her neck and pepper kisses along her collarbone as the wispy fabric skates over her curves and pools at her feet.

She shoves my shirt down my arms, but gives up when it doesn't fall from my wrists. Before I release her to unbutton the cuffs, her hands are at the front of my belt. A swish and flick, the buckle releases. She whips the belt from the loops and tosses it behind her.

I want to laugh at her obvious eagerness, but can't.

Dexterous fingers unfasten my slacks. Jerk down the zipper. Hook into the waistband of my pants and send the cotton to the floor before I take my next breath.

Shanti leans back just enough to take in the sight of me. To visually traverse my body in a different light. For years, she has seen me shirtless. Seen me in skintight apparel. Felt my body pressed to hers. But this is new. An intimacy we've never shared. And she wants to remember each moment as much as I do.

Until recently, most contact between us was impersonal. Staged. A show we put on for an audience. At least it was for Shanti.

I've always held Shanti with reverence. With utmost care. Like the treasure she is. The day I knew I loved her, I saw her in a different light. Overnight, she'd become more than my best friend. She'd become the most important person in my life. My world.

Now she sees me through the same lens, and the feeling is heady as hell.

Both our chests bare and heaving, I strain against my black

boxer briefs as I take in her almost nonexistent lacy silver satin panties.

"Fuck," I bite out as I reach for her hips and haul her into my body.

Before I take her mouth again, she shoves at my chest and forces me onto the bed. Wild, unrestrained hunger swirls in her golden eyes. I refuse to look away. Refuse to miss a single moment.

One of her knees hits the mattress, then the other.

I scoot up the bed as she gets closer.

Agile and calculated, she crawls up my body. Plants her hands on my chest and straddles my hips.

I stare up at the woman who has held my heart captive more years than not. Ogle the goddess I've wanted to call mine for so long.

And now, I can.

Reaching up, I thread my fingers through her hair, make a fist, and yank her down. Our lips a breath apart, her amber irises locked on my grays, my tongue darts out and licks her lips. "Mine." The single syllable is a growl, a declaration, a permanent mark on her soul. An irreversible claim.

Her eyes roll closed as a sigh leaves her lips, her entire body melting into mine. "Yours." On the next heartbeat, her eyes are on mine again. "I've always been yours."

Those four words flip a switch in my mind and make me feral.

Shifting to grip her hips, I roll mine and flip her onto her back. Take her wrists in my hands and pin them above her head.

The cutest fucking squeal echoes through the room as she wraps her legs around my waist and hooks her feet over my ass. Hair fanned out around her head, brilliant smile plumping her cheeks, she stares up at me as if her biggest wish finally came true.

In this time-stopping moment, I fall deeper and harder for her.

Bringing a hand to her cheek, I caress the length of her jaw with my knuckles. Take her chin between my thumb and finger and tip it up. Lower my mouth to hers and kiss her slowly, reverently, profoundly. When our gazes meet again, the gravity of what is about to happen glimmers in her eyes.

"I love you," I say, voice soft yet resolute.

She wiggles one of her hands free, reaches up, and cups my cheek. "I love you, too."

My lips are back on hers, the kiss morphing from slow worship to savage obsession in a matter of seconds. I rock my hips. Stroke her clit with my painfully hard cock once, twice, a third time before I drift down her body. Kiss the length of her neck. Trace the hollow of her throat with my tongue.

Her hands are in my hair. Fingers woven through my thick strands. Nails scratching my scalp.

I dip lower. Memorize every freckle I discover on her light-brown skin. Trail my lips and tongue down her midline as my fingertips skim the outer swells of her breasts. Inhale deeply when I detect a hint of her sweet orange-blossom-and-honey scent.

Staring up her body, I pin her with my gaze. Lick my lips. Then kiss the inner swell of her breast once, twice, again and again until I reach the crest. My tongue darts out and circles the tight peak of her tawny nipple before I wrap my mouth around the tight bud and suck.

Her back bows off the bed. "Oh god."

A grin curves my lips, but I don't let up. If anything, I suck harder. Graze her skin with my teeth. Roll the other nipple between my fingers. Tease her body until the sweetest whimper falls from her lips.

A guttural moan vibrates my chest as I release her nipple with a *pop* and kiss my way to the other, repeating the delicious torture.

Her body hums beneath me, her fingers wrenching my hair. But I don't dare let up. With each tweak of her nipple, her cries grow louder. Raspier. Greedier.

Precum leaks from my tip as my balls beg for relief. But they'll just have to fucking wait.

I've waited years for this moment. No chance in hell I'm ruining our first time together by rushing it.

Freeing her from my mouth, I hum against her skin. "One day, I'll suck these pretty nipples until you come."

She whimpers and thrusts her breast toward my mouth. "Yes, please."

I tweak her nipples with my fingers once, twice, then release them. "Not today, baby." I lower my lips and kiss farther down her body. "But I promise, one day."

"I'll hold you to it."

Pressing a kiss beneath her navel, I say, "You better."

One kiss after another, I sink lower down her body and down the bed. When I reach the thick satin waistband of her panties, I push up on my elbows to get a better view. Stare at the very sheer fabric and intricately stitched pale-blue flowers.

These damn panties.

Were it not for the waistband and occasional finely stitched flower, I'd think she wasn't wearing panties. Add in that she is bare beneath the silky material…

"Fuck," I say on a groan.

She lifts her head and waits until I meet her gaze. "Is it a bad time to tell you there's a matching bra and garter belt?"

I fist her lush hips and growl. "You wicked little minx." I tug at the thin fabric beneath my fingers and inch her panties down. "Next time you put these on, you put it all on." I rise from the bed, peel her panties off, and toss them aside. Then, I hook my fingers in the waistband of my briefs and shove them to the floor. "I need the full experience."

Her gaze drops from mine and lands on my hand, now stroking my cock. Squirming and needy, she licks her lips then captures the bottom one between her teeth. I watch with bated breath as she palms her breasts. Pinches and tweaks her nipples. Slowly spreads her legs and exposes herself fully.

I crawl back onto the bed. Stroke myself as I stare at her perfect, glistening pussy. With my free hand, I run a finger down her wet lips.

She shivers then rocks into my touch.

"So fucking wet." I trail my finger back up, circling her clit when I reach it. "Is this for me?"

Back bowing off the bed, she tweaks her nipples harder. "Yes."

Ignoring my cock, I grip her waist and shove her farther up the bed. Then I scoot back, lower myself to the mattress, and hook her thighs over my shoulders. "Such a pretty little pussy," I say, tongue peeking out to wet my lips. "Hot and wet and all fucking mine."

My tongue darts out as I lower myself. A beat later, I lick the seam of her pussy. Taste her salty tang for the first time. Moan as her flavor hits my taste buds. Tighten my hold on her legs and pin her in place.

"Better than I imagined."

And then I'm back between her thighs, devouring every inch of her wet cunt. Flicking her clit like it's a fucking sport and I'm going for gold.

She writhes beneath me, her fingers woven in my hair, fisting, yanking, holding me to her. Over and over, she rolls her hips. Grinds herself against my mouth. Chases her orgasm.

It's the most magnificent and addictive sight I've witnessed.

And fuck, if it doesn't make me want to spread her thighs daily and worship every inch of her.

Quaking beneath me, her breathy moans come faster. Deeper. Louder.

My dick weeps for her. Begs for the soft skin of her hand, the welcome heat of her mouth, the greedy tightness of her cunt. But it will have to wait a little longer.

I want to wear her cum as a face mask first.

Wrapping my lips around her clit, I suck the tight, swollen bud. Insert a finger in her pussy. Pump once, twice, then insert another. I suck faster. Pump harder. Hit the spot deep inside her that has her ripping my hair from my scalp.

"Oh fuck," she cries out on repeat. Breath ragged, her thighs clamp down.

My fingers piston in and out of her with quick, perfect precision. I flick her clit with my tongue once, twice, and on the third time, a deep, guttural moan roars through the room as she soaks my fingers, my hand.

Pulling my fingers free, I release her clit and drop lower. Lick and suck and drink every fucking drop of her cum.

Gaze trailing up her body, I stare at the blotchy patches of redness as they spread from her breasts to her cheeks. Stare at her parted lips and the rapid rise and fall of her chest as she fists the bedding. Gawk the impossibly tight peaks of her nipples as her back arches higher.

Absolute, utter perfection.

As she comes down from her orgasm, I crawl up her body. Take one nipple, then the other between my lips and suck.

Her hiss fills the air, but she doesn't tell me to stop. No, she frames my face with her hands and hauls me up her body until my lips crash down on hers. A moan rumbles in her chest as she tastes herself on my tongue.

"I need to be inside you," I say when the kiss breaks.

Her legs circle my hips and squeeze with brutal strength. "What are you waiting for?" She digs her heels into my ass and thrusts up, soaking my dick with her orgasm.

I shift to get up. "Condom."

She digs her heels in further. "I'm on the pill, and I've been tested. I'm clean."

My eyes dart between hers. "I'm clean, too… and I had a vasectomy years ago."

I wait for a look of bewilderment to cross her face. Wait for her to ask me a dozen questions. Because how many guys elect to get a reversible vasectomy at eighteen? None that I know. But it was the right move for my future. By no means am I promiscuous. Not that it would matter if I was. All it takes is one time, one malfunctioning condom, one missed pill, or one faulty batch of birth control. I've known people who got pregnant while the pill, a condom, and spermicide were involved.

No thanks.

I want to have a say in when or if I decide to have children. And because my family is incredible, they encouraged my choice.

"Again, what are you waiting for?"

Before I have the chance to answer, she rolls us until my back hits the bed. Thighs bracketing my hips and hands planted on my chest, she glides her slick cunt up the length of my cock.

I bruise her hips with my fingers. "Fuck, you feel good."

Nails pierce my pecs as she rolls her hips again. And again. When her opening hits the head of my cock again, she leans forward and sinks her weight. One quick shift of her hips and my tip eases in. But then she rolls her hips and releases me to glide down and up the underside of my length again.

She repeats this over and over, driving me wild.

More than once, I open my mouth to argue. To tell her I need to feel her tight cunt around my cock. But I keep my mouth shut. I keep my hands on her hips and move with her. While Shanti teases me for what feels like hours, I ogle her body. Survey her gorgeous brown nipples and how they beg for attention. Scan every inch of her as she not only rolls her hips but her entire body.

Her lips part as her fiery amber eyes meet and hold mine. On her next roll up my length, she tilts her hips a little different. Takes the head of my cock inside her. Then another inch. And another until she is fully seated on my dick.

I shoot up and wrap my arms around her. Clutch the nape of her neck with one hand and pin her in place with my other hand pressed to her ass.

My back stings as her nails bite the skin. "So deep," she says on a moan.

Every hormone surging through my body yells at me to move. To roll my hips. To pump in and out of her. To fist her hips and fuck her hard until everyone in this hotel hears her scream my name.

But I stay still. Let her adjust to the feel of me inside her. Let her make the next move.

She doesn't make me wait long.

Arms draped over my shoulders, her fingers dive into my hair a beat before she rears back then drives forward.

We moan in unison.

My grip on her neck tightens. I ease out of her, then press down on her ass as I thrust my hips up.

The sting on my back intensifies as her nails return to my skin. It's the most delicious fucking pain. "More," I bite out as I palm both her ass cheeks and spread them. "Mark me."

Her nails dig deeper, and it sets me off. In a single move, we become a frenzy of hands and mouths and two bodies colliding in the most electric, intense, euphoric way.

Frantic and rough, she takes me again and again, deeper and deeper. I meet each drop of her hips with an upward thrust of mine.

Her head tips back, her lips parting as she bobs up and down my length. Her breasts in my face, I drop my mouth to one of her nipples and suck the tight bud with a little teeth.

"Yes." She drops her chin, her gaze falling to watch.

The sight of her staring at me sucking her nipple gives me another idea.

I release her with a *pop*. Slow the pace of my hips and hers in my hands. Lean back, drop a hand to the bed behind me, and lower my gaze to where my cock disappears inside her.

"Look how well you take me." I bring my thumb to her clit and roll circles around the tight bud. "This perfect, sweet pussy is mine."

Tucking her chin to her chest, lips parted, skin reddening and slick, she watches in fascination as she swallows every thick inch of my length.

"Say it."

Hooded eyes meet mine as she reaches up and pinches her nipples. "My pussy is yours."

"Fucking right it is."

She reaches between us, her fingers wrapping around the base of my cock as I slide out. "And this is mine," she states, her tone not to be argued with.

I thrust up and hit that spot deep inside her. "Only yours."

With a shove, my back hits the mattress. She slaps her palms to my chest and rides me hard and fast.

I fist her hips. Add to her speed. Jut up and meet her again and again.

And then her sweet whimpers echo through the room. Telling me she is close. So fucking close.

Her movements turn jerky as her body tightens around me. I hold her steady. Thrust her up and down my cock. Hold out just a little longer.

"Come on, baby. Get there."

The delicious, painful sting of her nails returns as she anchors herself to my chest. On my next upward thrust, she detonates with a roar and soaks my thighs.

Before she has a chance to come down, I sit up, clutch her to my chest, and flip her onto her back.

Hiking her leg up, her knee to her chest, I piston my hips and fuck her like a man out of control. My panting breaths mingle with hers, the smell of sex and sweat clinging to the air. Fire and urgency curl around my spine and settle low in my balls.

Her fingers comb through my hair and tighten into a fist and yank hard as she says, "Fill me up."

Those three words are my tipping point. A feral growl rumbles in my chest as I let go and spill inside her.

Lifting off the mattress, she takes my mouth with hers. Swallows my moans with gentle yet hungry swipes of her tongue.

When the kiss breaks, I brush away the hair stuck to her cheek. Trail my knuckles along the line of her jaw. Sigh at how absolutely perfect our first time was.

"I love you." I drop a chaste kiss to her lips.

The corners of her eyes crinkle as a soft smile tugs at her lips. "I love you, too." She reaches down and takes my ass in both of her hands. "Now, let me know when you're ready to go again."

THIRTY-SEVEN
DON'T MESS WITH WHAT IS MINE
SHANTI

Slower than what seems humanly possible, I peel my limbs from Jet's body. Scoot back one inch at a time until I reach the edge of the mattress. Then, in a swift move, I roll off the bed and pad out of the bedroom.

Exhausted from driving two days on the road, I leave Jet to sleep. With today comes a whole new bout of stress, and he needs as much rest and strength as he can get.

Closing the door behind me, I move through the guesthouse for the bathroom off the living room rather than disrupt Jet using the en suite. After I take care of business, I head for the kitchen and riffle through the fridge and cabinets in search of breakfast.

The eggs are almost finished cooking when Jet wanders out of the bedroom, one hand in his hair and the other scratching his stomach.

Dear god, he is the most beautiful man I've seen.

Jogger shorts slung low on his hips, bed head for days, pillow crease marks on half his face, and a smirk tugging at his lips that'd wet my panties... if I was wearing any. Jet is a fantasy come to life.

Mine.

"Something smells good," he says, voice raspy and low. He

steps up behind me, circles my waist with his arms, and drops his lips to my shoulder. "Thanks for making breakfast."

Turning my head, I give him a chaste kiss that feels anything but. Since the shift in our relationship, everything feels different. Bigger. More meaningful. More intense.

His love is everything I've always wanted but was too scared to believe I deserved. And every single day, I count my lucky stars he is part of my life. Thank every deity for giving him the patience to wait until I was ready.

After what feels like a lifetime, I am eager for the next phase of our journey. Thrilled and a touch antsy for what the future has in store. But no matter what happens, it will be wonderful so long as I have Jet.

"No problem." Heat blooms on my cheeks. "Will you grab plates and bowls?"

Pressing a kiss to my temple, he unwinds his arms from my waist and fetches dishes from the cabinet. He helps me divvy the oatmeal, diced fruit, cubed cheese, and scrambled eggs. Then he grabs the maple syrup and jar of sliced almonds.

"Coffee, tea, or something else?" He sets our plates on the breakfast bar.

"What are my tea options?"

He rattles off so many flavors I forget more than half.

"Earl Grey is good."

"Hot or iced?"

"Iced with oat milk."

He winks then spins around to make our drinks.

I slide onto the stool, drop my elbows to the counter, rest my chin on my clasped hands, and watch him move about. This all feels so domestic, so normal. Like we've been doing it for years instead of days.

Part of me wishes I'd given in earlier. Told him I loved him when he first said it to me. But another part of me is glad I didn't. Although I've loved Jet a long time, I was a mess for years. Angry with my parents for dictating every minute of my life. Upset at never getting the support or approval I craved from the people I deemed important. Frustrated when I worked hard and was told it wasn't enough.

I've done things I'm not proud of, but I wouldn't change any of them. The dark moments of my past shape who I am now. They allow me to see how precious life is. Without the bad, I wouldn't appreciate or be grateful for the good.

Jet sets the fanciest homemade iced latte next to my plate. "Added some vanilla-lavender simple syrup. Hope that's okay."

I narrow my eyes at him. "Did I totally miss you working as a barista at some point?"

He laughs. "No." He takes the stool next to mine. "Mom loves tea. She's the only reason I have so many options and know how to make that."

At the mention of his mom, awareness creeps in. And I know he feels it too.

There is no escaping what will happen today. After we clean up and dress, Jet plans to tell his parents about Vivienne. Although I'll be by his side, it won't be easy—for him or his family. But if I've learned anything about the Fox clan over the years, it's that they are the strongest, most resilient family in this town.

I lean into his side. "Lucky me." I press a kiss to his cheek. "Now, eat before it gets cold. I worked really hard at not burning anything."

His smirk in response exactly what I'd hoped for. With a silly little statement, I've eased some of his stress. Given him something else to focus on. Taken some of his anxiety. It's nowhere near enough, but it's a start.

Tears rim Aurora's eyes as a hand covers her mouth. August wraps an arm around her shoulders and hauls her into his chest, a hurt I've never seen before etched in the lines of his face.

Jet tightens his hold on my hand as his parents shatter on the couch across from us. I don't miss the faint tremble rippling through his body. The random quiet sniffles as he tries to hold it together.

I want to tell him it's okay to let go, to cry until his eyes get puffy, to scream until he loses his voice, to throw something and break it. Whatever he is feeling, the actions that follow are justified.

Jet didn't ask for this to happen. Nothing he said or did was an open invitation for Vivienne to take advantage of him. To overstep her role and his boundaries. Yet, Vivienne still did as she pleased and used her position of power to her advantage.

Now, unfortunately, Jet has to deal with the emotional domino effect on his feelings and those of his loved ones.

And I swear to every god in existence, Vivienne Bellecourt will pay gravely for what she has done.

Still in August's hold, Aurora sits straighter as she wipes at her cheeks. She blinks her red, glassy eyes a few times then looks to Jet. "My sweet, sweet boy." She extends a hand to him, and he takes it. "Wish I would've known about this from the beginning." Her gaze momentarily darts to her husband. "How did I not see this, Auggie?"

August runs a hand up and down her arm. "I missed it too, baby." He presses a kiss to her head then shifts his attention to Jet. "But none of us is to blame," he says, tone resolute. "And whatever it takes, I will make sure this woman never has an easy day for the rest of her life."

Well, *damn.*

The Fox family is notorious for their kindness and positivity. For generations, they have welcomed others with open arms and big hearts. Given so much of themselves to family, friends, and the community. And someone took advantage of their empathy and generosity.

An unidentifiable, intense emotion blooms and ignites in my chest. It urges me to not only fight for Jet but the whole Fox clan.

They are the only people who have ever felt like family, a real family, and I will not let a bitch like Vivienne steal their light.

"I just want her away from kids, Dad."

August's expression softens. "Yes, we've instilled you and your siblings with love and decency. But that doesn't mean we let anyone walk all over us. It doesn't mean they get to hurt us and be free from punishment." August stands, moves around the coffee table, and sits next to Jet. "What this woman did was wrong. Period. And now, she will pay the consequences."

Jet's knee starts to bounce, something I've never seen him do.

I lean more into his side, give him more of my weight. "It's the right thing to do," I say softly.

A heavy sigh leaves his chest. "I know." Jet peeks up at me, his gray eyes lighter. "Still twists me up inside."

Aurora pops up from her spot on the couch and darts around the table to kneel in front of him. She rests her hands on his knees and looks up at her son, so much love in her deep-blue eyes. "That just means you're human, sweetheart." A sympathetic smile curves her lips. "You have the biggest heart. And even though this woman did things she shouldn't have, it hurts you to not find a kinder way to deal with the situation." Aurora lifts her hands to frame his face. "But you did try. More than once." Her thumbs stroke his cheeks. "Now we do things differently."

Indecision still lingers on Jet's aura. He wants to do the right thing, but he doesn't want to stir up unnecessary trouble. He doesn't want to be the center of town gossip. He doesn't want to be hated, even if it's by a woman who wronged him.

So I try one last time to make him see what we are about to do is the way forward. Our next step is how we ensure this never happens again.

"What if Cedric or Stephanie or Manuel approached you after class and told you the same thing happened to them?"

My goal isn't to guilt Jet into taking legal action. I want to give him another perspective. The point of view of those of us indirectly involved. Because if Vivienne is allowed to carry on without being held accountable, this will happen again with someone else. And that child could easily be one of Jet's students if they attend dance camp.

"This can't keep happening. Not when we have the ability to stop it."

What I keep to myself is that I want to ruin Vivienne. Whatever accolades she has received, I want them tarnished. Whatever reputation she has earned over the years, I want it burned to ashes. And whatever joy she has experienced because of the dance community, I want to replace it with pain.

The woman deserves to rot. To be exiled. To sit in a dark cave, all alone, for the rest of her days. Recalling the ways she fucked up so many times, it's all she knows.

Vivienne Bellecourt messed with what is mine, and now she will pay the ultimate price.

With a gentle nod, Jet mumbles, "Yeah. Okay." He looks at each of us in turn but stays focused on his dad when he speaks again. "What's the next step?"

Shoulders sagging, relief washes over both Aurora and August.

"We file a report with the police. Then we visit Barron Law."

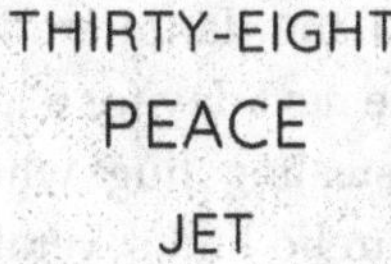

THIRTY-EIGHT
PEACE
JET

EXHAUSTING IS NOWHERE NEAR A STRONG ENOUGH WORD TO DESCRIBE the past ten days.

After opening up to my parents about Vivienne, Dad reached out to Chief Emerson at the police station. Then he called Barron Law. Knowing we'd have to go over every detail, and both would ask a long list of questions, each visit would likely be hours rather than minutes.

To save me from rehashing my story repeatedly, Emery Barron offered to meet us at the police station. She also asked if we'd invite Neesa and Aurelio to the meeting. This would help her get a bigger picture of Vivienne and her role.

An hour later, we took over the SBPD conference room. One horrible memory at a time, I spilled my history with Vivienne. Answered countless questions that made my stomach churn nonstop. By the end, I felt more violated, not by anyone in the room, but by the woman at the center of it all.

The more I talked about what happened, the more questions I answered, the more apparent it became I'd downplayed what actually happened. Maybe it was how my juvenile mind perceived things when it all started. Maybe I didn't *want* to believe it was worse—it's in my nature to find the positive and

keep the peace. Or maybe it was a method of mental protection or self-preservation.

Regardless, when we left the police station hours later, restraining orders had been filed for Vivienne from me, Shanti, Neesa, Aurelio, and the Fox family. A trespassing order was in place for our homes and the dance studio. Emery promised to have papers drawn up the next day for a lawsuit.

Delivering a breath-stealing hug when we finished, Neesa informed me she and Aurelio had several contacts to touch base with. By the time they reached the end of their list, no one would want Vivienne anywhere near their studio or dancers.

Two days after the lawsuit was officially on the books, a dancer in central Washington came forward and said they were also a victim of Vivienne's abuse. The next day, two dancers from Rhythm and Flow spoke up. A couple days later, two former dancers from the studio shared their stories.

The news broke my heart and gave me some respite simultaneously.

With every fiber of my being, I hate that this happened, not only to me but others as well. I hate that we were subjected to this sick woman's manipulation and misconduct. That none of us felt safe enough to come forward when it started.

A shadowy cloud of guilt also hangs over my head.

A small part of me is happy I'm not alone in this. That I have others to talk with. That we can heal from this together. Yes, I have Shanti, my family, and the studio in my corner. But it isn't the same.

It's difficult to truly comprehend the gravity and impact of a situation you haven't experienced firsthand. Trauma changes you. It makes you question everyone and their intentions, even the people you love and trust most. It forces you to put on a brave face, so no one sees your pain or asks questions.

We want to be seen for our personality, for what we have to offer the world, not our scars.

With Shanti in my life, I have no doubt I'll heal eventually. But it's nice to know I can call or text someone who has experienced similar circumstances. That we can chat freely and not worry about judgment or criticism.

"What're you thinking about so hard?" Sitting on the opposite end of the couch, Shanti rests her feet in my lap as she peeks over the top of her book.

Taking her foot in my hands, I massage all the places I know bother her. "How this will all be over soon."

The three days after we went to the police, Shanti and I tried to work at the studio. But I was too distracted. Shanti taught most of the lessons while I zoned out intermittently, my mind racing over what would happen next. At the end of the third day, Neesa told us to take a couple weeks off.

Naturally, we argued. I told her I was fine, but she saw through the lie and put her foot down.

I'm glad she did.

"Yes, it will." She slips a bookmark between the pages and sets her book down. "You seem less than happy about that."

I twist to face her better, keeping her foot in my lap to massage. I open my mouth, close it, then open it again to mutter, "It's weird."

"What is?"

I purse my lips as I figure out how to articulate what I'm feeling. Oddly, I *know* the feeling. Have felt something comparable to it. But it's almost as if my mind won't translate the emotion into words.

"I am happy." I hold her steady gaze. "So damn happy." Lifting her feet, I stretch my legs out on either side of hers then lower her feet to my lap again. "But there's also this foreign feeling here." I press a hand to the spot between my heart and throat. The flutter vibrates beneath my palm. "It's not relief, but something close to it."

I've always been open with Shanti. Always told her how much she means to me. How much I love her. But as the stress from the mess with Vivienne slowly evaporates, it dawns on me more each day how I've still kept pieces of myself from Shanti.

I've given so much of myself to her, but out of fear, I haven't given her my whole heart. Now I can.

"Peace," I say after a moment.

"Peace?" Shanti tilts her head.

"Yeah."

I start rubbing her other foot and think about my last therapy session. How a figurative light came on when we talked about more recent incidents. How things I'd bottled up for so long erupted because I was no longer worried only for myself, but also for Shanti.

"I've been holding back with everyone, and not just about what happened. My therapist says it's a defense mechanism. A way to shield myself from hard things. So whenever I was ready and willing to process those past hurts, I would have a safe space within myself. A quiet place unaffected by any of it."

Eyes narrowed and lips puckered, Shanti is as thoroughly confused as I was when my therapist told me this.

I chuckle. "It took days for it to click. Once it did, it made sense."

Everyone hides a piece of themselves away, and not for nefarious reasons. We all need a place no one else can touch. A place we can go to when we close our eyes and need to reset. A place all our own. Somewhere to mull over our thoughts without judgment or prejudice. A true safe space.

"I'll take your word for it."

"With Vivienne in police custody until the trial in a couple weeks, I no longer need my guard up all the time. I don't need to look over my shoulder."

And damn, it feels good—to not worry, to not wonder when her next visit will be, to be free from her intimidation.

On a deep inhale, I say, "For the first time in years, I finally feel like I can be *me*. All of me."

Shanti sits up, shifts her feet to the outside of my legs, and scoots across the couch until she's in my lap. Framing my face with her hands, those stunning golden eyes hold mine. "I love you, Jet." She presses a chaste kiss to my lips. "As you are now. Who you'll be five or ten or twenty years from now."

My heart jolts in my chest, my pulse whooshing loudly in my ears.

She rests her forehead on mine, her thumbs stroking my cheeks. "I. Love. You." She punctuates each word, making sure they strike and resonate.

And they do. They really do.

It's on the tip of my tongue to ask her again to move in with me. Yes, we have been inseparable since the start of our San Francisco trip. Yes, she has stayed every night with me since returning to Stone Bay. But I want to make it official. I want this, us, to be permanent in every possible way.

Winding my arms around her waist, I haul her forward until nothing exists between us. "I love you, too. So fucking much." I seal my lips to hers and emphasize just how much. Lick the seam of her lips a beat before my tongue dives in to stroke hers.

Her hands are in my hair, fingers curling and tugging as she tilts her head and kisses me deeper. Every taste, every roll of her hips, every delicious inch of her molded to my body drives my need for her higher. I've spent countless years falling emotionally in love with this woman. Now I get to fall just as much in love with other parts of her.

Move in with me. The thought runs on repeat through my mind as we kiss and claim and love each other more.

As I'm about to break the kiss and say the words, my phone vibrates in my pocket. I groan at whoever dares to interrupt this perfect moment.

Shanti breaks the kiss with a laugh and leans back only enough for me to retrieve my phone. "To be continued."

"Definitely."

Tapping on the text notification, my phone unlocks and opens the message.

MOM
Family dinner at 5. Is Shanti coming?

I turn the phone so Shanti can see the message. "You in for family dinner?"

Shanti's eyes glaze over as she stares at the screen, her bottom lip trapped between her teeth. It's cute that she's nervous. Over the years, she joined family dinners here and there. But this time is different because her role in my life is different.

We haven't declared as much, but Shanti is mine. My best friend, my partner, my person, and now, my girlfriend.

Releasing her lip, she nods. "I'm in."

My cheeks sting with a wide smile as I type out a response and hit send.

We'll be there.

Then I drop my phone on the couch cushion, wrap my arms back around Shanti, and pin her to my chest. "Move in with me," I say before I lose the nerve.

Her breath hitches as her eyes blow wide. "Jet…" My name is a choked whisper on her tongue.

"I've waited a lifetime for you, Shanti." My hands slip under her shirt, my fingers caressing her soft skin and supple curves. "Now is our time." I lean in and kiss the tip of her nose. "You and me against the world. What do you say?"

She reaches up and combs her fingers through my hair, her nails grazing my scalp. As the seconds tick by, her expression softens, warms, glows. And then, she nods. "Yes." She slaps a hand to her mouth, but I still see the radiant smile beneath it.

"Love you," I say as I crush her to my chest.

Her arms wring my neck as she lightly bounces in my lap. "Love you, too."

"Get over here and hug me," Grandma Amelia says as she extends her arms and waves me closer.

In two strides, I wrap my arms around Grandma's waist and lift her off the ground.

Muffled laughter shakes her chest as she clutches my shoulders. "Best hugs ever."

"Hey," Grandpa Zach says with mock affront. "I heard that."

As I set Grandma on her feet, she side-eyes him, the tease of a smile on her lips. "Good." The full force of her smile is unleashed, but only I can see it.

I love their light banter and easy affection. Their relationship has stood the test of time for many reasons, but their playful and lovable nature with each other is a major contributing factor.

My only hope is Shanti and I will have a love as passionate and timeless as theirs.

Releasing her hold on me, Grandma shuffles sideways and takes Shanti's hands. "It's been too long since I've seen you, darling girl." Then Shanti is in Grandma's arms. "Welcome home."

Tears rim Shanti's eyes as she hugs my grandma. "Th-thank you."

Grandpa hauls me into a quick, firm embrace, then holds me at arm's length and looks me over. "Something about you is different." His expression gentles as he leans in and drops his voice. "Must be the beautiful young lady at your side." He tilts his head toward Shanti. "Love is a powerful creature. It will either shred you or make you whole." Cupping my cheek, he nods. "Good to see you whole."

Grandma and Grandpa tug us farther into the house to exchange more hugs. Everyone embraces Shanti as if she has always been part of the Fox family. And in a way, she has.

Since our first year of ballet, we have shared the most incredible bond. A connection so powerful and rare. We've experienced highs and lows—individually and together. We've hurt each other as much as we've loved each other.

It took time for us to reach this point. For both of us to be emotionally ready for the future we deserve. But it's finally our time, and I can't wait to see what the future holds.

We settle around the table as we do for every family dinner. Food is passed, plates are filled, chatter and laughter fill the room. I glance across the table to see Delilah kiss Phoebe's cheek. A soft smile Phoebe only reserves for my sister tugs at the corners of her mouth. Then I shift my attention to June and their girlfriend, Fern. Tonight is Fern's introduction to the whole Fox crew, and I already know she's overwhelmed.

We may be one of the kindest families in Stone Bay, but there are still a lot of us, especially for someone as shy as Fern.

Once the dinner dishes are cleared from the table, Mom and Delilah return from the kitchen with a chocolate cake with dollops of peanut butter frosting and a banana cream pie. Dad hot on their heels with coffee and tea.

Shanti's gaze shoots to mine, silent questions swirling in her amber eyes.

I shrug then lean in and drop my voice. "Mom texted me and June to ask what you and Fern like for dessert."

"So she made me a cake and Fern a pie?" she whisper-asks, a touch awestruck.

"She may have picked it up at the bakery."

"Still..." The way the word floats out, it's obvious she is perplexed as to why.

Reaching for her hand under the table, I lace my fingers with hers. "Mom wanted to do something special for you and Fern, but not make it a huge display." I press my lips to her temple. "Think of it as a subtle, unspoken I love you."

She gives my hand a tight squeeze but doesn't say a word. She doesn't need to. If anyone at this table can read Shanti, it's Mom.

As the dessert plates clear, the gathering starts to thin. One round after another of hugs, we say our goodbyes until the next family dinner. When it's my turn to hug Mom, she holds me with a little more strength than usual.

"Love looks good on you, Jet." Releasing the hug, she meets my gaze. "Never take it for granted. Never stop working to keep her heart."

I nod. "Thank you, and I promise."

Mom winks then moves to hug Shanti. "So glad you're here." Mom tucks a loose strand behind Shanti's ear. "Right where you belong."

And before Shanti starts to cry, I take her hand and lead her back to the guesthouse. *Our* house.

THIRTY-NINE
THE GAVEL CLAPS
JET

SHANTI RESTS A HAND ON MY BOUNCING LEG AS WE WAIT FOR THE final day of the trial to begin. "I'm here," she whispers. "It's almost over."

Those words, combined with her touch, are the comfort I need right now.

According to Emery, we'll finish the last cross-examination this morning, then each attorney gives their closing arguments, and the jury goes off to deliberate. It could take hours or days, but I hope the evidence is clear enough to put this all behind us tonight.

When the bailiff walks toward the side door in the courtroom, I direct my gaze forward. I ignore everything in my periphery except for Shanti. Take slow, steadying breaths and focus my attention on each inhale and subsequent exhale.

After today, you never have to be in the same room as her again. Today, it ends.

"All rise," the bailiff's booming voice calls, snapping me out of my breathing exercises.

The judge enters the courtroom and sits behind the bench. "You may be seated."

As I have the previous three days, I zone out when others take

the witness stand. I've already heard their stories. Already know their pain. Already know their struggles and how what Vivienne did impacted their lives.

The only reason I'm here is to see this through to the end. Plus, Emery said it would look good for as many of us to be here as possible. A united front fighting for justice.

"Thank you for your testimony," the judge says to the witness. "You are excused."

The witness leaves the stand and comes to sit behind me next to the others. Each of us offers them a hand of support. A silent way to say, *after this, we can breathe again.*

In a pantsuit that costs more than I make in three months at the studio, Vivienne's attorney rises and glides across the room to stand in front of the jury box.

Again, I zone out.

I don't need a fancy degree to know this woman is going to preach about her client's accolades and reputation in the dance community prior to my "false" accusations. She will blather on about all of us being children when the "supposed" incidents started, and how we must have misinterpreted the situation. How we are not remembering correctly because it occurred so long ago. She will do her damnedest to convince the jury that we all have some preposterous vendetta against this woman because we didn't rise to the top in ballet.

My blood boils.

How can someone defend a person like Vivienne? How can they stand in a crowded room and say Vivienne did nothing wrong? More importantly, how do they live with themselves?

Nausea roils in my belly, and I press a hand to my mouth as I take more deep breaths.

The clicking of heels echoes through the room and Vivienne's attorney resumes her seat.

"Ms. Barron, if you'll give your closing argument," the judge says, gesturing toward the jury.

For whatever reason, this time, I pay attention.

"Thank you, Your Honor." Emery rises from her seat, buttons her suit jacket, and crosses to stand near the jury.

The entire room falls silent.

"When a parent signs their child up for a program, the last thing they want to worry about is if the adult is a safe person. Each of my clients was taught to speak up when something out of the ordinary happened, whether at school or dance or a friend's house. They were taught to protect themselves and their peers from harm by talking with a trusted adult."

With slow, purposeful strides, Emery traverses from one end of the jury box to the other, catching each juror's eye.

"But what happens when a trusted adult has ulterior motives? What should a *child* do when they fear the repercussions of speaking up against said trusted adult?" Emery pauses at the heart of the jury box and gives her words a moment to sink in. "Why do victims always have to fight harder to be heard? Especially the most vulnerable."

Taking a deep breath, Emery stands taller but manages to look relaxed.

"Mr. Fox waited nine years to come forward with his truth. When I asked him why, he said, and I quote, 'Police and courts rarely believe girls or women when they file these types of charges. Why would they believe me, a grown man who was a boy when it first started?' Let those words sink in."

She pauses and clasps her hands behind her back.

"Shortly after Mr. Fox had the courage to speak his truth, after word spread within the community, more came forward. More shared their harrowing stories, some darker and more dubious than others." Emery points toward Vivienne and her attorney. "Their abuser and her lawyer continue to deny the truth. Continue to claim the victims are doing this as a form of revenge. They claim this supposed vengeance is because they didn't excel in dance. I am here to tell you they are wrong."

Emery begins to pace the length of the jury box again.

"Of my clients who applied to dance companies, more than

half were accepted to six or more premier companies. Others were accepted by more than one but fewer than five. Each chose the best path for their future. The reason news of Ms. Bellecourt's behavior came to light is that, after years of no interaction, she began to heavily pursue Mr. Fox. Made him an offer he couldn't refuse, especially in front of his boss. Then she proceeded to confront him, even after she was asked to stay away. And finally, Ms. Bellecourt threatened Mr. Fox and Ms. Mahal, stating she would ruin them if they spoke a word to anyone."

Taking a couple steps back, Emery glances from one juror to the next.

"My clients, both as children and adults, were spoken to in a sexual manner by Ms. Bellecourt. My clients, both as children and adults, were touched in an unprofessional and explicit manner, without permission, by Ms. Bellecourt. A clear abuse of power. And each of my clients, both as children and adults, has been threatened in some capacity that if they were to mention any of their interactions with Ms. Bellecourt to anyone, she would enact her own form of vengeance."

With another step back, Emery nods.

"Ladies and gentlemen of the jury, Ms. Bellecourt used her role to exploit children and adults for her own deviant, inexcusable means. Ms. Bellecourt assaulted them and felt no remorse regarding her actions. How many more children need to be subjected to her abuse before action is taken? None, if you do the right thing and find her guilty on all charges."

Stomach in knots, I poke at the food on my plate, unable to eat while the jury deliberates.

Next to me, Shanti loads her fork with lettuce, chicken, and veggies, and brings it to her mouth. We've been in the café next to the courthouse for almost an hour and she has eaten maybe three bites of her salad.

Across the table, Emery's plate is close to empty.

I continue to poke.

"Would you like a box?"

Glancing up, an older woman with kind green eyes gives me a warm, sympathetic smile. A blue apron is cinched around her waist, straws and napkins filling two of the pockets. The nametag on her shirt reads *Joan*, a dish towel slung over her shoulder.

"That would be great, Joan. Thank you."

"You got it." She winks then looks to Shanti. "How about you?"

"Yes, please."

"Two boxes coming up." And then she turns to the other two tables in our group and asks the same.

Eating feels impossible right now. Like I can't even force my hand to load the fork and lift it to my mouth.

Emery's phone buzzes as the server returns with boxes. She taps the screen a couple times, her eyes scanning. Minute-long seconds pass before Emery glances up. "Can I get the check, please?"

"Give me one sec, sweetheart." The server is gone less than a minute, returning with the bill.

Emery does a quick scan and hands it back with her card.

"Everything okay?" I ask when the server walks off.

"The jury has decided. We're due back in thirty minutes."

So quick. Is that normal? Does that mean they sided with Vivienne?

My stomach roils.

"Okay," I manage to choke out.

Emery doesn't give us false hope as we walk back to the court-room. It'd be a foolish move. She did her part. She helped us share our story.

Now it is up to a jury of our peers.

My ears ring as we walk back into the courtroom. The walls feel like they are closing in on me as the jury takes their seats. My hands shake at my sides as Vivienne enters. My stomach constricts as the judge comes in and takes their seat.

Vision hazy, I watch as the bailiff takes a paper from a juror, hands it to the judge, and resumes his place in the room.

"So say you one, so say you all?" the judge asks the jurors.

"Yes, Your Honor."

The judge nods then reads the verdict. "In the case of Jet Fox and additional claimants versus Vivienne Bellecourt, in the matter of sexual misconduct with a minor, we, the jury, find Vivienne Bellecourt guilty on all six counts. In the matter of exploitation of a minor, we, the jury, find Vivienne Bellecourt guilty on all six charges. In the matter of felony stalking, we, the jury, find Vivienne Bellecourt guilty on four counts."

With a signal from the judge, the bailiff sidles up to Vivienne.

"I hereby sentence you, Vivienne Bellecourt, to the Washington Corrections Center for Women. Court will commence at a later date to determine the length of your sentence." The judge claps the gavel. "Jurors, thank you for your service. Court is adjourned."

Struck speechless, my vision blurs as the judge disappears into their chambers.

Guilty. Vivienne Bellecourt is guilty on all charges. She is going to jail, probably for the rest of her life.

And finally, I am free.

FORTY
ONE LAST TRY
SHANTI

One Month Later

Clasping the feather charm on my necklace, I slide it back and forth, over and over, as I stare up at the ceiling. My mind spins and spins, my thoughts churning in a wild vortex.

For weeks, a faint voice in the deep recesses of my mind has whispered incoherent drivel. But recently, the voice has grown louder. The message has become clearer. And my anxiety has ratcheted tenfold.

Because that voice is getting harder to ignore.

Something is missing.

Without a shadow of doubt, the niggling voice and aching gap in my heart have nothing to do with Jet. If anything, he has stitched my tattered pieces back together. He has shown me I am worthy of love and happiness and a future of my choosing. With Jet, I feel alive, truly alive, for the first time.

Yet, a chasm still exists beneath my breastbone. A pang I'm unable to shake. An inkling of sadness lingering in the periphery. And I can only think of one reason why it is there. One reason why I don't feel whole.

My parents.

It's been years since I've seen or spoken with them. Years since my father put his foot down regarding my future, since my mother lost her backbone and sided with him, since I shoved most of my belongings into suitcases and bags and left my parents behind without a word.

Now that I'm in a better place, now that I have love and peace in my life, I need to try to make things right with my parents. The keyword is *try*.

I have no preconceived notions all will end well. But I'll never know unless I make an effort.

The comforter shifts as a low groan fills the air. Jet stretches into a starfish, his hand and foot nudging my limbs a beat before he rolls onto his side to cuddle with me.

"Mm," he mumbles against my skin as he peppers kisses up my neck. "Morning, baby."

I love how raspy his voice is in the morning.

With a slight turn of my head, I press a kiss to his cheek. Before I can pull away, his lips are on mine. Soft and warm and perfect. "Morning."

He wiggles an arm free, reaches up, and gently presses between my eyebrows. "What has my girl flustered so early?" Dropping his finger, he kisses the same spot.

I roll onto my side to face him, tucking my hands under my cheek on the pillow. "Can I tell you later?"

He toys with the end of my braid. "Of course." Then he kisses me more thoroughly.

With his mouth on mine, every thought, every worry, every thread of anxiety disappears.

Needing more, I glide a hand up his cheek and into his hair as I take him deeper. I hook a leg over his hip, and he grips the underside of my thigh, hiking it higher.

We grind and groan as hands wander and fingers knead. Jet inches my shirt up, up, up, breaking the kiss long enough to jerkily yank it off and toss it aside. As soon as my arms are free, my hands go to his hips, my fingers slipping beneath the elastic of his boxer briefs and shoving them down his thighs.

I wrap my fingers around the base of his thick, pulsing length and stroke up.

His fingers bruise my ass as a sharp hiss echoes through the room. A beat later, I'm on top of him, his hands working my panties down my legs. The moment I kick them away, I straddle his hips and sit up, ready to take him.

But he has other plans.

Gripping my ass, he hauls me up his body. "Get up here." His tongue darts out and licks his bottom lip before he traps it between his teeth.

A low throb pulses at the junction of my thighs, arousal soaking my pussy lips. I crawl up his body until my knees bracket his head. And then I lower myself within an inch of his mouth.

Looping his arms around my legs, he tries to tug me down more. "Sit."

My brows twitch as I stare down at him, unsure. "Erm... what if I smother you?"

A, *Are you serious right now?* look takes over his expression. "You won't." He nips at the inside of my thigh, and I shriek. "Sit. Down."

This time, when he hauls me closer, I don't resist. I do as he says and sit on his face. His tongue darts out, licks up the seam of my pussy, then flicks my clit like it's his goddamn job.

"Holy shit." Dropping my head back, my eyes roll closed.

His mouth feels so fucking good like this. The pressure on my clit... blissful perfection. The way his tongue dips down and plunges inside me... absolutely euphoric.

I roll my hips. Grind my pussy against his mouth. Moan as his stubble bites then stings my sensitive skin. Drive my body faster. Crush him with more of my weight. Chase the mind-warping orgasm only Jet delivers.

He draws back, and I open my mouth to complain. But he cuts me off and commands, "Grab the headboard."

A guttural moan vibrates my chest.

"Fuck my face like a good girl."

"*Jesus.*"

A loud *whack* fills the air just before my ass stings. "The only name I want on those lips while I take you is mine." Another harsh, delicious slap. "And with these earmuffs"—he taps my thighs—"it's best you scream it."

He yanks me back to his mouth and eats my pussy like it's his last meal.

My hands go to the headboard, my nails scraping the wood. Above him, I slowly find my rhythm as I rock my body. Back and forth, again and again, I glide over his face. Seek out more pressure. Piston my hips faster.

Fire scorches my skin. An exquisite ache blooms low in my belly. Stroke after deliciously libidinous stroke, he devours my cunt. Dominates my clit. Growls against my pussy when I start to whimper. Tremble. Edge closer to orgasm.

The wood of the headboard complains as my nails dig deeper. "Oh fuck." My thighs shake as my hips move slower. "Jet, I..." I drop my chin and stare down at him. Greed and desperation and something inherently primal swirl in those fiery gray eyes.

My thighs trapped in his hold, he pins me to his face. Wraps his lips around my clit. Sucks and sucks and sucks until I'm writhing and mewling and begging to come.

On a hoarse scream of his name, I shatter. Fist the headboard until my hands go numb. Quake as I soak his face, my legs, the pillow.

Jet releases my thighs and slides me down his body. Flips me onto my back and settles in the cradle of my hips. Hikes my leg up until my knee grazes the bed. And then he slams into me, hitting so deep.

We both moan.

Then his mouth takes mine, the strokes of his tongue matching the rhythm of his thrusts.

My taste on his lips is sinful and addictive and something I never thought I'd crave. But god, I want more. Need more. Silently demand more.

Nipping a path along my jaw, he stops near my pulse point. "Your cunt is absolutely divine," he purrs, licking the shell of my ear. "So fucking sweet." He sucks my lobe between his lips. "Perfect."

I palm the globes of his ass. Sink my nails into his skin. Meet him thrust for thrust. "You feel so good." I claw my way up his back, latching my arms near his neck.

"Yeah?" He shifts his hips, his cock hitting from a different angle. "How about now? Does that feel good?"

Pleasure rolls through me as Jet plunges impossibly deeper. "Yes," I pant out, wrecking his back with my nails. "Whatever you do, don't stop."

A hand wrapped around my ankle, he hooks his free arm under my shoulders and pins me in place. Pistons his hips harder. Faster. Breath heating my skin, he slams into me over and over. Grunting. Growling.

He's feral, but I want him barbaric.

"Harder," I cry out.

Skin slaps skin with brutal force as his body pummels mine again and again. "You want harder, baby?"

"Yes." I send a hand into his hair, curl my fingers into a tight fist, and yank. "Own me."

A husky moan hits my ears. Then his fiery gray eyes meet my ambers as he says, "You are fucking mine, Shanti. *Mine.*"

And then he claims my body with his. Marking me with his mouth. Bruising me with his fingers. Ruining me with each thrust of his hips.

When he hits that spot deep within me again, I spiral into oblivion. Cry out his name as light dances in my vision, my orgasm pulsing in wave after blissful wave. A delicious buzz dances under my skin. A persistent ringing echoes in my ears.

"Exquisite," he coos, his lips ghosting mine. Then he pistons his hips once, twice, and on the third, he comes with a roar.

———

As Jet pops a forkful of food into his mouth, I say, "I've been thinking about reaching out to my parents." When I twist to meet his waiting gaze, his expression is exactly what I anticipated.

Really? You had to wait until my mouth was full?

Yes. I did. Because I wanted to get the whole thing out and give him a moment to mull over it before speaking.

Swallowing the bite, he washes it down with juice. "You know I'll support your decision, but is there a particular reason why?"

I've brewed over this for days. Asked myself the exact same question countless times. Because after all the heartache they've put me through, after the painful rejection they delivered, I needed to know this was the right move.

Every time it popped into my thoughts, that subtle hollow feeling in my chest throbbed more. Ignoring it is pointless. It won't go away until I have my answer. Until they give me a direct answer. Whether good or bad, in the end, I can say I tried one last time. I made an effort. And then, I can heal and move forward.

"Just feels like I'm not quite whole, if that makes sense."

He nods.

"I don't know if it's possible for us to forgive and move on, but I want to try." I push around the food on my plate with my fork. "If they refuse to let go of the past, if they can't accept me for who I am now, then I'll have my answer. Sad as it is, I'll accept it and move on without them."

Cupping my jaw, his thumb gently strokes my cheek. "You are one of the strongest, bravest people I know." He leans in and presses a tender kiss to my forehead. "I am honored and so damn proud to call you mine."

Heat hits my cheeks as he pulls back, and I drop my gaze. "Thank you," I say just above a whisper. "Don't know who I'd be without you."

Taking my chin, he lifts it until our eyes meet. "One, you never need to thank me." He tucks a fallen lock of hair behind my ear then trails the length of my braid until he reaches the ribbon at the end, giving it a gentle tug. "Two, you'd still be an incredible woman. I just help you shine brighter." He winks. "And three, I love that you're trying to repair something you didn't break in the first place. You have the biggest heart. It's a shame they can't look past their narrow focus to see that."

My insides turn to warm honey at his words. I don't know what I did to earn Jet's love, but I will never take it or him for granted. "If they agree to meet, will you go with me?"

"Of course. Nowhere else I'd rather be." He takes my hand in his and brings it to his lips.

"I'm not sure what to expect, but in case things don't go well, it'd be nice to have you there."

"Hey." He waits until our eyes lock. "I want you to promise me something."

"Okay."

His expression takes a more serious tone. "More than anything, I'd love for them to be a part of your life." He pauses and takes a breath. "But if they aren't willing to love you for who you are, you promise me that you'll do what's best for *you* and not them."

A lump forms in my throat, and I swallow.

"Baby, you're allowed to be you. To be genuine. To enjoy what makes you happy." His thumb strokes the back of my hand. "You deserve to live the best life without an ounce of guilt."

"Okay," I mutter, not knowing what else to say.

Jet twists in his seat, yanks my stool closer, and wraps me in a tight embrace. "I've seen so many of your facets, Shanti Mahal, and I love every single one of them." He relaxes his hold. "You wouldn't be the woman I fell in love with years ago without those moments."

The backs of my eyes sting. "Jet…"

He reaches up and caresses my cheek with the backs of his knuckles. "Promise me you'll choose you first."

I close the distance between us and press my lips to his. "I promise."

FORTY-ONE
IN YOUR CORNER, ALWAYS
JET

Fingers toying with her necklace, Shanti's knee bounces in the passenger seat as we drive off the Fox estate.

On instinct, I rest a hand on her thigh. Stroke the silky fabric of her knee-length dress once, twice, before tightening my hold on her. I want to tell her everything will work out, that when we leave the restaurant tonight, this rift between her and her parents will be resolved.

But I refuse to give her false hope. I refuse to make promises it isn't my place to keep.

If the only thing I can do is stand by her side, support her, and protect her heart, then that is what I'll do.

"If you want to go home, just say the word," I say, hoping it eases her anxiety.

Her eyes dart to my profile, and I see her shake her head in my periphery. "Thanks." She rests her hand on mine and gives it a squeeze. "But I need to see this through."

The call to her parents two days ago was brief. Less than five minutes. Only long enough for generic greetings, detached inquisitions of how the other person was doing, and to set up tonight's dinner plans.

Gods, I want to grab each of her parents and shake some sense

into them. I want to tell them how brilliant and talented and loving their daughter is. How my life is better because she is in it.

For the time being, I keep those thoughts to myself. But if they crush her soul with hurtful words or actions, I will step in. I will act.

All Shanti wants is love and happiness, and I will shield her from anyone who tries to rob her of that.

I turn my palm up to kiss hers and lace our fingers. "Love you, baby."

She leans across the console and kisses my cheek. "I love you, too."

Minutes later, I steer the SUV into the lot for Gigi's Italian and find a parking space a couple down from Reema. The relief I feel at seeing her is nothing compared to the way Shanti's whole body melts into the seat.

"She's early," Shanti says as she unbuckles her seat belt.

I cut the engine and hit the button on my seat belt. "Maybe she wanted a little time with you before we head inside."

Shanti nods. "You're probably right." Tugging the handle, she slips out of the car.

Doing the same, I meet her at the back of the car, take her hand, and let her lead us toward Reema.

A wide, toothy smile brightens Reema's face when we reach her. "Hi." Her arms instantly go around Shanti and wrap her in a breath-stealing hug. "I've missed you." Reema releases the hug and holds Shanti at arm's length. "How are you? I still need to hear all about San Francisco."

For the first time today, a genuine smile lights Shanti's expression. And with that simple reaction, relief and hope bubble to the surface.

Reema and Shanti chat and catch up until it is time to head inside the restaurant. When we reach the door, I hold it open for them. I press a kiss to Shanti's cheek, then excuse myself to let the host know we are waiting on the rest of our party.

The host offers to seat us now, and Shanti agrees. Honestly, I'm glad she does. It gives her and Reema a chance to figure out where they want to sit without their parents present. Reema takes the head of the table, and Shanti and I take one side of the table, leaving the other for their parents.

It may not be much, but at least there is some distance between our side and theirs. A little more than an arm's length of barrier. Hopefully, we won't need it.

As the server sets glasses of water on the table, Vishnu and Indira Mahal approach. The air turns thick with anticipation and apprehension. But when I glance up to make eye contact, I don't miss the way Indira looks at Shanti with a hint of sadness.

She misses her daughter.

Maybe this will go better than expected.

Before the server walks off, they take our drink orders. "I'll give you time to look over the menu," they say as they jot down the last drink on a small notepad.

The music and quiet conversation around us are drowned out by an awkward bubble of friction and uncertainty. Shanti lifts her menu, hiding her face from everyone but me. Reema follows suit, followed by her parents. I pick up mine with one hand, dropping my other to rest on her leg beneath the table.

"Breathe," I whisper.

Shanti closes her eyes, inhales deeply, holds it for a beat, then opens her eyes on a slow exhale. Her shoulders are still stiff, her fingers still have a death grip on the menu, but the slight softening of her expression tells me all I need to know.

This is probably one of the most difficult situations in her life, but she has it under control. With support from me and Reema, she will get through the evening with her head high.

I am in pure awe of her strength and bravery.

Reema sets her menu on the table a moment later. She reaches for her water, spinning the glass in place. "So, Shanti, how are things at the studio?"

One of Reema's most admirable qualities is that she has this uncanny ability to bring levity to any situation. To lighten the mood and be a buffer with ease. I'm beyond grateful she joined us tonight and have no doubt Shanti is too. Reema effortlessly erases some of the stress just by being herself.

Shanti closes her menu and sets it on the table. "Good. Fall classes started today and we've got a few new students."

When she doesn't say anything further, I open my mouth to brag about my beautiful girlfriend. Because her parents should hear about all of the incredible things she has accomplished and plans to do. They should know what they've missed because of their cruelty and inflexibility.

"Shanti's being humble." I turn to meet her golden eyes, the corner of my mouth tipping up in a gentle half smile. "She currently has fifteen students under her tutelage and is choreographing their first performance." I give her thigh a reassuring squeeze. "It's an absolute honor to work beside her."

Shanti's cheeks flush the prettiest shade of pink, her bottom lip quivering slightly. "Jet…" she admonishes, but it falls short.

"That's wonderful, Shanti."

My gaze drifts across the table to see Indira smiling at her daughter. It may be the low lighting messing with my eyes, but it looks as if Indira's on the cusp of tears.

Another spark of hope soars in my chest.

The server returns with our drinks then jots down our dinner orders. For a beat, everyone is all smiles and outspoken. But the moment the server walks off, the entire table goes silent.

Shanti wanted to resolve the grievances between her and her parents tonight. To put an end to the devastation and estrangement. To figure out a path toward peace and the future.

And no matter how badly I want to nudge her to speak up, to make the next move, I won't. I am here to support her. To lift her up when her confidence wanes. To step in momentarily when she can't find her words. But that is all.

Shanti is at the helm and needs full control of the situation. I'm simply here to help her sparkle and keep her from falling.

"Why are we here, Shanti?" Expression void of emotion, Vishnu cuts straight to the point as he takes a sip of water.

"Dad," Reema chastises.

Lips in a tight line, Shanti shakes her head. "It's fine, Reema."

Reema's gaze darts from Vishnu to Shanti. "No, it's not." Her silverware rattles on the table as she slams her hand down. "Shanti, you've sacrificed so much to make Mom and Dad proud. You've been through hell." Reema's attention is aimed at Vishnu once more. "And I will not let anyone, not even our parents, speak to you with such inhumanity. You deserve more respect."

Thank you, Reema.

Shanti takes Reema's hand on the table and gives it a fierce squeeze. Taking a deep breath, she covers my hand on her thigh with hers. Anchored by her two biggest champions, Shanti meets her father's waiting gaze and exhales.

"I asked you to dinner because I've done a lot of healing over the past few years."

Her leg starts to bounce beneath the table. I flip my hand over and lace our fingers. The moment we're palm to palm, her grip turns brutal. I don't flinch, don't try to pull away or loosen her hold. I simply let her release her anxiety on me in whatever way helps.

"But the more I heal," Shanti continues after a beat, "the more I feel incomplete."

Empathy tugs at Reema's expression, her eyes glazing with unshed tears.

"I've spent weeks trying to pinpoint why and it finally came to me." Shanti swallows. "We didn't always see eye to eye. Hell, we fought more than we agreed."

Vishnu opens his mouth, likely to scold Shanti for saying the word hell, but Reema narrows her eyes at him and says, "Don't."

Shanti gives her sister a clipped smile. "It won't happen overnight, but I want to repair our relationship, if possible. I want to let go of the past and start over." She pauses and inhales a shaky breath. "But the only way that can happen is if you're willing to do the same. You have to put in equal effort." Straightening her spine, Shanti holds her chin a little higher. "Because this won't work otherwise."

I stare at the woman next to me, my entire universe, with undiluted awe. Every damn day, she takes me by surprise. Every day, I fall harder for her. My fearless, resilient woman.

"We've done nothing wrong."

My gaze flies across the table to Vishnu, his arms folded over his chest, hands clamped above his elbows, and lips pursed.

"Haven't we?" Indira glares at her husband. Before he can answer her, she continues. "I miss my girls." Her voice cracks. "I want them in my life." Indira's face softens as she shifts her attention to Reema then Shanti. "These past few years have been awful." She reaches across the table and rests her hand atop Reema and Shanti's. "I will do whatever it takes to make this right. No matter how long it takes."

Beside me, Shanti sniffles.

Arms still crushed to his chest, the muscles of Vishnu's jaw flex as he narrows his eyes. His rigidity and cloudy red aura are a lit match to my fuse.

I refuse to hold back any longer.

But I also won't stoop to his level. I will counter his indignation with maturity and passion.

"I love Shanti," I say, all eyes shooting my way. "I've been in love with her since I understood what the word meant." I meet Vishnu's unwavering glare and square my shoulders. "And I will do anything and everything to protect her and her heart." With a tilt of my head, I arch a brow. "Even from you."

Shanti cuts off the circulation to my fingers, but I continue, needing to get this out.

"She was so nervous to do this. And a little scared. I could've discouraged her. Could've told her to forget about you. But I didn't because that's not what she needs." I shake my head. "I also won't make her choices for her. She's had so many of them stolen from her."

Vishnu's eyes flare with anger.

"Don't waste this chance," I say, not giving him a chance to speak. "Life's too short. Tomorrow isn't promised." I shrug. "You have a choice to make." Turning to face Shanti, I give her hand a quick squeeze. "Love and accept your daughters for who they are or lose them because you refuse to let go of some antiquated way of thinking." I meet Vishnu's gaze one last time. "If I were you, I'd choose love and acceptance."

Shanti leans into my side. "I love you."

Not giving a damn that her entire family is at the table, I twist, cup her cheek, and drop a chaste kiss to her lips. My thumb caresses her soft skin as I pull away. "Love you, too."

A heavy sigh fills the air.

"Vishnu…" Indira admonishes, her voice louder, bolder. "I will not lose them." Expression stern, she shakes her head. "I will not."

Seconds feel like hours as we all wait for Shanti's father to make his decision. It's subtle, but eventually the energy at the table shifts. Goes from tense and unclear to somewhat pliant and committed.

Shoulders caving, hands falling to his lap, Vishnu deflates in his seat. He takes Indira's hand and brings it to his lips, kissing her knuckles as he nods. "I will make mistakes."

Indira weeps, her bottom lip quivering as she tries to smile.

"It's all I know. All I was taught," he adds.

"I've made mistakes. It's called being human," Shanti says. "But I choose to try again. To do things differently. To constantly work on being a better version of myself." She takes a deep breath, so much stress leaving her body on the exhale. "Old habits can be unlearned if you want something bad enough."

My skin warms as Shanti takes in my profile.

"It took too long, but I finally saw what I'd been missing for years. I saw the love that'd been there all along. A love I'd denied myself because I didn't think I was worthy of it." Shanti tightens her grip on my hand. "But Jet showed me otherwise. He never gave up on me. Through thick and thin, he stuck by my side. Loved every one of my flaws. Healed almost all of my scars. Told me he loved me over and over until I believed him."

A tear spills down her cheek.

"Were it not for him, I'd be lost. Maybe worse." Shanti looks across the table, her attention bouncing between her parents. "The path you choose is up to you. Change isn't easy, and that's a good thing. But if you want to make this work, you have to put in the effort."

"We will do our part," Indira declares. "Whatever it takes."

Happiness radiates off Shanti in waves as she and Reema exchange smiles. "And we'll be here every step of the way."

As the server reaches the table with our meal, Indira bolts out of her chair and rushes around Reema to wrap her arms around both her daughters. "I love you girls with my whole heart."

"Love you too, Mom," they say in unison.

After the server sets the last plate on the table, Vishnu gets up and hugs Reema and Shanti in turn. "How did I end up with two beautiful, tenacious daughters?"

Shanti and Reema laugh a moment before Shanti looks up at her dad and shrugs. "Who do you think we got it from?"

The entire table erupts in laughter, and it feels so good. Right. Perfect.

My gaze flits from one smiling face to the next as warmth blooms in the center of my chest. Tonight could've gone so many ways, but it went the direction I manifested on repeat.

Tonight, love won.

Tonight, the last tether in Shanti's heart stitched back together.

EPILOGUE PART ONE – OUR BRAND OF LOVE

JET

Six Months Later

I follow Shanti with my eyes as she twirls around the room, chin high, shoulders back, spine straight, eyes trained on her target. The epitome of grace and beauty, of strength and tenacity, she dazzles me more and more each day. Makes me fall deeper and harder.

Shanti would tease me relentlessly if she knew how often I ogled her. The way I study the slope of her nose, the faint dusting of freckles, and her perfect pouty lips every time I wake before her. The way I ghost my fingers over her curves and memorize every perfect inch of her after we're both spent from orgasms.

But I'd take every one of her taunts with a wide smile on my face. Because I am so gone for her. Thoroughly, madly, and so fucking deeply in love with her.

Hitting her final mark, the song ends and applause echoes through the studio. Shanti curtsies, all while doing her best—and failing—to hide her beaming smile.

Since the dinner with her parents in September, Shanti has been more effervescent. Affable. Alive. They may have a way to go, but they have already made great strides.

And I'm so damn happy to see my girl relaxed and free.

"We'll pick up from here tomorrow," Shanti announces to the small group of preteens in the room. "Great class, everyone."

As the kids shuffle off to collect their belongings, I cross the room to sidle up to my girl. This is our third class with this age group, and we've opted to alternate lead instruction for the first couple of weeks. It gives us a chance to showcase our strengths as well as our weaknesses. To explain how vital we are to each other. How what affects one of us affects all of us.

I wrap Shanti in my arms and hoist her off the floor, spinning her in circles. "Incredible as always."

Soft giggles assault my ears as she clutches my shoulders and ducks her chin. "Put me down."

"Never." I pepper kisses along her neck.

Snickering echoes through the room, and I turn to see a few of the girls lingering.

Shanti pats my shoulders. "Please, Jet. At least wait until everyone's gone."

Reluctantly, I set her on her feet and unwind my arms from her waist. "You're no fun," I say, sticking out my bottom lip.

With a playful roll of her eyes, she shakes her head. "And you're a troublemaker."

A corner of my mouth curves up. "Nah. Just a fool in love."

Heat colors Shanti's cheeks, and gods, I love the effect I have on her.

While we wait for the last of the students to leave, I scroll through my music in search of the perfect song. The moment we're alone, I hit play, lock my phone, stuff it in the pocket of my leggings, and extend a hand to Shanti.

"May I have this dance?"

Lips pinned between her teeth, Shanti takes my hand and bows. "I'd be honored."

Taking the lead, I sweep us across the dance floor to a slow melody. Tuck Shanti impossibly close to my chest. Rest my free hand at the small of her back as my feet move in a one-two-three pattern again and again.

Ballroom dancing isn't something we do often, but we learned it early on to expand our talents. To give us a different perspective of dance. To boost our creativity when coming up with new routines. For the same reasons, we've also dabbled with the tango, foxtrot, swing, and hip-hop. It keeps our minds fresh and our creative juices flowing.

Pressing my cheek to hers, I close my eyes and sway to the music. "Have I told you lately that I love you?"

Shanti hums. "Yes, but you can tell me again."

"I love you."

"And I love you." Her fingers tangle in my hair at the nape of my neck and for the rest of the song, we get lost in each other.

My mind flits through all the people I am grateful for and the wonderful things that've happened recently.

Shanti and her parents have worked hard to rekindle their relationship. It's gotten a little rocky here and there, as was expected, but nothing they couldn't smooth out with an open, honest conversation.

The organizers for the West Coast Ballet Competition reached out in January and invited us to join them again this summer, and a few of our students. I lost my hearing for a few minutes with all the shrieking in the studio, but I'm so damn proud of my woman and our students.

Last month, Neesa and Aurelio sat us down and offered us Rhythm and Flow when they retire in roughly seven years. After much deliberation, we said yes. Shanti worried if we'd have the means to run a studio, but I assured her we'd be fine. For Shanti, for our shared love of dance, I will tap into my inheritance. I will always make exceptions for who and what I love.

Dance has always had a piece of my soul. I thought it was all I needed to be happy. When I met Shanti, I learned early on that she held another, more significant piece, as well as my heart. In no time, Shanti became my world. Our fate was sealed. My heart was tethered to hers and nothing would change that. Without one, the other doesn't matter.

It sounds cliché, but I count and thank every one of my lucky stars for her.

"Hungry?" I ask when the song ends.

"Is that a real question?"

I laugh. "My apologies." Bending at the waist, I bow. "Thank you for the dance, m'lady."

She playfully slaps me. "Come on." She jerks her head toward our bags. "I'm famished."

Sweats on over our dance clothes, I remote start the SUV, turn on the heat, and grab our dance bags. Spring is days away, but there's still a chill in the air. The colder temperatures don't bother me, but I like to make sure Shanti is comfortable.

"Where to?" Shanti asks as she closes the passenger door and flips on her seat heater.

"What if I want it to be a surprise?"

Shanti glances at me skeptically. "There're only so many places to eat in Stone Bay, but sure. Whatever." She shrugs, a smirk teasing her mouth. "Should I put on a blindfold?"

"Ha ha." I stick my tongue out at her. "No. That won't be necessary."

Exiting the parking lot, I drive through town without hurry. Residents mill about the sidewalks on Granite Parkway, enjoying a night out after a long week. But we won't be joining in on their evening. I pass the busiest streets in town, garnering a little side-eye from Shanti.

Turning right on Garnet Road, I head north. The only restaurant in this direction is the sushi place, but that isn't our destination either. Shanti's confusion is evident when we pass it. Still, she remains quiet in the passenger seat.

A moment later, I flip on my blinker then turn onto the driveway for one of the Fox family rental properties.

"Erm… what's going on?"

Pulling up to the cabin, I put the car in park and cut the engine. "Dinner," I say as if it's obvious.

She narrows her eyes. "You're up to something."

I open the door and slip out of the car. "Maybe. Maybe not. But you'll never know if you stay in the car." I shut the door and trek up the driveway for the short sidewalk that leads to the porch.

Gravel crunches behind me as I near the front door, and there's no use in fighting my smile. I enter the code on the keypad and step aside to let her go in first.

Candles flicker throughout the living and dining space of the cabin, the crackle of burning logs coming from the fireplace. Hints of rose and peony float in the air, followed by the savory scent of dinner staying warm in the oven.

Shanti whirls around, eyes wide and brimming with tears. "How?"

I shrug. "I know people."

"This is"—she slowly spins to take in everything—"very romantic." When her eyes meet mine again, she swallows.

Closing the distance between us, I frame her face in my hands. "What can I say? You bring out the best in me."

EPILOGUE PART TWO – THE WAY HE LOVES ME

SHANTI

I AM WARM HONEY IN HIS CAPABLE HANDS.

"Right back at ya," I whisper, voice hoarse with emotion.

Jet erases those pesky few inches between us and takes my mouth in a slow, sensual, deep kiss. Then his hands are in my hair, fingers curling as he switches the angle of the kiss. Each stroke of his tongue, each moan vibrating his chest, makes me melt further.

Fisting his hoodie, I haul him impossibly closer. Anchor myself to him. And when my knees quiver, he drops his hands to my waist, banding his arms around my middle.

On the next breath, Jet breaks the kiss and drops his forehead to mine.

A soft whimper leaves my lips. "Why'd you stop?"

The tip of his nose caresses the length of mine. "Because if I didn't, my plan for tonight would fall apart."

"We can eat after sex," I whisper like it's a secret.

Jet chuckles. "True." He kisses me chastely then adds a few more inches between us. "But there's more than food."

My gaze locks on his, trying to see what he's not telling me. But it's no use. I've never been as good at reading people as Jet. What I do see is a mischievous twinkle in his eye. How he's trying to fight a smile.

So rather than deflate his excitement, I let him take the lead on the romantic evening he planned.

I reach up and tug on his hoodie strings. "Alright then." I push up on my toes and kiss his cheek. "I'm ready to be wooed."

A bright, wide smile stretches across his face as he takes my hand and leads me toward a small table with two chairs. "M'lady." He takes an exaggerated bow and gestures for me to sit. When I do, he unfolds the cloth napkin on my place setting and sets it in my lap.

"Such fine dining," I tease.

"Nothing but the best for my girl." He winks then walks off for the kitchen.

A *pop* fills the air a moment before he comes back with a bottle of wine. He fills my glass then his, setting the bottle on the table before disappearing again. A few clanking noises and a *shit* hit my ears before he returns with two plates.

"The plate's really hot," he says, a black oven mitt with illustrated foxes on it covering his hand.

I clamp my lips between my teeth and swallow down my laugh. "Thank you."

He eyes me suspiciously but doesn't call me out. Setting his own plate down, he ditches the oven mitts and takes the seat across from me.

When I finally glance down to see what's for dinner, my jaw drops. This isn't just a meal, it's freaking art on a plate. "Oh my god." My eyes dart up to meet his. "Did you make this?"

He shakes his head. "Didn't have the time. I've been with you all day." Bringing his glass to his lips, he takes a sip of wine and leaves it at that.

"It's almost too pretty to eat."

I stare down at the golden-brown Cornish hen, jasmine rice with pine nuts, currants, and pomegranate seeds, and roasted Brussel sprouts with purple onion, rainbow carrots, and whole cranberries. At the top of the plate is a spiral-shaped bread roll coated in melted butter and sesame seeds.

"There's extra if you want more. Or we can take it home for leftovers." Jet picks his fork up and digs in, a moan falling from his lips when the first bite hits his tongue.

That is all the encouragement I need.

Taking our time, we savor every bite. He asks if there is anything I'd like to do over the weekend, and I tell him outside of teaching, I just want to lounge around with him. When our plates are empty, he takes them to the kitchen and returns with two thick slices of dark chocolate cake topped with fresh berries, whipped cream, and a mint leaf.

Saliva pools in my mouth and I'm surprised I'm not drooling.

"The night keeps getting better," I say as Jet takes his seat.

He winks. "And it's still early."

I narrow my eyes at him, but only for a beat. I need this cake in my mouth.

The fork goes through the dark chocolate sponge with ease. I make sure to get some of the silky frosting between the layers too. When the bite hits my tongue, a throaty moan vibrates my chest. It isn't frosting, it's chocolate-peanut-butter mousse.

"An orgasm for my mouth," I mutter, hand over my still-full mouth. "Dear god."

Jet chokes on a laugh, a brilliant smile on his face as he shakes his head. "Glad you approve."

I point to the slice of heaven on my plate and say, "Don't know where this came from, but we need more."

"Lucky for you, I think ahead. There's more than half a cake left, and I can order it anytime you want."

I shove another forkful in my mouth. "If that's not love, I don't know what is."

He laughs harder. "Anything to make my girl happy."

An exaggerated frown tugs the corners of my mouth down when I take the last bite. But Jet promises to make it better after he clears the table.

Taking my hand, he leads me through the cabin to the back door. As we step out onto the back porch, my eyes go wide as they land on the roaring fire in the stone pit in the middle of the yard.

Halting, I gape at him. "How?"

Lifting his free hand to his mouth, he pinches his thumb and finger together, dragging them across his lips.

This is the first time anyone has truly surprised me, and I have to say, I love it.

"Come on." He tugs my hand and guides us over to the fire.

We take a seat on an outdoor loveseat a couple feet from the fire. I kick off my shoes, tuck my feet under my butt, and curl into Jet's side. He wraps an arm around my shoulders and rests his cheek on my head. As the flames flicker and dance, we simply hold each other and enjoy this perfect blip in time.

"I remember the first day we met like it was yesterday."

I straighten in my seat and gape at him. "You do not."

His gentle gray eyes meet mine, the fire flickering in them as he nods. "I do. We'd just started our warm-ups when Neesa asked for everyone's attention." He reaches up and tucks a wayward strand of hair behind my ear. "With that silky pink ribbon in your hair, you looked so sad and nervous and uncomfortable as we welcomed you to class."

From day one, Jet read me like a book. "I was sick to my stomach with nerves," I admit. "My parents thought ballet would help make me *a proper lady*." I use air quotes on the last part. "Whatever the heck that means."

"Your guess is as good as mine," he says as he drops his gaze and takes my hand. "My favorite part of that day was making you smile." His thumb strokes my knuckles as he lifts his eyes to mine. "I liked that you only smiled at me."

My skin warms at the memory. It was years before either of us realized how strong our bond was, but it was there from the beginning. I may not love dance on the same level as Jet, but it will always hold a special place in my heart. Without dance, we may have never met.

"I think I loved you back then, but in the way young kids love their friends. Does that make sense?"

I nod, the backs of my eyes stinging. Were it not for Jet, I truly believe I wouldn't know what real love feels like.

"Shanti, I have loved you in every possible way there is to love another person. Through the ups and downs, the heartache and triumphs, the constant wondering when our time would come, my heart was always yours." He inhales deeply, holds it for a beat, then continues. "You've always been more than the woman I love. Our hearts, our souls, are irrevocably tethered. From one life to the next, we will always find each other. We will always love each other."

"Jet…" A tear spills down my cheek.

Cupping my jaw, he strokes my cheek with his thumb, wiping at the wetness. "Oddly, I don't remember much of my childhood before you. But every moment with you"—he taps his temple—"I remember with perfect clarity."

"Is your mission tonight to make me cry? Cause if it is, it's working."

With a shake of his head, he chuckles. "No, baby." Turning to face me better, he reaches into his pocket but leaves his hand closed when it comes out. "But I'm not mad about you crying over how much you love me."

I playfully shove him. "Of course you aren't."

Straightening in his seat, he swallows. "Shanti, I want all my memories to include you. The past, the present, and beyond."

He takes my hand, and I can feel a slight tremor in his.

Oh my god. Is he…

"You are all I've ever wanted. All I'll ever want." He shakes harder. "I want to explore the world with you. Grow old with you. Make enough memories to fill thousands of scrapbooks."

Tears stream down both my cheeks because without a shadow of doubt, I know what's coming next.

"Shanti, I want you forever."

He opens his clasped hand and holds up a curved, rose gold

band adorned with countless small diamonds and a stunning, large pearl at the heart. It's a match to the bracelet he bought me in San Francisco. *Last year.*

"Will you marry me?"

My hand flies to my mouth as tears soak my cheeks. Sniffling, I lower my hand and nod. "Yes," I choke out. "A million times, yes."

He slides the ring on my finger, then frames my face with his hands, and claims my mouth with a kiss that outshines every one before it.

BONUS CONTENT – MADLY, DEEPLY

JET

Five Years Later

PEOPLE WILL SAY IT'S IMPOSSIBLE, BUT EVERY DAY, I FALL MORE IN love with my wife.

From the juvenile love I felt when I first told her I loved her at fifteen to the love I experienced when she first said those three words back to me. From the heart-stopping love I felt the night I asked her to marry me to the breath-stealing love I endured as she walked down the aisle toward our forever.

A couple weeks into fall, eighteen months after I proposed, under a dusting of orange, red, and yellow foliage, Shanti and I exchanged our vows.

The months leading up to that moment were a tad stressful.

Shanti and I wanted the wedding small and simple. Intimate. Less than fifty people, including the wedding party. Getting our parents to agree was a struggle. When they finally realized we weren't backing down on our terms, they conceded. So long as we let them take charge of the venue, decor, and finances, they would adhere to the rest. In turn, we agreed, but only if they gave us the final say in what mattered most to us—color palette and Shanti's dress.

It was so hard to hand over the reins, but we did. When Indira showed us the first picture of how she envisioned the ceremony setup, our nerves settled.

A three-inch-thick album sits on our bookshelf, loaded with memories of our wedding. Some posed, others candid. Our parents harped on the importance of pictures because the bride and groom often forget pivotal moments of the day.

I remember them all.

Every time I close my eyes and think of that early October day, I see Shanti in her blush gown, gold-sequined flowers and vines stitched into the sand-colored tulle on the skirt, jacket, and dupatta. The gown was the perfect blend of traditional and modern—what Shanti wanted. The skirt dusted the floor as she walked down the aisle on her father's arm. The white bouquet in her hand was no match for how bright her smile was when our eyes locked. And when her father placed her hand in mine, I told her she looked like a goddess.

Every now and then, I still tell her she is a goddess. *My goddess.*

Because anything else would be a lie.

"Can I help with anything?" I ask as I take a seat at the foot of the bed.

Shanti groans from inside the closet, shoving hangers aggressively from one side to the other. "Got a shirt that won't make me look like a whale?"

We are currently in the phase of our relationship where most of what I say is wrong. I don't take her clipped words and momentary frustration to heart. If I had a beach-ball-sized belly and a mini human regularly jabbing my organs, I'd be pretty irritable too.

"What about one of my V-necks?" I suggest.

"Hmm." A hanger smacks the shelf above the rack a moment before she exits the closet and goes to the floor-length mirror. With the shirt draped over her chest, she tugs at the sides to see if it's worth the effort to put it on. "This might work."

Moving to the bed, she sets my shirt next to her bra as she takes off her partially buttoned pajama top. Sliding the straps up her arms, she finagles her bra into place then reaches around to latch it.

I consider offering to help, but I know better. Were she not utterly frustrated with her seven-month-pregnant body, she would appreciate the gesture. Hell, she'd probably swoon over it.

But not right now.

About a month ago, I quickly learned to stop lending a hand unless asked. We were getting dressed to go shopping and I noticed it wasn't as easy for her to tie her shoes. Naturally, I wanted to help. So, I asked.

Wrong move.

The muscles of her jaw flexed as she pressed her lips together so tight they paled. And then she said, *"What, because I'm pregnant, I'm incapable of doing things on my own?"*

I was so taken aback by the bite in her tone, I didn't know how to respond. Fumbling over what to say, I mumbled, *"Of course not. But I'm here if you need me."*

Thankfully, she didn't behead me for that one. And since then, I've tiptoed around what to say or do.

Her body is going through so many changes, and I feel guilty for not being able to do more. We may have planned this pregnancy—would've been difficult to make a baby without reversing my vasectomy—but with it being our first, we could only anticipate so much.

Tugging the black cotton over her head, she wiggles the hem over her round belly and then returns to the mirror.

The sight of her ample cleavage and swollen belly in my shirt makes me hard. Another surprise I didn't expect. But something about seeing my wife like this, her curves more pronounced and belly round with our child, makes me feral.

We are both reaping those rewards.

"This works," she says, relief in her tone. "Just need to put on my necklace, then I'm ready to go."

"I'll get the bag."

Rising from the bed, I exit the room, unlock my phone, and tap the screen a few times to open the garage door and remote start the car. Then I go to the kitchen and grab the packed grocery tote on the counter.

Our mothers insisted we didn't need to do or bring anything today, but Shanti dug in her heels. Said she didn't feel right coming to the baby shower empty-handed, knowing we would come home with so much.

The past two days, our kitchen looked like a flour bomb had detonated in it. I've never seen so many cookies and brownies at once in my life. Red velvet cookies, Cookie Monster cookies, sugar cookie bars smothered in unicorn frosting (her term, not mine), peanut butter pie brownies, and ube brownies with white chocolate chips. Everything looked so damn good. But her in the stained apron with blue food dye on her cheek... cute as fuck.

"I've got the goods," I say, patting the bag slung over my shoulder as she enters the room.

She grabs her coat off the hook by the door and shrugs it on. "Ready when you are."

In the car, I turn on the heat and let her adjust it to her comfort level. We drive off the Fox estate and head east on Opal Trail for the social center.

"Sorry I've been bitchy recently," she says after a few minutes.

I glance in her direction long enough to see the crestfallen look on her face. Eyes back on the road, I reach across the console and rest my hand on her thigh. "You know, if I was creating life in my body, I'd be way bitchier."

In my periphery, she turns her head in my direction. Unfortunately, I can't see her expression. But I don't need to. A moment later, she howls with laughter.

And damn, I love the sound.

When her laughter quiets, she swipes at her cheeks. "Yeah, you're kind of a wimp when it comes to pain."

"I am." I turn enough for her to see me wink. "But you still love me."

She laces my fingers with hers. "I really do."

The mood feels lighter, and I'm glad we cleared the air. If there is one thing Shanti and I are good at, it's talking about our feelings. Especially after one of us has a bad day. With all we've endured, we never want to walk away from each other upset.

Life is fleeting, and we want to make every moment count. So we vowed to always settle any disagreements after we take a minute to cool down.

"Do you really think we'll get everything we added to the registry?" I swear we put a couple hundred things on that list.

She scoffs. "Wouldn't put anything past our parents. I told my mom I wanted the shower small like our wedding. Last time I asked how many people were coming, she said close to a hundred." She pauses, and I picture her rolling her eyes. "I told her to cut the list in half. Most of the family on the list doesn't live within driving distance. They can mail gifts or cards."

"Glad you stood your ground." I stroke her hand with my thumb. "Today isn't about them. I get that they're excited, and they want to share the news with everyone, but your comfort matters most."

"Thank you."

"Baby, you don't need to thank me." I bring her hand to my lips and kiss her knuckles in turn. "I will do anything to keep you happy."

"Are you trying to make my mascara run?" she asks, a slight warble in her voice.

"Only happy tears. Then, I'd clean you up."

"You're so gone for me, Mr. Fox."

"Damn right I am, Mrs. Fox."

Before the wedding, Shanti and I never discussed her changing her name. Whether her last name stayed Mahal or changed to Fox didn't matter. The only thing that did matter was that she would always be mine. Some people get possessive over things like names, but that wasn't me. Shanti is her own person, fully capable of making her own decisions. The moment she said *I do*, our future was sealed.

A month after the wedding, she decided to hyphenate her last name, adding Fox.

I won't lie. The moment was pretty fucking euphoric. I smiled so much my face hurt the next day.

Entering the lot for the social center, I park in the closest space to the main entrance. I grab the bag from the back then offer my arm to Shanti when I reach her. She takes it without hesitation.

A large sign greets us when we enter the building. *Welcome to the Fox-Mahal baby shower* is in large, swirly, charcoal letters. The rest of the sign embellished with gray watercolor stars, clouds, and a crescent moon. It's perfect and exactly what we wanted.

Early in the pregnancy, Shanti and I decided we didn't want to know the baby's gender. It isn't important. All we care about is our little one being healthy and happy and feeling loved.

That said, we asked everything for the baby to be neutral tones. Black, white, shades of gray, and light wood. We're also doing a blend of celestial and woodland creatures for the accents. At first, we weren't sure how they'd look together. But after hours of internet scrolling, we were convinced and had a mile-long registry to prove it.

Shanti gasps as we step through glass French doors, entering another realm. Driftwood, greenery, twinkling lights, and pale blooms highlight the room. White window treatments and cloudy-gray tablecloths are the perfect offset to the pops of color.

"Incredible," she murmurs as our mothers cross the room for us.

I hook an arm around her shoulders and hug her to my side. "Our baby will be so loved." I press a kiss to her hair. "And probably a little spoiled."

"So spoiled." She laughs under her breath.

The next hour goes by way too fast as I help with the final touches before guests arrive. Our mothers insist Shanti sit and relax, but she doesn't. Unless the doctor puts her on bed rest or she feels like absolute garbage, Shanti only rests on her own terms.

Family and friends crowd the room in no time. Gifts are stacked on a large table off to the side. Quiet music floats in the background. Easy conversation and frequent laughter lightens the mood. We eat our weight in Shanti's favorite foods and sip on sparkling apple cider.

When it is time to open gifts, a gray, tufted wingback chair that looks more like a throne is set near the large table stacked high with packages. Shanti is handed boxes and bags, paper flung aside as she reveals each gift in turn. But after a handful, she asks for another chair to be brought in and for me to open gifts too.

It takes nearly an hour, but we reach the bottom of the stack. We had no reservations about getting a lot of the items on the registry, but we didn't think we would get them all, plus money and gift cards. Of course, our parents spoil us with all of the furniture. But one gift we don't expect comes from Neesa and Aurelio. On top of clothes, a crocheted blanket, and some of the cutest stuffed animals, they also "gift" us a lower price on the studio when we take over in a couple years.

"These people are seriously out to see me cry," Shanti mutters as we move back to our table for cake.

I weave my fingers with hers. "Only because they love us and our baby so much."

When we take our seats, Shanti leans in and kisses my cheek. "Thank you."

My brow furrows as I meet her gaze. "For what?"

Tears rim her amber eyes as her chin starts to wobble. "For loving me. For never giving up. For being the light in my darkest days." She sniffles. "For our beautiful, adventurous life. None of this would matter without you."

I cup her cheek, drop my forehead to hers, and close my eyes. "Ditto, baby." And then, I kiss her as if no one else is in the room.

FOX
family tree

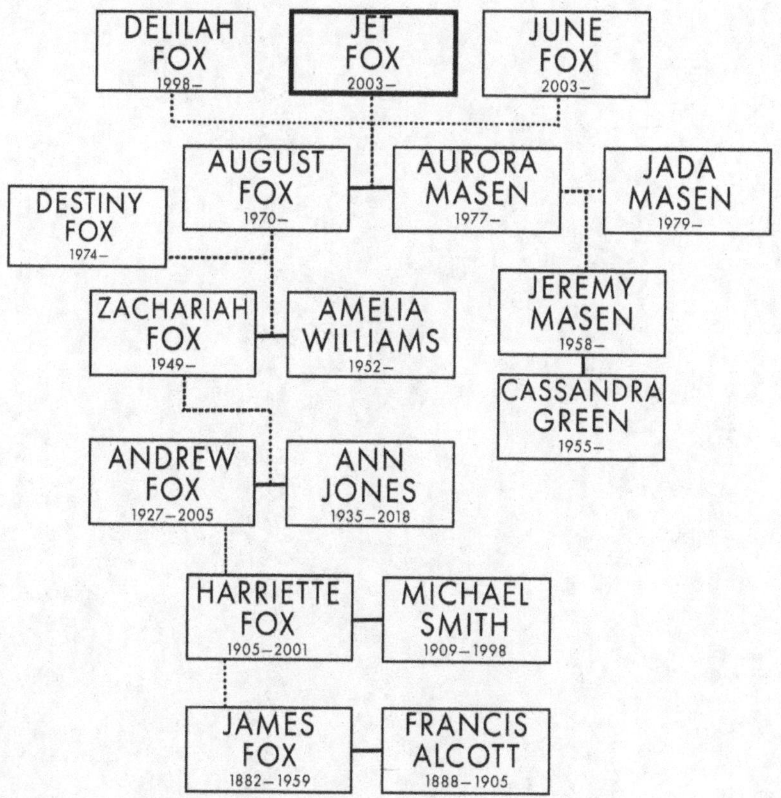

MORE BY PERSEPHONE

Every Thought Taken

As young children, an unshakable friendship brought them together. As teens, they discovered an undeniable love. Then life pulled them in different directions–into darkness and light–and slowly ripped them apart. Years later, he returns home in the hopes of a second chance with his first love and to conquer the demons of his past.

Transcendental

A musician in search of his muse and a woman grieving the loss of her husband. Two weeks at an exclusive retreat and their connection rivals all others. Until she leaves early without notice. But he refuses to give up until he finds her again.

The Click Duet

High school sweethearts torn apart. When fate gives them a second chance, one doesn't trust they won't be hurt again. Through the Lens (Click Duet #1) and Time Exposure (Click Duet #2) is an angsty, second chance, friends to lovers romance with all the feels.

Shattered Sun

When your heart is split in two, how do choose who to love more? While Ben, her childhood best friend, and Travis, the hottest cop in Stone Bay, fight for Kirsten's affection, someone else has their eye on her. When she questions everyone and everything, Ben and Travis vow to protect her. In the process, she falls for both men. Before it's too late, she needs to decide which man she loves more.

Fractured Night

Shallow. Heartless. Egocentric. The top three words people use to describe Phoebe Graves. Somehow, I've always seen past her icy facade. Seen beyond her callous exterior. And those minor glimpses… they make me want her more. The moment my fantasies start becoming reality, I question how long it'll last before Phoebe abandons me for something bigger.

Fallen Stars

An underlying current has always existed between us. An undeniable bond that keeps me tethered to my best friend. My person. The man I have loved in secret for years. I've wanted to tell him how I feel. Countless times, I've considered crossing the line but have resisted. I'd rather love him in secret than lose him forever. As our love story begins, one test after another is thrown at us. As we fall deeper in love, our world becomes a living, breathing nightmare.

Stolen Dreams

For years, I've had a clear picture of my life. College. Career. And eventually, love. My family insists on playing matchmaker. My best friend says to have more fun before settling down. All I want is to focus on work, help my students, and make a difference in the community. But a night out to celebrate the end of the school year rewrites my entire future. And if anyone's going to make me break my own rules, I'm glad it's him.

Raptured Souls

Love is the only thing I've given up on. Until I meet the broody, secret son of Stone Bay's biggest recluse. Maddox Freeman. Our connection is instantaneous and undeniable, but I ignore it and guard my heart. But the more time I spend with him, the more I let him in. I say yes to his dinner invitations and to helping him repair the house he inherited. As I clean, I find photos and documents that paint a different picture of the town I've always known. Paperwork someone else wants destroyed.

TETHERED HEARTS PLAYLIST

Here are some of the songs from the **Tethered Hearts** playlist. It is most definitely a vibe. You can find and listen to the entire playlist on Spotify!

Guilty as Sin? | Taylor Swift
loml | Taylor Swift
i love you | Billie Eilish
Sad Beautiful Tragic (TV) | Taylor Swift
She Is Poetry | Benjamin Gustafsson, Christopher Dennis
Coleman
tolerate it | Taylor Swift
Spellbound | Ballet L'école
Chloe or Sam or Sophia or Marcus | Taylor Swift
No Time To Die | Billie Eilish
12 to 12 | sombr

The scene where Shanti walks in on Jet dancing in contorted moves is inspired by a dance video on YouTube featuring "The Grotto" by AudioMachine. It can only be found of AudioMachine's website and YouTube.

CONNECT WITH PERSEPHONE

<u>Connect with Persephone</u>
www.persephoneautumn.com

<u>Subscribe to Persephone's newsletter</u>
www.persephoneautumn.com/newsletter

<u>Join Persephone's reader's group</u>
Persephone's Playground

<u>Follow Persephone online</u>

instagram.com/persephoneautumn

facebook.com/persephoneautumnwrites

tiktok.com/@persephoneautumn

bookbub.com/authors/persephone-autumn

goodreads.com/persephoneautumn

amazon.com/author/persephoneautumn

pinterest.com/persephoneautumn

threads.com/@persephoneautumn

ACKNOWLEDGMENTS

To my family and friends… I love you so fucking much. The last year has been the hardest of my life. I wouldn't be here if not for you and your endless, unconditional love and support.

Rose at Fairy Proofmother Proofreading—I am eternally grateful for your expertise, insight, and that you came back out of retirement. My books wouldn't be the same without you and your magic. Love you!!

Abi of Pink Elephant Designs—the past year has been hard for you too. I wish I could reach through the screen and hug you so hard. You are strong and incredible and one of the kindest souls I know. Thank you for making my books gorgeous on the outside. They wouldn't be the same without you.

Christopher John of CJC Photography—thank you for helping me find the perfect photo for my cover. Tethered Hearts wouldn't be as stunning without your artistic eye.

Alli & Taylor!! The moment I saw this album, I knew one of the photos would be on my book. And honestly, it was difficult to choose which one. They're all too perfect. Sending virtual hugs!

Huge shout out to Mahida, Mary, and Shannon!! Tethered Hearts needed too many names for side characters, and I was a bit dizzy trying to come up with more. So I asked my reader group for help, and you all came through. I am so thankful for you xoxo

To all the readers, bloggers, influencers, and ARC readers that continuously promote my stories, get excited about books I'm terrified of putting out in the world, or read and love my words. I love you all so much!! Your support means more than you know. I love seeing your posts, your joy about my books, and pics of my books on your shelves and in your bookstacks.

To every person who picks up one of my books, I love you! Whether Tethered Hearts is your first Persephone Autumn book or your 30+ book, I never take a single one of you for granted. All the obnoxious fucking hugs!!!!

ABOUT THE AUTHOR

USA Today Bestselling Author Persephone Autumn is a proud mom with a cuckoo grandpup. An ethnic food enthusiast who has fun discovering ways to vegan-ize her favorite non-vegan foods. Most days, you'll find her with a tea latte or fruity concoction in her hand. If given the opportunity, she would intentionally get lost in nature.

For years, Persephone did some form of writing; mostly journaling or poetry. After pairing her poetry with images and posting them online, she began the journey of writing her first novel.

She mainly writes romance and poetry but on occasion dips her toes in other works. Look for her non-romance novel publications under P. Autumn.